Mary Jane Holmes

Dora Deane, or The East India uncle

and Maggie Miller, or Old Hagar's Secret

Mary Jane Holmes

Dora Deane, or The East India uncle
and Maggie Miller, or Old Hagar's Secret

ISBN/EAN: 9783743372733

Manufactured in Europe, USA, Canada, Australia, Japa

Cover: Foto ©Andreas Hilbeck / pixelio.de

Manufactured and distributed by brebook publishing software (www.brebook.com)

Mary Jane Holmes

Dora Deane, or The East India uncle

DORA DEANE,

OR

THE EAST INDIA UNCLE;

AND

MAGGIE MILLER,

OR

OLD HAGAR'S SECRET.

BY MRS. MARY J. HOLMES,

AUTHOR OF "LENA RIVERS," "THE HOMESTEAD ON THE HILL-SIDE," "MEADOW BROOK, OR ROSA LEE," "TEMPEST AND SUNSHINE," ETC., ETC.

NEW YORK:

Carleton, Publisher, Madison Square.

LONDON: S. LOW, SON & CO

M DCCC LXXII.

CONTENTS OF DORA DEANE.

CONTENTS.

DORA DEANE;

OR,

THE EAST INDIA UNCLE.

———•••———

CHAPTER I.

DORA AND HER MOTHER.

POOR little Dora Deane! How utterly wretched and desolate she was, as she crouched before the scanty fire, and tried to warm the little bit of worn-out flannel, with which to wrap her mother's feet; and how hard she tried to force back the tears which would burst forth afresh whenever she looked upon that pale, sick mother, and thought how soon she would be gone!

It was a small, low, scantily furnished room, high up in the third story of a crazy old building, which Dora called her home, and its one small window looked out on naught save the roofs and spires of the great city whose dull, monotonous roar was almost the only sound to which she had ever listened. Of the country, with its bright green grass, its sweet wild flowers, its running brooks, and its shady trees, she knew but little, for only once had she looked on all these things, and then her heart was very sad, for the

1*

right green grass was broken, and the sweet wild flowers were trampled down, that a grave might be made in the dark, moist earth for her father, who had died in early man hood, leaving his wife and only child to battle with the selfish world as best they could. Since that time, life had been long and dreary to the poor widow, whose hours were well-nigh ended, for ere to-morrow's sun was risen, *she* would have a better home than that dreary, cheerless room, while Dora, at the early age of twelve, would be an orphan.

It was a cold December night, the last one of the year, and the wintry wind, which swept howling past the curtain-less window, seemed to take a sadder tone, as if in pity for the little girl who knelt upon the hearthstone, and with the dim firelight flickering over her tear-stained face, prayed that she, too, might die, and not be left alone.

"It will be so lonely—so cold without my mother!" she murmured. "Oh, let me go with her; I *cannot* live alone."

"Dora, my darling," came faintly from the rude couch, and in an instant the child was at her mother's side.

Winding her arms fondly about the neck of her daughter, and pushing the soft auburn hair from off her fair, open brow, Mrs. Deane gazed long and earnestly upon her face.

"Yes, you are like me," she said at last, "and I am glad that it is so, for it may be Sarah will love you better when she sees in you a look like one who once called her sister. And should *he* ever return "——

She paused, while her mind went back to the years long ago—to the old yellow farm-house among the New England hills—to the grey-haired man, who had adopted her as his own when she was written *fatherless*—to the dark-eyed girl, sometimes kind, and sometimes overbearing, whom she had called her sister, though there was no tie of blood between them. Then she thought of the red house just across the way, and of the three brothers, Nathaniel, Richard, and John. Very softly she repeated the name of the latter, seeming to see him again as he was on the day when, with the wreath of white apple blossoms upon her brow, she sat on the mossy bank and listened to his low spoken words of love. Again she was out in the pale starlight, and heard the autumn wind go moaning through the locust trees as *Nathaniel*, the strange, eccentric, woman-hating Nathaniel, but just returned from the seas, told her how madly he had loved her, and how the knowledge that she belonged to another would drive him from his fatherland forever—that in the burning clime of India he would make gold his idol, forgetting, if it were possible, the mother who had borne him ! Then she recalled the angry scorn with which her adopted sister had received the news of her engagement with John, and how the conviction was at last forced upon her that Sarah herself had loved him in secret and that in a fit of desperation she had given her hand to the rather inefficient Richard, ever after treating her rival with a cool reserve, which now came back to her with painful distinctness.

"But she will love my little Dora for *John's* sake, if not for mine," she thought, at last ; and then, as if she had all the time been speaking to her daughter, she continued, "And you must be very dutiful to your aunt, and kind to your cousins, fulfilling their slightest wishes."

Looking up quickly, Dora asked, "Have you written to Aunt Sarah ? Does she say I can come ?"

"The letter is written, and Mrs. Gannis will send it as soon as I am dead," answered Mrs. Deane. "I am sure she will give you a home. I told her there was no alternative but the almshouse ;" then, after a pause, she added : " wrote to your uncle Nathaniel some months ago, when knew that I must die. It is time for his reply, but I bade him direct to Sarah, as I did not then think to see the winter snow."

"Did you tell him of me ?" eagerly asked Dora, on whom the name of Uncle Nathaniel, or "Uncle Nat," as he was more familiarly called, produced a more pleasant impression than did that of her aunt Sarah.

"Yes," answered the mother, "it was of you that I wrote, commending you to his care, should he return to America. And if you ever meet him, Dora, tell him tha, on my dying bed I thought of him with affection—that my mind wandered back to the years of long ago, when I was young, and ask him, for the sake of one he called his brother, and for her who grieves that ever she caused him a moment's pain, to care for you, their orphan child."

Then followed many words of love, which were very precious to Dora in the weary years which followed that sad night ; and then, for a time, there was silence in that little room, broken only by the sound of the wailing tempest. The old year was going out on the wings of a fearful storm, and as the driving sleet beat against the casement, while the drifting snow found entrance through more than one wide crevice and fell upon her pillow, the dying woman murmured, "Lie up closer to me, Dora, I am growing very cold."

Alas ! 'twas the chill of death ; but Dora did not know it, and again on the hearthstone before the fast dying coals she knelt, trying to warm the bit of flannel, on which her burning tears fell like rain, when through the empty wood-box she sought in vain for chip or bark with which to increase the scanty fire.

"But I will not tell her," she softly whispered, when satis-fied that her search was vain, and wrapping the flannel around the icy feet, she untied the long-sleeved apron which covered her own naked arms, and laying it over her mother's shoulders, tucked in the thin bedclothes; and then, herself all shivering and benumbed, she sat down to wait and watch, singing softly a familiar hymn, which had some times lulled her mother into a quiet sleep.

At last, as her little round white arms grew purple with the cold, she moved nearer to the bedside, and winding them lovingly around her mother's neck, laid her head upon the pillow and fell asleep. And to the angels, who were hovering near, waiting to bear their sister spirit home, there was given charge concerning the little girl, so that she did not freeze, though she sat there the live-long night, calmly sleeping the sweet sleep of childhood, while the mother at her side slept the long, eternal sleep of death !

CHAPTER II.

THE FIRST AND LAST NEW YEAR'S CALL.

It was New Year's morning, and over the great city lay the deep, untrodden snow, so soon to be trampled down by thousands of busy feet. Cheerful fires were kindled in many a luxurious home of the rich, and "Happy New Year" was echoed from lip to lip, as if on that day there were no aching hearts—no garrets where the biting cold looked in on pinching poverty and suffering old age—no low, dark room where Dora and her pale, dead mother lay, while over them the angels kept their tireless watch till human aid should come. But one there was who did not forget—one about whose house was gathered every elegance which fashion could dictate or money procure ; and now, as she sat at her bountifully-furnished breakfast table sipping her fragrant chocolate, she thought of the poor widow, Dora's mother, for whom her charity had been solicited the day before, by a woman who lived in the same block of buildings with Mrs. Deane.

"Brother," she said, glancing towards a young man who, before the glowing grate, was reading the morning paper, 'suppose you make your first call with me ?"

"Certainly," he answered; "and it will probably be in some dreary attic or dark, damp basement ; but it is well, I suppose, to begin the New Year by remembering the poor."

Half an hour later, and the crazy stairs which led to the chamber of death were creaking to the tread of the lady and her brother, the latter of whom knocked loudly for admission. Receiving no answer from within, they at last raised the latch and entered. The fire had long since gone out, and the night wind, as it poured down the chimney, had scattered the cold ashes over the hearth and out upon the floor. Piles of snow lay on the window sill, and a tumbler in which some water had been left standing, was broken in pieces. All this the young man saw at a glance, but when his eye fell upon the bed, he started back, for there was no mistaking the rigid, stony expression of the upturned face, which lay there so white and motionless.

"But the child—the child," he exclaimed, advancing forward—"can she, too, be dead?" and he laid his warm hand gently on Dora's brow.

The touch aroused her, and starting up, she looked around for a moment bewildered; but when at last she turned towards her mother, the dread reality was forced upon her, and in bitter tones she cried, "Mother's dead, mother's dead, and I am all alone! Oh! mother, mother, come back again to me!"

The young man's heart was touched, and taking the child's little red hands in his, he rubbed them gently, trying to soothe her grief; while his sister, summoning the inmates from the adjoining room, gave orders that the body should receive the necessary attention; then, learning as much as was possible of Dora's history, and assuring her that she should be provided for until her aunt came, she went away, promising to return next morning and be present at the humble funeral.

That evening, as Dora sat weeping by the coffin in which her mother lay, a beautiful young girl, with eyes of deepest blue, and locks of golden hair, smiled a joyous welcome to him whose *first* New Year's call had been in the chamber of death, and whose *last* was to her, the petted child of fashion.

"I had almost given you up, and was just going to cry," she said, laying her little snow-flake of a hand upon the one which that morning had chafed the small, stiff fingers of Dora Deane, and which now tenderly pressed those of Ella Grey as the young man answered, "I have not felt like going out to-day, for my first call saddened me ;" and then, with his arm around the fairy form of Ella, his affianced bride, he told her of the cold, dreary room, of the mother colder still, and of the noble little girl, who had divested herself of her own clothing, that her mother might be warm.

Ella Grey had heard of such scenes before—had cried over them in books ; but the idea that *she* could do anything to relieve the poor, had never entered her mind. It is true, she had once given a *party dress* to a starving woman, and a *pound of candy* to a ragged boy who had asked for aid, but here her charity ended ; so, though she seemed to listen with interest to the sad story, her mind was wandering elsewhere, and when her companion ceased, she merely said, "*Romantic*, wasn't it."

There was a look of disappointment on the young man's face, which was quickly observed by Ella, who attributed it to its right source, and hastened to ask numberless questions about Dora—"How old was she ? Did he think her pretty, and hadn't she better go to the funeral the next day and bring her home for a waiting-maid ?—she wanted one sadly, and from the description, the orphan girl would just suit."

"No, Ella," answered her lover ; "the child is going to live in the country with some relatives, and will be much better off there."

"The country," repeated Ella. "*I* would rather freeze lu New York than to live in the dismal country."

Again the shadow came over the gentleman's brow, as he said, "Do you indeed object so much to a home in the country ?"

Ella knew just what he wanted her to say ; so she answered, " Oh, no, I can be happy anywhere with you, but do please let me spend just one winter in the city after "——

Here she paused, while the bright blushes broke over her childish face. She could not say, even to him, "after we are married," so he said it for her, drawing her closer to his side, and forgetting Dora Deane, as he painted the joyous future when Ella would be all his own. Eleven o'clock sounded from more than one high tower, and at each stroke poor Dora Deane moaned in anguish, thinking to herself, "Last night at this time *she* was here." Eleven o'clock, said Ella Grey's diamond set watch, and pushing back her wavy hair, the young man kissed her rosy cheek, and bade her a fond good-night. As he reached the door, she called him back, while she asked him the name of the little girl who had so excited his sympathy.

" I do not know," he answered. " Strange that I forgot to inquire. But no matter. We shall never meet again ;" and feeling sure that what he said was true, he walked away.

CHAPTER III.

DORA'S RELATIVES.

THREE hundred miles to the westward, and the storm, which, on New Year's eve, swept so furiously over all parts of the State, was perceptible only in the dull, grey clouds which obscured the wintry sky, shutting out the glimmering starlight, and apparently making still brighter the many cheerful lights which shone forth from the handsome dwellings in the village of Dunwood. Still the night was intensely cold, and, as Mrs. Sarah Deane, in accordance with her daughter Eugenia's request, added a fresh bit of coal to the already well-filled stove, she sighed involuntarily, wishing the weather would abate, for the winter's store of fuel was already half gone, and the contents of her purse were far too scanty to meet the necessity of her household, and at the same time minister to the wants of her extravagant daughters.

"But I can economize in one way," she said, half aloud, and crossing the room she turned down the astral lamp which was burning brightly upon the table.

"Don't, pray mother, make it darker than a dungeon!" petulantly exclaimed Eugenia, herself turning back the lamp. "I do like to have rooms light enough to see one's self;" and glancing complacently at the reflection of her handsome face, in the mirror opposite, she resumed her former lounging attitude upon the sofa.

Mrs. Deane sighed again, but she had long since ceased to oppose the imperious Eugenia, who was to all intents and purposes the mistress of the house, and who oftentimes led her mother and weaker-minded sister into the commission of acts from which they would otherwise have shrunk. Possessed of a large share of romance, Eugenia had given to their place the name of "Locust Grove ;" and as Mrs. Deane managed to keep up a kind of outside show by practising the most pinching economy in everything pertaining to the actual comfort of her family, they were looked upon as being quite wealthy and aristocratic by those who saw nothing of their inner life—who knew nothing of the many shifts and turns in the kitchen to save money for the decoration of the parlors, or of the frequent meagre meals eaten from the pantry shelf, in order to make amends for the numerous dinner and evening parties which Eugenia and Alice insisted upon giving, and which their frequent visits to their friends rendered necessary. Extensive servant-hire was of course too expensive, and, as both Eugenia and Alice affected the utmost contempt for anything like *work*, their mother toiled in the kitchen from morning until night, assisted only by a young girl, whose mother constantly threatened to take her away, unless her wages were increased, a thing which seemed impossible.

It was just after this woman's weekly visit, and in the midst of preparations for a large dinner party, that Mrs. Deane received her sister's letter, to which there was added a postscript, in a strange handwriting, saying she was dead. There was a moisture in Mrs. Deane's eyes as she read the touching lines ; and leaning her heated forehead against the cool window pane, she, too, thought of the years gone by—of the gentle girl, the companion of her childhood, who had never given her an unkind word— of *him*—the only man she had ever loved—and Dora was their child—Fanny's child and John's.

"Yes," she said, half aloud, "I will give her a home," but anon there came stealing over her the old bitterness of feeling, which she had cherished since she knew that Fanny was preferred to herself, and then the evil of her nature whispered, "No, I will not receive their child. We can hardly manage to live now, and it is not my duty to incur an additional expense. Dora must stay where she is, and if I do not answer the letter, she will naturally suppose I never received it."

Thus deciding the matter, she crushed the letter into her pocket and went back to her work; but there was an added weight upon her spirits, while continually ringing in her ears were the words, "Care for John's child and mine." "If I could only make her of any use to me," she said at last, and then as her eye fell upon *Bridget*, whose stay with her was so uncertain, the dark thought entered her mind, "Why could not Dora fill her place? It would be a great saving, and of course the child must expect to work."

Still, reason as she would, Mrs. Deane could not at once bring herself to the point of making a menial of one who was every way her equal; neither could she decide to pass the letter by unnoticed; so for the present she strove to dismiss the subject, which was not broached to her daughters until the evening on which we first introduced them to our readers. Then taking her seat by the brightly burning lamp, she drew the letter from her pocket and read it aloud, while Alice drummed an occasional note upon the piano and Eugenie beat a tattoo upon the carpet with her delicate French slipper.

"Of course she won't come," said Alice, as her mother finished reading. "It was preposterous in Aunt Fanny to propose such a thing!" and she glanced towards Eugenie for approbation of what she had said.

Eugenia's quick, active mind had already looked at the subject in all its bearings, and in like manner with her mother she saw how Dora's presence there would be a benefit ; so to Alice's remark she replied : "It will sound well for us to have a *cousin* in the *poorhouse*, won't it ? For my part, I propose that she comes, and then be made to earn her own living. We can dismiss Bridget, who is only two years older than Dora, and we shall thus avoid quarrelling regularly with her vixenish mother, besides saving a dollar every week "——

" So make a *drudge* of Dora," interrupted Alice. " Better leave her in the poorhouse at once."

" Nobody intends to make a *drudge* of her," retorted Eugenia. " Mother works in the kitchen, and I wonder if it will hurt Dora to help her. Every girl ought to learn to work !"

" Except Eugenia Deane," suggested Alice, laughing, to think how little her sister's practice accorded with her theory.

At this point in the conversation, Bridget entered, bringing a letter which bore the India post-mark, together with the unmistakable handwriting of Nathaniel Deane !

" A letter from Uncle Nat, as I live !" exclaimed Eugenia. " What *is* going to happen ? He hasn't written before in years. I do wish I knew when he expected to quit this mundane sphere, and how much of his money he intends leaving me !"

· By this time Mrs. Deane had broken the seal, uttering an exclamation of surprise as a check for $500 fell into her lap.

" Five hundred dollars !" screamed Eugenia, catching up the check and examining it closely, to see that there was no mistake. "The old miser has really opened his heart Now, we'll have some *genuine* silver forks for our best company, so we shan't be in constant terror lest some one should discover that they are only plated. I'll buy that set of *pearls* at Mercer's, too, and, Alice, you and I will have some new furs. I'd go to Rochester to-morrow, if it were not Sunday. What shall we get for you, mother ? A web of cloth, or an ounce of sewing silk ?" and the heartless girl turned towards her mother, whose face was white as ashes, as she said faintly : "The money is not ours. It is Dora's—— to be used for her benefit."

"Not ours ! What do you mean ? It can't be true !" cried Eugenia, snatching the letter, and reading therein a confirmation of her mother's words.

After a slight apology for his long silence, Uncle Nat had spoken of Fanny's letter, saying he supposed she must be dead ere this, and that Dora was probably living with her aunt, as it was quite natural she should do. Then he expressed his willingness to defray all the expense which she might be, adding that though he should never see her, as he was resolved to spend his days in India, he still wished to think of her as an educated and accomplished woman.

"Accompanying this letter," he wrote, "is a check for $500, to be used for Dora's benefit. Next year I will make another remittance, increasing the allowance as she grows older. I have more money than I need, and I know of no one on whom I would sooner expend it than the child of Fanny Moore."

"Spiteful old fool !" muttered Eugenia, "I could relieve him of any superfluous dimes he may possess."

But even Eugenia, heartless as she was, felt humbled and subdued for a moment, as she read the latter part of her uncle's letter, from which we give the following extract :

"I am thinking, to-day, of the past, Sarah, and I grow a very child again as I recall the dreary years which have gone over my head, since last I trod the shores of my father-land. You, Sarah, know much of my history. You know that I was awkward, eccentric, uncouth, and many years older than my handsomer, more highly gifted brother; and yet with all this fearful odds against me, you know that I ventured to love the gentle, fair-haired Fanny, your adopted sister. You know this, I say, but you do not know how madly, how passionately such as I can love—did love ; nor how the memory of Fanny's ringing laugh, and the thought of the sunny smile, with which I knew she would welcome me home again, cheered me on my homeward voyage, when in the long night-watches I paced the vessel's deck, while the stars looked coldly down upon me, and there was no sound to break the deep stillness, save the heavy swell of the sea. At the village inn where I stopped for a moment ere going to my father's house, I first heard that her hand was plighted to another, and in my wild frenzy, I swore that my rival, whoever it might be, should die !

" It was my youngest brother—he, who, on the sad night when our mother died, had laid his baby head upon my bosom, and wept himself to sleep—he whose infant steps I had guided, bearing him often in my arms, lest he should ' dash his foot against a stone.' And *his* life I had sworn to take, for had he not come between me and the only object I had ever loved ? There was no one stirring about the house, for it was night, and the family had retired. But the door was unfastened, and I knew the way up-stairs. I found him, as I had expected, in our old room, and all alone ; for Richard was away. Had he been there, it should make no difference, I said, but he was absent, and John was calmly sleeping with his face upturned to the soft moonlight which came in through the open window. I had not seen him for two long years, and now there was about him a look so much like that of my dead mother when she lay in her coffin bed, that the demon in my heart was softened, and I seemed to hear her dying words again, 'I can trust you, Nathaniel ; and to your protection, as to a second mother, I commit my little boy.'

" The little boy, whose curls were golden then, was now a brown-haired man—my brother—the son of my angel mother, whose spirit, in that dark hour of my temptation, glided into the silent room, and stood between me and her youngest born, so that *he* was not harmed, and *I* was saved from the curse of a brother's blood.

" ' Lead us not into temptation,' came back to me, just as I had said it kneeling at my mother's side ; and covering my face with my hands, I thanked God, who had kept me from so great a sin. Bending low, I whispered in his ear his name, and in a moment his arms were around my neck, while he welcomed me back to the home, which, he said, was not home without me. And then, when the moon had gone down, and the stars shone too faintly to reveal his blushes, he told me the story of his happiness, to which I listened, while the great drops of sweat rolled down my face and moistened the pillow on which my head was resting.

" But why linger over those days of anguish, which made me an old man before my time ? I knew I could not stand by and see her wedded to another—neither could I look upon her after she was another's wife ; so, one night, when the autumn days were come, I asked her to go with me out beneath the locust trees, which skirted my father's yard. It was there I had seen her for the first time, and it was there I would take my final leave. Of the particulars of that interview I remember but little, for I was terribly ex cited. We never met again, for ere the morrow's daylight dawned, I had left my home forever " ——

Then followed a few more words concerning Dora, with a request that she should write to him, as he would thus be able to judge something of her character ; and there the letter ended.

For a time there was silence, which was broken at last by Eugenia, whose active mind had already come to a decision. Dora would live with them, of course—it was best that she should, and there was no longer need for dismissing Bridget. The five hundred dollars obviated that necessity, and it was *theirs*, too—theirs by way of remuneration for giving Dora a home—theirs to spend as they pleased. And she still intended to have the *furs*, the *pearls*, and the *silver forks*, just the same as though the money had been a special gift to her !

" Suppose *Uncle Nat* should happen to come home, and Dora should tell him ?" suggested Alice, who did not so readily fall in with her sister's views.

" He'll never do that in the world," returned Eugenia. " And even if he should, Dora will have nothing to tell, for she is not supposed to know of the money. If we feed, clothe, and educate her, it is all we are required to do."

" But would that be exactly just ?" faintly interposed Mrs. Deane, whose perceptions of right and wrong were not quite so blunted as those of her daughter, who, in answer to her question, proceeded to advance many good reasons why Dora, for a time at least, should be kept in ignorance of the fact that her uncle supported her, and not her aunt.

" We can manage her better if she thinks she is dependent upon us And then, as she grows older, she will not be continually asking what has become of the money, which, as I understand the matter, is really *ours*, and not *hers* "

2

Still, Mrs. Deane was not quite convinced, but she knew how useless it would be to argue the point; so she said nothing, except to ask how Dora was to get there, as she could not come alone.

"I have it," answered Eugenia. "I have long wished to spend a few days in New York, but that bane of my life, poverty, has always prevented. Now, however, as old Uncle Nat has kindly furnished us with the means, I propose that Alice and I start day after to-morrow, and return on Saturday. That will give us ample time to see the *lions* and get the city fashions."

"It will cost a great deal for you both to stay at those large hotels," said Mrs. Deane; and Eugenie replied—

"One hundred dollars will cover all the expense, and pay Dora's fare besides. What is the use of money, if we can't use it? I shall get my furs, and jewelry, and forks while I'm there, so I'll better take along three hundred and fifty dollars, for fear of any accident. We are not obliged to spend it all, of course;" she added, as she saw the look of dismay on her mother's face. "And we can bring back whatever there is left."

For nineteen years Eugenia Deane had been suffered to have her way, and her mother did not like to thwart her now, for her temper was violent, and she dreaded an outbreak; so she merely sighed in reply, and when, on Monday morning, Eugenia started for New York, her purse contained the desired $350, which, after her arrival in the city, was spent as freely as if it really belonged to her, and not to the orphan Dora, who was now staying with Mrs. Grannis, a kind-hearted woman in the same block where her mother had died. The furs were bought, the pearls examined, the forks priced, and then Alice ventured to ask when they were going to find Dora.

"I shall leave that for the last thing," answered Eugenia "She can't run away, and nobody wants to be bothered with a child to look after."

So for three more days little Dora looked out of the dingy window upon the dirty court below, wishing her aunt would come, and wondering if she should like her. At last, towards the close of Friday afternoon, there was a knock at the door, and a haughty-looking, elegantly dressed young lady inquired if a little orphan girl lived there.

"That's her—Aunt Sarah," exclaimed Dora, springing joyfully forward; but she paused and started back, as she met the cold, scrutinizing glance of Eugenia's large black eyes.

"Are you the child I am looking for?" asked Eugenia, without deigning to notice Mrs. Grannis's request that she would walk in.

"I am Dora Deane," was the simple answer; and then, as briefly as possible, Eugenia explained that she had been sent for her, and that early the next morning she would call to take her to the depot.

"*Did* you know mother? Are you any relation?" asked Dora, trembling with eager expectation; and Alice, who, without her sister's influence, would have been a comparatively kind-hearted girl, answered softly, "We are your cousins."

There was much native politeness, and natural refinement of manner about Dora, and instinctively her little chubby hand was extended towards her newly found relative, who pressed it gently, glancing the while at her sister, who, without one word of sympathy for the orphan girl, walked away through the winding passage, and down the narrow stairs, out into the sunlight, where, breathing more freely, she exclaimed, "What a horrid place! I hope I haven't caught anything. Didn't Dora look like a Dutch doll in that long dress, and high-neck apron ?"

"Her face is pretty, though," returned Alice, "and her eyes are beautiful—neither blue nor black, but a mixture of both. How I pitied her as they filled with tears when you were talking ! Why didn't you speak to her ?"

"Because I'd nothing to say," answered Eugenia, stepping into the carriage which had brought them there, and ordering the driver to go next to Stuart's, where she wished to look again at a velvet cloak. "It is so cheap, and so becoming, too, that I am half tempted to get it," she exclaimed.

"Mother won't like it, I know," said Alice, who herself began to have some fears for the $350.

"Fudge !" returned Eugenia, adding the next moment, "I wonder if she'll have to buy clothes for Dora the first thing. I hope not," and she drew around her the costly fur, for which she had paid fifty dollars.

Of course the cloak was bought, together with several other articles equally *cheap* and becoming, and by the time the hotel bills were paid, there were found in the purse just twenty-five dollars, with which to pay their expenses back to Dunwood.

————

There were bitter tears shed at the parting next morning in Mrs. Grannis's humble room, for Dora felt that the friends to whom she was going, were not like those she left behind; and very lovingly her arms wound themselves around the poor widow's neck as she wept her last adieu, begging Mrs. Grannis not to forget her, but to write sometimes, and tell her of the lady who had so kindly befriended her.

"We can't wait any longer," cried Eugenia, and will

ore more farewell kiss, Dora went out of the house where she had experienced much of happiness, and where had come to ner her deepest grief.

"Forlorn! What is that old thing going for! Leave it," said Eugenia, touching with her foot a square, green trunk or chest, which stood by the side of the long, sack like carpet-bag containing Dora's wardrobe.

"It was father's—and mother's clothes are in it," answered Dora, with quivering lips.

There was something in the words and manner of the little girl, as she laid her hand reverently on the offending trunk, that touched even Eugenia ; and she said no more. An hour later, and the attention of more than one passenger in the Hudson River cars was attracted towards the two stylish-looking ladies who came in, laden with bundles, and followed by a little girl in black, for whom no seat was found save the one by the door where the wind crept in, and the unmelted frost still covered the window pane.

"Won't you be cold here ?" asked Alice, stopping a moment, ere passing on to her own warm seat near the stove.

"No matter ; I am used to it," was Dora's meek reply ; and wrapping her thin, half-worn shawl closer about her, and drawing her feet up beneath her, she soon fell asleep, dreaming sweet dreams of the home to which she was going, and of the Aunt Sarah who would be to her a second mother !

God help thee, Dora Deane !

CHAPTER IV.

DORA'S NEW HOME.

ONE year has passed away since the night when, cold, weary and forlorn, Dora followed her cousins up the gravelled walk which led to her new home. Onè whole year, and in that time she has somewhat changed. The merry hearted girl, who, until a few weeks before her mother's death, was happier far than many a favored child of wealth, has become a sober, quiet, self-reliant child, performing without a word of complaint the many duties which have gradually been imposed upon her.

From her aunt she had received a comparatively welcome greeting, and when Eugenia displayed her purchases, which had swallowed up the entire three hundred and fifty dollars, Mrs. Deane had laid her hand on the little girl's soft, auburn hair, as if to ask forgiveness for the injustice done her by the selfish Eugenia, whose only excuse for her extravagance was, that "no one in her right mind need to think of bringing back any money from New York."

And Dora, from her seat on a little stool behind the stove, understood nothing, thought of nothing, except that Eugenia looked beautifully in her velvet cloak and furs, and that her aunt must be very rich, to afford so many handsome articles of furniture as the parlor contained.

"And I am glad that she is," she thought, "fcr she will not be so likely to think me in the way."

As time passed on, however, Dora, who was a close ob
server, began to see things in their true light, and her life
was far from being happy. By her cousin Alice she was
treated with a tolerable degree of kindness, while Eugenia,
without any really evil intention, perhaps, seemed to take
delight in annoying her sensitive cousin, constantly taunting
her with her dependence upon them, and asking her sometimes how she expected to repay the debt of gratitude she
owed them. Many and many a night had the orphan wept
herself to sleep, in the low, scantily furnished chamber
which had been assigned her; and she was glad when at
last an opportunity was presented for her to be in a measure out of Eugenia's way, and at the same time feel that
she was doing something towards earning her living.

The oft-repeated threat of Bridget's mother that her
daughter should be removed, unless her wages were increased, was finally carried into effect; and one Saturday
night, Mrs. Deane was startled by the announcement that
Bridget was going to leave. In a moment, Dora's resolution was taken, and coming to her aunt's side, she
said:

"Don't hire another girl, Aunt Sarah. Let *me* help you.
I can do almost as much as Bridget, and you won't have to
pay me either. *I* shall only be paying you."

Unclasping the handsome bracelet which had been purchased with a portion of the remaining one hundred and
fifty dollars, Eugenia, ere her mother had time to reply,
exclaimed:

"That is a capital idea! I wonder how you happened
to be so thoughtful."

And so it was decided that Dora should take Bridget's
place, she thinking how much she would do, and how hard
she would try to please her aunt, who quieted her own con

science by saying "it was only a temporary arrangement, until she could find another servant."

But as the days went by, the temporary arrangement bid fair to become permanent, for Mrs. Deane could not be insensible to the vast difference which Bridget's absence made in her weekly expenses. Then, too, Dora was so will- ing to work, and so uncomplaining, never seeking a word of commendation, except once, indeed, when she timidly ven- tured to ask Eugenia if " what she did was enough to pay for her board ?"

" Just about," was Eugenia's answer, which, indifferent as it was, cheered the heart of Dora, as, day after day, she toiled on in the comfortless kitchen, until her hands, which, when she came to Locust Grove, were soft and white as those of an infant, became rough and brown, and her face gradually assumed the same dark hue, for she could not always stop to tie on her sun-bonnet, when sent for wood or water.

With the coming of summer, arrangements had been made for sending her to school, though Mrs. Deane felt at first as if she could not be deprived of her services. Still for appearance's sake, if for nothing more, she must go ; and with the earliest dawn the busy creature was up, work- ing like a bee, that her aunt and cousins might not have so much to do in her absence. At first she went regularly, but after a time it became very convenient to detain her at home, for at least two days in every week, and this wrung from her almost the only tears she had shed since the morn- ing, when, of her own accord, she had gone into the kitchen to perform a servant's duties.

Possessing naturally a fondness for books, and feeling ambitious to keep up with her class, she at last conceived the idea of studying at home ; and many a night, long after her aunt and cousins were asleep, she sat up alone, poring over her books, sometimes by the dim light of a lamp, and again by the light of the full moon, whose rays seemed to fall around her more brightly than elsewhere. It was on one of these occasions, when tracing upon her map the boundary lines of India, that her thoughts reverted to her uncle Nathaniel, whose name she seldom heard, and of whom she had never but once spoken. Then in the presence of her aunt and cousins she had wondered why he did not answer her mother's letter.

"Because he has nothing to write, I presume," said Eugenia, who would not trust her mother to reply.

And Dora, wholly unsuspecting, never dreamed of the five hundred dollars sent over for her benefit, and which was spent long ago—though not for her—never dreamed of the letter which Eugenia had written in reply, thanking her uncle again and again for his generous gift, which she said "was very acceptable, for *ma* was rather poor, and it would aid her materially in providing for the wants of Dora," who was represented as being "a queer, old-fashioned child, possessing but little affection for any one, and who never spoke of her uncle Nathaniel, or manifested the least gratitude for what he was doing!"

In short, the impression left upon the mind of Uncle Nat was that Dora, aside from being cold-hearted, was uncommonly dull, and would never make much of a woman, do what they might for her! With a sigh, and a feeling of keen disappointment, he read the letter, saying to himself, as he laid it away, "Can this be true of Fanny's child?"

But this, we say, *Fanny's child* did not know; and as her eye wandered over the painted map of India, she resolved to write and to tell him of her mother's dying words—tell

2*

him how much she loved him, because he was her father's
brother, and how she wished he would come home, that
she might know him better.

"If I only had some keepsake to send him—something
he would prize," she thought, when her letter was finished.
And then, as she enumerated her small store of treasures,
she remembered her mother's beautiful hair, which had been
cut from her head, as she lay in her coffin, and which now
held a place in the large square trunk. "I will send him a
lock of that," she said; and kneeling reverently by the
old green trunk, the shrine where she nightly said her
prayers, she separated from the mass of rich, brown hair,
one long, shining tress, which she inclosed within her letter,
adding, in a postscript, "It is mother's hair, and Dora's
tears have often fallen upon it. 'Tis all I have to give."

Poor little Dora ! Nathaniel Deane would have prized
that simple gift far more than all the wealth which he called
his, but it was destined never to reach him. The wily
Eugenia, to whom Dora applied for an envelope, unhesitatingly showing what she had written, knew better than to
send that note across the sea, and feigning the utmost
astonishment, she said : "I am surprised, Dora, that after
your mother's ill-success, you should think of writing to
Uncle Nat. He is a suspicious, miserly old fellow, and will
undoubtedly think you are after his money !"

"I wouldn't send it for the world, if I supposed he'd fancy
such a thing as that," answered Dora, her eyes filling with
tears

"Of course you wouldn't," continued Eugenia, perceiving
her advantage and following it up "You can do as you
like, but my advice is that you do not send it; let him
write to *you* first, if he wishes to open a correspondence !"

This decided the matter, and turning sadly away, Dora went back to her chamber, hiding the letter and the lock of hair in the old green trunk.

"How *can* you be so utterly void of principle?" asked Alice, as Dora quitted the room; and Eugenia replied : "It isn't a lack of principle, it's only my good management. I have my plans, and I do not intend they shall be frustrated by that foolish letter, which would, of course, be followed by others of the same kind. Now I am perfectly willing that Uncle Nat should divide his fortune between us and Dora, but unfortunately he is a *one idea* man, and should he conceive a fancy for our cousin, our hopes are blasted forever ; so I don't propose letting him do any such thing. Mother has given up the correspondence to me, and I intend making the old gentleman think I am a most perfect specimen of what a young lady should be, saying, of course, an occasional good word for *you !* I believe I understand him tolerably well, and if in the end I win, I pledge you my word that Dora shall not be forgotten. Are you satisfied ?"

Alice could not say yes, but she knew it was useless to reason with her sister, so she remained silent; while a curious train of thoughts passed through her mind, resulting at last in an increased kindness of manner on her part towards her young cousin, who was frequently relieved of duties which would otherwise have detained her from school. And Dora's step grew lighter, and her heart happier, as she thought that Alice at least cared for her welfare.

On New Year's Day there came a letter from Uncle Nat, containing the promised check, which Eugenia held up to view, while she read the following brief lines :

"Many thanks to Eugenia for her kind and welcome letter, which I may answer at some future time, when I have anything interesting to say."

"Have you written to Uncle Nat, and did you tell him

of me, or of mother's letter ?" exclaimed Dora, who had been sitting unobserved behind the stove, and who now sprang eagerly forward, while her cheeks glowed with excitement.

Soon recovering her composure, Eugenia answered, " Yes, I wrote to him, and, of course, mentioned you with the rest of us. His answer you have heard."

" But the other paper," persisted Dora. " Doesn't that say anything ?"

For a moment Eugenia hesitated, and then, deciding that no harm could come of Dora's knowing of the money, provided she was kept in ignorance of the object for which it was sent, she replied, carelessly, " Oh, that's nothing but a check. The old gentleman was generous enough to send us a little money, which we need badly enough."

There was not one particle of selfishness in Dora's disposition, and without a thought or wish that any of the money should be expended for herself, she replied, " Oh, I am so glad, for now Aunt Sarah can have that shawl she has wanted so long, and Alice the new merino."

Dear little Dora! she did not know why Eugenia's eyes so quickly sought the floor, nor understand why her aunt's hand was laid upon her head so caressingly. Neither did she know that Alice's sudden movement towards the window was to hide the expression of her face ; but when, a few days afterwards, she was herself presented with a handsome merino, which both Eugenia and Alice volunteered to make, she thought there was not in Dunwood a happier child than herself. In the little orphan's pathway there were a few sunny spots, and that night when, by the old green trunk, she knelt her down to pray, she asked of God that he would reward her aunt and cousins according to their kindnesses done to her !

Need we say that childish prayer was answered to the letter !

CHAPTER V.

ROSE HILL.

A LITTLE way out of the village of Dunwood, and situated upon a slight eminence, was a large, handsome building, which had formerly been owned by a Frenchman, who, from the great profusion of roses growing upon his grounds, had given to the place the name of "Rose Hill." Two years before our story opens, the Frenchman died, and since that time Rose Hill had been unoccupied, but now it had another proprietor, and early in the summer Mr. Howard Hastings and lady would take possession of their new home.

Of Mr. Hastings nothing definite was known, except that he was a man of unbounded wealth and influence— "and a little peculiar withal," so said Mrs. Leah, the matron, who had come up from New York to superintend the arrangement of the house, which was fitted up in a style of elegance far surpassing what most of Dunwood's inhabitants had seen before, and was for two or three weeks thrown open to the public. Mrs. Leah, who was a servant in Mr. Hastings's family and had known her young mistress's husband from childhood, was inclined to be rather communicative, and when asked to explain what she meant by Mr. Hastings's peculiarities, replied, "Oh, he's queer every way—and no wonder, with his kind of a mother. Why, she is rich as a Jew, and for all that, she made her only daughter learn how to do all kinds of work. It would make her a better wife, she said, and so, because *Ella* had rather lie on the sofa and read a nice novel than to be pokin' round in the kitchen and tending to things, as he calls it, Mr. Hastings looks blue and talks about *woman's* duties, and all that nonsense. Recently he has taken it into his head that late hours are killing her—that it isn't healthy for her to go every night to parties, concerts, operas, and the like o' that, so he's going to bury her in the stupid country, where she'll be moped to death, for of course there's nobody here that she'll associate with."

"The wretch!" exclaimed Eugenia, who formed one of the group of listeners to this precious bit of gossip ; but whether she intended this cognomen for the cruel husband, or Mrs. Leah, we do not know, as she continued to question the old lady of Mrs. Hastings herself, asking if her health were delicate and if she were pretty.

"Delicate! I guess she is," returned Mrs. Leah. "If she hasn't got the consumption now, she will have it. Why, her face is as white as some of them lilies that used to grow on the ponds in old Connecticut ; and then to think her husband won't let her take all the comfort she can, the little time she has to live! It's too bad," and the corner of Dame Leah's silk apron went up to her eyes, as she thought how her lady was aggrieved. Soon recovering her composure, she reverted to Eugenia's last question, and hastened to reply, "*Pretty*, don't begin to express it. Just imagine the least little bit of a thing, with the whitest face, the bluest eyes and the yellowest curls, dressed in a light blue silk wrapper, all lined with white satin, and tied with a tassel as big as my fist ; wouldn't such a creature look well in the kitchen, telling Hannah it was time to get dinner, and seeing if Tom was cleaning the vegetables !"

And Mrs. Leah's nose went up at the very idea of a blue silk wrapper being found outside of the parlor, even if the husband of said wrapper *did* have to wait daily at least two hours for his badly cooked dinner !

"Oh, but you ought to see her dressed for a party," continued Mrs. Leah, "she looks like a queen, all sparkling with diamonds and pearls ; but she'll never go to many more, poor critter !"

And as the good lady's services were just then needed in another part of the building, she bade good morning to her audience, who commented upon what they had heard, each according to their own ideas—some warmly commending Mr. Hastings for removing his delicate young wife from the unwholesome atmosphere of the city, while others, and among them Eugenia, thought he ought to let her remain in New York, if she chose. Still, while commiserating Mrs. Hastings for being obliged to live in "that *stupid village*," Eugenia expressed her pleasure that she was coming, and on her way home imparted to Alice her intention of being quite intimate with the New York lady, notwithstanding what "the spiteful old Mrs. Leah" had said about there being no one in Dunwood fit for her to associate with. In almost perfect ecstasy Dora listened to her cousin's animated description of Rose Hill, its handsome rooms and elegant furniture, and while her cheeks glowed with excitement, she exclaimed, "Oh, how I wish I could *really* live in such a house !"

"And I shouldn't wonder if you did. Your present prospects look very much like it," was Eugenia's scornful reply, which Dora scarcely heard, for her thoughts were busy elsewhere.

She had an eye for the beautiful, and, strange to say, would at any time have preferred remaining in her aunt's pleasant parlor, to washing dishes from off the long kitchen table; but as this last seemed to be her destiny, she submitted without a murmur, contenting herself the while by building *castles,* just as many a child has done before her, and will do again. Somehow, too, Dora's castles, particularly the one of which she was mistress, were always large and beautiful, just like Eugenia's description of Rose Hill, to which she had listened with wonder, it seemed so natural, so familiar, so like the realization of what she had many a time dreamed, while her hands were busy with the dish-towel or the broom.

Dora was a strange child—so her mother and her aunt Sarah both had told her—so her teachers thought, and so her companions said, when she stole away by herself to *think,* preferring her own thoughts to the pastime of her schoolmates. This *thinking* was almost the only recreation which Dora had, and as it seldom interfered with the practical duties of her life, no one was harmed if she did sometimes imagine the most improbable things ; and if for a few days succeeding her cousin's visit to Rose Hill, she did seem a little inattentive, and somewhat abstracted, it was merely because she had for a time changed places with the fashionable Mrs. Hastings, whose blue silk morning-gown, while discussed in the *parlor,* was worn in fancy in the *kitchen.*

Dream on, Dora Deane, dream on—but guard this, your last imagining, most carefully from the proud Eugenia, who would scarce deem you worthy to take upon your lips the name of Mrs. Hastings, much less to be even in fancy the mistress of Rose Hill.

CHAPTER VI.

MR. AND MRS. HASTINGS.

In blissful ignorance of the gossip which his movements were exciting in Dunwood, Mr. Hastings in the city went quietly on with the preparations for his removal, purchasing and storing away in divers baskets, boxes and bags, many luxuries which he knew he could not readily procure in the country, and which would be sadly missed by his young girl-wife, who sat all day in her mother's parlor, bemoaning her fate in being thus doomed to a life in the "horribly vulgar country." She had forgotten that she could live anywhere with *him*," for the Ella Hastings of to-day is the Ella Grey of little more than a year ago, the same who had listened to the sad story of *Dora Deane*, without ever thinking that some day in the future she should meet the little girl who made such an impression upon her husband.

Howard Hastings was not the only man who, with a grand theory as to what a wife ought to be, had married from pure fancy; finding too late that she whom he took for a companion was a mere plaything—a doll to be dressed up and sent out into the fashionable world, where alone her happiness could be found. Still the disappointment to such is not the less bitter, because others, too, are suffering from the effect of a like hallucination, and Howard Hastings felt it most keenly. He loved, or fancied he loved, Ella Grey devotedly, and when in her soft flowing robes of richly embroidered lace, with the orange blossoms resting upon her golden curls, and her long eye-lashes veiling her eyes of blue, she had stood at the altar as his bride, there was not in all New York a prouder or a happier man. Alas, that in the intimate relations of married life, there should ever be brought to light faults whose existence was never suspected! Yet so it is, and the honey-moon had scarcely waned, ere Mr. Hastings began to feel a very little disappointed, as, one after another, the peculiarities of his wife were unfolded to his view.

In all *his* pictures of domestic bliss, there had ever been a home of his own, a cheerful fireside, to which he could repair, when the day's toil was done, but Ella would not hear of housekeeping. To be sure, it would be very pleasant to keep up a grand establishment and give splendid dinner-parties, but she knew that Howard, with his peculiar notions, would expect her to do just as his " dear, fussy old mother did," and that, she wouldn't for a moment think of, for she really " did not know the *names* of one half the queer looking things in the kitchen."

" She will improve as she grows older—she is very young yet, but little more than eighteen," thought Mr. Hastings; and his heart softened toward her, as he remembered the kind of training she had received from her mother, who was a pure slave of fashion, and would have deemed her daughters degraded had they possessed any knowledge of work

And still, when the aristocratic Howard Hastings had sued for Ella's hand, she felt honored, notwithstanding that both his mother and sister were known to be well skilled in everything pertaining to what she called "drudgery." To remove his wife from her mother's influence, and at the same time prolong her life, for she was really very delicate, was Mr. Hastings's aim ; and as he had always fancied a home in the country, he at last purchased Rose Hill farm in spite of Ella's tears, and the frowns of her mother, who declared it impossible for her daughter to live without society, and pronounced all country people "rough, ignorant and vulgar."

All this Ella believed, and though she was far too amiable and sweet-tempered to be really angry, she came very near *sulking* all the way from New York to Dunwood But when at the depot, she met the new carriage and horses which had been purchased- expressly for herself, she was somewhat mollified, and telling her husband "he was the best man in the world," she took the reins in her own little soft, white hands, and laughed aloud as she saw how the spirited creatures obeyed her slightest wish. From the parlor windows of Locust Grove, Eugenia and her sister looked out upon the strangers, pronouncing Mr. Hastings the most elegant-looking man they had ever seen, while his wife, the girlish Ella, was thought far too pale to be very beautiful.

Near the gate at the entrance to Rose Hill, was a clear limpid stream, where the school-children often played, and where they were now assembled. A little apart from the rest, seated upon a mossy bank, with her bare feet in the running water, and her rich auburn hair shading her brown cheeks, was Dora Deane, not dreaming this time, but watching so intently a race between two of her companions, that she did not see the carriage until it was directly opposite. Then, guessing who its occupants were, she started up, coloring crimson as she saw the lady's eyes fixed upon her, and felt sure she was the subject of remark.

"Look, Howard," said Ella. "I suppose that is what you call a rural sight—a bare-foot girl, with a burnt face and huge sun-bonnet ?"

Ere Mr. Hastings could reply, Dora, wishing to redeem her character, which she was sure she had lost by having been caught with her feet in the brook, darted forward and opening the gate, held it for them to pass.

"Shall I give her some money?" softly whispered Ella, feeling for her purse.

"Hush-sh!" answered Mr. Hastings, for he knew that money would be an insult to Dora, who felt more than repaid by the pleasant smile he gave her as he said, "Thank you, miss."

"I have seen a face like his before," thought Dora, as she walked slowly down the road, while the carriage kept on its way, and soon carried Ella to her new home.

Not to be pleased with Rose Hill was impossible, and as the young wife's eye fell upon the handsome building, with its cool, vine-wreathed piazza—upon the shaded walks, the sparkling fountains and the thousands of roses which were now in full bloom, she almost cried with delight, even forgetting, for a time, that she was in the "horrid country." But she was ere long reminded of the fact by Mrs. Leah, who told of the "crowds of gaping people," who had been up to see the house. With a deprecating glance at the village where the "gaping people" were supposed to live, Ella drew nearer to her husband, expressing a wish that the good folks of Dunwood would confine their calls to the house and grounds, and not be troubling her. But in this she was destined to be disappointed, for the inhabitants of Dunwood were friendly, social people, who knew no good reason why they should not be on terms of equality with the little lady of Rose Hill; and one afternoon, about a week after her arrival at Dunwood, she was told that some ladies were waiting for her in the parlor.

"Dear me! Sophy," said she, while a frown for an

instant clouded her pretty face, "tell them I'm not at home."

"But I just told them you were," answered Sophy, adding that "the ladies were well-dressed and fine looking," and suggesting that her young mistress should wear down something more appropriate than the soiled white muslin wrapper in which she had lounged all day, because "it was not worth her while to dress, when there was no one but her *husband* to see her."

This, however, Ella refused to do. "It was good enough for country folks," she said, as she rather reluctantly descended to the parlor, where her first glance at her visitors made her half regret that she had not followed Sophy's advice. Mrs. Judge Howell and her daughter-in-law were refined, cultivated women, and ere Ella had conversed with them five minutes, she felt that if there was between them any point of inferiority, it rested with herself, and not with them. They had travelled much, both in the Old and New World; and though their home was in Boston, they spent almost every summer in Dunwood, which Mrs. Howell pronounced a most delightful village, assuring Ella that she could not well avoid being happy and contented. Very wonderingly the large childish blue eyes went up to the face of Mrs. Howell, who, interpreting aright their expression, casually remarked that when she was young, she fell into the foolish error of thinking there could be *nobody* outside the walls of a city. "But the experience of sixty years has changed my mind materially," said she, "for I have met quite as many refined and cultivated people in the country as in the city."

This was a new idea to Ella, and the next visitors, who came in just after Mrs. Howell left, were obliged to wait while she made quite an elaborate toilet.

"Oh, Ella, how much better you are looking than you were 'au hour or two since," exclaimed Mr. Hastings, who entered the chamber just as his wife was leaving it.

"There's company in the parlor," answered Ella, trip ping lightly away, while her husband walked on into the dressing-room, where he stepped first over a pair of slippers, then over a muslin wrapper, and next over a towel, which Ella in her haste had left upon the floor, her usual place for everything.

This time the visitors proved to be Eugenia and Alice, with the first of whom the impulsive Ella was perfectly delighted, she was so refined, so genteel, so richly dressed, and assumed withal such a *patronizing* air, that the short-sighted Ella felt rather overawed, particularly when she spoke of her "Uncle in India," with whom she was "*such* a favorite." During their stay, *servants* were introduced as a topic of conversation, and on that subject Eugenia was quite as much at home as Mrs. Hastings, descanting at large upon the many annoyances one was compelled to endure, both from the "ignorance and impertinence of hired help." Once or twice, too, the words "my waiting-maid" escaped her lips, and when at last she took her leave, she had the satisfaction of knowing that Mrs. Hastings was duly impressed with a sense of her importance.

"Such charming people I never expected to find in the country, and so elegantly dressed too," thought Ella, as from her window she watched them walking slowly down the long avenue. "That silk of Miss Eugenia's could not have cost less than two dollars a yard, and her hands, too, were as soft and white as mine. They must be wealthy—those Deanes : I wonder if they ever give any parties."

And then, as she remembered sundry gossamer fabrics which were dignified by the title of party dresses, and which, with many tears she had folded away as something she should never need in the country, she exclaimed aloud, "Why, can't *I* have a party here as well as at home? The house is a great deal larger than the long narrow thing on which mamma prides herself so much. And then it will be such fun to show off before the country people, who, of course, are not all as refined as the Deanes. I'll speak to Howard about it immediately."

"Speak to me about what?" asked Mr. Hastings, who had entered the parlor in time to hear the last words of his wife.

Very briefly Ella stated to him her plan of giving a large party as soon as a sufficient number of the village people had called.

"You know you wish me to be sociable with them," she continued, as she saw the slightly comical expression of her husband's face; "and how can I do it better than by inviting them to my house?"

"I am perfectly willing for the party," answered Mr. Hastings, "but I do rather wonder what has so soon changed your mind."

"Oh, nothing much," returned Ella, "only the people don't seem half as vulgar as mamma said they would. I wish you could see Eugenia Deane. She's perfectly magnificent—wears a diamond ring, Valenciennes lace, and all that. Her mother is very wealthy, isn't she?"

"I have never supposed so—if you mean the widow Deane, who lives at the place called 'Locust Grove,'" answered Mr. Hastings; and Ella continued, "Yes, she is, I am sure, from the way Eugenia talked. They keep servants, I know, for she spoke of a waiting-maid. Then, too, they have an old bachelor uncle in India, with a million or more, and these two young ladies will undoubtedly inherit it all at his death."

"Miss Deane must have been very communicative," said Mr. Hastings, who understood the world much better than his wife, and who readily guessed that Miss Eugenia had passed herself off for quite as much as she was.

"It was perfectly natural for her to tell me what she did," answered Ella, "and I like her so much! I mean to drive over there soon, and take her out riding."

Here the conversation was interrupted by the ringing of the door-bell, and it was not again resumed until the Monday morning following, when, at the breakfast-table Ella asked for the carriage to be sent round, as "she was going to call at Mrs. Deane's, and take the young ladies to ride."

"But it is washing-day," suggested Mr. Hastings, wishing to tease his wife. "And nothing," I am told, "mortifies a woman more than to be caught with her hair in papers, and her arms in the suds. So, if you value your friend Eugenia's feelings, you had better wait until to-morrow."

"Suds, Howard! What do you mean?" asked the indignant Ella. "Eugenia Deane's hands never saw a wash-tub! Why, they are almost as white as mine." And the little lady glanced rather admiringly at the small snowy fingers, which handled so gracefully the heavy knife and fork of silver.

"You have my permission to go," said Mr. Hastings, "but I am inclined to think you'll have to wait a long time for your friends to make their appearance."

Mentally resolving not to tell him if she did, Ella ran up to her room, where, leaving her morning dress in the middle of the floor, and donning a handsome plaid silk, she descended again to the parlor, and suggested to her husband the propriety of bringing the young ladies home with her to dinner, alleging, as one reason, that "there was no use of having a silver dining set and nice things, unless there was somebody to see them."

"And am not *I* somebody?" asked Mr. Hastings, playfully winding his arm around the little creature, who answered, "Why, yes—but mamma never thought it worth her while always to have *the best things* and fix up when there was no one to dinner but us and father ; and I don't think I need to be so particular as when I was Ella Grey and you were Mr. Hastings, for now I am your wife, and you are"——

Here she paused, while she stooped down to caress a huge Newfoundland dog, which came bounding in. Then, remembering she had not finished her sentence, she added, after a moment, "And you are *only Howard!*"

Silenced, if not convinced, Mr. Hastings walked away, wondering if every husband, at the expiration of fifteen months, reached the enviable position of being "only Howard!" Half an hour later, and Ella Hastings, having left orders with Mrs. Leah for a "company dinner," was riding down the shaded avenue into the highway, where she bade the coachman drive in the direction of Locust Grove

CHAPTER VII.

THE VISIT.

THE plain though comfortable breakfast of dry toast, baked potatoes and black tea was over. This morning it had been eaten from the kitchen table; for, as Mr. Hastings had surmised, it was *washing day*, and on such occasions, wishing to save work, Mrs. Deane would not suffer the dining-room to be occupied. To this arrangement the proud Eugenia submitted the more readily, as she knew that at this hour they were not liable to calls; so, she who had talked of her *waiting-maid* and wealthy uncle to Mrs. Hastings, sat down to breakfast *with* her waiting-maid, eating her potatoes with a knife and cooling her tea in her saucer; two points which in the parlor she loudly denounced as positive marks of ill breeding, but which in the kitchen, where there was no one to see her, she found vastly convenient! Piles of soiled clothes were scattered over the floor, and from a tub standing near, a volume of steam was rising, almost hiding from view the form of Dora Deane, whose round red arms were diving into the suds, while she to herself was softly repeating the lesson in History, that day to be recited by her class, and which she had learned the Saturday night previous, well knowing that Monday's duties would keep her from school the entire day.

In the chamber above—her long, straight hair plaited up in braids, so as to give it the wavy appearance she had so much admired in Mrs. Hastings—her head enveloped in a black silk apron and her hands incased in buckskin gloves, was Eugenia, setting her room to rights, and complaining with every breath of her hard lot, in being thus obliged to exert herself on hot summer mornings.

"Don't you wish you were rich as Mrs. Hastings," asked Alice, who chanced to come in.

"That I do," returned Eugenia. "I have been uncomfortable and discontented ever since I called upon her, for I can't see why there should be such a difference. She has all the money, servants and dresses which she wants, besides the handsomest and most elegant man for a husband ; while I, Eugenia Deane, who am ten times smarter than she, and could appreciate these things so much better, am obliged to make all sorts of shifts, just to keep up appearances. But didn't I impress her with a sense of my *greatness !*" she added, after a pause, and Alice rejoined, "Particularly when you talked of your *waiting-maid !* I don't see, Eugenia, how you dare do such things, for of course Mrs. Hastings will eventually know that you mean Dora."

"I'm not so sure of that," returned Eugenia ; "and even if she does, I fancy I have tact enough to smooth it over with her, for she is not very deep."

For a moment Alice regarded her sister intently, and then said, "I wonder from whom you take your character for deception."

"I've dwelt upon that subject many a time myself," answered Eugenia, "and I have at last come to the conclusion that as father was not famous for sense of any kind, I must be a second and revised edition of mother—but hark, don't you hear the roll of wheels ?" And springing up, she reached the window just as Mrs. Hastings alighted from her carriage, which stood before the gate.

"Great goodness!" she exclaimed, "there's M's. Hastings coming here to call—and *I* in this predicament. What *shall* I do?"

"Let her wait, of course, until we change our dresses," answered Alice, and rushing down the stairs, Eugenia bade Dora "show the lady into the parlor," adding, "and if she asks for me, say I am suffering from a severe headache, but you presume I will see her."

Perfectly delighted at the idea of standing face to face with a person of whom she had heard so much, Dora removed her high-necked apron, and throwing it across the tub so that the sleeves trailed upon the floor, was hurrying away, when her foot becoming accidentally entangled in the apron, she fell headlong to the floor, bringing with her *tub*, *suds*, *clothes* and all! To present herself in this drenched condition was impossible, and in a perfect tremor lest Mrs. Hastings should go away, Eugenia vibrated, brush in hand, between her own chamber and the head of the kitchen stairs, scolding Dora unmercifully in the one place, and pulling at the long braids of her hair in the other.

At last, just as Mrs. Hastings was about despairing of being heard, and was beginning to think that possibly her husband might be right and Eugenia in the *suds* after all, a chubby, brown-faced girl appeared, and after giving her a searching, curious glance, showed her into the parlor.

"Are the young ladies at home?" asked Mrs. Hastings; and Dora, who had never told a falsehood in her life, and had no intention of doing so now, replied that they were, and would soon be down; after which, with a low courtesy she went back to the scene of her late disaster, while Mrs. Hastings busied herself awhile by looking around the room, which, though small, was very handsomely furnished.

At last, beginning to grow sleepy, she took up a book

and succeeded in interesting herself so far as to nod quite
approvingly, when the rustle of female garments aroused
her, and in a moment Eugenia and Alice swept into the
room. Both were tastefully dressed, while about Eugenia
there was an air of languor befitting the *severe headache*, of
which Mrs. Hastings was surprised to hear.

"Then *that girl* didn't tell you as I bade her to do," said
Eugenia; adding, that " Mrs. Hastings must have thought
her very rude to keep her so long waiting."

But Mrs. Hastings was too good-natured to think anything, and, after a few common-place remarks, she told the
object of her call, saying, that " the fresh air would, undoubtedly, do Eugenia good." In this opinion the young
lady fully concurred, and, half an hour later, she was slowly
riding through the principal streets of Dunwood, wondering
if her acquaintances did not envy her for being on such
terms of intimacy with the fashionable Mrs. Hastings. Very
politely were the young ladies received by Mr. Hastings, on
their arrival at Rose Hill, and throughout the entire day
their admiration, both for the place and its owner, increased,
though Eugenia could not conceal from herself the fact, that
she stood very much in fear of the latter, whose keen black
eyes seemed to read her very thoughts. How such a man
came to marry Ella Grey, was to her a puzzle; and if occasionally she harbored the thought that Eugenia Deane was
far better suited to be the mistress of Howard Hastings's
home than the childish creature he had chosen, she was only
guilty of what had, in a similar manner, been done by more
than one New York belle. Dinner being over, Ella led the
way to an upper balcony, which opened from her chamber,
and which was a cool, shaded spot. Scarcely were they
seated, when remembering something she had left in the
parlor, she went back for it, and in returning, she ran up

the stairs so swiftly that a sudden dizziness came over her, and with a low cry she fell half fainting into the arms of her husband, who bent tenderly over her, while Eugenia made many anxious inquiries as to what was the matter, and if she were often thus affected.

"Yes, often," answered Ella, who began to revive; then, as the perspiration gathered thickly about the white lips, she pressed her blue-veined hand upon her side, and cried, "The pain—the pain! It has come again. Country air won't do me any good. I shall die of consumption, just as mother said." And as if she saw indeed the little grave, on which the next summer's sun would shine, she hid her face in her husband's bosom, and sobbed aloud. Instantly a dark thought flashed upon Eugenia—a thought which even *she* would not harbor, and casting it aside, she drew nearer to the weeping Ella, striving by an increased tenderness of manner to atone for having dared to think of a time when the little willow chair on the balcony would be empty, and Howard Hastings free. Soon rallying, Ella feigned to smile at her discomposure, saying that " consumption had been preached to her so much that she always felt frightened at the slightest pain in her side," thoughtlessly adding, as she glanced at her husband, " I wonder if Howard would miss me any, were I really to die."

A dark shadow settled upon Mr. Hastings's face, but he made no reply; and Eugenia, who was watching him, fancied she could read his thoughts; but when they at last started for home, and she saw how tenderly he wrapped a warm shawl around his delicate young wife, who insisted upon going with them, she felt that however frivolous and uncompanionable Ella might be, she was Howard Hastings's wife, and as such, he would love and cherish her to the last.

By her window in the attic sat Dora Deane, poring over to-morrow's lessons; but as the silvery voice of Ella fell upon her ear, she arose, and going to her cousin's chamber, looked out upon the party as they drew near the gate.

"How beautiful she is!" she whispered to herself, as, dropping her shawl, and flinging back her golden curls, Ella sprang up to reach a branch of locust blossoms, which grew above her head.

Then, as she saw how carefully Mr. Hastings replaced the shawl, drawing his wife's arm within his own, she stole back to her room, and, resuming her seat by the window, dreamed, as maidens of thirteen will, of a time away in the future, when she, too, might perhaps be loved even as was the gentle Ella Hastings.

CHAPTER VIII.

THE PARTY.

ONE pleasant July morning, the people of Dunwood were electrified by the news that on Thursday evening, Mrs Howard Hastings would be at home to between one and two hundred of her *friends*. Among the first invited was Eugenia, who had been Mrs. Hastings's chief adviser, kindly enlightening her as to the *somebodies* and *nobodies* of the town, and rendering herself so generally useful, that, in a fit of gratitude, Mrs. Hastings had promised her her brother Stephen, a fast young man, who was expected to be present at the party. To appear well in his eyes was, therefore, Eugenia's ambition; and the time which was not spent in giving directions at Rose Hill, was occupied at home in scolding, because her mother would not devise a way by which she could obtain a new pink satin dress, with lace overskirt, and flowers to match.

It was in vain that Mrs. Deane sought to convince her daughter how impossible it was to raise the necessary funds. Eugenia was determined; and at last, by dint of secretly selling a half-worn dress to one Irish girl, a last year's bonnet to another, and a broché shawl to another, she succeeded in obtaining enough for the desired purchase, lacking five dollars, and this last it seemed impossible to procure. But Eugenia never despaired; and a paragraph read one evening in a city paper, suggested to her a plan which she resolved to execute immediately.

It was nearly dark ; her mother and sisters were in the village ; Dora was gone on an errand, and she was alone. Half reluctantly, she opened the stair door which led to Dora's room, the low room in the attic. Up the steep stair-case, and through the narrow hall she went, treading softly, and holding her breath, as if she feared lest the dead, from her far-off grave in the great city, should hear her noiseless footfall, and come forth to prevent the wrong she meditated. But no, Fanny Deane slept calmly in her coffin, and Eugenia kept on her way unmolested, until the chamber was reached. Then, indeed, she hesitated, for there was, to her, something terrifying in the darkness which had gathered in the cor-ners of the room, and settled like a pall upon the old green trunk. To reach that and secure the treasure it contained, would have been the work of a moment ; but, wholly pow-erless to advance, Eugenia stood still, while the cold perspi-ration started from every pore.

"I can do anything but *that*," she said, at last, and, as if the words had given her strength to move, she turned back, gliding again through the narrow hall, and down the steep stairway, out into the open air ; and when, that night, as she often did, Dora looked for her mother's beautiful *hair*, it lay in its accustomed place, unruffled and unharmed ; and the orphan child, as she pressed it to her lips, dreamed not of the danger which had threatened it, or of the snare about to be laid for herself by Eugenia, who could not yet give up the coveted dress.

Next morning, as Dora stood before the mirror, arrang-ing her long, luxuriant hair, which she usually wore in braids, hanging down her back, Eugenia came up, and with an unusual degree of kindness in her manner, offered to fix it for her, commenting the while on the exceeding beauty of the rich auburn tresses, and saying, that if she were in

3*

Dora's place she would have it *cut off*, as by the means she
would, when grown up, have much handsomer hair than it
it were suffered to remain long.   Dora remembered having
heard her mother say the same; but she had a pride in her
hair, which was longer and thicker than any of her companions' ; so she said nothing until Eugenia, who, to serve her
own purpose, would not hesitate to tell a falsehood, and who
knew how much Dora admired Mrs. Hastings, spoke of that
lady's beautiful curls, saying they were all the result of her
having worn her hair quite short until she was sixteen years
of age.   Then, indeed, Dora wavered.   She had recently
suffered much from the headache, too, and it might relieve
that ; so that when Eugenia offered her a coral bracelet in
exchange for her hair, she consented, and Alice entered the
room just as the last shining braid dropped upon the floor.

"What upon earth !" she exclaimed, stopping short, and
then bursting into a loud laugh at the comical appearance which Dora presented ; for Eugenia had cut close to
the head, leaving the hair so uneven that shingling seemed
the only alternative, and to this poor Dora finally submitted.
When at last the performance was ended, and she glanced
at herself in the mirror, she burst into a paroxysm of tears,
while Alice tried to soothe her by saying that it really would
eventually benefit her hair, and that she would not always
look so strangely.

But Dora, who began to suspect that it was pure selfishness on Eugenia's part, which had prompted the act,
felt keenly the injustice done her, and refused to be comforted, keeping her room the entire day, and weeping until
her eyelids were nearly blistered.   Meantime, Eugenia had
hurried off to the city with her ill-gotten treasure, on which
the miserly old Jew, to whom it was offered, looked with
eager, longing eyes, taking care, however, to depreciate its

value, lest his customer should expect too much. But Eugenia was fully his equal in management, and when at night she returned home, she was in possession of the satin, the lace, and the flowers, together with several other articles of finery.

The next day was the party, and as Dora, besides being exceedingly tasteful, was also neat, and handy with her needle, she was kept from school, stitching the livelong day upon the dainty fabric, a portion of which had been pur ;hased with her hair! Occasionally, as Eugenia glanced at the swollen eyelids and shorn head, bending so uncomplainingly over the cloud of lace, her conscience smote her for what she had done ; but one thought of *Stephen Grey*, and the impression she should make on him, dissipated all such regrets ; and when at length the hour for making her toilet arrived, her jaded cousin was literally made to perform all the offices of a waiting-maid. Three times was the tired little girl sent down to the village in quest of something which the capricious Eugenia *must* have, and which, when brought, was not " the thing at all," and must be exchanged. Up the stairs and down the stairs she went, bringing pins to Alice and powder to Eugenia, enacting, in short, the part of a second Cinderella, except that in her case no kind old godmother with her potent wand appeared to her relief!

They were dressed at last, and very beautifully Eugenia looked in the pink satin and flowing lace, which harmonized so well with her complexion, and which had been bought with the united proceeds of a velvet bonnet, a delaine dress, a broché shawl, and Dora's hair!

" Why don't you compliment me ?" she said to the weary child, who, sick with yesterday's weeping, and the close confinement of to-day, had laid her aching head upon the arm of the lounge.

Slowly unclosing her eyes, and fixing them upon her cousin, Dora answered—

"You do look beautifully. No one will excel you, I am sure, unless it be Mrs. Hastings. I wish I could see how she will dress."   •

"You might go up and look in at the window ; or, if I'd thought of it, I could have secured you the office of door-waiter," said the thoughtless Eugenia, adding, as she held out her shawl for Dora to throw around her, "Don't you wish you could attend a party at Rose Hill ?"

There was a sneer accompanying this question, which Dora felt keenly. Her little swelling heart was already full, and, with quivering lips and gushing tears, she answered, somewhat bitterly—

"I never expect to be anybody, or go anywhere ;" then, as her services were no longer needed, she ran away to her humble room, where from her window she watched the many brilliant lights which shone from Rose Hill, and caught occasional glimpses of the airy forms which flitted before the open doors and windows. Once she was sure she saw Eugenia upon the balcony, and then, as a sense of the difference between herself and her cousins came over her, she laid her down upon the old green trunk, and covering her face with her hands, cried out, "Nobody cares for me, or loves me either. I wish I had died that winter night. Oh, mother ! come to me, I am so lonely and so sad."

Softly, as if it were indeed the rustle of an angel's wings, came the evening air, through the open casement, cooling the feverish brow and drying the tears of the orphan girl, who grew strangely calm ; and when at last the moon looked in upon her, she was sleeping quietly, with a placid smile upon her lips. Years after, and Dora Deane remembered that summer night, when, on the hard green trunk,

she slept so soundly as not to hear the angry voi.e of Eugenia, who came home sadly out of humor with herself and
the world at large.

At breakfast, next morning, she was hardly on speaking
terms with her sister, while *Stephen Grey* was pronounced " a
perfect bore—a baboon, with more hair than brains."

"And to that I should not suppose you would object,"
said Alice, mischievously. "You might find it useful in case
of an emergency."

To this there was no reply, save an angry flash of the
black eyes, which, it seems, had failed to interest Stephen
Grey, who was far better pleased with the unassuming
Alice, and who had paid the haughty Eugenia no attention
whatever, except, indeed, to plant his patent leather boot
upon one of her lace flounces, tearing it half off, and leaving
a sad rent, which could not well be mended. This, then,
was the cause of her wrath, which continued for some time;
when really wishing to talk over the events of the evening,
she became a little more gracious, and asked Alice how she
liked *Mrs. Elliott*, who had unexpectedly arrived from New
York.

"I was delighted with her," returned Alice; "she was
such a perfect lady. And hadn't she magnificent hair !
Just the color of Dora's," she added, glancing at the little
cropped head, which had been so suddenly divested of its
beauty.

"It wasn't all hers, though," answered Eugenia, who in-
variably saw and spoke of every defect. "I heard her tell
ing Ella that she bought a braid in Rochester as she came
up. But what ails you ?" she continued, speaking now to
Dora, whose eyes sparkled with some unusual excitement,
and who replied—

"You said Mrs. Elliott, from New York. And that was

the name of the lady who was so kind to me.   Oh, if I only thought it were she, I'd "——

"Make yourself ridiculous, I dare say," interrupted Eugenia, adding, that " there was more than one Mrs. Elliott in the world, and she'd no idea that so elegant a lady as Mr. Hastings's sister ever troubled herself to look after folks in such a miserable old hovel as the one where Dora had lived."

This, however, did not satisfy the child, who, during the week that Mrs. Elliott remained in the neighborhood, cast many longing glances in the direction of Rose Hill, gazing oft with tearful eyes upon a female figure which sometimes walked upon the balcony, and which, perhaps, was her benefactress.   One night it was told at Locust Grove that Mrs. Elliott had gone, and then, with a feeling of desolation for which she could not account, Dora again laid her face on the old green trunk and wept.

Poor Dora Deane !   The path she trod was dark, indeed, but there was light ahead, and even now it was breaking upon her, though she knew it not.

CHAPTER IX.

DORA AT ROSE HILL

Summer was over. The glorious September days were gone. The hazy October had passed away, and the autumn winds had swept the withered leaves from the tall trees which grew around Rose Hill; when one cold, rainy November morning, a messenger was sent to Mrs. Deane, saying that Mrs. Hastings was sick, and wished to see her.

"Mrs. Hastings sent for mother! How funny! There must be some mistake," said Eugenia, putting her head in at the door. "Are you sure it was mother?"

"Yes, quite sure," answered the man. "Mrs. Hastings thought she would know what to do for the baby, which was born yesterday, and is a puny little thing."

This silenced Eugenia, who waited impatiently until nightfall, when her mother returned with a sad account of affairs at Rose Hill. Mrs. Hastings was sick and nervous, Mrs. Leah was lazy and cross, the servants ignorant and impertinent, the house was in disorder; while Mr. Hastings, with a cloud on his face, ill befitting a newly-made father, stalked up and down the sick-room, looking in vain for an empty chair, so filled were they with blankets, towels, baby's dresses, and the various kinds of work which Ella was always beginning and never finishing.

"Such an ignorant, helpless creature I never saw," said

Mrs. Deane. "Why, she *don't know anything*—and such looking rooms! I don't wonder her servants give her so much trouble; but my heart ached for him, poor man, when I saw him putting away the things, and trying to make the room a little more comfortable."

It was even as Mrs. Deane had said. Ella, whose favorite theory was, "a big house, a lot of things, and *chairs* enough to put them in," was wholly unprepared for sickness, which found her in a sad condition. To be sure there were quantities of French embroidery, thread lace and fine linen, while the bed, on which she lay, cost a hundred dollars, and the rosewood crib was perfect of its kind, but there was a great lack of neatness and order; and as day after day Mr. Hastings stood with folded arms, looking first from one window and then from the other, his thoughts were far from being agreeable, save when he bent over the cradle of his first-born, and then there broke over his face a look of un-utterable tenderness, which was succeeded by a shade of deep anxiety as his eye rested upon his frail young wife, whose face seemed whiter even than the pillow on which it lay.

After a few weeks, during which time Ella had gained a little strength and was able to see her friends, Eugenia came regularly to Rose Hill, sitting all day by the bedside of the invalid, to whom she sometimes brought a glass of water, or some such trivial thing. Occasionally, too, she would look to see if the baby were asleep, pronouncing it "a perfect little cherub, just like its mother;" and there her services ended, for it never occurred to her that she could make the room much more cheerful by picking up and putting away the numerous articles which lay scattered around, and which were a great annoyance to the more orderly Mr. Hastings. Once, when Ella, as usual, was expatiating upon her goodness, asking her husband if she were not the best girl in the world, and saying "they must make her some handsome present in return for all she had done," he replied, "I confess, I should think more of Miss Deane, if she did you any real good, or rendered you any actual service ; but, as far as I can discover, she merely sits here talking to you until you are wearied out."

"Why, what would you have her do?" asked Ella, her large blue eyes growing larger and bluer.

"I hardly know myself," answered Mr. Hastings ; "but it seems to me that a genuine woman could not sit day after day in such a disorderly room as this."

"Oh, Howard!" exclaimed Ella, "you surely cannot expect Eugenia Deane to do a servant's duty. Why, she has been as delicately brought up as I, and knows quite as little of work."

"More shame for her if this is true," answered Mr. Hastings somewhat bitterly, and Ella continued, "You've got such queer ideas, Howard, of *woman's duties*. I should suppose you would have learned, ere this, that few ladies are like your mother, who, though a blessed good soul, has the oddest notions."

"But they make a man's home mighty comfortable, those odd notions of mother's," said Mr. Hastings ; then, knowing how useless it would be to argue the point, he was about changing the subject, when the new nurse who had been there but a few days (the first one having quarrelled with Mrs. Leah, and gone home), came in and announced her intention of leaving also, saying, "she would not live in the same house with old mother Leah!"

It was in vain that Mr. Hastings tried to soothe the angry girl—she was determined, and for a second time was Ella left alone.

"Oh, what will become of me?" she groaned, as the door closed upon her late nurse. "Do, pray, Howard, go to the kitchen and get me some—some—*I don't know what,* but get me *something!*"

With a very vague idea as to what he was to get or to do, Mr. Hastings left the room just as it was entered by Eugenia, to whom Ella detailed her grievances. "Her head ached dreadfully, Howard was cross, and her nurse gone. Oh, Eugenia!" she cried, "what shall I do? I wish I could die. Don't ever get married. What shall I do?"

And hiding her face in the pillow, poor Ella sobbed bitterly. For a time Eugenia stood, revolving the propriety of offering Dora as a substitute in the place of the girl who had just left. "Mother can work a little harder," she thought. "And Alice can help her occasionally. It will please Mr. Hastings, I know. Poor man, *I pity him!*"

So, more on account of the *pity* she felt for Mr. Hastings, than for the *love* she bore his wife, she said at last, "We have a little girl at our house, who is very capable for one of her years. I think she would be quite handy in a sick room. At all events, she can rock the baby. Shall I send her up until you get some one else?"

"Oh, if you only would," answered Ella. "I should be so glad."

So, it was arranged that *Dora* should come next morning, and then Eugenia, who was this time in a hurry, took her leave, having first said that Mrs. Hastings "needn't think strange if Dora called *her* cousin, and her mother *aunt,* for she was a poor relation, whom they had taken out of charity!"

At first Mrs. Deane objected to letting her niece go, "for she was needed at home," she said; but Eugenia finally prevailed, as she generally did, and the next morning

Dora, who was rather pleased with the change, started bundle in hand for Rose Hill. She had never been there before, and she walked leisurely along, admiring the beautiful house and grounds, and thinking Mrs. Hastings must be very happy to live in so fine a place. Ella was unusually nervous and low-spirited this morning, for her husband had gone to Rochester ; and when Dora was shown into the room she was indulging in a fit of crying, and paid no attention whatever when Mrs. Leah said, "This is the new girl." "She'll get over it directly," muttered the housekeeper, as she went from the room, leaving Dora inexpressibly shocked at witnessing such grief in one whom she had thought so happy.

"Can I do anything for you ?" she said at last, drawing near, and involuntarily laying her hand on the golden curls she had so much admired.

There was genuine sympathy in the tones of that childish voice, which touched an answering chord in Ella's heart, and lifting up her head she gazed curiously at the little brown-faced girl, who stood there neatly attired in a dress of plain dark calico, her auburn hair, which had grown rapidly, combed back from her open brow, and her dark-blue eyes full of tears. No one could mistake Dora Deane for a menial, and few could look upon her without being at once interested ; for early sorrow had left a shade of sadness upon her handsome face, unusual in one so young. Then, too, there was an expression of goodness and truth shining out all over her countenance, and Ella's heart yearned towards her. at once as towards a long-tried friend. Stretching out her white, wasted hand, she said, "And you are *Dora.* I am glad you have come. The sight of you makes me feel better already," and the small, rough hand she held was pressed with a fervor which showed that she was sin-

cere in what she said.   It was strange how fast they grew
to liking each other—those two children—for in everything
save years, Ella was younger far than Dora Deane ; and it
was strange, too, what a change the little girl's presence
wrought in the sick-chamber.   Naturally neat and orderly,
she could not sit quietly down in the midst of disorder, and
as far as she was able, she put things in their proper places;
then, as her quick-seeing eye detected piles of dust which
for days had been unmolested, she said, " Will it disturb
you if I sweep ?"

" Not at all.   Do what you like," answered Ella, her own
spirits rising in proportion as the appearance of her surroundings was improved.

Everything was in order at last.   The carpet was swept,
the furniture dusted, the chairs emptied, the curtains looped
back, and the hearth nicely washed.   Fresh, clean linen
was put upon the pillows, while Ella's tangled curls were
carefully brushed and tucked under her tasteful cap, and
then for the first time Dora took the baby upon her lap.   It
was a little thing, but very beautiful to the young mother,
and beautiful, too, to Dora, when she learned that its name
was " Fannie."

" *Fannie!*" how it carried her back to the long ago,
when her father had spoken, and her precious mother had
answered to that blessed name !   And how it thrilled her
as she repeated it again and again, while her tears fell like
rain on the face of the unconscious infant.

" Why do you cry ?" asked Ella, and Dora answered, " I
am thinking of mother.   Her name was Fannie, and I shall
love the baby for her sake."

" Has your mother long been dead ?   Tell me of her,"
said Ella ; and drawing her chair close to the bedside, Dora
told the sad story of her life, while Ella Hastings's tears fell

fast and her eyes opened wide with wonder as she heard of
the dreary room, the dead mother, the bitter cold night, and
of the good lady who brought them aid.

Starting up in bed and looking earnestly at Dora, Ella
said, "And *you* are the little girl whom Howard and Mrs.
Elliott found sleeping on her mother's neck that New Year's
morning. But God didn't let you freeze. He saved you
to live with me, which you will do always. And I will be
to you a sister, for I know you must be good."

And the impulsive creature threw her arms around the
neck of the astonished Dora, who for some time could not
speak, so surprised and delighted was she to learn that her
benefactress was indeed the sister of Mr. Hastings. After
a moment, Ella continued, "And you came to live with
some distant relatives—with Mrs. Deane?"

"Yes, with Aunt Sarah," answered Dora, stating briefly
the comparatively double relationship that existed between
herself and her cousins, and casually mentioning her uncle
Nathaniel, whom she had never seen.

"Then he is *your* uncle, too—the old East India man,
whose heir Eugenia is to be. I should think he would send
you money."

"He never does," said Dora, in a choking voice. "He
sent some to Eugenia once, but none to me," and a tear at
her uncle's supposed coldness fell on the baby's head.

Ella was puzzled, but she could not doubt the truth of
what Dora had said, though she wisely refrained from be-
traying Eugenia, in whom her confidence was slightly
shaken, but was soon restored by the appearance of the
young lady herself, who overwhelmed her with caresses,
and went into ecstasies over the little Fannie, thus surely
winning her way to the mother's heart. Owing to a severe
cold from which Eugenia was suffering, she left for home

about dark, and soon after her departure, Ella began to ex
pect her husband.

"If you will tell me where to find his dressing-gown and
slippers, I'll bring them out for him," said Dora, wheeling
up before the glowing grate the large easy-chair which she
felt almost sure was occupied by Mr. Hastings.

"His gown and slippers!" repeated Ella. "It's an age
since I saw them, but I guess they are in the dressing-room,
either behind the door, or in the black trunk, or on the
shelf—or, stay, I shouldn't wonder if they were on the *closet
floor.*"

And there, under a promiscuous pile of other garments,
Dora found them, sadly soiled, and looking as if they had
not seen the light for many a day. Shaking out the gown,
and brushing the dust from off the slippers, she laid them in
the chair, and Ella, who was watching her, said, "Pray,
what put that into your mind?"

"I don't know," returned Dora; "only I thought, perhaps, you did so, when you were well. Ever so long ago,
before pa died, mother made him a calico dressing-gown, and
he used to look so pleased when he found it in his chair."

"Strange I never thought of such things," softly whispered Ella, unconsciously learning a lesson from the little
domestic girl, who brushed the hearth, dropped the curtains,
lighted the lamp, and then went out to the kitchen in quest
of milk for Fannie.

"He will be so happy and pleased!" said Ella, as, lifting
up her head, she surveyed the cheerful room.

And happy indeed he was. It was the first time he had
left his wife since her illness, and with a tolerable degree of
satisfaction he took his seat in the evening cars. We say
tolerable, for though he was really anxious to see Ella and
the baby, he was in no particular haste to see the room in

which he had left them ; and rather reluctantly he entered his handsome dwelling, starting back when he opened the door of the sick chamber, and half thinking he had mistaken another man's house for his own. But Ella's voice reassured him, and in a few moments he had heard from her the story of Dora Deane, who ere long came in, and was duly presented. Taking her hand in his, and looking down upon her with his large black eyes, he said, " I have seen you before, I believe, but I did not then think that when we met again I should be so much indebted to you. I am glad you are here, Dora."

Once before had he held that hand in his, and now, as then, the touch sent the warm blood bounding through her veins. She had passed through much since that wintry morning, had grown partially indifferent to coldness and neglect, but the extreme kindness of Mr. and Mrs. Hastings touched her heart ; and stammering out an almost inaudible reply, she turned away to hide her tears, while Mr. Hastings, advancing towards the fire, exclaimed, " My double gown! And it's so long since I saw it! To whose thoughtfulness am I indebted for this ?"

" 'Twas Dora," answered Ella. " She thinks of everything. She is my good angel, and I mean to keep her always, if she will stay. Will you, dear ?"

" Oh, if I only could," answered Dora; " but I can't. They need me at home !"

" Why need you ? They have servants enough," said Ella, who had not yet identified Eugenia's waiting-maid with the bright, intelligent child before her.

" We have no servants but *me*," answered the truthful Dora. " We are poor, and I help Aunt Sarah to pay for my board; so, you see, I can't stay. And then, too, I must go to school."

Perfectly astonished at this fresh disclosure, Ella glanced towards her husband, whose quizzical expression kept her silent, for it seemed to say, "I told you all the time, that Miss Eugenia was not exactly what you supposed her to be."

"How could she deceive me so?" thought Ella, while Mr Hastings was mentally resolving to befriend the child, in whom he felt such a strong interest.

Wishing to know something of her education, he questioned her during the evening concerning her studies, and the books she had read, feeling surprised and pleased to find how good a scholar she was, considering her advantages.

"There's the germ of a true, noble woman there. I wish my sister could have the training of her," he thought, as he saw how animated she became when he mentioned her favorite books, and then watched her as she hovered round the bedside of his wife.

Very swiftly and pleasantly passed the three following days, and during all that time Eugenia did not once appear; but at the close of the fourth day, a note was brought to Ella, saying that both Eugenia and her mother were sick, and Dora must come home.

"Oh, how can I let you go?" cried Ella, while Dora crept away into a corner and wept.

But there was no alternative, and just at dark she came to say, good bye. Winding her feeble arms around her neck, Ella sobbed out her adieu, and then, burying her face in her pillow, refused to be comforted. One kiss for the little Fannie—one farewell glance at the weeping Ella, and then, with a heavy heart, Dora went out from a place where she had been so happy—went back to the home where no one greeted her kindly, save the old house cat, who purred a joyous welcome, and rubbed against her side as she kindled a fire in the dark, dreary kitchen, where, on the table, were piles of dishes left for her to wash. That night, when, at a late hour, she stole up to bed, the contrast between her humble room and the cozy chamber where she had recently slept, affected her painfully, and, mingled with her nightly prayer, was the petition, that "sometimes she might go back and live with *Mr. Hastings!*"

Meantime at Rose Hill there was sorrowing for her, Ella refusing to be comforted unless she should return. Mr. Hastings, who had spent the day in the city, and did not come home until evening, felt that something was wrong the moment he entered the door of his chamber. The fire was nearly out, the lamp was burning dimly, and Ella was in tears.

"What is it, darling?" he asked, advancing towards her ; and laying her aching head upon his bosom, she told him of her loss, and how much she missed the little brown-faced girl, who had been so kind to her.

And Howard Hastings missed her, too—missed the tones of her gentle voice, the soft tread of her busy feet, and more than all, missed the sunlight of comfort she had shed over his home. The baby missed her, too; for over her Dora had acquired an almost mesmeric influence, and until midnight her wailing cry smote painfully upon the ear of the father, who, before the morning dawned, had concluded that Rose Hill was nothing without Dora Deane. "She shall come back, too," he said, and the sooner to effect this, he started immediately after breakfast for the house of Mrs. Deane. Very joyfully the deep blue eyes of Dora, who met him at the door, looked up into his, and her bright face flushed with delight when he told her why he had come. Both Eugenia and her mother were convalescent, and sitting by the parlor fire, the one in a shilling calico, and the other in a plaid silk morning gown. At first Mrs. Deane objected, when she heard Mr. Hastings's errand, saying, with a sudden flash of pride, that "it was not necessary for her niece to work out."

"And I assure you, it is not our intention to make a servant of her," answered Mr. Hastings. "We could not do otherwise than treat so near a relative of yours as an equal."

This last was well timed, and quite complacently Mrs. Deane listened, while he told her that if Dora were allowed to stay with them until his wife was better, she should be well cared for, and he himself would superintend her studies, so she should lose nothing by being out of school. "Come, Miss Eugenia," he continued, "please intercede for me, and, I assure you, both Ella and myself will be eternally grateful."

He had touched the right chord at last. Rumor said that Ella Hastings would never see another summer, and if before her death the husband was eternally grateful, what would he not be after her death? Then, too, but the day before they had received a remittance from Uncle Nat, and with that they could afford to hire a servant; so, when Eugenia spoke, it was in favor of letting "*Mr. Hastings have Dora just when he wanted her*, if it would be any satisfaction to poor dear Ella!"

A while longer Mr. Hastings remained, and when at last he arose to go, he was as sure that Dora Deane would again gladden his home as he was next morning, when from his library window he saw her come tripping up the walk, her cheeks flushed with exercise, and her eyes sparkling with joy, as, glancing upward, she saw him looking down upon her. In after years, when Howard Hastings's cup was full of blessings, he often referred to that morning, saying "he had seldom experienced a moment of deeper thankfulness than the one when he welcomed back again to his fireside and his home the orphan Dora Deane."

CHAPTER X.

ELLA.

Very pleasantly to Dora did the remainder of the winter pass away. She was appreciated at last, and nothing could exceed the kindness of both Mr. and Mrs. Hastings, the latter of whom treated her more like a sister than a servant, while even Eugenia, who came often to Rose Hill, and whose fawning manner had partially restored her to the good opinion of the fickle Ella, tried to treat her with a show of affection, when she saw how much she was respected. Regularly each day Dora went to the handsome library, where she recited her lessons to Mr. Hastings, who became deeply interested in watching the development of her fine, intellectual mind.

One thing, however, troubled her. Ella did not improve, and never since Dora came to Rose Hill had she sat up more than an hour, but lay all day on her bed, while her face grew white almost as the wintry snow, save when a bright red spot burned upon her cheeks, making her, as Dora thought, even more beautiful than she had been in health. Once in the gathering twilight, when they sat together alone, she startled Dora with the question, "Is everybody afraid to die ?"

"Mother was not," answered Dora, and Ella continued, "But she was good, and I am not. I have never done a worthy act in all my life. Never thought of *death*, or even looked upon it, for mother told us there was no need of harrowing up our feelings—it would come soon enough, she said ; and to me, who hoped to live so long, it has come *too soon*—all too soon ;" and the hot tears rained through the transparent fingers, clasped so convulsively over her face.

For many weeks Dora had felt an undefined presentiment of coming evil—had seen it in Ella's failing health—in the increased tenderness of Mr. Hastings's manner, whenever he bent over the pillow of his young wife, or bore her in his arms, as he sometimes did, to the window, that she might look out upon the garden, and the winding walks which she would never tread again. And now Ella herself had confirmed it—had spoken of death as something very near.

" Oh, she must not die !" was Dora's mental cry of anguish, as moving nearer to the bedside she grasped the little wasted hand which lay outside the counterpane, and this was her only answer, for she could not speak. There was a numbness at her heart, a choking sensation in her throat, which prevented her utterance. But Ella understood her, and returning the warm pressure, she continued, "You, too, have seen it then, and know that I must die ; but oh ! you do not know how I dread the lonesome darkness of the grave, or the world which lies beyond. If somebody would go with me, or teach me the way, it wouldn't be so hard."

Poor Ella ! Her life had been one round of fashionable folly, and now that the world was fading from her view, her fainting soul cried out for light to guide her through the shadowy valley her feet were soon to tread. And light came at last, through the word of God and the teachings of the faithful clergyman, who was sent for at her request.

and who came daily up to see her. There was no more fear now—no more terror of the narrow tomb, for there was *One* to go with her—one whose arm was powerful to save ; and on him Ella learned to lean, clinging still with an undying love to her husband, with whom she often talked of the time when he would be alone and she be far away.

"It is so hard to give you up," she said one day, when as usual he was sitting by her side ; "so hard to say good bye forever, and know that though you will miss me at first, and mourn for me too, there *will* come a time when another will take my place—another than Ella can call you hers ; but I am willing," she continued, as she saw him about to speak, "willing that it should be so. I have loved you, Howard, more than you can know, or I can ever tell ; but I am not worthy of you. I do not satisfy the higher feelings of your heart ; I am not what *your* wife should be, and for this I must die. Many a night, when you were sleeping at my side, have I lain awake, asking myself why *I*, to whom the world was so beautiful and bright, must leave it so soon ; and as I thought over the events of our short married life, the answer came to me, 'I cannot make you happy as you ought to be, and for your sake I am taken away.'"

"Oh, Ella, Ella !" groaned Mr. Hastings, laying his head beside hers, upon the pillow.

From his inmost soul he knew that what she said was true ; but for this he would not that she should die. She had been to him a gentle, loving wife, the one he had chosen from all others to share his home ; and though he had failed to find in her the companion he had sought, she was very dear to him—was the mother of his child ; and the strong man's heart was full of anguish as he thought of giving her up so soon. Who would comfort him when she was gone, or speak to him words of love ?

Softly the chamber door unclosed, and Dora Deane looked in; but seeing them thus together, she stole away into the garden, where the early spring grass was just starting into life, and there, weeping bitterly, she too prayed that Ella might not die. But neither tears nor prayers were of avail to save her. Still, for weeks she lingered, and the soft June air, stealing in through the open window, had more than once lifted the golden curls from off her fading brow, and more than one bouquet of sweet wild blossoms had been laid upon her pillow, ere the midnight hour, when, with anguish at their hearts, Howard Hastings and Dora Deane watched together by her side, and knew that she was dying. There had been long, dreary nights of wakefulness, and the worn-out sufferer had asked at last that she might die— might sleep the dreamless sleep from which she would never waken. And Howard Hastings, as night after night went by, and the laughing blue eyes which had won his early love grew dim with constant waking, had felt that it would be better when his loved one was at rest. But death, however long expected, is sudden at the last, and so it was to him, when he saw the shadow creeping over her face, which cometh once to all. She would not suffer them to rouse the household, she would rather die with them alone, she said, with Dora standing near, and her husband's arms about her, so that the tones of his voice should be the last sound which would fall upon her ear, and Dora's hand the last to minister to her wants.

"I have loved you so much, Howard, oh, so much!" and the white clammy fingers, so soon to be laid away beneath the summer flowers, strayed lovingly through the raven locks of her husband, who could answer only with his tears, which fell fast upon her face. "And you too, Dora," she continued, motioning the weeping girl to advance, "I have

loved you too, for you have been kind to me, and when I
am gone, you will live here still and care for my child,
whom we have called *Fannie*. It is a beautiful name, Dora
—your mother's name, and for your sake, I would fain let
her keep it—but," turning to Mr. Hastings, and laying her
hand caressingly upon his head, " when I no longer live, I
would rather you should call my baby *Ella Grey;* and if,
my husband "—here she paused to gather strength for what
she was about to say, and after a moment continued, " if in
coming years, another sits beside you in my chair, and the
voices of other children shall call you father, you will not
forget your first-born, I know, but will love her better, and
think, perchance, the oftener of me, if she bears my name ;
for however truly you may hereafter love, it was Ella Grey
that won your first affection.

Again she paused, and there was no sound heard in the
chamber of death, save the sobs of those about to be bereaved, and the faint rustling of the leaves without, which
were gently moved by the night wind.

"Bring me my baby," she said at last; and Dora laid the
sleeping child in the arms of the young mother, who, clasping it fondly to her bosom, breathed over it a dying mother's
blessing, and with a dying mother's tears baptized it Ella
Grey.

There was a long, deep silence then, and when at last
Howard Hastings lifted up his head from the pillow where
it had been resting, and Dora Deane came timidly to his
side, they gazed together on the face of the sweetly sleeping
dead

CHAPTER XI.

THE HOUSE OF MOURNING.

ELLA HASTINGS was dead. The deep-toned bell proclaimed it to the people of Dunwood, who, counting the nineteen strokes, sighed that one so young should die. The telegraphic wires carried it to her childhood's home, in the far-off city ; and while her tears were dropping fast for the first dead of her children, the fashionable mother did not forget to have her mourning in the most expensive and becoming style. The servants in the kitchen whispered it one to the other, treading softly and speaking low, as if aught could disturb the slumber of her who lay so motionless and still, unmindful of the balmy summer air which kissed her marble cheek. The grief-stricken husband repeated it again and again as he sat by her side in the darkened room ;. and only they who have felt it, can know with what a crushing weight they fell upon his heart, the three words—"She is dead !"

Yes, Ella was dead, and Eugenia Deane, with hypocritical tears upon her cheek, gathered fresh, white rose-buds, and twining them in the golden curls which shaded the face of the beautiful dead, dared even there to think that *Howard Hastings was free;* and as she saw the silent grief of the stricken man, who, with his head upon the table, sat hour after hour, unmindful of the many who came to look on what had been his wife, her lip curled with scorn, and she marvelled that one so frivolous as Ella should be so deeply mourned. Once she ventured to speak, asking him some trivial thing concerning the arrangement of affairs, and without looking up, he answered, " Do as you like, until her mother comes. She will be here to-morrow."

So, for the remainder of the day, Eugenia flitted from the parlor to the chamber of death, from the chamber of death to the kitchen, and from the kitchen back again to the parlor, ordering the servants, admitting visitors, and between times scolding Dora for " being so foolish as to cry herself sick for a person who, of course, cared nothing for her, except as a waiter !"

Since the night of her mother's death, Dora's heart had not been half so sore with pain. The girlish Ella had been very dear to her, and the tears she shed were genuine. To no one else would the baby go, and after dinner was over, the dinner at which Eugenia presided, and of which Mr. Hastings could not be induced to partake, she went into the garden with her little charge, seating herself in a pleasant summer-house, which had been Ella's favorite resort. It was a warm, drowsy afternoon, and at last, worn out with weeping, and the fatigue of the last night's watching, she fell asleep, as the baby had done before. Not long had she sat thus, when Mr. Hastings, too, came down the gravelled walk, and stood at the arbor door. The constant bustling in and out of Eugenia annoyed him, and wishing to be alone, he had come out into the open air, which he felt would do him good. When his eye fell on Dora, who was oo soundly sleeping to be easily aroused, he murmured, " Poor child ! she is wearied with so many wakeful nights;" then, fearing lest the slender arms should relax their hold and drop the babe, he took it gently from her, and folding

4*

it to his bosom, sat down by her side, so that her drooping head could rest upon his shoulder.

For two long hours she slept, and it was not until the baby's waxen fingers gave a vigorous pull to her short, thick hair, that she awoke, feeling greatly surprised when she saw Mr. Hastings sitting near.

"I found you asleep," he said, by way of explanation, " and knowing how tired you were, I gave you my arm for a pillow;" then, as the baby wished to go to her, he gave it up, himself going slowly back to the lonesome house, from which Ella was gone forever.

The next morning, the mother and her three youngest daughters, all draped in deepest black, arrived at Rose Hill, prepared to find fault with everything which savored at all of the "horrid country." Even Eugenia sank into nonentity in the presence of the cold, city-bred woman, who ignored her existence entirely, notwithstanding that she loudly and repeatedly expressed so much affection for the deceased.

" Perhaps your daughter wrote to you of me (Miss Deane); we were great friends," she said, when they stood together in the presence of the dead, and Mrs. Grey's emotions had somewhat subsided.

" Possibly; but I never remember names," returned the haughty lady, without raising her eyes.

" There are so few people here with whom she could be intimate," continued Eugenia, " that I saw a great deal of her."

But to this Mrs. Grey made no reply, except to ask, " Whose idea was it dressing Ella in this plain muslin wrapper, when she has so many handsome dresses ? But it don't matter," she continued, as Eugenia was about to disclaim all participation in that affair. " It don't matter, for no one here appreciates anything better, I dare say. Where's the baby? "I haven't seen that yet," she asked, as they were descending the stairs.

"She's with Dora, I presume," answered Eugenia; and Mrs. Grey continued—

"Oh, the nurse girl, whom Ella wrote so much about. Send her in."

But Eugenia was not one to obey orders so peremptorily given, and, for a long time, Madam Grey and her three daughters waited the appearance of the nurse girl, who, not knowing that they were in the parlor, entered it at last, of her own accord, and stood before them with such a quiet, self-possessed dignity, that even Mrs. Grey treated her with far more respect than she had the assuming Eugenia, whose rule, for the time being, was at an end. Everything had been done wrong; and when Mr. Hastings spoke of having Ella buried at the foot of the spacious garden, in a quiet, grassy spot, where trees of evergreen were growing, she held up her hands in amazement at the idea that her daughter should rest elsewhere than in the fashionable precincts of Greenwood. So Mr. Hastings yielded, and on the morning of the third day, Dora watched with blinding tears the long procession winding slowly down the avenue, and out into the highway towards the village depot, where the shrieking of the engine, and the rattling of the car bell would be the only requiem tolled for Ella Hastings, as she was borne rapidly away from a spot which had been her home for one brief year.

The little Ella was in Dora's arms, and as she, too, saw the handsome steeds and moving carriages, she laughed aloud, and patted the window-pane with her tiny baby hands. Dear little one! she did not know—would never know, how much she was bereaved; but Dora knew, and her tears fell all the faster when she thought that she, too, must leave her, for her aunt had said to Mr. Hastings, that after the funeral Dora must go home, adding, that Mrs. Leah would take care of Ella until his return. So, when the hum of voices and the tread of feet had ceased, when the shutters were closed and the curtains dropped, Eugenia came for her to go, while Mrs. Leah came to take the child, who refused to leave Dora, clinging so obstinately to her neck, and crying so pitifully, that even Eugenia was touched, and bade her cousin remain until Mr. Hastings came home. So Dora staid, and the timid servants, as they sat together in the shadowy twilight, felt not half so lonely when they heard her gentle voice singing the motherless babe to sleep.

CHAPTER XII.

WAYS AND MEANS.

With all the showy parade and empty pomp of a fashionable city funeral, Ella was laid to rest in Greenwood,
and, in their darkened parlor, arrayed in the latest style of
mourning, the mother and sisters received the sympathy of
their friends, who hoped they would try to be reconciled,
and were so sorry they could not now go to the Springs, as
usual. In another parlor, too, far more elegant but less
showy than that of Mrs. Grey, another mother wept for her
only son, speaking to him blessed words of comfort in his
bereavement, and telling him of the better world, where
again he would meet the loved and lost. Once she ventured
to hope that he would come back again to her fireside, now
that his was desolate, but he refused. Rose Hill henceforth
would be his home, and though it was lonely and drear, he
must in a few days go back to it ; for the sake of the little
one, doubly dear to him now that its mother was gone. Oh,
how sad was that journey back, and what a sense of desolation came over him, as he drew near his home, and knew
that Ella was not there !—that never more would she come
forth to meet him—never again would her little feet stray
through the winding walks, or her fairy fingers pluck the
flowers she had loved so well.

It was near the first of July. The day had been rainy,

and the evening was dark and cold. Wet, chilly, and forlorn, he entered the hall and ascended the stairs, but he could not that night go to the old room and find it empty ; and he was passing on to his library, when the sound of some one singing made him pause, while a thrill of joy ran through his veins, for he knew that childish voice, knew it was Dora Deane singing to his child. Another moment and he stood within the room where Ella had died. All traces of sickness and death had been removed, and everything was in perfect order. Vases of flowers adorned the mantel and the stands, seeming little out of place with the rain which beat against the window, and the fire which burned within the grate. In her crib lay Fannie, and sitting near was Dora Deane, her rich auburn hair combed smoothly back, and the great kindness of her heart shining out from the depths of her clear blue eyes.

There are people whose very presence brings with it a feeling of comfort, and such a one was Dora. Mr. Hastings had not expected to find her there ; and the sight of her bright face, though it did not remove the heavy pain from his heart, took from him the sense of utter desolation, the feeling of being alone in his sorrow.

"Dora," he exclaimed, coming to her side, "I did not expect this ! How happened you to stay ?"

"The baby cried so hard," answered Dora, "that Eugenie told me I might remain until your return."

"It was very kind and thoughtful in her, and I thank her very much. Will you tell her so ?" he said, involuntarily laying his hand on Dora's head.

Divesting himself at last of his damp overcoat, and donning the warm dressing gown, which Dora brought him, he sat down before the fire, and listened while she told him how she had staid in that room and kept it in order for him, because she thought it would not seem half so bad to him if he came into it at once and found it comparatively pleasant.

"You are a very thoughtful girl," he said, when she had finished, "and I hope I shall some time repay you for your kindness to myself and Ella."

But Dora did not wish for any pay, and at the mention of Ella's name her tears burst forth afresh. The next morning, when news of Mr. Hastings's return was received at Locust Grove, Eugenia at once suggested that Dora be sent for immediately. "It did not look well," she said, "for a good sized girl, fourteen and a half years of age, to be staying in the same house with a widower. Folks would talk!"

And growing suddenly very careful of her cousin's reputation, she dispatched a note to Rose Hill, requesting her immediate return. Not that she really thought there would be any impropriety in Dora's staying with Mr. Hastings, but because she had a plan by which she hoped herself to see him every day. And in this plan she succeeded. As she had expected, her note brought down Mr. Hastings himself, who, on his child's account, objected to parting with Dora, unless it were absolutely necessary.

"She is as well off there as here," said he; "and why can't she stay?"

"I am perfectly willing she should take care of little Ella," answered the previously instructed Mrs. Deane, who, in a measure, shared her daughter's ambitious designs; "but it must be done here, if at all. I can't suffer her to remain alone with those gossiping servants."

"Oh, yes!" exclaimed Eugenia, speaking as if this were the first she had heard of it. "That is a good idea. It will be delightful to have the dear little creature here, and so much better for her too in case of *croup*, or anything like that, to be with an experienced person like mother!"

"But," said Mr. Hastings, "this would keep Dora entirely from her studies, and that ought not to be."

' It need not," hastily interrupted Eugenia. "She can go to school every day, for nothing will give me greater pleasure than to take care of our dear Ella's child ;" and the pocket-handkerchief went up to her face to conceal the tears which might have been there, but probably were not.

It was finally arranged, and in the course of a few days the parlor of Locust Grove was echoing sometimes to the laughter, and sometimes to the screaming of Little Ella Grey, who, from some unaccountable freak of babyhood, conceived a violent fancy for Eugenia, to whom she would go quite as readily as to Dora, whose daily absence at school she at last did not mind. Regularly each day, and sometimes twice a day, Mr. Hastings came down to Locust Grove, and his manner was very kind toward Eugenia, when he found her, as he often did, with his baby sleeping in her arms. He did not know how many times, at his approach, it was snatched from the cradle by Eugenia, who, in reality, was not remarkably fond of baby-tending, and who, in the absence of the father, left the child almost wholly to the care of her mother and sister. Management, however, was everything, and fancying she had found the shortest avenue to Mr. Hastings's heart, she, in his presence, fondled, and petted, and played with his child, taking care occasionally to hint of neglect on the part of Dora, whom he now seldom saw, as, at the hour of his calling, she was generally in school. It was by such means as this, that Eugenia sought to increase Mr. Hastings's regard for herself, and, in a measure, she succeeded; for though his respect for Dora was undimin

Ished, he could not conceal from himself the fact that Eugenia was very agreeable, very interesting, and very *kind to his daughter!*

As the autumn advanced, and the cold rainy weather precluded out-door exercise, it was but natural that he should spend much of his time at Locust Grove, where his tastes were carefully studied, his favorite books read, and his favorite authors discussed, while Eugenia's handsome black eyes smiled a welcome when he came, and drooped pensively beneath her long eyelashes when he went away. Thus the autumn and the winter passed, and when the spring had come, the village of Dunwood was rife with rumors concerning the attraction which drew Mr. Hastings so often to Locust Grove ; some sincerely pitying him if, indeed, he entertained a serious thought of making Eugenia Deane his wife, while others severely censured him for having so soon forgotten one whose grave had not been made a twelvemonth. But he had not forgotten, and almost every hour of his life was her loved name upon his lips, and the long golden tress his own hand had severed from her head was guarded as his choicest treasure, while the dark hours of the night bore witness to his lonely grief. And it was to escape this loneliness—to forget for a brief time the sad memories of the past—that he went so often to Locust Grove, where as yet his child was the greater attraction, though he could not be insensible to the charms of Eugenia, who spared no pains to interest him in herself.

He was passionately fond of music, and many an hour she sat patiently at the piano, seeking to perfect herself in a difficult piece, with which she thought to surprise him. But nothing, however admirably executed, could sound well upon her old-fashioned instrument, and how to procure a new one was the daily subject of her meditations. Occasionally, as she remembered the beautiful rosewood piano standing useless and untouched in the parlors of Rose Hill, something whispered her to "wait and it would yet be hers." But this did not satisfy her present desire, for aside from the sweet sounds, with which she hoped to entrance Mr. Hastings, was the wish to make him think them much wealthier than they were. From one or two circumstances, she had gathered the impression that he thought them poor, and, judging him by herself, she fancied her chances for becoming Mrs. Hastings 2d, would be greatly increased if by any means he could be made to believe her comparatively rich. As one means of effecting this, she must and would have a new piano, costing not less than four hundred dollars. But how to procure the money was the question ; the remittance from Uncle Nat, which had come on the first day of January, was already half gone, and she could not, as she had once done before, make Dora's *head* keep her out of the difficulty. At last, a new idea suggested itself, and springing to her feet she exclaimed aloud, for she was alone, "I have it ; strange I didn't think of that before. I'll write to the old man, and tell him that as Dora is now fifteen, we would gladly send her away to school, if we had the means, but our expenses are so great it is impossible, unless the money comes from him. And he'll do it too, the old miser ! —for in his first letter he said he would increase the allowance as Dora grew older."

Suiting the action to the word, she drew out her writing-desk, and commenced a letter to her "dearest Uncle Nathaniel," feelingly describing to him their straitened circumstances, and the efforts of herself and her sister to keep the family in *necessaries*, which they were enabled to do very comfortably with the addition of the allowance he so generously sent them every year. But they wished now to send Dora to school, to see if anything could be made of her ! She had improved latterly, and they really hoped a change of scene would benefit her. For Dora's sake, then, would "her dear uncle be so kind as to send them, on the receipt of that letter, such a sum as he thought best. If so, he would greatly oblige his loving niece."

"There ! That will do," she said, leaning back in her chair, and laughing as she thought what her mother and Alice would say, if they knew what she had done. "But they needn't know it," she continued aloud, "until the money comes, and then they can't help themselves."

Then it occurred to her that if Dora herself were to send some message, the coming of the money might be surer ; and calling her cousin into the room, she said :

"I am about writing to old Uncle Nat—have you any word or anything to send him ?"

"Oh, yes," answered Dora. "Give him my love, and tell him how much I wish he would come home—and stay !" she added, leaving the room, and soon returning with a lock of soft brown hair, which she laid upon the table. "Give him that, and tell him it was mother's."

Had a serpent started suddenly into life before Eugenia, she could not have turned whiter than she did at the sight of that hair. It brought vividly to mind the shadowy twilight, the darkness in the corners, and the terror which came over her on that memorable night, when she had thought to steal Dora's treasure. Soon recovering her composure, however, she motioned her cousin from the room, and, resuming her pen, said to herself, "I sha'n't write all that nonsense about his coming home, for nobody wants him here ; but the love and the hair may as well go."

Then, as she saw how much of the latter Dora had brought, she continued, "There's no need of sending all this

It would make beautiful hair ornaments, and I mean to keep a part of it ; Dora won't care, of course, and I shall tell her."

Dividing off a portion of the hair for her own use, she laid it aside, and then in a postscript wrote, "Dora sends"—here she paused ; and thinking that "Dora's *love*" would please the old man too much, and possibly give him too favorable an opinion of his niece, she crossed out the "sends," and wrote, "Dora wishes to be remembered to you, and sends for your acceptance a lock of her mother's hair."

Thus was the letter finished, and the next mail which left Dunwood bore it on its way to India, Eugenia little thinking how much it would influence her whole future life.

CHAPTER XIII.

UNCLE NAT

IT was a glorious moonlight night, and, like gleams of burnished silver, the moonbeams flashed from the lofty domes and minarets of Calcutta, or shone like sparkling gems on the sleeping waters of the bay. It was a night when the Hindoo lover told his tale to the dusky maiden at his side, and the soldier, wearing the scarlet uniform, talked to his blue-eyed bride of the home across the waters, which she had left to be with him.

On this night, too, an old man in his silent room, sat thinking of *his* home far beyond the shores of " Merrie England." Near him lay a letter, Eugenia's letter, which was just received. He had not opened it yet, for the sight of it had carried him back across the Atlantic wave, and again he saw, in fancy, the granite hills which had girded his childhood's home—the rock where he had played—the tree where he had carved his name, and the rushing mountain stream, which ran so swiftly past the red house in the valley—the home where he was born, and where had come to him the heart grief which had made him the strange, eccentric being he was. Thoughts of the dead were with him, too, to-night, and with his face buried in his broad, rough hands, he thought of *her*, whose winsome smile and gentle ways had woven around his heart a mighty and undying love, such as few men ever felt. Of Dora, too, he thought—Dora, whom he had never seen, and his heart yearned towards her with a deep tenderness, because his Fannie had been her mother.

"I should love her, I know," he said, "even though she were cold-hearted and stupid as they say;" then, as he remembered the letter, he continued, "I will open it, for it may have tidings of the child."

The seal was broken, the letter unfolded, and a tress of shining hair dropped on the old man's hand, clinging lovingly, as it were, about his fingers, while a low, deep cry broke the stillness of the room. He knew it in a moment—knew it was *Fannie's hair*—the same he had so oft caressed when she was but a little girl and he a grown-up man. It was Fannie's hair, come to him over land and sea, and his eyes grew dim with tears, which rained over his thin, dark face as he kissed again and again the precious boon, dearer far to him than the golden ore of India. "Fannie's hair!" very softly he repeated the words, holding it up to the moonlight, and then turning it toward the lamp, as if to assure himself that he really had it in his possession. "Why was it never sent before?" he said at last, "or why was it sent at all?" and taking up the letter, he read it through, lingering long over the postscript, and grieving that Dora's message, the first he had ever received, should be comparatively so cold.

"Why couldn't she have sent her *love* to her poor old uncle, who has nothing in the wide, wide world to love save this one lock of hair! God bless you, Dora Deane, for sending that," and again he raised it to his lips, saying as he did so, "And she shall have the money, too, aye, more than Eugenia asked; *one golden dollar for every golden hair*, will be a meet return!" And the old man laughed aloud at the novel idea, which no one but himself would have con‧ceived.

It was a long, weary task, the counting of those hairs; for more than once, when he paused in his work to think of her whose head they once adorned, he forgot how many had been told, and patiently began again, watching carefully, through blinding tears, to see that none were lost, for he would not that one should escape him. It was strange how childish the strong man became, counting those threads of hair; and when at last the labor was completed, he wept because there were no more. Fifteen hundred dollars seemed too small a sum to pay for what would give him so much joy; and *he* mourned that the tress had not been larger, quite as much as did Eugenia, when she heard of his odd fancy.

The moon had long since ceased to shine on the sleeping city, and day was breaking in the east, ere Nathaniel Deane arose from the table where he had sat the livelong night, gloating over his treasure, and writing a letter which now lay upon the table. It was addressed to Dora, and in it he told her what he had done, blessing her for sending him that lock of hair, and saying that the sight of it made his withered heart grow young and green again, as it was in the happy days when he so madly loved her mother. Then he told her how he yearned to behold her, to look upon her face and see which she was like, her father or her mother. Both were very dear to him, and for their sake he loved their child.

"No one will ever call me *father*," he wrote, "and I am lonely in my Indian home, lined all over, as it is, with gold, and sometimes, Dora, since I have heard of you, orphaned thus early, I have thought I would return to America, and seeking out some pleasant spot, would build a home for you and me. And this I would do, were I sure that I was wanted there—that you would be happier with me than with your aunt and cousins. Are they kind to you, my child? Sometimes, in my reveries, I have fancied they were not—have dreamed of a girlish face, with locks like that against which my old heart is beating, and eyes of deep dark blue, looking wistfully at me, across the waste of waters, and telling me of cruel neglect and indifference. Were this indeed so, not all India would keep me a moment from your side.

"Write to me, Dora and tell me of yourself, that I may judge something of your character. Tell me, too, if you ever think of the lonesome old man, who, each night of his life, remembers you in his prayers, asking that if on earth he may never look on *Fannie's* child, he may at last meet and know her in the better land. And now farewell, my *daughter*, mine by adoption, if from no other cause.

"Write to me soon, and tell me if at home there is one who would kindly welcome back

"Your rough old
"UNCLE NAT."

"She'll answer that," the old man said, as he read it over. "She'll tell me to come home," and, like a very child, his heart bounded with joy as he thought of breathing again the air of the western world.

The letter was sent, and with it we, too, will return to America, and going backward for a little, take up our story at a period three months subsequent to the time when Eugenia wrote to Uncle Nat.

CHAPTER XIV.

MANAGEMENT.

ONE year had passed away since the night waen **Ella Hastings** died, and alone in his chamber the husband was musing of the past, and holding, as it were, communion with the departed, who seemed this night to be so near that once he said aloud, "Ella, are you with me now?" But to his call there came no answer, save the falling of the summer rain ; and again, with his face upon the pillow, just as it had lain one year ago, he asked himself if to the memory of the dead he had thus long been faithful ; if no thought of another had mingled with his love for her ; and was it to ascertain this that she had come back to him to-night, for he felt that she was there, and again he spoke aloud, "I have not forgotten you, darling ; but I am lonesome, oh, so lonesome, and the world looks dark and drear. Lay your hand upon my heart, dear Ella, and you will feel its weight of pain."

But why that sudden lifting of the head, as if a spirit hand had indeed touched him with its icy fingers? Howard Hastings was not afraid of the dead, and it was not this which made him start so nervously to his feet. His ear had caught the sound of a light footstep in the hall below, and coming at that hour of a stormy night, it startled him, for he remembered that the outer door had been left unlocked

5

Nearer and nearer it came, up the winding stairs, and on through the silent hall, until it reached the threshold of his chamber, where it ceased, while a low voice spoke his name.

In an instant he was at the door, standing face to face with Dora Deane, whose head was uncovered, and whose hair was drenched with the rain.

"Dora," he exclaimed, "how came you here and where-fore have you come ?"

"Your child !" was her only answer, and in another moment he, too, was out in the storm with Dora Deane, whose hand he involuntarily took in his, as if to shield her from the darkness.

In a few words she told him how she had been aroused from her sleep by her aunt, who said the baby was dying with the *croup ;* that the servant was timid and refused to go either for him or the physician, and so she had come herself.

"And were you not afraid ?" he asked ; and the heroic girl answered, "No ; I fancied Ella was with me, cheering me on, and I felt no fear."

Mr. Hastings made no reply, but, when he reached the house, and saw the white, waxen face of the child, he felt that Ella had indeed been near to him that night ; that she had come for her little one, who, with a faint, moaning cry, stretched its hands towards Dora, as she entered the room. And Dora took it in her arms, holding it lovingly there, until the last painful struggle was over, and the father, standing near, knew that wife and child had met together in heaven.

At the foot of the garden, beneath the evergreens, where he had wished to lay his other Ella, they buried the little girl, and then Howard Hastings was, indeed, alone in the

world--alone in his great house, which seemed doubly desolate now that all were gone. For many weeks he did not
go to Locust Grove, but remained in his quiet rooms, brood
ing over his grief, and going often to the little grave be
neath the evergreens. There, once, at the hour of sunset,
he found *Eugenia Deane* planting flowers above his sleeping
child! She had marvelled much that he staid so long
away, and learning that the sunset hour was always spent
in the garden, she had devised a plan for meeting him. It
succeeded, and with well-feigned embarrassment she was
hurrying away, when he detained her, bidding her tarry
while he told her how much he thanked her for her kindness
to his child.

"I have wished to come to Locust Grove," he said, "and
thank you all, but I could not, for there is now no baby
face to greet me."

"But there are those there still who would welcome you
with pleasure," softly answered Eugenia; and then with
her dark eyes sometimes on the ground and sometimes looking very pityingly on him, she acted the part of a consoler,
telling him how much better it was for the child to be at
rest with its mother.

And while she talked, darkness fell upon them, so that
Howard Hastings could not see the look of triumph which
the dark eyes wore when he said, "You must not go home
alone, Miss Deane. Let me accompany you."

So the two went together very slowly down the long
avenue, and when over an *imaginary* stone the fair Eugenia
stumbled, the arm of Howard Hastings was offered for her
support, and then more slowly still they continued on their
way. From that time Mr. Hastings was often at Eugenia's
side, and before the autumn was gone, he had more than
once been told she was to be his wife. And each time that

he heard it, it affected him less painfully, until at last he
himself began to wonder how it were possible for him ever
to have disliked and distrusted a person so amiable, so intelligent and so agreeable as Eugenia Deane ! Still he could
never quite satisfy himself that he loved her, for there was
omething which always came up before him whenever he
seriously thought of making her his wife. This something
he could not define, but when, as he sometimes did, he
fancied Eugenia the mistress of his house, there was always
in the background the form of Dora Deane, gliding noiselessly about him, as she did that night when first she came
to Rose Hill. He saw but little of her now, for whenever
he called, Eugenia managed to keep from the room both
mother, sister and cousin, choosing to be alone with the
handsome widower, who lingered late and lingered long,
dreading a return to his lonely home.

Eugenia was now daily expecting an answer to her letter,
and feeling sure that it would bring the money, she began
to talk to Mr. Hastings of her new piano, playfully remark-
ing, that as he was a connoisseur in such matters, she believed she should call on him to aid in her selection ; and
this he promised to do, thinking the while of the unused
instrument in his deserted parlor, and feeling strongly
tempted to offer her its use. Thus the weeks passed on,
while Eugenia became more and more impatient for the letter.

"It is an age since I had anything from the post-office.
I wish you'd call and inquire," she said to Dora one afternoon, as she saw her preparing to go out.

Scarcely was she gone, however, when, remembering something which she wanted, and, thinking she might possibly
meet with Mr. Hastings, she started for the village herself,
reaching the office door just as Dora, accompanied by Mr
Hastings, was crossing the street in the same direction.

"I shan't have to go in now," said Dora; and, fancying her companion would prefer waiting for her cousin to walking with her, she passed on, all unconscious of what she had lost by being a minute too late.

"A letter from Uncle Nat—directed to Dora, too!" and Eugenia grew alternately red and white, as, crushing the missive into her pocket, she went out into the street, where she was joined by Mr. Hastings.

"Dora left me rather unceremoniously," said he, as he bade her good evening, "and so I waited to walk with you."

But Eugenia could not appear natural, so anxious was she to know what the letter contained. Up to the very gate Mr. Hastings went, but for once she did not ask him to stop; and he turned away, wondering at her manner, and feeling a little piqued at her unusual coolness. Hastening to her chamber, and crouching near the window, Eugenia tore open Dora's letter, and clutching eagerly at the draft, almost screamed with delight when she saw the amount. FIFTEEN HUNDRED DOLLARS! She could scarcely believe her senses; and drawing still nearer the window, for the daylight was fading fast, she sought for the reason of this unexpected generosity. But the old man's childish fancy, which would have touched a heart less hard than hers, aroused only her deepest ire—not because he had counted out the hairs, but because there had not been more to count. Bounding to her feet in her wrath, she exclaimed, "Fool that I was, to have withheld one, when the old dotard would have paid for it so richly. But it cannot now be helped," she continued, and resuming her seat, she read the letter through, exploding but once more, and that at the point where Uncle Nat had spoken of returning, asking if there was one who would welcome him home.

"Gracious heavens!" she exclaimed, growing a little faint. "Wouldn't I be in a predicament? But it shall never be, if I can prevent it, and I fancy I can. As Dora will not read this letter, it is not reasonably to be expected that she will answer it, and it will be some time, I imagine, before *I* invite him to come and see if we are kind to her! What a childish old thing he must be, to pay so much for one little lock of hair! I'd send him all of mine, if I thought it would bring me fifteen hundred dollars."

It did seem a large sum to her, that fifteen hundred dollars, more than she dared to appropriate to herself; but the piano she was determined to have, and, as she dreaded what her mother might say, she resolved upon keeping the letter a secret until the purchase was made, and then Mrs. Deane could not do otherwise than indorse the draft, and let her have the money.

They had been talking of going to Rochester for some time past, and if she could manage to have Mr. Hastings go with her, she could leave her mother at the hotel, or dispose of her elsewhere, while she went with him to the music rooms, and made the selection. As if fortune were, indeed, favoring her, Mr. Hastings called the next night, and they were, as usual, left together alone. She was looking uncommonly well this evening; and as she saw how often, and how admiringly his eyes rested upon her, hope whispered that the prize was nearly won. After conversing awhile on different subjects, she spoke of her new piano, asking him if he remembered his promise of assisting her in a selection, and saying she thought of going to the city some day that week. Again Mr. Hastings remembered the beautiful rosewood instrument, whose tones had been so long unheard in his silent home, and he said, "Do you not like Ella's piano?" while a feeling, shadowy and undefined, stole over him, that possibly it might, some day, be hers; and Eugenia, divining his thoughts, answered artfully, "Oh, very much. I used to enjoy hearing dear Ella play, but that don't do me any good. It isn't mine, you know."

Very softly and tenderly the beautiful black eyes looked into his, and the voice was low and gentle, as it breathed the sacred name of Ella. It was the hour of Howard Hastings's temptation; and, scarce knowing what he did, he essayed to speak—to offer *her* the piano, whose keys had been so often touched by the fairy fingers, now folded away beneath the winter snow. But his lips refused to move; there was a pressure upon them, as if a little hand were laid upon his mouth to prevent the utterance of words he had better far not speak. Thus was he saved, and when Eugenia, impatient at his delay, cast towards him an anxious glance, she saw that his thoughts were not of her, and, biting her lips with vexation, she half petulantly asked, "if he had any intention of going to the city that week?"

"Yes—no—certainly," said he, starting up as if from a deep reverie. Then, as he understood what was wanted of him, he continued, "excuse me, Miss Deane. I was thinking of Ella, and the night when she died. What were you saying of Rochester? I have business there to-morrow, and if you go down, I will aid you all I can. By the way," he continued, "that is the night of ——'s grand concert. How would you like to attend it?"

"Oh, so much!" answered Eugenia, her fine eyes sparkling with delight.

"But stop," said he, "now I think of it, I have an engagement which may possibly prevent me from attending it, as I would like to do with you, for I know you would enjoy it. Still, it may be that I can, and if so, I'll call for you at the hotel. We can come home on the eleven o'clock train.'

So, ere Mr. Hastings departed, it was arranged that Eugenia and her mother should next morning go down with him to the city, and that in the evening he would, perhaps, accompany them to the concert.

"I am progressing fast," thought Eugenia, as she sat alone in her chamber that night, after Alice had retired, " but still I wish he'd come to the point, and not keep me in such suspense. I thought once he was going to, and I believe now he would if he hadn't gone to thinking of Ella, and all that nonsense ; but never mind, he's worth waiting for, with his fine house and immense wealth ; I shan't care so much about Uncle Nat's money then, though goodness knows I don't want him turning up here some day and exposing me, as I dare say the meddlesome old thing would do."

This reminded her of the letter, and, as Alice was asleep, she thought this as favorable an opportunity for answering it as she would probably have. Opening her writing-desk, and taking her pen, she framed a reply, the substance of which was, that *ma*, *Alice* and *herself* were very, very thankful to her dear uncle for his generous gift to Dora, who, strange to say, manifested no feeling whatever !

"If she is grateful," wrote Eugenia, " she does not show it in the least. I hardly know what to make of her, she's so queer. Sometime, perhaps, she will appreciate your goodness, and meanwhile, rest assured that I will see that your gift is used to the best advantage."

Not a word of coming home to the expectant old man, whose heart each day grew lighter as he thought of the letter which *Dora* would write bidding him to come to the friends who would welcome him back. Not one line from Dora to the kind uncle who, when he read the cruel lines, laid his weary head upon his pillow and wept bitterly that this, his last fond hope, was crushed !

There is such a thing as Retribution, and Eugenia Deane, sitting there alone that night, shuddered as the word seemed whispered in her ear. But it could not deter her from her purpose. Howard Hastings must be won. "The object to be gained was worthy of the means used to gain it," she thought, as she sealed the letter ; then, placing the draft for the $1,500 safely in her purse, she crept softly to bed, sleeping ere long as soundly as if the weight of a guilty conscience had never rested upon her.

CHAPTER XV.

THE NEW PIANO.

THE next morning, at the appointed time, Mr. Hastings, Mrs. Deane and her daughter stood together in the Dunwood Depot, awaiting the arrival of the train. Eugenia was in high spirits, chatting gaily with Mr. Hastings, whose manner was so unusually lover-like, that more than one looker-on smiled meaningly, as they saw how very attentive he was. On reaching the city he parted from the ladies for a time, telling Eugenia, as he bade her good morning, that he should probably not see her again until about three o'clock in the afternoon, when he would meet her at the music-rooms.

"Meet you at the music-rooms for what?" asked Mrs. Deane, who, though she had frequently heard her daughter talking of a new piano, had never for a moment believed her to be in earnest.

"What do you suppose he would meet me for, unless it were to look at pianos?" answered Eugenia, and her mother replied, "Look at pianos ! A great deal of good that will do, I imagine, when both of us together have but twenty-five dollars in the world !"

A curious smile flitted over Eugenia's face, as she thought of the draft, but she merely replied, "And suppose we haven't any money, can't I *make believe*, and by looking at expensive instruments induce Mr. Hastings to think we are richer than we are? I don't accuse him of being at all mercenary, but I do think he would have proposed ere this, if he hadn't thought us so wretchedly poor."

Mrs. Deane could not understand how merely looking at a costly piano indicated wealth; but feeling herself considerable interest in her daughter's success, she concluded to let her pursue her own course, and the subject was not resumed again until afternoon, when, having finished their shopping, they sat alone in a private room, opening from the public hall, and opposite the ladies' parlor in the hotel. They had taken this room, because in case she attended the concert, Eugenia would wish to rearrange her hair, and make some little change in her personal appearance. "Then, too, when Mr. Hastings came," she said, "they would be by themselves, and not have everybody listening to what they said. By the way, mother," she continued, as she stood before the glass, "if Mr. Hastings can attend the concert, suppose you go home at half-past six. You don't care for singing, you know, and besides that, you stumble so in the dark, that it will be so much pleasanter for Mr. Hastings to have but one in charge."

"And much pleasanter for you, too, to be alone with him," suggested Mrs. Deane, who really cared but little for music, and was the more willing to accede to Eugenia's proposal."

"Why, yes," answered the young lady. "I think it would be pleasanter—so if he says he can accompany me, you go home, like a dear good old woman as you are." And tying on her bonnet, Eugenia went out to keep her appointment, finding Mr. Hastings there before her, as she had expected.

Several expensive pianos were examined, and a selection

at last made of a very handsome one, whose cost was $450.
"I care but little what price I pay, if it only suits me," said
Eugenia, with the air of one who had the wealth of the
Indies at her disposal. "You will see that it is carefully
boxed and sent to Dunwood, will you not?" she continued,
turning to the man in attendance, who bowed respectfully,
and stood waiting for the money, while Mr. Hastings, too, it
may be, wondered a very little if it would be forthcoming.
"I did not know certainly as I should make a purchase,"
continued Eugenia, "so I left the money with mother at the
hotel : I will bring it directly ;" and she tripped gracefully
out of the store, followed by Mr. Hastings, who felt almost
as if he had done wrong in suffering her to buy a new piano,
when *Ella's* would have suited her quite as well, and .the
name upon it, "E. Hastings," would make no difference !

Once, in the street, he thought to say something like this
to her and prevent the purchase, but again an unseen hand,
as it were, sealed his lips ; and when he spoke, it was to tell
her that he could probably escort her to the concert,
and would see her again about dark. Here having reached
the hotel, he left her, and walked on a short distance, when,
remembering something concerning the concert, which he
wished to tell her, he turned back, and, entering the hotel,
went to the parlor, where he expected to find her. But she
was not there, and thinking she had gone out for a moment
and would soon return, he stepped into the hall, and as the
day was rather cold, stood over the register, which was very
near Eugenia's room. He had been there but an instant,
when he caught the sound of his own name, and looking up,
he saw that the ventilator over the door opposite was turned
back, so that everything said within, though spoken in a low
tone, could be distinctly heard without. It was Eugenia
who was speaking, and not wishing to listen, he was about

turning away, when the words she uttered aroused his curiosity and chained him to the spot.

They were, " And what if Mr. Hastings *did* give it to me? If he marries me, and I intend that he shall, 'twill make no difference whether the piano was bought afterward or a little in advance. He knows, or ought to know, that I would not use Ella's old one."

" But has he ever said a word to you on the subject of marriage?" queried Mrs. Deane, and Eugenia answered, " Not directly, perhaps, but he has had it in his mind a hundred times, I dare say. But pray don't look so distressed. I never knew before that scheming mothers objected to their daughters receiving costly presents from the gentlemen to whom they were engaged."

" You are not engaged," said Mrs. Deane, and Eugenia replied, " But expect to be, which is the same thing ;" then after a pause, she continued, " but, jesting aside, Mr. Hastings did not buy the piano. I bought it myself and expect to pay for it, too, that is, if you will indorse this draft. Look !". and she held to view the draft, of which Mrs. Deane was, until that moment, wholly ignorant.

Wiping from his white brow the heavy drops of perspiration which had gathered thickly upon it, Mr. Hastings attempted to · leave the place, but the same hand which twice before had sealed his lips, was interposed to keep him there, and he stood silent and immovable, while his surprise and indignation increased as the conversation proceeded.

In great astonishment Mrs. Deane examined the draft, and then questioned her daughter as to how she came by it. Very briefly Eugenia told of the letter she had sent her Uncle Nat. "I knew there was no surer way of gaining his good will," said she, " than by thrusting Dora in his face so I asked her if she had any message, and she sent her love, together with a lock of her mother's hair, which I verily believe turned the old fellow's heart. I have not the letter with me which he wrote in reply, and directed to Dora, but it was a sickish, sentimental thing, prating about his love for her mother, and how much he prized that lock, which he said he would pay for at the rate of one dollar a hair! And, don't you believe, the silly old fool sat up all night, crying over and counting the hairs, which amounted to fiftceen hundred! 'Twould have been more if I hadn't foolishly kept back some for hair ornaments. I was so provoked I could have thrown them in the fire."

"But if the letter was directed to Dora, how came you by it?" asked Mrs. Deane, who, knowing Eugenia as well as she did, was still wholly unprepared for anything like this.

"'Twas the merest chance in the world," answered Eugenia, stating the circumstance by which the letter came into her possession, and adding that "Mr. Hastings must have thought her manner that night very strange; but come," she continued, "do sign your name quick, so I can get the money before the bank closes."

But this Mrs. Deane at first refused to do, saying it was not theirs, and Dora should no longer be defrauded; at the same time, she expressed her displeasure at Eugenia's utter want of principle.

"Grown suddenly very conscientious, haven't you!" scornfully laughed the young lady, reminding her of the remittance anually sent to them for Dora's benefit, but which had been unjustly withheld; "very conscientious indeed; but I am thankful I parted company with that commodity long ago.

Then followed a series of angry words, and bitter recriminations, by which the entire history of Eugenia's selfish treatment of her cousin, even to the cutting off her hair more than two years before, was disclosed to Mr. Hastings, who, immeasurable shocked and sick at heart, turned away just as Mrs. Deane, to avoid further altercation, expressed her readiness to indorse the draft, on condition that the balance after paying for the piano, should be set aside for Dora.

"And haven't I told you repeatedly that the piano was all I wanted? and I shouldn't be so particularly anxious about that, if I did not think it would aid me in securing Mr. Hastings."

"Which you never shall, so help me Heaven!" exclaimed the indignant man, as he strode noiselessly down the hall, and out into the open air, where he breathed more freely, as if just escaping from the poisonous atmosphere of the deadly upas.

It would be impossible to describe his emotion, as he walked on through one street after another. Astonishment, rage, horror, and disgust each in turn predominated, and were at last succeeded by a deep feeling of thankfulness that the veil had been removed, and he had escaped from the toils of one, who, slowly but surely, had been winding herself around his fancy—he would not say affections, for he knew he had never loved her. "But she might have duped me," he said, "for I am but human;" and then as he thought what a hardened, unprincipled woman she was, he shuddered and grew faint at the mere idea of taking such a one to fill the place of his gentle, loving Ella. "I cannot meet her to-night," he continued, as he remembered the concert. "I could not endure the sound of her voice, for I should say that to her which had better not be said. I will go home—back to Dunwood, leaving her to wait for me as long as she chooses."

With him, to will was to do, and having finished his business, he started for the depot, whither Mrs. Deane had preceded him, having been coaxed by Eugenia to return at half past six, and thus leave her the pleasure of Mr. Hastings's company alone. The piano had been paid for, and as it was quite dark, and beginning to rain, the now amiable young lady accompanied her mother to the depot, and having seen her safely in the cars, which would not start in some minutes, was on her way back to the hotel, her mind too intently occupied with thoughts of coming pleasure to heed the man, who, with dark lowering brow, and hat drawn over his face, met her on the sidewalk, and who at sight of her started suddenly as if she had been a crawling serpent.

"Will the Deanes always cross my path?" he exclaimed, as, opening the car door, he saw near the stove the brown satin hat and black plumes of the mother, who was sitting with her back towards him, and consequently was not aware of his presence.

To find a seat in another car was an easy matter, and while Eugenia, at the hotel, was alternately admiring herself in the glass, and peering out into the hall to see if he were coming, he was on his way to Dunwood, breathing more and more freely, as the distance between them increased.

"Yes, I have escaped her," he thought, and mingled with thankfulness for this, was a deep feeling of sympathy for Dora, to whom such injustice had been done.

He understood perfectly her position—knew exactly the course of treatment, which, from the first, she had received, and while trembling with anger, he resolved that it should not continue. "I *can* help her, and I *will*," he said emphatically; though how, or by what means he could not, in his present state of excitement, decide. Arrived at Dunwood, he stepped hastily from the car and walked rapidly down the street until he came opposite Locust Grove

Then, indeed he paused, while an involuntary shudder ran through his frame as he thought of the many hours he had spent within those walls with one who had proved herself un-worthy even of the name of woman.

"But it is over now," he said, "and when I cross that threshold again, may "——

The sentence was unfinished, for a light flashed suddenly out upon him, and a scene met his view which arrested his foot-steps at once, and, raining as it was, he leaned back against the fence and gazed at the picture before him. The shut-ters were thrown open, and through the window was plainly discernible the form of Dora Deane, seated at table, on which lay a book which she seemed to be reading. There was nothing elegant about her dress, nor did How-ard Hastings think of this ; his mind was intent upon *her* who had been so cruelly wronged, and whose young face, seen through the window on that winter night, looked very fair, so fair that he wondered he had never thought before how beautiful was Dora Deane.

At this point, Mrs. Deane, who had been slower in her movements, reached the gate, and, resigning his post near the fence, Mr. Hastings walked slowly home, bearing in his mind that picture of Dora Deane as he saw her through the window, with no shadows on her brow, save those left there by early grief, and which rendered her face still more attractive than it would otherwise have been. That night, all through the silent hours, there shone a glimmering light from the room where Howard Hastings sat, brooding upon what he had heard, and meditating upon the best means for removing Dora from the influence of her heartless cousin. Slowly over him, too, came memories of the little brown-faced girl who, when his home was cheerless, had come to him with her kindly acts and gentle ways, diffusing over all an air

of comfort and filling his home with sunlight. Then he re
membered that darkest hour of his desolation—that first coming home from burying his dead ; and, now as then he felt
creeping over him the icy chill which had lain upon his heart
when he approached the house whence they had borne his
fair girl wife. But he had found *her* there—Dora Deane—
folding his motherless baby to her bosom, and again in imagi-
nation he met the soft glance of her eye as she welcomed him
back to Ella's room which seemed not half so lonely with
Dora sitting by his side. Again he was with her in the storm
which she had braved on that night when his child lay dying—
the child whom she had loved so much, and who had died
upon her lap. Anon, this picture faded too, and he saw her
as he had seen her but a few hours before—almost a woman
now, but retaining still the same fair, open brow, and sunny
smile which had characterized her as a child. And *this* was the
girl whom Eugenia would trample down—would misrepre-
sent to the fond old uncle, far away. "But it shall never
be," he said aloud ; "I will remove her from them by force
if need be." But "where would she go ?" he asked. Then
as he remembered Ella's wish that he should care for her—
a wish which his foolish fancy for Eugenia had for a time
driven from his mind, he felt an intense longing to have her
there with him ; there, in his home, where he could see her
every day—not as his wife, for at that time, Howard Hastings had never thought it possible for him to call her by
that name, she seemed so much a child ; but she should
be his sister, and his manly heart throbbed with delight, as
he thought how he would watch over and protect her from
all harm. He would teach her, and she should learn, sitting at his feet as she sat two years before ; and life
would seem no longer sad and dreary, for he would have a
pleasant home, and in it *Dora Deane !* Ere long, however,

his better judgment told him that the censorious, curious world would never suffer this to be ; *she couldn't come as his sister—she couldn't come at all*—and again there came over him a sense of desolation, as if he were a second time bereaved.

Slowly and steadily the rain drops pattered against the window pane, while the lamp upon the table burned lower and lower, and still Mr. Hastings sat there, pondering another plan, to which he could see no possible objection, provided Mrs. Deane's consent could be obtained ; "and she shall consent," he said, "or an exposure of her daughter will be the consequence."

Then, it occurred to him, that in order to succeed, he must for a time at least appear perfectly natural—must continue to visit at Locust Grove, just as he had been in the habit of doing—must meet Eugenia face to face, and even school himself to listen to the sound of her piano, which he felt would grate so harshly on his ear. And all this he could do if in the end Dora would be benefited.

For the more immediate accomplishment of his purpose, it seemed necessary that he should visit New York, and as, in his present excitement, he could not rest at home, he determined upon going that very morning, in the early train. Pushing back the heavy drapery which shaded the window, he saw that daylight was already breaking in the east, and, after a few hurried preparations, he knocked at Mrs. Leah's door, and telling her that important business required his presence in New York, whither he should be gone a few days, he started for the depot, just as the sun was rising ; and, that night, Mrs. Elliott, his sister, was surprised to hear that he was in the parlor, and wished to see her.

"Why, Howard !" she exclaimed, as she entered the room, and saw how pale and haggard he was, "what is the matter, and why have you come upon me so suddenly ?"

"I have come, Louise, for aid," he answered, advancing

towards her, and drawing her to his side. "Aid for an injured orphan. Do you remember Dora Deane?"

"Perfectly well, answered Mrs. Elliott. I was too muc' interested in her to forget her soon. Ella wrote me that she was living in Dunwood, and when next I visited you, I intended seeking her out. But what of her, and how can I befriend her?"

In as few words as possible, Mr. Hastings told what he knew of her history since his sister saw her last, withholding not even the story of his own strange fancy for Eugenia. "But that is over, thank Heaven," he continued; "and now, Louise, you must take Dora to live with you. You have no child, no sister, and she will be to you both of these. You must love her, educate her, make her just such a woman as you are yourself; make her, in short, what that noble-hearted old man in India will wish her to be when he returns, as he shall do, if my life is spared; and Louise," he added, growing more and more earnest, "she will well repay you for your trouble. She brought sunshine to my home; she will bring it to yours. She is naturally refined and intelligent. She is amiable, ingenuous, open-hearted, and will one day be beautiful.

"And you, my brother, love her?" queried Mrs. Elliott, looking him steadily in his face, and parting the thick, black hair from off his high, white forehead.

"*Love her*, Louise!" he answered, "*I love Dora Deane!* Why, no. Ella loved her, the baby loved her, and for this I will befriend her, but to *love her*, I never thought of such a thing!" and walking to the window, he looked out upon the night, repeating to himself, "*Love Dora Deane!* I wonder what put that idea into Louise's brain?"

Returning ere long to his seat, he resumed the conversation, which resulted at last in Mrs. Elliott's expressing her perfect willingness to give Dora a home, and a mother's care, to see that she had every possible advantage, to watch over and make her not only what Uncle Nat would wish to find her, but what Howard Hastings himself desired that she should be. Of Mrs. Elliott, we have said but little, neither is it necessary that we should dwell upon her character at large. She was a noble, true-hearted woman, finding her greatest happiness in doing others good. Widowed in the second year of her married life, her home was comparatively lonely, for no second love had ever moved her heart. In Dora Deane, of whom Ella had written so enthusiastically, she felt a deep interest, and when her brother came to her with the story of her wrongs, she gladly consented to be to her a mother, nay, possibly a sister, for, with woman's ready tact, she read what Mr. Hastings did not even suspect, and she bade him bring her at once.

A short call upon his mother, to whom he talked of Dora Deane ; a hasty visit to Ella's grave, on which the winter snow was lying ; a civil bow across the street to Mrs. Grey, who had never quite forgiven him for having *killed her daughter ;* and he started back to Dunwood, bearing with him a happier, healthier, frame of mind, than he had experienced for many a day. There was something now worth living for—the watching Dora Deane grow up into a woman, whose husband would delight to honor her, and whose children would rise up and call her blessed. This picture, however, was not altogether pleasing, though why the thoughts of Dora's future husband should affect him unpleasantly, he could not tell. Still it did, and mentally hoping she would never marry, he reached Dunwood at the close of the third day after his departure from it.

Here for a moment we leave him, while, in another chapter, we look in upon Eugenia, whom we left waiting for him at the hotel.

CHAPTER XVI.

FAILURE AND SUCCESS.

In a state of great anxiety, which increased each moment, Eugenia looked for the twentieth time into the long hall, and seeing no one, went back again to the glass, wondering if her new hat, which, without her mother's knowledge, had that afternoon been purchased, and now adorned her head, were as becoming as the milliner had said, and if fifteen dollars were not a great price for one in her circumstances to pay for a bonnet. Then she thought if Mr. Hastings proposed soon, as she believed he would, she should never again feel troubled about the trivial matter of money, of which she would have an abundance. But where was he and why did he not come? she asked herself repeatedly, caring less, however, for the delay, when she considered that if they were late, more people would see her in company with the elegant Mr. Hastings, who was well known in the city.

"Eight o'clock as I live," she exclaimed at last, consulting her watch, "and the concert was to commence at half-past seven. What can it mean?" and with another glance at her bonnet, she walked the length of the hall, and leaning far over the balustrade looked anxiously down into the office below, to see if by any chance he were there.

But he was not, and returning to her room, she waited another half hour, when, grown more fidgety and anxious she descended to the office, inquiring if Mr. Hastings had been there that evening. Some one thought they had seen him in the ladies' parlor that afternoon, but further information than that, she could not obtain, and the discomfited young lady went back to her room in no very enviable frame of mind, particularly as she heard the falling of the rain, and thought how dark it was without.

"What can have kept him?" she said, half crying with vexation. "And how I wish I had gone home with mother!"

Wishing, however, was of no avail, and when that night at half-past ten, the hotel omnibus as usual went to the depot, it carried a very cross young lady, who, little heeding what she did, and caring less, sat down beneath a crevice in the roof, through which the rain crept in, lodging upon the satin bows and drooping plumes of her fifteen-dollar hat, which, in her disappointment, she had forgotten to exchange for the older one, safely stowed away in the band-box she held upon her lap. Arrived at Dunwood station, she found, as she had expected, no omnibus in waiting, nor any one whose services she could claim as an escort, so, borrowing an umbrella, and holding up her dress as best she could, she started, band-box in hand, for home, stepping once into a pool of water, and falling once upon the dirty sidewalk, from which the mud and snow were wiped by her rich velvet cloak, to say nothing of the frightful pinch made in her other bonnet by her having crushed the band-box in her fall.

In a most forlorn condition, she at last reached home, where to her dismay she found the door was locked and the fire gone out, her mother not having expected her to return on such a night as this. To rouse up Dora, and scold her unmercifully, though for what she scarcely knew, was under the circumstances quite natural, and while Mr. Hastings at Rose Hill was devising the best means of removing Dora from her power, she at Locust Grove, was venting the entire weight of her pent-up wrath upon the head of the devoted girl, who bore it uncomplainingly. Removing at last her bonnet, she discovered the marks of the omnibus leak, and then her ire was turned towards him as having been the cause of all her disasters.

"I'll never speak to him again, never," she exclaimed, as she crept shivering to bed.

But a few hours, quiet slumber dissipated in a measure her wrath, and during the next day she many times looked out to see him coming, as she surely thought he would, laden with apologies for his seeming neglect. But nothing appeared except the huge box containing the piano, and in superintending the opening of that her mind was for a time diverted. Greatly Alice and Dora marvelled whence came the money with which the purchase had been made, and both with one consent settled upon Mr. Hastings as having been the donor. To this suggestion Eugenia made no reply, and feeling sure that it was so, Dora turned away and walking to the window sighed as she wondered what Ella would say if she could know who was to take her place in the heart of Howard Hastings.

The instrument was finely toned, and Eugenia spent the remainder of the day in practising a very difficult piece, which she knew Mr. Hastings admired, and with which she intended to surprise and charm him. But he did not come, either that day or the next, and on the morning of the next, which was Saturday, feigning some trivial errand to Mrs. Leah, she went herself to Rose Hill, casting anxious glances towards the windows of his room to see if he were in sight. Dame Leah was a shrewd old woman, and readily guessing that Eugenia's visit was prompted from a desire to see her master, rather than herself, she determined to tantalize her by saying nothing of him unless she were questioned. Continually hoping he would appear, Eugenia lingered until there was no longer a shadow of excuse for tarrying, and then she arose to go, saying as she reached the door, "Oh, now I think of it, Mr. Hastings has a book in his library which I very much wish to borrow. Is he at home?"

"No," answered Mrs. Leah, "he went to New York, Thursday morning, on the early train."

"To New York!" repeated Eugenia, "for what? and when will he be home?"

"He said he had important business," returned Mrs. Leah, adding that "maybe he'd be home that night."

Eugenia had heard all she wished to know, and forgetting entirely the *book*, bade Mrs. Leah good morning, and walked away, feeling in a measure relieved, for the *business* which took him so suddenly to New York, had undoubtedly some connection with his failing to call at the hotel for her! He had never called upon Sunday evening, but thinking that after so long an absence he might do so now, she sat in state from six o'clock till nine, starting nervously at every sound, and once when sure, she heard him, running from the room, so he would not find her there, and think she had been waiting for him. But he did not come, and the next day, feeling exceedingly anxious to know if he had returned, and remembering the book, which she had failed to get, and *must* have, she towards night sent *Dora* to Rose Hill, bidding her if she saw Mr. Hastings tell him that her piano had come and she wished him to hear it.

In the long kitchen by a glowing stove, Dame Leah sat, busy with her knitting, which she quickly suspended when she saw Dora, who was with her a favorite.

6

"So Eugenia sent you for that book?" she said, when told of Dora's errand. "I'll see if he will lend it."

Mr. Hastings was alone in his library. All that day he had been making up his mind to call at Locust Grove, where he knew Eugenia was impatiently expecting him, for Mrs. Leah had told him of her call, winking slily as she spoke of the *forgotten book!*

"Yes, I will go and have it over," he thought, just as Mrs. Leah entered, telling him that "Miss Deane wanted that book."

Thinking that Eugenia was in the house, he answered hastily. "Take it to her, and pray don't let her in here."

"It's Dora, not Eugenia," said Mrs. Leah, and instantly the whole expression of his countenance changed

"*Dora!*" he exclaimed. "It's a long time since I saw her in this room. Tell her to come up."

Very gladly Dora obeyed the summons, and in a moment she stood in the presence of Mr. Hastings.

"I am glad to see you," he said, motioning her to the little stool, on which she had often sat when reciting to him her lessons, and when she now sat down, it was so near to him that, had he chosen, his hand could have rested on her beautiful hair, for she held her hood upon her lap.

Two months before and he would not have hesitated to smooth these shining tresses, but the question of his sister, "Do you love her?" had produced upon him a curious effect, making him half afraid of the child-woman who sat before him, and who, after waiting a time for him to speak, looked up into his face, and said, "Do you want me for anything in particular, Mr. Hastings?"

"Want you, Dora? Want you?" he said, abstractedly, as if that question, too, had puzzled him; then remembering himself, and why he had sent for her, he ans-

wered, "I want to talk with you, Dora—to tell you something. Do you remember my sister Mrs. Elliott?"

The eager, upward glance of Dora's eyes, was a sufficient
answer, and he continued. "I saw her last week and
talked with her of you. She wishes you to come and live
with her. Will you go?"

Dora could never tell why she cried, but the thought of
living with Mrs. Elliott, whom she regarded as an almost
superior being, overcame her, and she burst into tears,
while Mr. Hastings looked at her, quite uncertain as to what,
under the circumstances, it was proper for him to do. If
his sister had never bothered him with that strange question, he would have known exactly how to act; but
now in a state of perplexity, he sat motionless, until, thinking he must do something, he said gently, "*Dora, my child.*"
The last word removed his embarrassment entirely. She
was a child, and as such he would treat her. So he said
again, "Dora, my child, why do you cry?" and Dora answered impulsively, "It makes me so glad to think of living
with Mrs. Elliott, for you do not know how unhappy I have
been since she found me four years ago.

"I know more than you suppose. But it is over now,"
he said; and stretching out his arm, he drew her nearer to
him, and resting her head upon his knee, he soothed her as
if she were indeed the child he tried to believe she was, and
he her grey-haired sire, instead of a young man of twenty-
seven!

And Dora grew very calm sitting there with Mr. Hastings's
hand upon her head, and when he told her it was all arranged, and she should surely go, she sprang to her feet,
and while her cheeks glowed with excitement, exclaimed, "It
is too good to come true. Something will happen, Aunt
Sarah will not let me go"

"Yes, she will," said Mr. Hastings decidedly. "I am going there to-night to talk with her."

Then, as it was already growing dark, he arose to accompany Dora home, both of them forgetting the book, which Eugenia seemed destined never to receive. But she did not think to ask for it in her joy at meeting Mr. Hastings, who succeeded in appearing natural far better than he had expected, telling her, not that he was sorry for having failed to keep his appointment, but that it was not consistent for him to do so, and adding that he hoped she was not very much disappointed.

"Oh, no," she said, "I know of course that business detained you;"—then, as she saw him looking at her piano, she advanced towards it, and seating herself upon the stool, asked, "if he would like to hear her play?"

He could not conscientiously answer "yes," for he felt that the sound would sicken him; but he stood at her side and turned the leaves of her music as usual, while she dashed through the piece she had practised with so much care.

"How do you like it?" she said, when she had finished; and he answered, "I always admired your playing, you know, but the tone of the instrument does not quite suit me. It seems rather muffled, *as if the wires were made of hair!*" and his large black eyes were bent searchingly upon her.

Coloring crimson, she thought, "Can he have learned my secret?" then, as she remembered how impossible it was for him to know aught of the money, she answered, "Quite an original idea," at the same time seating herself upon the sofa. Sitting down beside her as he had been in the habit of doing, he commenced at once upon the object of his visit, asking if her mother were at home, and saying he wished to see her on a matter of some importance; then, knowing who was really the ruling power there, he added, as Eugenia arose to leave the room in quest of her mother, "perhaps I had better speak of my business first to you!"

Feeling sure now of a proposal, the young lady resumed her seat, involuntarily pulling at her fourth finger, and mentally hoping the *engagement ring* would be a diamond one! What then was her surprise when she found that not herself, but Dora was the subject of his remarks! After telling her of his visit to his sister, and of her wishes with regard to Dora, he said, "since the death of my wife and baby, I have felt a deep interest in your family, for the kindness shown to me in my affliction. I promised Ella that I would befriend Dora, and by placing her with Louise, I shall not only fulfill my word, but shall also be relieved of all care concerning her. Do you think I can persuade your mother to let her go?"

Eugenia did not know. She would speak to her about it after he was gone, and tell him on the morrow.

" I shall rely upon you to plead my cause," he continued ; " Louise's heart is quite set upon it, and I do not wish to disappoint her."

" I will do my best," answered Eugenia, never suspecting that Mr. Hastings was quite as anxious as his sister, who, she presumed, intended making a half companion, half waiting-maid of her cousin.

" But it will be a good place for her, and somewhat of a relief to us," she thought, after Mr. Hastings had gone. " She is getting to be a young lady now, and growing each year more and more expensive. I presume Mrs. Elliott will send her to school for a time at least, and in case our families should be connected, it is well for her to do so. I wrote to Uncle Nat that we wished to send her away to school, and this is the very thing. Mother won't of course insist upon her having all that money, for she will be

well enough off without it, and if Mr. Hastings ever does pro
pose, I can have a handsome outfit ! Fortune does favor
me certainly."

Thus Eugenia mused, and thus did she talk to her mother,
and she was the more easily persuaded when she saw how
eager Dora was to go."

"I shall be sorry to leave you, Aunt Sarah," said Dora,
coming to her side, and resting her hand upon her shoulder,
" but I shall be so happy with Mrs. Elliott, that I am sure
you'll let me go."

Mrs. Deane was naturally a cold, selfish woman, but the
quiet, unassuming Dora had found a place in her heart, and
she would be very lonely without her ; still it was better
for her, and better for them all that she should go ; so she
at last gave her consent, and when the next day Mr. Hastings called he was told that Dora could go as soon as he
thought best.

"Let it be immediately, then," he said. "I will write to
Louise to night, and tell her we shall come next week."

"I wish I could go to New York with her," said Eugenia.
"It's so long since I was there."

"You had better wait till some other time, for I could
not now show you over the city," answered Mr. Hastings,
who had no idea of being burdened with Eugenia.

"He expects me to go with him sometime, or he would
never have said that," thought Eugenia, and this belief
kept her good natured during all the bustle and hurry of
preparing Dora for her journey.

The morning came at last on which Dora was to leave,
and with feelings of regret Mrs. Deane and Alice bade her
good bye, while Eugenia accompanied her to the depot,
where she knew she should see Mr. Hastings.

"I've half a mind to go with you as far as Rochester," she

said to Dora, in his presence, as the cars came up, but he made no reply, and the project was abandoned.

Kissing her cousin good-bye, she stood upon the platform until the train had moved away, and then walked slowly back to the house, which even to her seemed lonesome.

CHAPTER XVII.

THE QUESTION ANSWERED.

IT was late in the evening when our travellers reached the city, which loomed up before Dora like an old familiar friend. They found Mrs. Elliott waiting to receive them, together with Mr. Hastings's mother, who, having heard so much of *Dora Deane*, had come over to see her. Very affectionately did Mrs. Elliott greet the weary girl, and after divesting her of her wrappings, she led her to her mother, whose keen eyes scrutinized her closely, but found no fault in the fair childish face which looked so timidly up to her. Half bewildered, Dora gazed about her, and then, with her eyes swimming in tears, whispered softly to Mr. Hastings, "I am so afraid it will prove to be a dream."

"I will see that it does not," said Mrs. Elliott, who had overheard her, and who, as time passed on, became more and more interested in the orphan girl.

For several days Mr. Hastings lingered, showing her all over the city, and going once with her to visit the room where he had found her. But the elements had preceded them—fire and water—and not a trace of the old building remained. At the expiration of a week, Mr. Hastings started for home, half wishing he could take Dora with him, and wondering if his sister were in earnest, when she asked him *if he loved her?*

A new world now seemed opened to Dora, who never thought it possible for her to be so happy. The ablest instructors were hired to teach her, and the utmost care bestowed upon her education, while nothing could exceed the kindness both of Mrs. Elliott and Mrs. Hastings, the latter of whom treated her as she would have done a young and favorite daughter. One evening when Mrs. Elliott was dressing for a party, Dora asked permission to arrange her soft glossy hair, which she greatly admired.

"It's not all my own," said Mrs. Elliott, taking off a heavy braid and laying it upon the table. " I bought it in Rochester, nearly two years ago, on the day of Ella's party. I have often wished I knew whose it was," she continued, "for to me there is something disagreeable in wearing other people's hair, but the man of whom I purchased it, assured me that it was cut from the head of a young, healthy girl."

For a moment Dora stood thinking—then catching up the beautiful braid and comparing it with her own, she exclaimed, " *It was mine! It was mine!* Eugenia cut it off, and sold it the day before the party. Oh, I am so glad," she added, "though I was sorry then, for I did not know it would come to you, the dearest friend I ever had," and she smoothed caressingly the shining hair, now a shade lighter than her own.

Mrs. Elliott had heard from her brother the story of Dora's shorn locks, and the braid of hair was far more valuable to her, now that she knew upon whose head it had grown. In her next letter to her brother, she spoke of the discovery, and he could not forbear mentioning the circumstances to Eugenia, who, not suspecting how much he knew of the matter, answered indifferently, " Isn't it funny how things do come round? Dora had so much of the headache that we thought it best to cut off her hair, which she

6*

wished me to sell for her in Rochester. I think she was always a little penurious!"

Wholly disgusted with this fresh proof of her duplicity. Mr. Hastings could scarcely refrain from upbraiding her for her perfidy, but thinking the time had not yet come, he restrained his wrath, and when next he spoke, it was to tell her of a *foreign tour* which he intended making.

"I have long wished to visit the old world," said he, "and as there is nothing in particular to prevent my doing so, I shall probably start the first of June. I should go sooner, but I prefer being on the ocean in the summer season."

For a moment Eugenia grew faint, fancying she saw an end of all her hopes, but soon rallying, she expatiated largely upon the pleasure and advantages to be derived from a tour through Europe, saying, "it was a happiness she had herself greatly desired, but should probably never realize."

"Not if you depend upon me for an escort," thought Mr. Hastings, who, soon after, took his leave.

Much Eugenia wondered whether he would ask the important question, and take her with him, and concluding at last that he would, she secretly made some preparations for the expected journey! But alas for her hopes! The spring went by, the summer came, and she was still Eugenia Deane, when one evening towards the middle of June, Mr. Hastings came over to say good-bye, as he was intending to start next morning for New York, or rather, for his sister's country seat on the Hudson, where she was now spending the summer. This was a death-blow to Eugenia, who could scarcely appear natural. Tears came to her eyes, and once when she attempted to tell him how lonely Rose Hill would be without him, she failed entirely for want of voice.

"How hoarse you are. Have you a cold," said Mr. Hastings, and that was all the notice he took of her emotion

Fearing lest he should suspect her real feelings, she tried to compose herself, and after a time said, jokingly. "I shouldn't wonder if you were going to take you a wife from some of the city belles."

"Oh, no," he answered lightly. "Time enough to think of that when I return."

This gave her hope, and she bore the parting better than she could otherwise have done.

"You will not forget me entirely, I trust," she said, as she gave him her hand.

"Oh, no," he answered. "That would be impossible. I have many reasons which you do not perhaps suspect, for remembering you! By the way," he continued, "have you any message for Dora! I shall probably see her as she is with my sister."

"Give her my love," answered Eugenia, "and tell her to write more definitely of her situation. She never particularizes, but merely says she is very happy. I do hope Mrs. Elliott will make something of her!"

The next moment Mr. Hastings's good bye was ringing in her ears, and he was gone. Seating herself upon the stairs, and covering her face with her hands, Eugenia wept bitterly, and this was their parting.

One week later and at the same hour in the evening, Mr. Hastings sat in his sister's pleasant parlor, looking out upon the blue waters of the Hudson, and wondering why, as the time for his departure drew near, his heart should cling so fondly to the friends he was to leave behind. "I shall see them again if I live," he said, "and why this dread of bidding them farewell?"

At this moment his sister entered the room, bringing to him a letter from a rich old Texan bachelor, who was spending the summer with some friends in the vicinity of her home. It was directed to the " Guardians of Dora Deane," and asked permission to address her ! He had seen her occasionally at Mrs. Elliott's house, had met her frequently in his morning rambles, and the heart which for forty-five years had withstood the charms of northern beauties and southern belles, was won by the modest little country girl, and he would make her his wife, would bear her to his luxurious home, where her slightest wish should be his law. With a curious smile upon her lip, Mrs. Elliott read this letter through, and then without a word to Dora, carried it to her brother, watching him while he read it, and smiling still more when she saw the flush upon his brow, and the unnatural light in his eye.

" Have you talked with Dora ?" he said, when he had finished reading.

" No, I have not," answered his sister. " I thought I would leave that to you, for in case she should ask my advice, my fear of losing her might influence me too much."

" *Louise*," he exclaimed, leaning forward so that his hot breath touched her cheek, " you surely do not believe that Dora Deane cares aught for that old man. She is nothing but a child."

" She is seventeen next November," said Mrs. Elliott, " almost as old as Ella was when first you were engaged, and how can we tell how often she has thought of matrimony ? Mr. *Trevors* is a man of unexceptionable character, and though old enough to be her father, he is immensely wealthy, and this, you know, makes a vast difference with some girls."

" But not with her—not with Dora Deane, I'm sure," he said. " Where is she ? Send her to me, and I will see."

Dora's governess, who had accompanied them to the country, was sometimes very exacting, and this day she had been unusually cross, on account of her pupil's having failed in one or two lessons.

"I'll report you to Mr. Hastings, and see what he can do," she had said, as she hurled the French Grammar back upon the table.

This threat Dora had forgotten, until told that Mr. Hastings had sent for her; then, fancying he wished to reprimand her, she entered the parlor reluctantly, and rather timidly took a seat upon an ottoman near the window, where he was sitting.

During Dora's residence with Mrs. Elliott, she had improved much, both in manner and personal appearance, and others than the Texan planter called her beautiful. The brownish hue, which her skin had acquired from frequent exposure, was giving way to a clearer and more brilliant complexion, while the peculiarly sweet expression of her deep blue eyes would have made a plain face handsome. But Dora's chief point of beauty lay in her *hair*— her beautiful hair of reddish brown. It had grown rapidly, fully verifying Alice's prediction, and in heavy shining braids was worn around her classically shaped head. And Dora sat there very still—demurely waiting for Mr. Hastings to speak, wondering if he would be severe, and at last laughing aloud when, in place of the expected rebuke, he asked if she knew Mr. Trevors.

"Excuse me," she said, as she saw his look of surprise. "Miss Johnson threatened to report me for indolence, and I thought you were going to scold me. Yes, I know Mr. Trevors. I rode horseback with him last week."

A pang shot through Mr. Hastings's heart, but he continued, holding up the letter. "He has sued for your hand. He asks you to be his wife. Will you answer yes?"

And trembling with excitement, he awaited her reply,

while the revelation of a new light was faintly dawning
upon him.

"Mr. Trevors wish *me* to be his wife—that old man !"
she exclaimed, turning slightly pale. "It cannot be ; let
me read the letter." And taking it from his hand, she stood
beneath the chandelier, and read it through, while Mr. Hastings scanned her face to see if he could detect aught to
verify his fears.

But there was nothing, and breathing more freely, he
said, as she returned to him the letter, "Sit down here,
Dora, and tell me what I shall say to him. But first consider well, Mr. Trevors is rich, and if money can make you
happy, you will be so as his wife."

Dora did not know why it was, but she could not endure
to hear him talk in such a calm unconcerned manner of
what was so revolting. It grieved her, and laying her
head upon the broad window seat, she began to cry.
Mr. Hastings did not this time say " Dora, my child," for
Louise had told him she was not a child, and he began to
think so, too. Drawing his chair nearer to her, and laying
his hand upon her hair, he said gently, "will you answer
me ?"

"Yes," she replied, somewhat bitterly. "If Mrs. Elliott is
tired of me, I will go away, but not with Mr. Trevors. I
would rather die than marry a man I did not love, because
of his gold."

"Noble girl !" was Mr. Hastings's involuntary exclamation, but Dora did not hear it, and looking him in his face,
she said, "do you wish me to marry him ?"

' Never, never," he answered, "him, nor any one else !"

"Then tell him so," said she, unmindful of the latter part
of the remark. "Tell him I respect him, but I cannot be
his wife."

And rising to her feet she left the room, to wash away in another fit of tears, the excitement produced by her first offer!

Very still sat Mr. Hastings when she was gone, thought after thought crowding fast upon him, and half bewildering him by their intensity. He could answer Louise's question now! It had come to him at last, sitting there with Mr. Trevor's letter in his hand, and Dora at his feet. *Dora* who was so dear to him, and his first impulse was to hasten to her side, and sue for the love she could not give the grey-haired Texan.

"And she will not tell me nay," he said. "It will come to her as it has to me—the love we have unconsciously borne each other."

He arose to leave the room, but meeting his sister in the door, he turned back. and seating himself with her in the deep recess of the window, he told her of the mighty love which had been so long maturing, and of whose existence he did not dream until another essayed to come between him and the object of his affection.

"And, Louise," he said, "Dora Deane must be mine. Are you willing—will you call her sister, and treat her as my wife?"

And Mrs. Elliott answered, "I know, my brother, that you love Dora Deane. I knew it when I asked you that question, and if to-night I tried to tease you by making you believe it possible that she cared for Mr. Trevors, it was to show you the nature of your feelings for her. And I am willing that it should be so—but not yet. You must not speak to her of love, until you return. 'Hear me out," she continued, as she saw in him a gesture of impatience. "Dora is no longer a child—but she is too young to be trammelled with an engagement. And it must not be. You must leave her free till she has seen more of the world, and her mind is more mature.

"Free till another wins her from me," interrupted Mr. Hastings, somewhat bitterly ; and his sister answered, "I am sure that will never be, though were you now to startle her with your love she probably would refuse you."

"*Never*," he said emphatically ; and Mrs. Elliott replied "I think she would. She respects and admires you, but as you have looked upon her as a child, so in like manner, has she regarded you as a father, or, at least the husband of Ella, and such impressions must have time to wear away. You would not take her with you, and it is better to leave her as she is. I will watch over her and seek to make her what your wife ought to be, and when you return she will be older, will be capable of judging for herself, and she will not tell you no. Do you not think my reasoning good ?"

"I suppose it is," he replied, "though it is sadly at variance with my wishes. Were I sure no one would come between us, I could more easily follow your advice, and were it not that I go for *her*, I would give up my journey at once, and stay where I could watch and see that no one came near."

"This I will do," said Mrs. Elliott, "and I fancy I can keep her safe for you."

Awhile longer they talked together, and their conversation was at last interrupted by the appearence of Dora herself, who came to say good night.

"Come and sit by me, Dora," said Mr. Hastings, unmindful of his sister's warning glance. "Let me tell you what I wish you to do while I am gone," and moving along upon the sofa, he left a place for her at his side.

Scarcely was she seated when a servant appeared, wishing to speak with Mrs. Elliott, and Mr. Hastings was left alone with Dora, with whom he merely talked of what he hoped to find her when he returned. Once, indeed, he told her how often he should think of her, when he was far away, and asked as a keepsake a lock of her soft hair.

Three days afterwards he went to New York accompanied by Mrs. Elliott and Dora. He was to sail next morning, and wishing to see as much of the latter as possible, he felt somewhat chagrined when, soon after their arrival, his sister insisted upon taking her out for a time, and forbade him to follow. For this brief separation, however, he was amply repaid when, on the morrow, his sister, who went with him on board the vessel, placed in his hand at parting a daguerreotype, which she told him not to open till she was gone. He obeyed, and while Dora in his sister's home was weeping that he had left them, he in his state-room was gazing rapturously on a fair young face, which, looking out from its handsome casing, would speak to him many a word of comfort when he was afar on the lonely sea.

CHAPTER XVIII.

MR. HASTINGS IN INDIA.

IT was night again in Calcutta, and in the same room where we first found him was Nathaniel Deane—not alone this time, for standing before him was a stranger—"an American," he called himself, and the old East Indiaman, when he heard that word, grasped again the hand of his unknown guest, whose face he curiously scanned to see if before he had looked upon it. But he had not, and pointing him to a chair, he too sat down to hear his errand. Wishing to know something of the character of the individual he had come so far to see, Mr. Hastings, for he it was, conversed awhile upon a variety of subjects, until, feeling sure that 'twas a noble, upright man, with whom he had to deal, he said, "I told you, sir, that I came from New York, and so I did; but my home is in Dunwood."

One year ago, and Uncle Nat would have started with delight at the mention of a place so fraught with remembrances of *Dora*, but Eugenia's last cruel letter had chilled his love, and now, when he thought of Dora, it was as one incapable of either affection or gratitude. So, for a moment he was silent, and Mr. Hastings, thinking he had not been understood, was about to repeat his remark, when Uncle Nat replied, "My brother's widow lives in Dunwood—Mrs. Richard Deane—possibly you may have seen her!" And with a slight degree of awakened interest, the little keen black eyes looked out from under their thick shaggy eyebrows at Mr. Hastings, who answered, "I know the family well. Dora is not now at home, but is living with my sister."

Many and many a time had Uncle Nat repeated to himself the name of *Dora*, but never before had he heard it from other lips, and the sound thrilled him strangely, bringing back in a moment all his olden love for one whose mother had been so dear. In the jet black eyes there was a dewy softness now, and in the tones of his voice a deep tenderness, as, drawing nearer to his guest, he said in a half whisper, "Tell me of *her*—of *Dora*—for though I never saw her, I knew her mother."

"And loved her too," rejoined Mr. Hastings, on purpose to rouse up the old man, who, starting to his feet exclaimed, "How knew *you* that? *You*, whom I never saw until to-night! Who told you that I loved Fannie Deane? Yes it is true, young man—true, though *love* does not express what I felt for her; she was my *all*—my very *life*, and when I lost her the world was a dreary blank. But go on—tell me of the child, and if she is like her mother. Though how should you know? You, who never saw my Fannie?"

"I *have* seen her," returned Mr. Hastings, "but death was there before me, and had marred the beauty of a face which once must have been lovely. Five years ago last January I found her dead, and at her side was Dora, sweetly sleeping, with her arms around her mother's neck."

"*You*—*you*," gasped the old man, drawing near to Mr. Hastings—"you found them thus! I could kneel at your feet, whoever you may be, and bless you for coming here to tell me this; I never knew before how Fannie died. They never wrote me that, but go on and tell me all you know.

Did Fannie freeze to death while in India I counted my gold by hundreds of thousands ?"

Briefly Mr. Hastings told what he knew of Mrs. Deane's sad death, while the broad chest of Uncle Nat heaved with broken sobs, and the big tears rolled down his sunken checks.

"Heaven forgive me for tarrying here, while she was suffering so much !" he cried ; "but what of *Dora?* She did not die. I have written to her, and sent her many messages, but never a word has she replied, save once "—here Uncle Nat's voice grew tremulous as he added, "and then she sent me this—look—'twas Fannie's hair," and he held to view a silken tress much like the one which lay next Howard Hastings's heart ! "Oh, what a child it made of me, the first sight of this soft hair," he continued, carefully returning it to its hiding-place, without a word of the generous manner in which it had been paid for.

"Shall I tell him now ?" thought Mr. Hastings, but Uncle Nathaniel spoke before him, and as if talking with himself, said softly, "Oh, how I loved her, and what a wreck that love has made of me. But I might have known it. Twenty-one year's difference in our ages, was too great a disparity, even had my face been fair as John's. She was seventeen, and I was almost forty ; I am *sixty* now, and with every year added to my useless life, my love for her has strengthened."

"Could you not transfer that love to her daughter ? It might make you happier," suggested Mr. Hastings, and mournfully shaking his head, Uncle Nat replied, "No, no, I've tried to win her love so hard. Have even thought of going home, and taking her to my bosom as my own darling child—but to all my advances, she has turned a deaf ear. I could not make the mother love me—I cannot make the child. It isn't in me, the way how, and I must live here all alone. I wouldn't mind that so much, for I'm used to it now, but when I come to die, there will be nobody to hold my head, or to speak to me a word of comfort, unless God sends Fannie back to me in the dark hour, and who knows but he will ?"

Covering his face with his hands, Uncle Nathaniel cried aloud, while Mr. Hastings, touched by his grief, and growing each moment more and more indignant, at the deception practised upon the lonesome old man, said slowly and distinctly: *"Dora Deane never received your letter—never dreamed how much you loved her—never knew that you had sent her money. She has been duped—abused—and you most treacherously cheated by a base, designing woman! To tell you this, sir, I have come over land and sea! I might have written it, but I would rather meet you face to face—would know if you were worthy to be the uncle of Dora Deane !"*

Every tear was dried, and bolt upright, his keen eyes flashing gleams of fire, and his glittering teeth ground firmly together, Nathaniel Deane sat, rigid and immovable, listening to the foul story of Dora's wrongs, till Mr. Hastings came to the withholding of the letter, and the money paid for Fannie's hair. Then, indeed, his clenched fists struck fiercely at the empty air, as if Eugenia had been there, and springing half way across the room, he exclaimed, *" The wretch ! The fiend ! The beast ! The Devil ! '* What *shall* I call her ? Help me to some name which will be appropriate."

" You are doing very well, I think," said Mr. Hastings, smiling in spite of himself at this new phase in the character of the excited man, who, foaming with rage, continued to stalk up and down the room, setting his feet upon the floor with vengeance, and with every breath denouncing Eugenia's perfidy.

"Curse her!" he muttered, "for daring thus to maltreat Fannie's child, and for making me to believe her so ungrateful and unkind. And she once cut off her hair to buy a party dress with, you say," he continued, stopping in front of Mr. Hastings, who nodded in the affirmative, while Uncle Nat, as if fancying that the few thin locks, which grew upon his own bald head, were Eugenia's long, black tresses, clutched at them savagely, exclaiming, "The selfish jade! But I will be avenged, and Madam Eugenia shall rue the day that she dared thus deceive me. That mother, too, had not, it seems, been wholly guiltless. She was jealous of my Fannie—she has been cruel to my child. I'll remember that, too!" and a bitter laugh echoed through the room, as the wrathful old man thought of revenge.

But as the wildest storm expends its fury, so Uncle Nat at last grew calm, though on his dark face there were still traces of the fierce passion which had swept over it. Resuming his seat and looking across the table at Mr. Hastings, he said, "It is not often that *old Nat Deane* is moved as you have seen him moved to-night; but the story you told me set me on fire, and for a moment, I felt that I was going mad. But I am now myself again, and would hear how you learned all this."

In a few words, Mr. Hastings told of his foolish fancy for Eugenia, and related the circumstance of his having overheard her conversation at the hotel in Rochester.

"And Dora, you say, is beautiful and good," said Uncle Nat; "and I shall one day know her and see if there is in her aught like her angel mother, whose features are as perfect to me now as when last I looked upon them beneath the locust trees."

Bending low his head, he seemed to be thinking of the past, while Mr. Hastings, kissing fondly the picture of Dora Deane, laid it softly upon the table, and then anxiously awaited the result. Uncle Nathaniel did not see it at first, but his eye ere long fell upon it, and, with a cry like that which broke from his lips when first he looked on his dead Fannie's hair, he caught it up, exclaiming, "'Tis *her*—'tis Fannie—my long lost darling, come back to me from the other world. Oh, Fannie, Fannie!" he cried, as if his reason were indeed unsettled, "I've been so lonesome here without you. Why didn't you come before?"

Again, for a time, he was silent, and Mr. Hastings could see the tears dropping upon the face of Dora Deane, who little dreamed of the part she was acting, far off in Hindostan. Slowly the reality dawned upon Uncle Nat., and speaking to Mr. Hastings, he said, "Who are you that moves me thus from one extreme to another, making me first a *fury* and then a *child*?"

"I have told you I am Howard Hastings," answered the young man, adding that the picture was not that of Fannie, but her child.

"I know—I know it," returned Uncle Nat, "but the first sight of it drove me from my senses, it is so like her. The same open brow, the same blue eyes, the same ripe lips, and more than all, the same sweet smile which shone on me so often 'mid the granite hills of New Hampshire. And it is mine," he continued, making a movement to put it away. "You brought it to me, and in return, if you have need for gold, name the sum, and it shall be yours, even to half a million."

Money could not buy that picture from Howard Hastings, and though it grieved him to do so, he said, very gently, "I cannot part with the likeness, Mr. Deane, but we will share it together until the original is gained."

Leaning upon his elbows and looking steadily at his visitor, Uncle Nathaniel said, "You have been married once?"

" Yes, sir," answered Mr. Hastings, while his countenance flushed, for he readily understood the nature of the
questioning to which he was to be subjected.

" What was the name of your wife ?" was the next
query, and Mr. Hastings replied, " Ella Grey."

" Will you describe her ?" said Uncle Nat, and almost
as vividly as the features of Dora Deane were delineated by
the artist's power, did Mr. Hastings portray by word the
laughing blue eyes, the pale, childish face, the golden curls,
and little airy form of her who had once slept upon his
bosom as his wife.

" And did you love her, this Ella Grey?" asked Uncle Nat.

" Love her ? Yes. But she is dead," answered Mr. Hastings, while Uncle Nat continued :

" And now if I mistake not, you love Dora Deane ?"

" *Yes, better than my life,*" said Mr. Hastings, firmly.
" Have you any objections ?"

" None whatever," answered Uncle Nat, " for, though you
are a stranger to me, there is that in your face which tells
me you would make my darling happy. But it puzzles me
to know how, loving one as you say you did, you can
forget and love another."

" I have not forgotten," said Mr. Hastings, sadly ; " God
forbid that I should e'er forget my Ella ; but, Mr. Deane,
though she was good and gentle, she was not suited to me.
Our minds were wholly unlike ; for what I most appreciated,
was utterly distasteful to her. She was a fair, beautiful
little creature, but she did not satisfy the higher, nobler feelings of my heart ; and she, too, knew it. She told me so
before she died, and spoke of a coming time when I would
love another. She did not mention *Dora*, who then seemed
like a child, but could she now come back to me, she would
approve my choice, for she, too, loved Dora Deane."

"Have you told her this?" asked Uncle Nat—"told Dora how much you loved her?"

"I have not," was Mr. Hastings's reply. "My sister would not suffer it until my return, when Dora will be more mature. At first I would not listen to this; but I yielded at last, consenting the more willingly to the long separation, when I considered that with Louise she was at least safe from Eugenia, and I hope, safe from any who might seek either to harm her, or win her from me."

"You spoke of having stopped in Europe on your way hither," said Uncle Nat. "How long is it since you left New York?"

"I sailed from there the latter part of June, almost ten months ago," was Mr. Hastings's answer, adding that, as he wished to visit some parts of Europe, and left home with the ostensible purpose of doing so, he had thought it advisable to stop there on his way, for he well knew that Mr. Deane, after learning why he had come, would be impatient to return immediately.

"Yes, yes; you are right," answered the old man. "I would go to-morrow if possible; but I shall probably never return to India, and I must make some arrangements for leaving my business in the hands of others. Were Dora still in Eugenia's power, I would not tarry a moment. I would sacrifice everything to save her, but as you say she is safe with your sister, and a few week's delay, though annoying to me, will make no difference with her. Do they know aught of this—those *wretches* in Dunwood?" he continued, beginning to grow excited.

"They suppose me to be in Europe, for to no one save my mother and sister, did I breathe a word of India," Mr. Hastings replied; and Uncle Nat rejoined, "Let them continue to think so, then. I would rather they should not

7

suspect my presence in America until I meet them face to
face, and taunt them with their treachery. It shall not be
long, either, before I do it. In less than a month, we are
homeward bound—and then, Miss Eugenia Deane—*we'll
see!*" and his hard fist came down upon the table, as he
thought of her dismay when told that he stood before her.

But alas for Uncle Nat ! The time was farther in the
distance than he anticipated. The excitement of what he
had heard, told upon a frame already weakened by constant
toil and exposure in the sultry climate of India, and one
week from the night of Mr. Hastings's arrival, the old
man lay burning with fever, which was greatly augmented
by the constant chafing at the delay this unexpected illness
would cause. Equally impatient, Mr. Hastings watched
over him, while his heart grew faint with hope deferred, as
weeks, and even months, glided by ; while vessel after vessel sailed away, leaving Uncle Nat prostrate and powerless
to move. He had never been sick before in all his life, and
his shattered frame was long in rallying, so that the summer, and the autumn and a part of the winter passed away,
ere, leaning heavily on Mr. Hastings's arm, he went on board
the ship which was to take him home—take him to Dora
Deane, who had listened wonderingly to the story of her
wrongs, told her by Mrs. Elliott at Mr. Hastings's request.

Indignant as she was at Eugenia, she felt more than repaid for all she had suffered, by the knowledge that Uncle
Nat had always loved her ; and many a cheering letter from
her found its way to the bedside of the invalid, who laid each
one beneath his pillow, beside the picture which Mr. Hastings suffered him to keep. More than once, too, had Dora
written to Mr. Hastings *kind, sisterly notes*, with which he
tried to be satisfied, for he saw that she was the same frank,
ingenuous girl he had left, and from one or two things which

she wrote, he fancied he was not indifferent to her. " She did not, at least, care for another," so Louise assured him. There was comfort in that, and during the weary days when their floating home lay, sometimes becalmed and sometimes tossed by adverse winds, he and Uncle Nat whiled away the tedious hours, by talking of the happiness which awaited them when home was reached at last.

During Mr. Deane's illness, Mr. Hastings had suggested that the annual remittance be sent to Dunwood, as usual, lest they should suspect that something was wrong, if it were withheld, and to this Uncle Nat reluctantly consented, saying, as he did so, " It's the last dime they'll ever receive from me. I'll see her starve before my eyes, that girl Eugenia."

Still, as the distance between himself and the young lady diminished, he felt a degree of satisfaction in knowing that the draft had as usual been sent, thus lulling her into a state of security with regard to himself. Rapturously he talked of the meeting with Dora, but his eye was fiery in its expression when he spoke of that other meeting, when Eugenia would be the accused and he the wrathful accuser. The invigorating sea breeze did him good, and when at last the Cape was doubled and he knew that the waves which dashed against the ship, bore the same name with those which kissed the shores of America, he stood forth upon the deck, tall and erect as ever, with an eager, expectant look in his eye, which increased as he each day felt that he drew nearer and nearer to his home—and *Dora Deane* !

CHAPTER XIX.

THE MEETING.

ONE bright, beautiful summer morning, a noble vessel was sailing slowly into the harbor of New York. Groups of passengers stood upon her deck, and a little apart from the rest were Uncle Nat and Howard Hastings, the former gazing eagerly towards the city, which had more than doubled its population since last he looked upon it.

"We are almost home," he said to his companion, joyfully, for though the roof that sheltered his childhood was further to the northward, among the granite hills, he knew that it was *America*, the land of his birth, which lay before him, and as a child returns to its mother after a long and weary absence, so did his heart yearn towards the shore they were fast approaching.

A crowd of memories came rushing over him, and when, at last, the plank was lowered, he was obliged to lean upon the stronger arm of Howard Hastings, who, procuring a carriage, bade the hackman drive them at once to his sister's. For some time Mrs. Elliott and Dora had been looking for the travellers, whose voyage was unusually long, and they had felt many misgivings lest the treacherous sea had not been faithful to its trust; but this morning they were not expecting them, and wishing to make some arrangements for removing to her country seat on the Hudson, Mrs. Elliott had gone out there and taken Dora with her. Mr. Hast ings's first impulse was to follow them, but knowing that they would surely be home that night, and remembering how weary Uncle Nathaniel was, he wisely concluded to remain in the city and suprise them on their return.

Like one in a dream, Uncle Nat walked from room to room, asking every half hour if it were not almost time for the train, and wondering if Dora would recognize him if no one told her who he was. Scarcely less excited, Mr. Hastins, too, waited and watched; and when, just at dark, he heard the door unclose, and Dora's voice in the hall without, the rapid beating of his heart was distinctly audible.

"That's *her*—that's *Dora*. I'll go to her at once," said Uncle Nat; but Mr. Hastings kept him back, and Dora passed on to her room, from which she soon returned, and they could hear the sound of her footsteps upon the stairs, as she drew near.

With his face of a deathlike whiteness, his lips apart, and the perspiration standing thickly about them, Uncle Nat sat leaning forward, his eyes fixed upon the door through which she would enter. In a moment she stood before them—Dora Deane—but far more lovely than Mr. Hastings had thought or dreamed. Nearly two years before, he had left her a school girl, as it were, and now he found her a beautiful woman, bearing about her an unmistakable air of refinement and high breeding. She knew him in an instant, and with an exclamation of surprised delight, was hastening forward, when a low, moaning cry, from another part of the room, arrested her ear, causing her to pause ere Mr. Hastings was reached.

Uncle Nat had recognized her—knew that she was Dora, and attempted to rise, but his strength utterly failed him, and stretching out his trembling arms towards her, he said, supplicatingly, "*me first, Dora—me first.*"

It was sufficient, and Dora passed on with a welcoming glance at Mr. Hastings, who feeling that it was not for him to witness that meeting, glided noiselessly from the room in quest of his sister. Fondly the old man clasped the young girl to his bosom, and Dora could hear the whispered blessings which he breathed over her, and felt the hot tears dropping on her cheek.

"Speak to me, darling," he said at last; "let me hear your own voice assuring me that never again shall we be parted, until your mother calls for me to come and be with her."

Looking lovingly up into his face, Dora answered, "I will never leave nor forsake you, my father, but wherever your home may be there will mine be also."

Clasping her still closer in his arms, he said, "God bless you, my child, for so I will call you, and never, I am sure, did earthly parent love more fondly an only daughter than I love you, my precious Dora. I have yearned so often to behold you, to look into your eyes and hear you say that I was loved, and now that it has come to me, I am willing, almost, to die."

Releasing her after a moment, and holding her off at a little distance, he looked earnestly upon her, saying, as he did so, "Yes, you *are* like her—like your mother, Dora. Some, perhaps, would call you even more beautiful, but to me there is not in all the world a face more fair than hers."

In his delight at seeing her, he forgot for the time being how deeply she had been injured, and it was well that he did, for now nothing marred the happiness of this meeting, and for half an hour longer he sat with her alone, talking but little, but looking ever at the face so much like her whom he had loved and lost. At last, as if suddenly remembering himself, he said, "Excuse me, Dora; the sight of you drove

ev other thought from my mind, and I have kept you
too long from one who loves you equally well with myself,
and who must be impatient at the delay. He is worthy of
you, too, my child," he continued, without observing how the
color faded from Dora's cheeks. "He is a noble young
man, and no son was ever kinder to a father than he has
been to me, since the night when I welcomed him to my
home in India. Go to him, then, my daughter, and ask him
to forgive my selfishness."

From several little occurrences, Dora had received the im
pression that a marriage between herself and Mr. Hastings
would not be distasteful to his sister, but she had treated
the subject lightly as something impossible. Still the
thought of his loving another was fraught with pain, and
when at last she knew that he was on the stormy sea, and
felt that danger might befall him—when the faces of his
mother and sister wore an anxious, troubled look as days
went by, bringing them no tidings—when she thought it just
possible that he would never return to them again, it came
to her just as two years before it had come to him, and sitting alone in her pleasant chamber, she, more than once,
had wept bitterly, as she thought how much she loved him,
and how improbable it was that he should care for her, whom
he had found almost a beggar girl.

In the first surprise of meeting him she had forgotten everything, save that he had returned to them in safety, and her
manner towards him then was perfectly natural ; but now,
when Uncle Nat, after telling what he did, bade her go to
him, she quitted the room reluctantly, and much as she
wished to see him, she would undoubtedly have run away
up stairs, had she not met him in the hall, together with
Mrs. Elliott, who was going to pay her respects to Uncle
Nat.

" I have not spoken with you yet, Dora," he said, taking her hand between both his. " Go in there," motioning to the room he had just left, "and wait until I present Louise to your uncle."

It was a habit of Dora's always to cry just when she wished to least, and now entering the little music room, she threw herself upon the sofa and burst into tears. Thus Mr. Hastings found her on his return, and sitting down by her side, he said gently, " Are you, then, so glad that I have come home ?"

Dora would not, for the world, let him know her real feelings, and she answered, " Yes, I am glad, but I am crying at what Uncle Nat said to me."

Mr. Hastings bit his lip, for this was not exactly the kind of meeting he had anticipated, and after sitting an awkward moment, during which he was wishing that she had not answered him as she did, he said : "Will you not look up, Dora, and tell me how you have passed the time of my absence ? I am sure you have improved it, both from your own appearance and what Louise has told me."

This was a subject on which Dora felt that she could trust herself, and drying her tears, she became very animated as she told him of the books she had read, and the studies she had pursued. " I have taken music lessons, too," she added. " Would you like to hear me play ?"

Mr. Hastings would far rather have sat there, watching her bright face, with his arm thrown lightly around her waist, but it was this very act, this touch of his arm, which prompted her proposal, and gracefully disengaging herself, she crossed over to the piano, which was standing in the room, and commenced singing the old, and on that occasion, very appropriate song of " Home again, home again, from a foreign shore." The tones of her voice were rich and full,

and they reached the ear of Uncle Nat, who in his eagerness to listen, forgot everything, until Mrs. Elliott said, ' It
is Dora singing to my brother: Shall we join them ?"

Leading the way she ushered him into the music room,
where, standing at Dora's side, he listened rapturously to
her singing, occasionally wiping away a tear, called forth
by the memories that song had awakened. The sight of
the piano reminded him of Eugenia, and when Dora had
finished playing, he laid his broad hand upon her shoulder
and said, " Do you ever hear from them—the villains ?"

Dora knew to whom he referred, and half laughing at his
excited manner, she replied, as she stole a mischievous
glance towards Mr. Hastings, " I received a letter from Eugenia not long since, and she seemed very anxious to know
in what part of Europe Mr. Hastings was now travelling, and
if he were ever coming home !"

" Much good his coming home will do _her_, the _trollop !_"
muttered Uncle Nat, whispering incoherently to himself as he
generally did, when Eugenia was the subject of his thoughts.
" Don't answer the letter," he said at last, " or, if you
do, say nothing of me ; I wish to meet them first as a
stranger."

Near the window Mr. Hastings was standing, revolving
in his own mind a double surprise which he knew would mortify Eugenia more than anything else. But in order to effect this, Uncle Nat must remain _incog._ for some time yet,
while Dora herself must be won, and this, with the jealous
fears of a lover, he fancied might be harder to accomplish
than the keeping Uncle Nat silent when in the presence of
Eugenia.

" To-morrow I will see her alone, and know the worst,"
he thought, and glancing at Dora, he felt a thrill of fear
lest she, in all the freshness of her youth, should refuse her

heart to one, who had called another than herself his wife.

But Ella Grey had never awakened a love as deep and absorbing as that which he now felt for Dora Deane, and all that night he lay awake, wondering how he should approach her, and fancying sometimes that he saw the cold surprise with which she would listen to him, and again that he read in her dark blue eyes the answer which he sought. The morrow came, but throughout the entire day, he found no opportunity of speaking to her alone, for Uncle Nat hovered near her side, gazing at her as if he would never tire of looking at her beautiful face. And Dora, too, had much to say to the old man, on this the first day after his return. With his head resting upon her lap, and her soft white hand upon his wrinkled brow, she told him of her mother, and the message she had left for him on the sad night when she died. Then she spoke of her aunt Sarah, of Eugenia and Alice, and the wrath of Uncle Nat was somewhat abated, when he heard *her* pleading with him not to be so angry and unforgiving—

"I can treat Alice well, perhaps," he said, "for she, it seems, was never particularly unkind. And for your sake, I may forgive the mother. But Eugenia *never!*—not even if Fannie herself should ask me!"

Thus passed that day, and when the next one came, Uncle Nat still staid at Dora's side, following her from room to room, and never for a moment leaving Mr. Hastings with her alone. In this manner nearly a week went by, and the latter was beginning to despair, when one evening as the three were together in the little music room, and Mrs. Elliott was with her mother, who was ill, it suddenly occurred to Uncle Nat that he had appropriated Dora entirely to himself, not giving Mr. Hastings a single opportunity for seeing her alone.

"I have wondered that he did not tell me he was en-gaged," he thought, "but how could he when I haven't given him a chance to speak to her, unless he did it before me ; strange, I should be so selfish : but I'll make amends now—though I do hope he'll be quick !"

Rising up, he walked to the door, when thinking that Mr. Hastings might possibly expect him to return every mo-ment, and so keep silent, he said, "I've been in the way of you young folks long enough, and I feel just as if something might happen if I left you together ! Call me when you want me ?" so saying he shut the door, and Mr. Hastings was alone at last with Dora Deane !

Both knew to what Uncle Nat referred, and while Dora fidgeted from one thing to another, looking at a book of prints wrong side up, and admiring the pictures, Mr. Hast-ings sat perfectly still, wondering why he was so much afraid of her. Two years before he felt no fear ; but a refusal at that time would not have affected him as it would do now, for he did not then know how much he loved her. Greatly he desired that she should speak to him—look at him—or do something to break the embarrassing silence ; but this Dora had no intention of doing, and she was just meditating the propriety of *running away*, when he found voice enough to say, "Will you come and sit by me, Dora ?"

She had always obeyed him, and she did so now, taking a seat, however, as far from him as possible, on the end of the sofa. Still, when he moved up closely to her side, and wound his arm about her, she did not object, though her face burned with blushes, and she thought it quite likely that her next act would be to cry ! And this she did do, when he said to her, "Dora, do you remember the night when Ella died ?"

He did not expect any answer yet, and he continued, "She told me, you know, of a time when, though not forgetting her, I should love another—should seek to call another my wife. And, Dora, she was right, for I do love another, better, if it be possible, than I did my lost Ella. 'Tis four years since she left me, and now that I would have a second wife, will the one whom I have chosen from all the world to be that wife, answer me *yes*? Will she go back with me in the autumn to my long deserted home, where her presence always brought sunlight and joy?"

There was no coquetry about Dora Deane, and she could not have practised it now, if there had been. She knew Mr. Hastings was in earnest—knew that he meant what he said—and the little hand, which at first had stolen partly under her dress, lest he should touch it, came back from its hiding-place, and crept slowly along until his was reached, and there she let it lay! *This* was her answer, and he was satisfied!

For a long, long time they sat together, while Mr. Hastings talked, not wholly of the future when she would be his wife, but of the New Year's morning, years ago, when he found her sleeping in the chamber of death—of the bright June afternoon, when she sat with her bare feet in the running brook—of the time when she first brought comfort to his home—of the dark, rainy evening, when the sight of her sitting in Ella's room, with Ella's baby on her lap, had cheered his aching heart—of the storm she had braved to tell him his baby was dying—of the winter night when he watched her through the window—of the dusky twilight when she sat at his feet in the little library at Rose Hill— and again in his sister's home on the Hudson, when he first knew how much he loved her. Of all these pictures so indelibly stamped upon his memory, he told her, and of the many, many times his thoughts had been of her when afur on a foreign shore.

And Dora, listening to him, did not care to answer, her neart was so full of happiness, to know that she should be thus loved by one like Howard Hastings. From a tower not far distant, a city clock struck *twelve*, and then, starting up, she exclaimed, " *So late!* I thought 'twas only ten ! We have kept Uncle Nat too long. Will you go with me to him ?" and with his arms still around her, Mr. Hastings arose to accompany her.

For half an hour after leaving the music-room Uncle Nat had walked up and down the long parlors, with his hands in his pockets, hoping Mr. Hastings *would* be brief, and expecting each moment to hear Dora calling him back ! In this manner an hour or more went by, and then grown very nervous and cold (for it was a damp, chilly night, such as often occurs in our latitude, even in summer) he began to think that if *Dora* were not coming, a fire would be acceptable, and he drew his chair near to the register, which was closed. Wholly unaccustomed to furnaces, he did not think to open it, and for a time longer he sat wondering why he didn't grow warm, and if it took everybody as long to propose as it did Mr. Hastings.

It " didn't take me long to tell my love to Fanny," he said, " but then she refused, and when they accept, as Dora will, it's always a longer process, I reckon !"

This point satisfactorily settled, he began to wish the atmosphere of the room would moderate, and hitching in his chair, he at last sat directly over the register ! but even this failed to warm him, and mentally concluding that, " though furnaces might do very well for New Yorkers, they were of no account whatever to an East India man," he fell asleep. In this situation, Dora found him.

" Poor old man," said she, " 'twas thoughtless in me to

leave him so long," and kissing his brow, she cried, " Wake up, Uncle Nat—wake up!" and Uncle Nat rubbing his eyes with his red stiff fingers, and looking in her glowing face, knew "that something had happened !"

CHAPTER XX.

THE SPRINGS.

Mr. Hastings and Dora were engaged. Mrs. Hastings, the mother, and Mrs. Elliott, the sister, had signified their entire approbation, while Uncle Nat, with a hand placed on either head of the young people, had blessed them as his children, hinting the while that few brides e'er went forth as richly dowered as should Dora Deane. The marriage was not to take place until the following October, as Mr. Hastings wished to make some improvements at Rose Hill, which was still to be his home proper, though Uncle Nat insisted upon buying a very elegant house in the city for a winter residence, whenever they chose thus to use it. To this proposal Mr. Hastings made no objection, for though he felt that his greatest happiness would be in having Dora all to himself in Dunwood, he knew that society in the city would never have the effect upon her which it did upon Ella, for her tastes, like his own, were domestic, and on almost every subject she felt and thought as he did.

Immediately after his engagement he imparted to Uncle Nat a knowledge of the double surprise he had planned for Eugenia, and the old gentleman at last consented, saying, though, that " 'twas doubtful whether he could hold himself together when first he met the young lady. Still, with Mr Hastings's presence as a check, he would try "

So it was arranged that in Dunwood, where Mr. Hastings's return was still unknown, Uncle Nat should pass as a *Mr Hamilton*, whom Mr. Hastings had picked up in his travels. Four years of his earlier life had been spent in South America, and whenever he spoke of any particular place of abode it was to be of *Buenos Ayres*, where he had once resided. By this means he could the more easily learn for himself the character and disposition of his relatives, and feeling now more eager than ever to meet them, he here started with Mr. Hastings for Dunwood. It was morning when they reached there, and with a dark, lowering brow, he looked curiously at the house which his companion designated as *Locust Grove*. It was a pleasant spot, and it seemed almost impossible that it should be the home of a woman as artful and designing as Eugenia. About it now, however, there was an air of desertion. The doors were shut and the blinds closed, as if the inmates were absent.

On reaching Rose Hill, where he found his servants overwhelmed with delight at his unexpected return, Mr. Hastings casually inquired of Mrs. Leah if the Deanes were at home. A shadow passed over the old lady's face, and folding her arms, she leaned against the door and began : " I wonder now, if you're askin' after them the first thing ! I don't know but they are well enough, all but Eugenia. I believe I never disliked anybody as I do her, and no wonder, the way she's gone on. At first she used to come up here almost every week on purpose to ask about you, though she pretended to tumble over your books, and mark 'em all up with her pencil. But when that scapegrace *Stephen Grey* came, she took another *tack*, and the way she and he went on was scandalous. She was a runnin' up here the whole time that he wasn't a streakin' it down there."

" *Stephen Grey been here* ? When and what for ?" inter

rupted Mr. Hastings, who, as his father-in-law, during his absence, had removed to Philadelphia, knew nothing of the family.

"You may well ask that," returned Mrs. Leah, growing very much excited as she remembered the trouble the fast young man had made her. "Last fall in shootin' time, he came here, bag, baggage, guns, dogs and all--said it didn't make a speck of difference, you being away--'twas all in the family, and so you'd a' thought, the way he went on, drinkin, swearin', shootin', and carousin' with a lot of fellers who staid with him here a spell, and then, when they were gone, he took a flirtin' with Eugenia Deane, who told him, I'll bet, more'n five hundred lies about an old uncle that, she says, is rich as a Jew, and has willed his property to her and Alice."

"The viper!" muttered Uncle Nat to himself; and Mrs. Leah continued, "I shouldn't wonder if old Mr. Grey was gettin' poor, and Steve, I guess, would marry anybody who had money; but Lord knows I don't want him to have her, for though he ain't an atom too good, I used to live in the family, and took care of him when he was little. I should a' written about his carryin's on to Mrs. Elliott, only I knew she didn't think any too much of the Greys, and 'twould only trouble her for nothin'."

"But where are they now—Mrs. Deane and her daughters?" asked Mr. Hastings; and Mrs. Leah replied, "Gone to Avon Springs; and folks do say they've done their own work, and ate cold victuals off the pantry shelf ever since last November, so as to save money, to cut a swell. I guess Eugenia'll be mighty glad if that old uncle ever dies. For my part, I hope he won't! or, if he does, I hope he won't leave her a dollar."

"*Not a dime!*" thought Uncle Nat, who, not being sup-posed to feel interested in Eugenia Deane, had tried to appear indifferent, holding hard the while upon the rounds of his chair "to keep himself together."

Alone with Mr. Hastings, his wrath burst forth, but after a few tremendous explosions, he grew calm, and proposed that they too should go at once to Avon. "We shall then see the lady in all her glory," said he, "and maybe hear something about her old uncle, though you'll have to keep your eye on me, or I shall go off on a sudden, and shake her as a dog would a snake! We'll send for Mrs. Elliott and Dora to join us there," he continued; "it will be fun to bring them together, and see what Eugenia will do."

"I am afraid you could not restrain yourself," said Mr. Hastings; but Uncle Nat was sure he could, and after a few days they started for Avon, where "Miss Eugenia Deane, the heiress," was quite a belle.

For a long time after Mr. Hastings's departure for Europe, she had remained true to him, feeding on the remembrance of his parting words, that "he had more reasons for remembering her than she supposed;" but when, as months went by, he sent her neither letter, paper nor message, she began to think that possibly he had never entertained a serious thought concerning her, and when Stephen Grey came, she was the more ready to receive his attentions, and forgive his former neglect. He was a reckless, unprincipled fellow, and feeling this time rather pleased with the bold dashing manner of Eugenia, backed as it was by the supposed will of Uncle Nat, he made some advances, which she readily met, making herself and him, as Mrs. Leah had said, "perfectly ridiculous." When he left Dunwood he went west, telling her playfully, that, "if he found no one there who suited him better than she, he would the next summer meet her at Avon, and perhaps propose! He was disgusted with Saratoga, Newport, Nahant, and all those stupid places," he said "and wished to try something new."

To spend several weeks at Avon, therefore, was now Eugenia's object. She had succeeded in coaxing her mother to withhold from Dora the thousand dollars, a part of which was safely invested for their own benefit, but this alone would not cover all their expenses, for Mrs. Deane, growing gay and foolish as she grew older, declared her intention of going to Avon also. "The water would do her good," she said, "and 'twas time she saw a little of society."

To this plan Eugenia did not particularly object, "for it would indicate wealth," she thought, for the whole family to spend the summer at a watering place. Still it would cost a great deal, and though Uncle Nat's remittance came at the usual time, they did not dare to depend wholly upon that, lest on their return there should be nothing left with which to buy their bread. In this emergency, they hit upon the expedient of dismissing their servant, and starving themselves through the winter and spring, for the purpose of making a display in the summer; and this last they were now doing. Eugenia fluttered like a butterfly, sometimes in white satin, sometimes in pink, and again in embroidered muslin; while her mother, a very little disgusted with *society*, but still determined to brave it through, held aside her cambric wrapper and made faces over *three glasses* of spring water in the morning, drowned herself in a hot bath every other day, rode twice a day in crowded omnibuses to and from the springs, through banks of sand and clouds of dust, and sat every evening in the heated parlors with a very red face, and a very tight dress, wondering if everybody enjoyed themselves as little in society as she did, and thinking ten dollars per week a great deal to pay for being as uncomfortable as she was!

For her disquietude, however, she felt in a measure repaid when she saw that Eugenia was the most showy young lady present, and managed to keep about her a cross-eyed widower, a near sighted-bachelor, a medical student of nineteen, a broken down merchant, a lame officer, a spiritualist, and Stephen Grey ! This completed the list of her admirers, if we except a gouty old man, who praised her dancing, and would perhaps have called her beautiful, but for his better half, who could see nothing agreeable or pleasing in the dashing belle. True to his promise, Stephen Grey had met her there, and they were in the midst of quite a flirtation, when Mr. Hastings and Uncle Nat arrived ; the latter registering his name as *Mr. Hamilton;* and taking care soon after to speak of *Buenos Ayres*, as a place where he formerly lived. The ruse was successful, and in less than half an hour, it was known through the house, that " the singular looking old gentleman was a South American, a bachelor, and rich undoubtedly, as such men always were !

The Deanes were that afternoon riding with Stephen Grey, and did not return until after supper, a circumstance which Eugenia greatly lamented when she learned that their numbers had been increased by the arrival of an elegant looking stranger from New York, together with an old South American, whose name was Hamilton. The name of the other Eugenia's informant did not know, for he had not registered it, but " he was a splendid-looking man," she said, and with more than usual care, Eugenia dressed herself for the evening, and between the hours of eight and nine, sailed into the parlor with the air of a queen.

From his window in an upper chamber Uncle Nat had seen the ladies, as they returned from their ride ; and when Mr. Hastings, who at that time was absent from the room, came back to it, he found the old gentleman hurriedly pacing the floor and evidently much excited.

"*I've seen her,*" said he, "*the very one herself—Eugenia Deane!* I knew her mother in a moment, and I knew *her* too, by her evil eyes. I could hardly refrain from pouncing upon her, and I believe I *did* shake my fist at her! But it's over now," he continued, "and I am glad I have seen her, for I can meet her and not betray myself; though, Hastings, if at any time I am missing, you may know that I've come up here to let myself off, for my wrath must evaporate somehow."

Feeling confident that he could trust him, Mr. Hastings ere long accompanied him to the parlor, where his gentlemanly manners, and rather peculiar looks procured for him immediate attention; and when Eugenia entered the room, he was conversing familiarly with some gentlemen whose notice she had in vain tried to attract. At a little distance from him and nearer the door was Mr. Hastings, talking to Stephen Grey. Eugenia did not observe him until she was directly at his side, then, turning pale, she uttered an exclamation of surprise, while he, in his usual polite, easy manner, offered his hand, first to her mother, and then to herself and Alice, saying, in reply to their many inquiries as to when he returned, that he reached Dunwood a few days before, and finding they were all at Avon, had concluded to follow. At this remark the pallor left Eugenia's cheek, and was succeeded by a bright glow, for "Mr. Hastings must feel interested in her, or he would not have followed her there;" and the black eyes, which a few hours before had smiled so bewitchingly upon Stephen Grey, now shone with a brighter lustre, as she talked with Mr. Hastings of his European tour, asking him why he had staid so long, and telling him how natural it seemed to have him home once more.

"By the way," she continued, "they say there is an old South American here—a queer old fellow—did he come with you?"

"Yes," answered Mr. Hastings, glancing towards Uncle Nat, whose eyes had never for a moment lost sight of Eugenia; "I found him in my travels, and liking him very much, brought him home with me. Allow me to introduce you, for though rather eccentric, he's a fine man, and quite wealthy, too."

"*Wealth is nothing!* I wouldn't think any more of him for that," returned Eugenia, taking Mr. Hastings's arm, and advancing toward Uncle Nat, whose left hand grasped tightly one side of his blue coat, while the other was offered to Eugenia.

With a slight shudder, he dropped her hand as soon as it was touched; then, pressing his fingers together so firmly, that his long nails left marks in his flesh, he looked curiously down upon her, eyeing her furtively as if she had been a wild beast. Nothing of all this escaped Eugenia, who, feeling greatly amused at what she thought to be his embarrassment, and fancying he had never before conversed with so fine a lady as herself, she commenced quizzing him in a manner excessively provoking to one of his excitable temperament. Lifting up first one foot, and then the other, he felt his patience fast giving way, and at last, as her ridicule became more and more marked, he could endure it no longer, but returned it with a kind of sarcasm far more scathing than anything she could say. Deeply chagrined, and feeling that she had been beaten with her own weapons, she was about to leave the "old bear," as she mentally styled him, when remembering that he was Mr. Hastings's friend, and, as such, worthy of more respect than she had paid him, she said play-fully, "I have a mother and sister here, whom you may like better than you do me. I'll introduce them," and tripping across the room, she made known her wishes to her mother, adding that "there was a chance for her, as he was an old bachelor."

Long and searchingly the old man looked in the face of the widow, thinking of the time when she had called *Fannie* her sister ; but of this Mrs. Deane did not know ; and remembering what Eugenia had said, she blushed crimson, and as soon as possible, stole away, leaving him alone with Alice, with whom he was better pleased, talking with her so long that Eugenia, who was hovering near Mr. Hastings, began to laugh at what she called her *sister's conquest.* Nothing had escaped Mr. Hastings, and thinking this a good opportunity for rebuking the young lady, he spoke of Mr. Hamilton in the highest terms, saying that "he should consider any disrespect paid to his friend a slight to himself." This hint was sufficient, and wishing to make amends for her rudeness, Eugenia ere long sought the stranger, and tried to be very agreeable ; but there was no affinity between them, and to Mr. Hastings, who was watching them, they seemed much like a fierce mastiff, and a spiteful cat, impatient to pounce upon each other !

During the evening the three were standing together, and Eugenia suddenly remembering Dora, asked Mr. Hastings how she was, saying she seldom wrote to them, and when she did, her letters amounted to nothing. With a warning glance at Uncle Nat, whose face grew very dark, Mr. Hastings replied that she was well, and had, he thought, improved under his sister's care.

"I am glad," said she, "for there was need enough of improvement. She was so unrefined, always preferring the kitchen to the parlor, that we couldn't make anything of her."

A sudden "*Ugh!*" from Uncle Nat stopped her, and she asked him what was the matter.

"Nothing, nothing," said he, wiping his face, "only I'm getting pretty warm, and must cool off."

The next moment he was gone, and when, at a late hour, Mr. Hastings repaired to his room, he knew by the chairs, boots, brushes, and books scattered over the floor, that Uncle Nat, snoring so loudly in bed, had cooled off!

"I had to hold on, to keep from falling to pieces right before her," he said, next morning, in speaking of the last night's adventure ; "but I shall do better next time. I am getting a little accustomed to it."

And he was right, for only twice during the entire day and evening did he disappear from the room. Once when Eugenia sat down to play, and once when he heard her telling Stephen Grey, who asked her to ride again, that, "he really must excuse her, as she had a letter to write to *Uncle Nat*, who undoubtedly wondered why she was so tardy. And you know," she said, "it won't do to neglect him!"

Uncle Nat knew it was a farce to get rid of Stephen Grey, who was nothing compared with his brother-in-law, but his indignation was not the less ; and Mr. Hastings, when he saw the long blue coat flying up the stairs, smiled quietly, though he pitied the poor old man, who was thus kept vibrating between his chamber and the parlor.

In this manner several days passed away, during which time Uncle Nat's temper was severely tested, both by Eugenia's remarks concerning Dora, and by what she said of himself, for he more than once heard her speaking of "*Old Uncle Nat*," who sent her money to buy the various articles of jewelry which she wore. On such occasions it seemed almost impossible for him to restrain his anger, and he often wished he had never promised to keep silent ; but by frequent visits to his chamber, which witnessed many a terrific storm, he managed to be quiet, so that Eugenia had no suspicion whatever, though she disliked him greatly, and wished he had never come there. Mr. Hastings troubled her, too, for she felt very uncertain as to the nature of his feelings towards her. He treated her politely, but that was all, and no management on her part could draw from him any particular attention.

"Maybe he's jealous of Stephen Grey," she thought, and then she became so cold towards the latter individual, that had he not remembered *Uncle Nat's will*, in which he firmly believed, he would have packed his trunk at once, and left her in disgust.

But Stephen's necessities were great. There was standing against him a long list of bills, which his father refused to pay, and he was ready to marry the first purse which was offered. Had Eugenia been altogether agreeable to him, he would have proposed ere this, but without knowing why, he felt afraid of her. Added to this was the memory of his mother's threat, that his father should disinherit him if he disgraced them by marrying *that Deane girl*, in whose expected fortune she did not believe. So halting between two opinions, he allowed himself to be taken up and cast off whenever the capricious Eugenia chose.

In the meantime, Uncle Nat had cultivated the acquaintance of Mrs. Deane and Alice, finding the latter quite a pleasant girl, and feeling disposed to think more favorably of the former when he heard her speak kindly of Dora, as she always did. Matters were in this state, when, one afternoon, in compliance with her brother's written request, Mrs. Elliott arrived, together with Dora. Most of the visitors were at the springs, and as Eugenia never let an opportunity pass for showing herself to the guests of the different

8

houses, she too was there, and thus failed to see how tenderly Dora was greeted by Mr. Hastings, and how fondly
Uncle Nat clasped her in his arms, holding her hand all the
way up the stairs, and only releasing her when she reached
the door of the room, which had been previously engaged
for them by Mr. Hastings. Feeling slightly indisposed,
Mrs. Elliott did not go down to supper, and as Dora chose
to remain with her, neither of them were seen until evening.
Eugenia had heard of the arrival of two aristocratic looking
·ladies, one of whom was young and very beautiful, and this
aroused her fears at once. Hitherto she had reigned without a rival, for aside from her beauty, the generally believed
rumor of her being an heiress, procured for her attention
from many who otherwise would have been disgusted with
her overbearing manner and boisterous conduct ; for, like
many others, she had fallen into the error of thinking that
to be *fashionable*, she must be bold and noisy, and no voice
in the drawing-room ever reached so high a note as hers
Still she was tolerated and flattered, and when the friend,
who told her of the new arrivals, and who had caught a
view of Dora's face, laughingly bade her beware lest her
star should begin to wane, she curled her lip in scorn, as
if anything in Avon could compete with her, who " had
spent so many seasons at *Saratoga* and *Newport*, and who
would have gone there this summer, only she wanted a
change, and then it was more quiet for *ma !*"

    This was one of her stereotyped remarks until Mr. Hast-
ings came, but he knew her, and in his presence she was less
assuming. She had heard that the new arrivals were his
friends, and thinking they must of course be *somebody*, she
arrayed herself for the evening with unusual care, wearing
her white satin and lace bertha, the most becoming and at
the same time the most expensive dress she had.

"I wish I had some pearls," she said, glancing at her raven hair; "they would look so much richer than these flowers."

"I should think an heiress like *you* would have everything she wanted," suggested Alice, mischievously, and Eugenia replied, "Oh, pshaw! We shall never get more than five hundred a year from Uncle Nat, but I don't much care. Old Mr. Grey is wealthy, and if Mr. Hastings don't manifest any more interest in me than he has since he came here, I shall let that foolish *Steve* propose, much as I dislike him."

So saying, she clasped upon her arm a heavy bracelet, for which the sum of forty dollars had been paid, and descended with her mother and sister to the parlor. Mrs. Elliott and Dora were there before her—the former leaning on Mr. Hastings's arm, while the latter was already surrounded by a group of admirers, a few of whom had met her before. She was standing with her back towards Eugenia, who singled her out in a moment, as her rival, noticing first her magnificent hair, in which an ornament of any kind would have been out of place, and which was confined at the back of the head by a small and elegantly wrought gold comb. Her dress was perfectly plain, consisting simply of white India muslin, which fitted her admirably and seemed well adapted to her youthful form.

"Who is she?" inquired Eugenia of Uncle Nat, who had stationed himself near the door, on purpose to see how the first sight of Dora would affect her.

"Who is she!" he replied. "Strange you don't know your own cousin *Dora Deane*," and a look of intense satisfaction danced in his keen eyes, as he saw the expression of astonishment which passed over Eugenia's face.

"Impossible!" she exclaimed, while a pang of envy shot

through her heart. "That stylish looking girl can't be Dora! Why, I always supposed Mrs. Elliott made a half servant, half companion of her. She never told us any different;" and with a vague hope that the old South Amer lean might be mistaken, she took a step or two forward, just as Dora turned round, disclosing to view her face.

There was no longer any doubt, and with mingled feelings of surprise, mortification, jealousy, and rage, Eugenia advanced to meet her, wisely resolving as she did so to make the best of it, and never let her cousin know how much annoyed she was. Both Mrs. Deane and Alice were greeted kindly by Dora, who could scarcely be more than polite to Eugenia, and when the latter made a movement to kiss her, she involuntarily drew back, feeling that she could not suffer it.

"Grown suddenly very proud," muttered Eugenia, at the same time determining that her mother should insist upon taking Dora home with them, and secretly exulting as she thought how she should again work in the dark kitchen at Locust Grove, as she had done before. "That'll remove some of her fine airs, I reckon," she thought, as, with bitter hatred at her heart, she watched her young cousin, who, throughout the entire evening, continued to be the centre of attraction.

Everybody asked who she was; everybody pronounced her beautiful, and everybody neglected Eugenia Deane, who, greatly enraged, retired early, and vented her wrath in tears, to think that the once despised Dora should now be so far above her.

But it shall not be," she said, and then to her mother she unfolded her plan of having Dora go home with them immediately. "I'd as soon be in Joppa as to stay here with her for a rival," she said. "Mr. Hastings don't care for me,

I know, and I hate that old codger of a Hamilton, with his sarcastic remarks and prying eyes. I've been here long enough, and I mean to go home."

To this proposition Mrs. Deane assented willingly ; but she expressed her doubts concerning her ability to *make* Dora accompany them.

"Of course she'll go," said Eugenia. "Her mother placed her under your control, and she is bound to obey."

Yielding at last, as she generally did, Mrs. Deane promised to see what she could do, and the next day she announced to Mrs. Elliott her intention of taking *Dora* home with her. "I am grateful for all you have done for her," said she ; "but we need her, and cannot spare her any longer, so, Dora dear," turning to her niece, "pack up your things, and we will start to-morrow morning."

Had Uncle Nat been there, he would, undoubtedly, have exploded at once ; but he was not present, neither was Mr. Hastings, and it remained for Mrs. Elliott alone to reply, which she did firmly and decidedly. "No, Mrs. Deane, Dora cannot go. She was committed to your care, I know, but you gave her up to me, and I shall not part with her unless I am legally compelled to do so, or she wishes to go. She can answer this last for herself," and she turned towards Dora, who, drawing nearer to her, replied, "I am sorry to disobey you, Aunt Sarah, but I cannot leave Mrs. Elliott."

Mrs. Deane was not very courageous, and unwilling to press her claim, she turned away and reported her ill-success to Eugenia, who heaped a torrent of abuse upon both Mrs Elliott, Dora, the old South American, and Mr. Hastings who, she declared, were all leagued against them.

"But I don't care," said she, "old Mr. Grey is quite as wealthy as Mr. Hastings, and by saying the word, I can marry *Steve* at any time ; and I will do it, too," she con tinued, "and that proud Mrs. Elliott shall yet be obliged to meet me on terms of equality, for she will not dare to neglect *the Greys!*"

Somewhat comforted by this thought, she dried her tears, and signified her willingness to start for home on the morrow, even if Dora did not accompany her. As yet, she had no suspicion whatever of the engagement existing between Mr. Hastings and her cousin. There was nothing in the manner of either to betray it, and when, next morning, attired in her travelling dress, she stood with them upon the piazza, she little thought how and where she would next meet them. At her side was Stephen Grey. He had been won over by her gracious smiles the night previous, and was now going with her as far as Rochester, where, if a favorable opportunity were presented, he intended offering himself for her acceptance. Uncle Nat was not present, and Eugenia was glad that it was so, for there was something about him exceedingly annoying to her, and she always felt relieved at his absence.

"Why do you go so soon? I thought you were intending to spend the summer," said one of her old admirers ; and with a scornful toss of her head, she replied, "It is getting so insufferably dull here, that I can't endure it any longer."

Just then the omnibus was announced, and with a hurried good bye, she followed her baggage down the stairs, and amid a cloud of dust was driven rapidly away, while Uncle Nat, from his chamber window, sent after her a not very complimentary or affectionate adieu. Arrived at the hotel in Rochester, where Eugenia had once waited in vain for Mr. Hastings, Stephen Grey managed to hear from her again, that she had well-founded hopes of being one of the heirs of Nathaniel Deane, who, she said, sent them annually a sum of money varying from five to fifteen hundred dollars

This was quite a consideration for one whose finances were low, and whose father, while threatening to disinherit him, was himself on the verge of bankruptcy, and thinking the annual remittances worth securing, even if the *will* should fail, Stephen found an opportunity to go down on his knees before her after the most approved fashion, telling her that "she alone could make him happy, and that without her he should be wretched;" and she, knowing just how much in earnest he was, promised to be his wife, intending the while to break that promise if she saw in Mr. Hastings any signs of renewed interest. So, when Stephen pressed her to name an early day, she put him off, telling him she could not think of being married until near the middle of autumn, and at the same time requesting him to keep their engagement a secret, for she did not wish it to be a subject of remark, as engaged people always were. To this, Stephen consented willingly, as he would thus escape, for a time, his mother's anger. And so when, tired, jaded, cross and dusty, Eugenia Deane reached Locust Grove, she had the satisfaction of knowing that her trip to the Springs had been successful, inasmuch as it procured for her " *a husband, such as he was.*"

CHAPTER XXI.

THE DOUBLE SURPRISE.

The Deanes had been home about two weeks when **Mr.** Hastings returned to Rose Hill, accompanied by the " Old South American," who seemed to have taken up his abode there. Being naturally rather reserved, the latter visited but little in the village, while at Locust Grove he never called, and seldom saw Eugenia when he met her in the street. Mr. Hastings, too, was unusually cool in his manner towards her, and this she imputed wholly to the fact of her having been rude to his friend on the night of her introduction. " He was never so before " she thought, and she redoubled her efforts to be agreeable, to no effect, as he was simply polite to her and nothing more. So after a series of tears and headaches, she gave him up, comforting herself with the belief that he would never marry anybody. After this, she smiled more graciously upon Stephen Grey, who, pretending to be a lawyer, had, greatly to her annoyance, hung out his sign in Dunwood, where his office proper seemed to be in the bar-room, or drinking-saloon, as in one of these he was always to be found, when not at Locust Grove.

One evening, towards the last of September, when he came as usual to see her, he startled her with the news, that there was ere long to be a new bride at Rose Hill ! Starting involuntarily, Eugenia exclaimed, " A new bride ! It can't be possible ! Who is it ?"

It was months since Stephen had been in New York, and he knew nothing, except that the lady was from the city, and he mentioned a *Miss Morton*, with whom he had several times seen Mr. Hastings walking, and who was very inti mate with Mrs. Elliott. At first Eugenia refused to believe it, but when she had remembered how extensively Mr. Hastings was repairing his place, and heard that the house was being entirely refurnished, and fitted up in a princely style, she wept again over her ruined hopes, and experienced many a sharp pang of envy, when from time to time she saw go by loads of elegant furniture, and knew that it was not for herself, but another. The old South American, too, it was said, was very lavish of his money, purchasing many costly ornaments, and furnishing entirely the chamber of the bride. For this the fair Eugenia styled him " a silly old fool," wondering " what business it was to him," and " why he need be so much interested in one who, if she had any sense, would, in less than two weeks, turn him from the house, with his heathenish ways." Still, fret as she would, she could not in the least retard the progress of matters, and one morning towards the last of October, she heard from Mrs. Leah, whom she met at a store in the village, that the wedding was to take place at the house of the bride on Tuesday of the next week, and that on Thursday evening following, there was to be a grand party at Rose Hill, far exceeding in splendor and elegance the one given there some years before.

" Crowds of folks," she said, " are coming from the city with the bridal pair, who would start on Wednesday, stay in Syracuse all night, and reach Dunwood about three o'clock on Thursday afternoon. The invitations for the village people," she added, " were already written and were left with her to distribute on Wednesday morning."

8*

Eugenia would have given much to know if she were invited, but she was too proud to ask, and assuming an air of indifference she casually inquired the name of the bride.

With the manner of one in a deep study, Mrs. Leah replied, "Let me see! It's a very common name. Strange I don't speak it!"

"*Morton?*" suggested Eugenia, but Mrs. Leah affected not to hear her, and, having completed her purchases, she left the store and walked slowly homeward, dropping more than one tear on the brown paper parcel she held in her hand.

Crying, however, was of no avail, and mentally chiding herself for her weakness, she resolved to brave it through, comforting herself again with the thought that *the Greys* were as aristocratic as the *Hastings's*, and as Stephen's wife she should yet shine in the best society, for in case she married him she was resolved that he should take her at once to Philadelphia, where she would compel his proud mother to notice her. This helped to divert her mind, and in the course of the day she was talking gaily of the party, and wondering if she should be as intimate with the second Mrs. Hastings as she had been with the first!

That night, Alice went down to the post-office, from which she soon returned, evidentally much excited; and rushing into the room where her mother and sister were sitting, she said, as she threw a letter into the lap of the latter, "It's from *Uncle Nat*, and postmarked *New York.*"

Turning whiter than ever she was before, Eugenia could scarcely command herself to break the seal, and read the few brief lines which told her that Uncle Nat had, at last, concluded to come home, that a matter of some importance would keep him from Locust Grove for a few days; but if nothing occurred, he would be with them on Saturday even-

Ing of next week! In the postscript, he added, that "he should expect to find Dora with them, and he hoped her going away to school had been a benefit to her."

So great was their consternation that for some minutes neither of them uttered a word, but each waited for the other to suggest some way of acting in the present emergency. As Eugenia's mind was the most active of the three she was the first to speak. After venting her indignation upon Uncle Nat, for intruding himself where he was not wanted, she continued : " We are in a sad dilemma, but we must make the best of it, and inasmuch as he is coming, I am glad that Dora is what she is. We can tell him how rapidly she has improved, and how rejoiced we are that it is so. I am glad I have said nothing about her for the last two years, except that she was away at school. I'll write to her to-night, and tell her to meet him here, and come immediately. You know, she is good-natured, and on my bended knees I'll confess what I have done, and beg of her not to betray me to him, or let him know that we did not pay for her education, and if she refuses, you, mother, must go down on your knees, too, and we'll get up between us such a scene that she will consent, I know—if not, why, wo must abide the consequence "—and with the look of one about to be martyred, Eugenia sat down and wrote to Dora, beseeching her to " come without delay, as there was something they must tell her before meeting Uncle Nat !"

This was Friday night, and very impatiently she awaited an answer, which, though written on Monday, did not come until the Wednesday following.

" What does she say ?" cried Mrs. Deane and Alice, crowding around her, while with a rueful face she read that Dora would be delighted to meet Uncle Nat at Locust Grove, but could not come quite so soon as they wished to have her.

"You have undoubtedly heard," she wrote, "of Mr. Hastings's approaching marriage, at which I wish to be present.
Mrs. Elliott will accompany the bridal party to Rose Hill on
Thursday, and she thinks I had better wait and come with
her.   I shall probably see you at the party.

"Yours in haste,

"DORA DEANE."

On Eugenia's mind there was not a shadow of suspicion
that *Dora Deane*, appended to that letter, had ere this
ceased to be her cousin's name—that Mr. Hastings, who,
together with Uncle Nat, had the Saturday previous gone
down to New York, had bent fondly over her as she wrote
it for the last time, playfully suggesting that she add to it
an H, by way of making a commencement, nor yet that
Uncle Nat, with an immense degree of satisfaction in his
face, had read the short note, saying as he did so, "We'll
cheat 'em, darling, won't we ?"

Neither did she dream that last night's moon shone down
on Dora Deane, a beautiful, blushing bride, who, with
orange blossoms in her shining hair, and the deep love-light
in her eye, stood by Mr. Hastings's side and called him her
husband.   Nothing of all this she knew, and hastily reading the letter, she exclaimed, "Plague on her ! a vast deal
of difference *her* being at the wedding would make.   But no
matter, the old codger will not be here until Saturday night
and there'll be time enough to coax her."

Just then the cards of invitation were left at the door,
and in the delightful certainty of knowing that she was
really invited, she forgot in a measure everything else   In
the evening she was annoyed as usual with a call from
Stephen Grey.   He had that day received news from home
that his father's failure could not long be deferred, and

judging Eugenia by himself, he fancied she would sooner
marry him now, than after he was the son of a bankrupt.
Accordingly he urged her to consent to a private marriage
at her mother's on Friday evening, the night following the
party.

"There was nothing to be gained by waiting," he said —
an opinion in which Eugenia herself concurred, for she feared
lest in some way her treachery should be betrayed, and she
should lose Stephen Grey, as well as Mr. Hastings.

Still she could hardly bring herself to consent until she
had seen Dora, and she replied that she would think of it,
and answer him at the party. Thursday morning came,
and passed, and about half-past two, Eugenia saw Mr.
Hastings's carriage pass on its way to the depot, together
with two more, which had been hired to convey the guests
to Rose Hill. Seating herself by her chamber window, she
waited impatiently for the cars, which came at last, and in
a few moments the roll of wheels announced the approach
of the bridal party. Very eagerly Eugenia, Alice, and their
mother gazed out through the half closed shutters upon the
carriage in front, which they knew was Mr. Hastings's.

"There's Mrs. Elliott looking this way. Don't let her see
us," whispered Alice, while her mother singled out old Mrs.
Hastings for Dora, wondering why she didn't turn that way.

· But Eugenia had no eye for any one, save the figure
seated next to Mr. Hastings, and so closely veiled as entirely
to hide her features.

"I wouldn't keep that old brown thing on my face, unless
It was so homely I was afraid of having it seen," she said ;
and hoping the bride of Howard Hastings might prove to be
exceedingly ugly, she repaired to Dora's room, and from the
same window where Dora once had watched the many lights
which shone from Rose Hill, she now watched the travellers

until they disappeared within the house. Then, rejoining her mother and sister she said, " I don't see why Dora can't come over here a little while before the party. There's plenty of time and I do want to have it off my mind. Besides that, I might coax her to assist me in dressing, for she has good taste, if nothing more ; I mean to write her a few lines asking her to come."

The note was accordingly written, and dispatched by the Irish girl, who soon returned, bearing another tiny note, which read as follows :

" I cannot possibly come, as I have promised to be present at the dressing of the bride.   DORA."

Forgetting her recent remark, Eugenia muttered something about " folks thinking a great deal of her taste," then turning to the servant girl, she asked " how Dora looked, and what she said ?"

" Sure, I didn't see her," returned the girl ; " Mistress Leah carried your letter to her, and brought hers to me. Not a ha'p'orth of anybody else did I see." And this was all the information which Eugenia could elicit concerning the people of Rose Hill.

The time for making their toilet came at last, and while Eugenia was missing the little *cropped head* girl, who, on a similar occasion, had obeyed so meekly her commands, a fair young bride was thinking also of that night, when she had lain upon her mother's old green trunk, and wept herself to sleep. Wishing to be fashionable, Eugenia and her party were the last to arrive. They found the parlors crowded, and the dressing-room vacant, so that neither of them received the slightest intimation of the surprise which awaited them. In removing her veil, Eugenia displaced one the flowers in her hair, and muttering about Alice's awk-wardness, she wished she could see Dora just a minute, and have her arrange the flowers!

But Dora was busy elsewhere, and pronouncing herself ready, Eugenia took the arm of Stephen Grey, and followed her mother and sister down stairs. At a little distance from the door was Mr. Hastings, and at his side was Dora, won-drously beautiful in her costly bridal robes. She had grace-fully received the congratulations of her Dunwood friends, who, while expressing their surprise, had also expressed their delight at finding in the new mistress of Rose Hill, the girl who had ever been a favorite in the village. Near her was Uncle Nat, his face wearing an expression of perfect happi-ness, and his eye almost constantly upon the door, through which Eugenia must pass. There was a rustle of silk upon the stairs, and drawing nearer to Dora, he awaited the result with breathless interest.

Mrs. Deane came first, but scarcely had she crossed the threshold, ere she started back, petrified with astonishment, and clutching Alice's dress, whispered softly, " am I deceived, or *is it Dora*?"

And Alice, with wild staring eyes, could only answer " *Dora;*" while Eugenia, wondering at their conduct, strove to push them aside. Failing in this, she raised herself on tiptoe, and looking over their heads, saw what for an instant chilled her blood, and stopped the pulsations of her heart. It was the *bride*, and fiercely grasping the arm of Stephen Grey to keep herself from falling, she said, in a hoarse, unnatural voice, " *Great Heaven—it is Dora!* DORA DEANE!"

Fruitful as she had hitherto been in expedients, she was now utterly powerless to act, and knowing that in her present state of excitement, she could not meet her cousin, she turned back and fleeing up the stairs, threw herself upon a chair in the dressing-room, where, with her hands clasped firmly together, she sat rigid as marble until the storm of passion had somewhat abated.

"And *she* has won him—*Dora Deane*, whom I have so ill-treated," she said at last, starting at the sound of her voice, it was so hollow and strange. Then, as she remembered the coming of Uncle Nat and the exposure she so much dreaded, she buried her face in her hands, and in the bitterness of her humiliation cried out, "It is more than I can bear!"

Growing ere long more calm, she thought the matter over carefully, and decided at last to brave it through—to greet the bride as if nothing had occurred, and never to let Mr. Hastings know how sharp a wound he had inflicted. "It is useless now," she thought, "to throw myself upon the mercy of Dora. She would not, of course, withhold my secret from her husband, and I cannot be despised by him. I have loved him too well for that. And perhaps he'll never know it," she continued, beginning to look upon the brighter side. "Uncle Nat may not prove very inquisitive—may not stay with us long; or, if he does, as the wife of Stephen Grey, I can bear his displeasure better," and determining that ere another twenty-four hours were gone, she would cease to be Eugenia Deane, she arose and stood before the mirror, preparatory to going down.

The sight of her white, haggard face startled her, and for a moment she felt that she could not mingle with the gay throng below, who would wonder at her appearance. But the ordeal must be passed, and summoning all her courage, she descended to her parlor, just as her mother and Alice, alarmed at her very long absence, were coming in quest of her. Crossing the room mechanically she offered her hand to Dora, saying, while a sickly smile played around her bloodless lips, "You have really taken us by surprise, but I congratulate you ; and you too," bowing rather stiffly to Mr. Hastings, who returned her greeting so pleasantly, that she began to feel more at ease, and after a little, was chatting familiarly with Dora, telling her she must be sure and meet, "Uncle Nat," on Saturday evening, and adding in a low tone, "If I've ever treated you badly, I hope you won't tell him."

"I shall tell him nothing," answered Dora, and comforted with this answer, Eugenia moved away.

"You are looking very pale and bad to-night. What is the matter ?" said Uncle Nat, when once he was standing near her.

"Nothing but a bad headache," she replied, while her black eyes flashed angrily upon him, for she fancied he saw the painful throbbings of her heart, and wished to taunt her with it.

Supper being over, Stephen Grey led her into a little side room, where he claimed the answer to his question. It was in the affirmative, and soon after, complaining of the intense pain in her head, she begged to go home. Alone in her room, with no one present but her mother and Alice, her pent-up feelings gave away, and throwing herself upon the floor she wished that she had died ere she had come to this humiliation.

"That Dora, a beggar as it were, should be preferred to *me* is nothing," she cried, "compared to the way which the whole thing was planned. That old wretch of a Hamilton had something to do with it, I know. How I hate him, with his sneering face !"

Becoming at length a little more composed, she told her mother of her expected marriage with Stephen Grey.

"But why so much haste?" asked Mrs. Deane, who, a

little proud of the alliance, would rather have given a large wedding.

Sitting upright upon the floor, with her long loose hair falling around her white face, Eugenia answered bitterly ; " Stephen Grey has no more love for me than I have for him. He believes that we are rich, or we will be when Uncle Nat is dead. For *money* he marries me, for money I marry him. I know old Grey is wealthy, and as the wife of his son, I will yet ride over Dora's head. But I must be quick, or I lose him, for if after Uncle Nat's arrival our real situation should chance to be disclosed, Steve would not hesitate to leave me.

> ' So to-morrow or never a bride I shall be,' "

she sang with a gaiety of manner wholly at variance with the worn, suffering expression of her countenance. Eugenia was terribly expiating her sins, and when the next night, in the presence of a few friends, she stood by Stephen Grey, and was made his wife, she felt that her own hands had poured the last drop in the brimming bucket, for; as she had said, there was not in her heart a particle of esteem or love for him who was now her husband.

"It's my destiny," she thought ; "I'll make the best of it," and her unnatural laugh rang out loud and clear, as she tried to appear gay and happy.

Striking contrast between the gentle bride at Rose Hill, who felt that in all the world, there was not a happier being than herself—and the one at Locust Grove, who with blood-shot eyes and livid lips gazed out upon the starry sky, almost cursing the day that she was born, and the fate which had made her what she was. Ever and anon, too, there came stealing on her ear the fearful word *retribution*, and the wretched girl shuddered as she thought for how much she had to atone

Marvelling much at the strange mood of his bride, Stephen Grey, on the morning succeeding his marriage, left her and went down to the village, where he found a letter from his father, telling him the crisis had come, leaving him more than 100,000 dollars in debt! Stephen was not surprised—he had expected it, and it affected him less painfully when he considered that his wife would inherit a portion of Uncle Nathaniel's wealth.

"I won't tell her yet," he thought, as he walked back to Locust Grove, where, with an undefined presentiment of approaching evil, Eugenia moved listlessly from room to room, counting the hours which dragged heavily, and half wishing that Uncle Nat would hasten his coming, and have it over!

*   *   *   *   *   *

The sun went down, and as darkness settled o'er the earth, a heavy load seemed pressing upon Eugenia's spirits. It wanted now but a few minutes of the time when the train was due, and trembling, she scarcely knew why, she sat alone in her chamber, wondering how she should meet her uncle, or what excuse she should render, if her perfidy were revealed. The door bell rang, and in the hall below she heard the voices of Mr. Hastings and Dora.

"I must go down, now," she said, and forcing a smile to her face, she descended to the parlor, as the shrill whistle of the engine sounded in the distance.

She had just time to greet her visitors and enjoy their surprise at the announcement of her marriage, when her ear caught the sound of heavy, tramping footsteps, coming up the walk, and a violent ringing of the bell announced another arrival.

"You go to the door, Stephen," she whispered, while an icy coldness crept over her.

He obeyed, and bending forward in a listening attitude, she heard him say, " Good evening, Mr. Hamilton."

Just then, a telegraphic look between Mr. Hastings and Dora caught her eye, and springing to her feet, she exclaimed, " *Mr. Hamilton!*" while a suspicion of the truth flashed like lightning upon her. The next moment he stood before them, Uncle Nat, his glittering black eyes fixed upon Eugenia, who quailed beneath that withering glance.

" *I promised you I would come to-night,*" he said, " *and I am here, Nathaniel Deane! Are you glad to see me?*" and his eyes never moved from Eugenia, who sat like one petrified, as did her mother and sister. " Have you no word of welcome?" he continued. " Your letters were wont to be kind and affectionate. I have brought them with me, as a passport to your friendship. Shall I show them to you?"

His manner was perfectly cool and collected, but Eugenia felt the sting each word implied, and, starting up, she glared defiantly at him, exclaiming, " Insolent wretch! What mean you by this? And what business had you thus to deceive us?"

" The fair Eugenia does not believe in *deceit*, it seems. Pity her theory and practice do not better accord," he answered, while a scornful smile curled his lips.

" What proof have you, sir, for what you say?" demanded Eugenia; and with the same cold, scornful smile, he replied, " Far better proof than you imagine, fair lady. Would you like to hear it?"

Not suspecting how much he knew, and goaded to madness by his calm, quiet manner, Eugenia replied, " I defy you, old man, to prove aught against me."

" First, then," said he, " let me ask you what use you made of that fifteen hundred dollars sent to Dora nearly three years ago? Was not this piano," laying his hand

upon the instrument, "bought with a part of that money?
Did Dora ever see it, or the five hundred dollars sent annually by me?"

Eugenia was confounded. He did know it all, but how
had she been betrayed? It must be through Dora's agency,
she thought, and turning fiercely towards her, she heaped
upon her such a torrent of abuse, that, in thunder-like tones,
Uncle Nat, now really excited, bade her keep silent; while
Howard Hastings arose, and confronting the angry woman,
explained briefly what he had done, and why he had done
it.

"Then you, too, have acted a traitor's part?" she hissed;
"but it shall not avail, I will not be trampled down by
either you, or this grey haired"——

"Hold!" cried Uncle Nat, laying his broad palm heavily upon her shoulder. "I am too old to hear such language from you, young lady. I do not wish to upbraid you
farther with what you have done. 'Tis sufficient that I
know it all, that henceforth we are strangers;" and he
turned to leave the room, when Mrs. Deane, advancing towards him, said pleadingly, "Is is thus, Nathaniel, that you
return to us, after so many years? Eugenia may have
been tempted to do wrong, but will you not forgive her for
her father's sake?"

"*Never!*" he answered fiercely, shaking off the hand she
had lain upon his arm. "Towards Alice I bear no ill will;
and you, madam, who suffered this wrong to be done, I
may, in time, forgive, but *that woman*," pointing towards
Eugenia, "*Never!*" And he left the room, while Eugenia,
completely overwhelmed with a sense of her detected guilt,
burst into a passionate fit of tears, sobbing so bitterly
that Dora, touched by her grief, stole softly to her side,
and was about to speak, when, thrusting her away, Eugenia

exclaimed, "Leave me, Dora Deane, and never come here again. The sight of you mocking my wretchedness is hateful and more than I can bear!"

There were tears in Dora's eyes, as she turned away, and offering her hand to her aunt and cousin, she took her husband's arm, and went out of a house, where she had suffered so much, and which, while Eugenia remained, she would never enter again.

Like one in a dream sat Stephen Grey. He had been a silent spectator of the exciting scene, but thought had been busy, and ere it was half over, his own position was clearly defined, and he knew that, even as he had cheated Eugenia Deane, so Eugenia Deane had cheated him. It was an even thing, and unprincipled and selfish as he was, he felt that he had no cause for complaint. Still the disappointment was not the less severe, and when the bride of a day, looking reproachfully at him through her tears, asked, "why he didn't say to her a word of comfort?" he coolly replied, 'because I have nothing to say. You have got yourself into a deuced mean scrape, and so have I!"

Eugenia did not then understand what he meant, and, when, an hour or two later, she dried her tears, and began to speak of an immediate removal to Philadelphia, where she would be more effectually out of Uncle Nat's way, she was surprised at his asking her, "what she proposed doing in the city, and if she had any means of support."

"Means of support!" she repeated. "Why do you ask that question, when your father is worth half a million, and you are his only son?"

With a prolonged whistle, he answered. "Father worth a copper cent and I a precious fool comes nearer the truth!"

"What do you mean?" she asked, in unfeigned astonishment; and he replied, "I mean that three days ago father *failed*, to the tune of $100,000, and if you or I have any bread to eat hereafter, one or the other of us must earn it!"

Eugenia had borne much to-day, and this last announcement was the one straw too many. Utterly crushed, she buried her face in her hands, and remained silent. She could not reproach her husband, for the deception had been equal, and now, when this last hope had swept away, the world indeed seemed dreary and dark.

"What shall we do?" she groaned at last, in a voice so full of despair, that with a feeling akin to pity, Stephen, who had been pacing up and down the room, came to her side, saying, "why can't we stay as we are? I can average a pettyfogging suit a month, and that'll be better than nothing."

"I wouldn't remain here on any account after what has happened," said Eugenia; "and besides that, we couldn't stay, if we would, for now that Uncle Nat's remittance is withdrawn, mother has nothing in the world to live on."

"Couldn't you take in *sewing*," suggested Stephen, "or *washing*, or *mopping*?"

To the sewing and the washing Eugenia was too indignant to reply, but when it came to the *mopping*, she lifted up her hands in astonishment, calling him "a fool and a simpleton."

"Hang me, if I know anything about woman's work," said Stephen, resuming his walk, and wondering why the taking in of *mopping* should be more difficult than anything else. "I have it," he said at length, running his fingers over the keys of the piano. "Can't you teach music? The piano got you into a fix, and if I were you, I'd make it help me out."

"I'll use it for kindling-wood first," was her answer, and Stephen resumed his cogitations, which resulted finally in his telling her, that on the prairies of Illinois there were a

few acres of land, of which he was the rightful owner
There was a house on it, too, he said, though in what condition he did not know, and if they only had a little money
with which to start, it would be best for them to go out
there at once. This plan struck Eugenia more favorably
than any which he had proposed.

Humbled as she was, she felt that the further she were
from Dunwood, the happier she would be, and after a consultation with Mrs. Deane, it was decided that the beautiful
rosewood piano should be sold, and that with the proceeds,
Stephen and Eugenia should bury themselves for a time at
the West. Two weeks more found them on their way to
their distant home, and when that winter, Dora Hastings, at
Rose Hill, pushed aside the heavy damask which shaded her
pleasant window, and looked out upon the snow-covered
lawn and spacious garden beyond, Eugenia Grey, in her
humble cabin, looked through her paper-curtained window
upon the snow-clad prairie, which stretched away as far as
eye could reach, and shed many bitter tears, as she heard
the wind go wailing past her door, and thought of her home,
far to the east, towards the rising sun.

CHAPTER XXII.

CONCLUSION.

THREE years have passed away, and twice the wintry storms have swept over the two graves, which, on the prairies of Illinois, were made when the glorious Indian summer sun was shining o'er the earth, and the withered leaves of autumn were strewn upon the ground. Stephen and Eugenia are dead—he, dying as a drunkard dies—she, as a drunkard's wife. Uncle Nat had been to visit the western world, and on his return to Rose Hill, there was a softened light in his eye, and a sadness in the tones of his voice, as, drawing Dora to his side, he whispered, "I have forgiven her—forgiven Eugenia Deane."

Then he told her how an old man in his wanderings came one day to a lonely cabin, where a wild-eyed woman was raving in delirium, and tearing out handfuls of the long black hair which floated over her shoulders. This she was counting one by one, just as the old East India man had counted the silken tress which was sent to him over the sea, and she laughed with maniacal glee as she said the numbering of all her hairs would atone for the sin she had done. At intervals, too, rocking to and fro, she sang of the fearful night when she had thought to *steal* the auburn locks concealed within the old green trunk ; on which the darkness lay so heavy and so black, that she had turned away in

9

terror, and glided from the room. In the old man's heart there was much of bitterness towards that erring woman for the wrong she had done to him and his, but when he found her thus, when he looked on the new-made grave beneath the buckeye tree, and felt that she was dying of starvation and neglect, when he saw how the autumn rains, dripping from a crevice in the roof, had drenched her scanty pillows through and through—when he sought in the empty cupboard for food or drink in vain, his heart softened towards her, and for many weary days he watched her with the tenderest care, administering to all her wants, and soothing her in her frenzied moods, as he would a little child, and when at last a ray of reason shone for a moment on her darkened mind, and she told him how much she had suffered from the hands of one who now slept just without the door, and asked him to forgive her ere she died, he laid upon his bosom her aching head, from which in places the long hair had been torn, leaving it spotted and bald, and bending gently over her, he whispered in her ear, " As freely as I hope to be forgiven of Heaven, so freely forgive I you."

With a look of deep gratitude, the dark eyes glanced at him for a moment, then closed forever, and he was alone with the dead.

Some women, whose homes were distant two or three miles, had occasionally shared his vigils, and from many a log cabin the people gathered themselves together, and made for the departed a grave, and when the sun was high in the heavens, and not a cloud dimmed the canopy of blue, they buried her beside her husband, where the prairie flowers and the tall rank grass would wave above her head.

This was the story he told, and Dora listening to it, wept bitterly over the ill-fated Eugenia, whose mother and sister never knew exactly how she died, for Uncle Nathaniel would not tell them, but from the time of his return from the West his manner towards them was changed, and when the New Year came round, one hundred golden guineas found entrance at their door, accompanied with a promise that when the day returned again, the gift should be repeated.

*   *   *   *   *   *

On the vine-wreathed pillars, and winding walks of Rose Hill, the softened light of the setting sun is shining. April flowers have wakened to life the fair spring blossoms, whose delicate perfume, mingling with the evening air, steals through the open casement, and kisses the bright face of Dora, beautiful now as when she first called him her husband who sits beside her, and who each day blesses her as his choicest treasure.

On the balcony without, in a large armed willow chair, is seated an old man, and as the fading sunlight falls around him, a bright-haired little girl, not yet two years of age, climbs upon his knee, and winding her chubby arms around his neck, lisps the name of " Grandpa," and the old man, folding her to his bosom, sings to her softly and low of *another Fannie*, whose eyes of blue were much like those which look so lovingly into his face. Anon darkness steals over all, but the new moon, " hanging like a silver thread in the western sky," shows us where Howard Hastings is sitting, still with Dora at his side.

On the balcony, all is silent; the tremulous voice has ceased ; the blue-eyed child no longer listens ; old age and infancy sleep sweetly now together ; the song is ended ; the story is done.

MAGGIE MILLER;

OR,

OLD HAGAR'S SECRET.

MAGGIE MILLER;

OR

OLD HAGAR'S SECRET.

———•••———

CHAPTER I.

THE OLD HOUSE BY THE MILL.

'MID the New England hills, and beneath the shadow of their dim old woods, is a running brook, whose deep waters were not always as merry and frolicsome as now; for years before our story opens, pent up and impeded in their course, they dashed angrily against their prison walls, and turned the creaking wheel of an old saw mill, with a sullen, rebellious roar. The mill has gone to decay, and the sturdy men who fed it with the giant oaks of the forest, are sleeping quietly in the village graveyard. The waters of the mill-pond, too, relieved from their confinement, leap gaily over the ruined dam, tossing for a moment in wanton glee their locks of snow-white foam, and then flowing on, half fearfully as it were, through the deep gorge overhung with the hemlock and the pine, where the shadows of twilight ever lie, and where the rocks frown gloomily down upon the stream below, which, emerging from the darkness, loses

itself at last in the waters of the gracefully winding Chicopee, and leaves far behind the moss-covered walls, of what
is familiarly known as the "Old House by the Mill."

'Tis a huge, old-fashioned building, distant nearly a mile
from the public highway, and surrounded so thickly by forest trees, that the bright sunlight, dancing merrily midst the
rustling leaves above, falls but seldom on the time-stained
walls of dark grey stone, where the damp and dews of more
than a century have fallen, and where now the green moss
clings with a loving grasp, as if 'twere its rightful resting
place. When the thunders of the Revolution shook the
hills of the Bay State, and the royal banner floated in the
evening breeze, the house was owned by an old Englishman,
who, loyal to his king and country, denounced as rebels the
followers of Washington. Against these, however, he
would not raise his hand, for among them were many long
tried friends, who had gathered with him around the festal
board ; so he chose the only remaining alternative, and
went back to his native country, cherishing the hope that
he should one day return to the home he loved so well, and
listen again to the musical flow of the water-brook, which
could be distinctly heard from the door of the mansion.
But his wish was vain, for when at last America was free,
and the British troops recalled, he slept beneath the sod of
England, and the old house was for many years deserted.
The Englishman had been greatly beloved, and his property
was unmolested, while the weeds and grass grew tall and
rank in the garden beds, and the birds of heaven built their
nests beneath the projecting roof, or held a holiday in the
gloomy, silent rooms.

As time passed on, however, and no one appeared to dis-
pute their right, different families occupied the house at intervals, until at last, when nearly fifty years had elapsed, news

was one day received that Madam Conway, a grand-daughter
of the old Englishman, having met with reverses at home,
had determined to emigrate to the New World, and remembering the "House by the Mill," of which she had heard so
much, she wished to know if peaceable possession of it
would be allowed her, in case she decided upon removing
thither, and making it her future home. To this plan no
objection was made, for the aged people of Hillsdale still
cherished the memory of the hospitable old man, whose
locks were grey while they were yet but children, and the
younger portion of the community hoped for a renewal of
the gaieties which they had heard were once so common at
the old stone house.

But in this they were disappointed, for Madam Conway
was a proud, unsocial woman, desiring no acquaintance whatever with her neighbors, who, after many ineffectual attempts
at something like friendly intercourse, concluded to leave
her entirely alone, and contented themselves with watching
the progress of matters at "Mill Farm," as she designated the
place, which soon began to show visible marks of improvement. The Englishman was a man of taste, and Madam
Conway's first work was an attempt to restore the grounds
to something of their former beauty. The yard and garden
were cleared of weeds ; the walks and flower-beds laid out
with care, and then the neighbors looked to see her cut
away a few of the multitude of trees, which had sprung up
around her home. But this she had no intention of doing.
"They shut her out," she said, "from the prying eyes of
the vulgar, and she would rather it should be so." So the
trees remained, throwing their long shadows upon the high,
narrow windows, and into the large square rooms, where
the morning light and the noon-day heat seldom found
entrance, and which seemed like so many cold, silent

9*

caverns, with their old-fashioned massive furniture, their dark, heavy curtains, and the noiseless footfall of the stately lady, who moved ever with the same measured tread, speaking always softly and low to the household servants, who, having been trained in her service, had followed her across the sea.

From these, the neighbors learned that Madam Conway had in London a married daughter, Mrs. Miller; that old Hagar Warren, the strange looking woman, who, more than any one else, shared her mistress's confidence had grown up in the family, receiving a very good education, and had nursed their young mistress, Miss Margaret, which of course entitled her to more respect than was usually bestowed upon menials like her; that Madam Conway was very aristocratic, very proud of her high English blood; that, though she lived alone, she attended strictly to all the formalities of high-life, dressing each day with the utmost precision for her solitary dinner; dining from off a service of solid silver, and presiding with great dignity in her straight, high-backed chair. She was fond, too, of the ruby wine, and her cellar was stored with the choicest liquors, some of which she had brought with her from home, while others, it was said, had belonged to her grandfather, and for half a century, had remained unseen and unmolested, while the cobwebs of time had woven around them a misty covering, making them still more valuable to the lady, who knew full well how age improved such things.

Regularly each day she rode in her ponderous carriage, sometimes alone, and sometimes accompanied by *Hester*, the daughter of old Hagar, a handsome, intelligent looking girl, who, after two or three years of comparative idleness at Mill Farm, went to Meriden, Connecticut, as seamstress in a family, which had advertised for such a person. With her,

departed the only life of the house, and during the following year there ensued a monotonous quiet, which was
broken at last for Hagar, by the startling announcement
that her daughter's young mistress had died four months
before, and the husband, a grey-haired, elderly man, had
proved conclusively that he was in his dotage, by talking of
marriage to Hester, who, ere the letter reached her mother,
would probably be the third bride of one, whose reputed
wealth was the only possible inducement to a girl like
Hester Warren.

With an immense degree of satisfaction, Hagar read the
letter through, exulting that fortune had favored her at
last. Possessed of many sterling qualities, Hagar Warren
had one glaring fault which had embittered her whole life.
Why others were rich while she was poor, she could not
understand, and her heart rebelled at the fate which had
made her what she was. But Hester would be wealthy,
nay, would, perhaps, one day rival the haughty Mrs.
Miller across the water, who had been her playmate ; there
was comfort in that, and she wrote to her daughter expressing her entire approbation, and hinting vaguely of the
possibility that she herself might sometime cease to be a
servant, and help do the honors of Mr. Hamilton's house !
To this there came no reply, and Hagar was thinking seriously of making a visit to Meriden, when one rainy autumnal
night, nearly a year after Hester's marriage, there came
another letter sealed with black. With a sad foreboding,
Hagar opened it, and read that Mr. Hamilton had *Failed;*
that his house and farm were sold, and that he, overwhelmed with mortification both at his failure, and the
opposition of his friends to his last marriage, had died suddenly, leaving Hester with no home in the wide world,
unless Madam Conway received her again into her family.

"Just my luck!" was Hagar's mental comment, as she finished reading the letter, and carried it to her mistress, who had always liked Hester, and who readily consented to give her a home, provided she put on no *airs*, from having been for a time the wife of a reputed wealthy man. 'Mustn't put on *airs!*" muttered Hagar, as she left the room. "Just as if *airs* wasn't for anybody but high bloods," and with the canker worm of envy at her heart, she wrote to Hester, who came immediately; and Hagar, when she heard her tell the story of her wrongs, how her husband's sister, indignant at his marriage with a sewing girl, had removed from him the children, one a step-child and one his own, and how of all his vast fortune there was not left for her a penny, experienced again the old bitterness of feeling, and murmured that fate should thus deal with her and hers.

With the next day's mail, there came to Madam Conway a letter, bearing a foreign postmark, and bringing the sad news that her son-in-law had been lost in a storm, while crossing the English Channel, and that her daughter Margaret, utterly crushed and heart-broken, would sail immediately for America, where she wished only to lay her weary head upon her mother's bosom and die.

"So, there is one person that has no respect for *blood*, and that is *Death*," said old Hagar to her mistress, when she heard the news. "He has served us both alike, he has taken my son-in-law first and yours next."

"Frowning haughtily, Madam Conway bade her be silent, telling her at the same time to see that the rooms in the north part of the building were put in perfect order for Mrs. Miller, who would probably come in the next vessel. In sullen silence Hagar withdrew, and for several days worked half reluctantly in the "north rooms," as Madam Conway termed a comparatively pleasant, airy suit of apartments, with a balcony above, which looked out upon the old mill-dam, and the water brook pouring over it.

"There'll be big doings when my lady comes," said Hagar one day to her daughter. "It'll be Hagar here, and Hagar there, and Hagar everywhere, but I shan't hurry myself. I'm getting too old to wait on a chit like her."

"Don't talk so, mother," said Hester. "Margaret was always kind to me. She is not to blame for being rich, while I am poor."

"But somebody's to blame," interrupted old Hagar. "You was always accounted the handsomest and cleverest of the two, and yet for all you'll be nothing but a drudge to wait on her and the little girl."

Hester only sighed in reply, while her thoughts went forward to the future, and what it would probably bring her. Hester Warren and Margaret Conway had been children together, and in spite of the difference of there stations they had loved each other dearly ; and when at last the weary traveller came, with her pale sad face and mourning garb, none gave her so heartfelt a welcome as Hester ; and during the week when from exhaustion and excitement, she was confined to her bed, it was Hester who nursed her with the utmost care, soothing her to sleep, and then amusing the little Theo, a child of two years. Hagar, too, softened by her young misstress's sorrow, repented of her harsh words, and watched each night with the invalid, who once when her mind seemed wandering far back in the past, whispered softly, "Tell me the Lord's prayer, dear Hagar, just as you told it to me years ago when I was a little child."

It was a long time since Hagar had breathed that prayer, but at Mrs. Miller's request she commenced it, repeating it correctly until she came to the words, "Give us this day our daily bread," then she hesitated, and bending forward said, "What comes next, Miss Margaret? Is it, 'Lead us not into temptation?'"

'Yes, yes," whispered the half unconscious lady. "'Lead us not into temptation,' that's it;" then, as if there were around her a dim foreboding of the great wrong Hagar was to do, she took her old nurse's hand between her own, and continued, "Say it often, Hagar, 'Lead us not into temptation;' you have much need for that prayer."

A moment more and Margaret Miller slept, while beside her sat Hagar Warren, half shuddering she knew not why, as she thought of her mistress's words, which seemed to her, so much like the spirit of prophecy.

"Why do *I* need that prayer more than any one else?" she said, at last. "I have never been tempted more than I could bear—never shall be tempted—and if I am, old Hagar Warren, bad as she is, can resist temptation, without that prayer."

Still, reason as she would, Hagar could not shake off the strange feeling, and as she sat, half dozing in her chair, with the dim lamplight flickering over her dark face, she fancied that the October wind, sighing so mournfully through the locust trees beneath the window and then dying away in the distance, bore upon its wing, "Lead us not into temptation Hagar you have much need to say that prayer."

"Aye, Hagar Warren, much need, much need !

CHAPTER II.

HAGAR'S SECRET.

THE wintry winds were blowing cold and chill around the old stone house, and the deep untrodden snow lay high piled upon the ground. For many days, the grey, leaden clouds had frowned gloomily down upon the earth below, covering it with a thick veil of white. But the storm was over now, with the setting sun it had gone to rest, and the pale moonlight stole softly into the silent chamber, where Madam Conway bent anxiously down to see if but the faintest breath came from the parted lips of her only daughter. There had been born to her that night another grandchild— a little, helpless girl, which now in an adjoining room was Hagar's special care ; and Hagar, sitting there with the wee creature upon her lap, and the dread fear at her heart that her young mistress might die, forgot for once to repine at her lot, and did cheerfully whatever was required of her to do.

There was silence in the rooms below—silence in the chambers above—silence everywhere—for the sick woman seemed fast nearing the deep, dark river, whose waters move onward but never return.

Almost a week went by, and then, in a room far more humble than that where Margaret Miller lay, another immortal being was given to the world ; and with a softened light in her keen black eyes, old Hagar told to her stately mistress, when she met her on the stairs, that she, too, was a grandmother.

"You must not on that account neglect Margaret's child," was Madam Conway's answer, as with a wave of her hand, she passed on ; and this was all she said—not a word of sympathy or congratulation for the peculiar old woman whose heart, so long benumbed, had been roused to a better state of feeling, and who in the first joy of her new-born happiness, had hurried to her mistress, fancying for the moment that she was almost her equal.

"Don't neglect Margaret's child for that !" How the words rang in her ears, as she fled up the narrow stairs and through the dark hall, till the low room was reached where lay the babe for whom Margaret's child was not to be neglected. All the old bitterness had returned, and as hour after hour went by, and Madam Conway came not near, while the physician and the servants looked in for a moment only and then hurried away to the other sick room, where all their services were kept in requisition, she muttered : "Little would they care if Hester died upon my hands. And she will die too," she continued, as by the fading daylight she saw the palor deepen on her daughter's face.

And Hagar was right, for Hester's sands were nearer run than those of Mrs. Miller. The utmost care might not, perhaps, have saved her, but the matter was not tested, and when the long clock at the head of the stairs struck the hour of midnight, she murmured, "It is getting dark here, mother—so dark—and I am growing cold. Can it be death ?"

"Yes, Hester, 'tis death," answered Hagar, and her voice was unnaturally calm as she laid her hand on the clammy brow of her daughter.

An hour later, and Madam Conway, who sat dozing in the parlor below, ready for any summons which might come from Margaret's room, was roused by the touch of a cold, hard hand, and Hagar Warren stood before her.

"Come," she said, "come with me ;" and thinking only of Margaret, Madam Conway arose to follow her. "Not there—but this way," said Hagar, as her mistress turned towards Mrs. Miller's door, and grasping firmly the lady's arm, she led to the room where Hester lay dead, with her young baby clasped lovingly to her bosom. "Look at her —and pity me now, if you never did before. She was all I had in the world to love," said Hagar passionately.

Madam Conway was not naturally a hard-hearted woman, and she answered gently, "I do pity you, Hagar, and I did not think Hester was so ill. Why haven't you let me know?" To this Hagar made no direct reply, and after a few more inquiries Madam Conway left the room, saying she would send up the servants to do whatever was necessary. When it was known throughout the house that Hester was dead, much surprise was expressed and a good deal of sympathy manifested for old Hagar, who, with a gloomy brow, hugged to her heart the demon of jealousy, which kept whispering to her of the difference there would be were Margaret to die. It was deemed advisable to keep Hester's death a secret from Mrs. Miller ; so, with as little ceremony as possible, the body was buried at the close of the day, in an inclosure which had been set apart as a family burying ground ; and when again the night shadows fell, Hagar Warren sat in her silent room, brooding o'er her grief, and looking oft at the plain pine cradle, where lay the little motherless child, her grand-daughter. Occasionally, too, her eye wandered towards the mahogany crib, where another infant slept. Perfect quiet seemed necessary for

Mrs. Miller, and Madam Conway had ordered her baby to
be removed from the ante-chamber where first it had been
kept, so that Hagar had the two children in her own
room.

In the pine cradle there was a rustling sound ; the baby
was awaking, and taking it upon her lap, Hagar soothed it
again to sleep, gazing earnestly upon it to see if it were like
its mother.   It was a bright, healthy-looking infant, and
though five days younger than that of Mrs. Miller, was quite
as large and looked as old.

"And you will be a *drudge*, while she will be a *lady*,"
muttered Hagar, as her tears fell on the face of the sleeping
child.   "Why need this difference be ?"

Old Hagar had forgotten the words "Lead us not into
temptation ;" and when the tempter answered "It need not
be," she only started suddenly as if smitten by a heavy blow ;
but she did not drive him from her, and she sat there reasoning with herself that, "it need not be."   Neither the physician nor Madam Conway had paid any attention to Margaret's child ; it had been *her* special care, while no one had
noticed hers, and newly born babies were so much alike
that deception was an easy matter.   But *could* she do it ?
Could she bear that secret on her soul ?   Madam Conway,
though proud, had been kind to her, and could she thus de-
cieve her !   Would her daughter, sleeping in her early
grave, approve the deed.   "*No, no*," she answered aloud,
"she would not ;" and the great drops of perspiration stood
thickly upon her dark haggard face, as she arose and laid
back in her cradle the child whom she had thought to make
an heiress.

For a time the tempter left her, but returned ere long,
and creeping into her heart sung to her beautiful songs of the
future which might be, were Hester's baby a lady.   And

Hagar, listening to that song, fell asleep, dreaming that the deed was done by other agency than hers—that the little face resting on the downy pillow, and shaded by the costly lace, was lowly born ; while the child, wrapped in the coarser blanket, came of nobler blood, even that of the Conways, who boasted more than one lordly title. With a nervous start she awoke at last, and creeping to the cradle of mahogany, looked to see if her dream were true ; but it was not. She knew it by the pinched, blue look about the nose, and the thin covering of hair. This was all the difference which even her eye could see, and probably no other person had noticed that, for the child had never been seen save in a darkened room. The sin was growing gradually less heinous, and she could now calmly calculate the chances for detection. Still, the conflict was long and severe, and it was not until morning that the tempter gained a point by compromising the matter, and suggesting that while dressing the infants she should change their clothes for once, just to see how fine cambrics and soft flannel would look upon a grandchild of Hagar Warren !   " She could easily change them again—'twas only an experiment," she said, as with trembling hands she proceeded to divest the children of their wrappings. But her fingers seemed all thumbs, and more than one sharp pin pierced the tender flesh of her little grandchild, as she fastened together the embroidered slip, teaching her thus early had she been able to learn the lesson, that the pathway of the rich is not free from thorns.

Their toilet was completed at last—their cradle beds exchanged, and then with a strange, undefined feeling, old Hagar stood back and looked to see how the little usurper became her new position.   She became it well, and to Hagar's partial eyes it seemed more mete that she should lie there beneath the silken covering, than the other one, whose nose looked still more pinched and blue in the plain white dress and cradle of pine. Still, there was a gnawing pain at Hagar's heart, and she would perhaps have undone the wrong, had not Madam Conway appeared with inquir- ies for the baby's health. Hagar could not face her mistress, so she turned away and pretended to busy, herself with the arrangement of the room, while the lady bending over the cradle, said, "I think she is improving, Hagar ; I never saw her look so well ;" and she pushed back the window curtain to obtain a better view.

With a wild startled look in her eye, Hagar held her breath to hear what might come next, but her fears were groundless ; for in her anxiety for her daughter, Madam Conway had heretofore scarcely seen her grand-child, and had no suspicion now that the sleeper before her was of plebeian birth, nor yet that the other little one, at whom she did not deign to look, was bone of her bone, and flesh of her flesh. She started to leave the room, but impelled by some sudden impulse turned back and stooped to kiss the child. Involuntarily old Hagar sprang forward to stay the act, and grasped the lady's arm, but she was to late ; the aristocratic lips had touched the cheek of Hagar Warren's grand-child, and the secret, if now confessed, would never be forgiven.

"It can't be helped," muttered Hagar, and then, when Mrs. Conway asked an explanation of her conduct, she ans- wered. " I was afraid you'd wake her up, and mercy knows I've had worry enough with both the brats."

Not till then had Madam Conway observed how haggard and worn was Hagar's face, and instead of reproving her for her boldness, she said gently, " you have, indeed, been sorely tried. Shall I send up Bertha to relieve you ?"

"No, no," answered Hagar hurriedly, "I am better alone."

The next moment Madam Conway was moving silently down the narrow hall, while Hagar on her knees was weeping passionately. One word of kindness had effected more than a thousand reproaches would have done; and wringing her hands she cried, "I will not do it; I cannot."

Approaching the cradle she was about to lift the child, when again Madam Conway was at the door. She had come, she said, to take the babe to Margaret, who seemed better this morning, and had asked to see it.

"Not now, not now. Wait till I put on her a handsomer dress, and I'll bring her myself," pleaded Hagar.

But Madam Conway saw no fault in the fine cambric wrapper, and taking the infant in her arms, she walked away, while Hagar followed stealthily. Very lovingly the mother folded to her bosom the babe, calling it her fatherless one, and wetting its face with her tears, while through the half closed door peered Hagar's wild dark eyes—one moment lighting up with exultation as she muttered, "it's *my* flesh, *my* blood, proud lady!" and the next, growing dim with tears, as she thought of the evil she had done.

"I did not know she had so much hair," said Mrs. Miller, parting the silken locks. "I think it will be like mine," and she gave the child to her mother, while Hagar glided swiftly back to her room.

That afternoon, the clergyman, whose church Mrs. Conway usually attended, called to see Mrs. Miller, who suggested that both the children should receive the rite of baptism. Hagar was accordingly bidden to prepare them for the ceremony, and resolving to make one more effort to undo what she had done, she dressed the child, whom she had thought to wrong, in its own clothes, and then anxiously awaited her mistress's coming.

"Hagar Warren! What does this mean? Are you crazy!" sternly demanded Madam Conway, when the old nurse held up before her the child with the blue nose.

"No, not crazy yet; but I shall be, if you don't take this one first," answered Hagar.

More than once that day Madam Conway had heard the servants hint that Hagar's grief had driven her insane; and now, when she observed the unnatural brightness in her eyes, and saw what she had done, she, too, thought it possible that her mind was partially unsettled; so she said gently, but firmly, "this is no time for foolishness, Hagar. They are waiting for us in the sick-room; so make haste and change the baby's dress."

There was something authoritative in her manner, and Hagar obeyed, whispering incoherently to herself, and thus further confirming her mistress's suspicions that she was partially insane. During the ceremony, she stood tall and erect like some dark, grim statue, her hands firmly locked together, and her eyes fixed upon the face of the little one, who was baptized "*Margaret Miller.*" As the clergyman pronounced that name, she uttered a low, gasping moan, but her face betrayed no emotion, and very calmly she stepped forward with the other child upon her arm.

"What name?" asked the minister, and she answered "her *mother's;* call her for her *mother!*"

"*Hester,*" said Madam Conway, turning to the clergyman, who understood nothing from Hagar's reply.

So "*Hester*" was the name given to the child, in whose veins the blood of English noblemen was flowing; and when the ceremony was ended, Hagar bore back to her room "Hester Hamilton," the child defrauded of her birthright, and "Maggie Miller," the heroine of our story.

CHAPTER III.

HESTER AND MAGGIE.

"It is over now," old Hagar thought, as she laid the children upon their pillows. "The deed is done, and by their own hands too. There is nothing left for me now but a confession, and that I cannot make ;" so with a heavy weight upon her soul, she sat down resolving to keep her own counsel and abide the consequence, whatever it might be.

But it wore upon her terribly—that secret—and though it helped in a measure to divert her mind from dwelling too much upon her daughter's death, it haunted her continually, making her a strange, eccentric woman, whom the servants persisted in calling crazy, while even Madam Conway failed to comprehend her. Her face, which was always dark, seemed to have acquired a darker, harder look, while her eyes wore a wild startled expression, as if she were constantly followed by some tormenting fear. At first, Mrs. Miller objected to trusting her with the babe ; but when Madam Conway suggested that the woman who had charge of little Theo should also take care of Maggie, she fell upon her knees and begged most piteously that the child might not be taken from her. Every thing I have ever loved has left me," said she, " and I cannot give her up."

"But they say you are crazy," answered Madam Conway, somewhat surprised that Hagar should manifest so much affection for a child not at all connected to her. "They say you are crazy, and no one trusts a crazy woman."

Crazy !" repeated Hagar, half scornfully, "*crazy*—'tis not *craziness*—'tis *the trouble*—*the trouble*—that's killing me. But I'll *hide* it closer than it's hidden now," she continued, "If you'll let her stay ; and 'fore Heaven, I swear, that sooner than harm one hair of Maggie's head, I'd part with my own life ;" and taking the sleeping child in her arms, she stood like a wild beast at bay.

Madam Conway did not herself really believe in Hagar's insanity. She had heretofore been perfectly faithful to whatever was committed to her care, so she bade her be quiet, saying they would trust her for a time.

"It's the talking to myself," said Hagar, when left alone. "It's the talking to myself, which makes them call me crazy ; and though I might talk to many a worse woman than old Hagar Warren, I'll stop it ; I'll be still as the grave, and when next they gossip about me, it shall be of something besides my craziness.

So Hagar became suddenly silent, and uncommunicative, mingling but little with the servants, but staying all day long in her room, where she watched the children with untiring care. Especially was she kind to Hester, who as time passed on, proved to be a puny, sickly thing, never noticing any one, but moaning frequently as if in pain. Very tenderly old Hagar nursed her, carrying her often in her arms, until they ached from very weariness, while Madam Conway, who watched her with a vigilant eye, complained that she neglected little Maggie.

"And what if I do ?" returned Hagar, somewhat bitterly, "Ain't there a vast difference between the two ? S'pose Hester was your own flesh and blood, would you think I could do too much for the poor thing ?" And she glanced compassionately at the poor wasted form, which lay upon her lap, gasping for breath, and presenting a striking contrast to the little Maggie, who, in her cradle, was crowing and laughing in childish glee, at the bright firelight which blazed upon the hearth.

Maggie was indeed a beautiful child. From her mother she had inherited the boon of perfect health, and she throve well in spite of the bumped heads and pinched fingers, which frequently fell to her lot, when Hagar was too busy with the feeble child to notice her. The plaything of the whole house, she was greatly petted by the servants, who vied with each other in tracing points of resemblance between her and the Conways; while the grandmother prided herself particularly on the arched eyebrows, and finely cut upper lip, which, she said, were sure marks of high blood, and never found in the lower ranks! With a most scornful expression on her face, old Hagar would listen to these remarks, and then, when sure that no one heard her, she would mutter, "*Marks of blood!* What nonsense! I'm almost glad I've solved the riddle, and know 'taint *blood* that makes the difference. Just tell her the truth once, and she'd quickly change her mind. Hester's blue pinched nose, which makes one think of *fits*, would be the very essence of *aristocracy*, while Maggie's *lip* would come of the little *Paddy* blood there is running in her veins!"

"And still, Madam Conway herself was not one half so proud of the bright, playful Maggie, as was old Hagar, who, when they were alone, would hug her to her bosom, and gaze fondly on her fair, round face, and locks of silken hair so like those now resting in the grave. In the meantime Mrs. Miller, who, since her daughter's birth, had never left her room, was growing daily weaker, and when Maggie was

nearly nine months old, she died, with the little one folded
to her bosom, just as Hester Hamilton had held it, when,
she, too, passed from earth.

"Doubly blessed," whispered old Hagar, who was present,
and then when she remembered that to poor little Hester a
mother's blessing would never be given, she felt that her load
of guilt was greater than she could bear. "She will perhaps
forgive me if I confess it to her over Miss Margaret's coffin,"
she thought ; and once when they stood together by the
sleeping dead, and Madam Conway, with Maggie in her
arms was bidding the child kiss the clay cold lips of its mother, old Hagar attempted to tell her. "Could you bear
Miss Margaret's death as well," she said, "if Maggie, instead
of being bright and playful as she is, were weak and sick,
like Hester?" and her eyes fastened themselves upon Madam Conway with an agonizing intensity which that lady
could not fathom. "Say, would you bear it as well—could
you love her as much—would you change with me, take
Hester for your own, and give me little Maggie?" she per
sisted, and Madam Conway, surprised at her excited manner, which she attributed in a measure to envy, answered
coldly. "Of course not. Still, if God had seen fit to give
me a child like Hester, I should try to be reconciled, but I
am thankful he has not thus dealt with me."

"'Tis enough. I am satisfied," thought Hagar. "She
would not thank me for telling her. The secret shall be
kept ;" and half exultingly she anticipated the pride she
should feel in seeing her grand-daughter grown up a lady,
and an heiress.

Anon, however, there came stealing over her a feeling of
remorse, as she reflected that the child defrauded of its birth-
right would, if it lived, be compelled to serve in the capacity
of a servant ; and many a night, when all else was silent in

the old stone house, she paced up and down the room, her
long hair, now fast turning grey, falling over her shoulders,
and her large eyes dimmed with tears, as she thought what
the future would bring to the infant she carried in her arms.
But the evil she so much dreaded never came, for when the
winter snows were again falling, they made a little grave
beneath the same pine tree where Hester Hamilton lay
sleeping, and while they dug that grave, old Hagar sat with
folded arms and tearless eyes, gazing fixedly upon the still,
white face, and thin blue lips, which would never again be
distorted with pain. Her habit of talking to herself had
returned, and as she sat there, she would at intervals
whisper, "poor little babe ! I would willingly have cared
for you all my life, but I am glad you are gone to Miss Margaret, who, it may be, will wonder what little thin-faced
angel is calling *her* mother ! But somebody'll introduce you,
somebody'll tell her who you are, and when she knows how
proud her mother is of Maggie, she'll forgive old Hagar
Warren !"

" Gone stark mad !" was the report carried by the servants to their mistress, who believed the story, when Hagar
herself came to her with the request that Hester might be
buried in some of Maggie's clothes.

Touched with pity by her worn, haggard face, Madam
Conway answered ; " yes, take some of her common ones,"
and choosing the cambric robe which Hester had worn on
the morning when the exchange was made, Hagar dressed
the body for the grave. When, at last, everything was
ready and the tiny coffin stood upon the table, Madam
Conway drew near, and looked for a moment on the ema-
ciated form which rested quietly from all its pain. Hovering at her side was Hagar, and feeling it her duty to say a
word of comfort, the stately lady remarked, that "'twas

best the babe should die ; that were it *her* grandchild, she should feel relieved ; for had it lived, it would undoubtedly have been physically and intellectually feeble."

"Thank you ! I am considerably comforted," was the cool reply of Hagar, who felt how cruel were the words, and who for a moment was strongly tempted to claim the beauti ful Maggie as her own, and give back to the cold, proud woman the senseless clay, ou which she looked so calmly.

But love for her grandchild conquered. There was nothing in the way of her advancement now, and when at the grave she knelt her down to weep, as the bystanders thought, over her dead, she was breathing there a vow that never so long as she lived should the secret of Maggie's birth be given to the world, unless some circumstance then unforeseen should make it absolutely and unavoidably neces- sary. To see Maggie grow up into a beautiful, refined and cultivated woman, was now the great object of Hagar's life ; and fearing lest by some inadvertent word or action the secret should be disclosed, she wished to live by herself, where naught but the winds of heaven could listen to her incoherent whisperings, which made her fellow servants accuse her of insanity.

Down in the deepest shadow of the woods, and distant from the old stone house nearly a mile, was a half-ruined cottage which, years before, had been occupied by miners, who had dug in the hillside for particles of yellow ore, which they fancied to be gold. Long and frequent were the night revels said to have been held in the old hut, which had at last fallen into bad repute and been for years deserted. To one like Hagar, however, there was nothing intimidating in its creaking old floors, its rattling windows and noisome chim- ney, where the bats and the swallows built their nests ; and when, one day, Madam Conway proposed giving little Mag gie into the charge of a younger and less nervous person than herself, she made no objection, but surprised her mistress by asking permission to live by herself in the " cottage by the mine " as it was called.

"It is better for me to be alone," said she, "for I may do something terrible if I stay here, something I would sooner *die* than do," and her eyes fell upon Maggie sleeping in her cradle.

This satisfied Madam Conway that the half-crazed woman meditated harm to her favorite grandchild, and she consented readily to her removal to the cottage, which by her orders was made comparatively comfortable. For several weeks, when she came, as she did each day to the house, Madam Conway kept Maggie carefully from her sight, until at last she begged so hard to see her, that her wish was gratified ; and as she manifested no disposition whatever to molest the child, Madam Conway's fears gradually subsided, and Hagar was permitted to fondle and caress her as often as she chose.

Here, now, for a time, we leave them ; Hagar in her cottage by the mine ; Madam Conway in her gloomy home ; Maggie in her nurse's arms ; and Theo, of whom as yet but little has been said, playing on the nursery floor ; while with our readers we pass silently over a period of time which shall bring us to Maggie's girlhood.

CHAPTER IV.

GIRLHOOD.

FIFTEEN years have passed away, and around the old stone house there is outwardly no change. The moss still clings to the damp, dark wall, just as it clung there long ago, while the swaying branches of the forest trees still cast their shadows across the floor, or scream to the autumn blast, just as they did in years gone by, when Hagar Warren breathed that prayer, " Lead us not into temptation." Madam Conway, stiff and straight and cold as ever, moves with the same measured tread through her gloomy rooms, which are not as noiseless now as they were wont to be, for girlhood, joyous, merry girlhood, has a home in those dark rooms, and their silence is broken by the sound of other feet, not moving stealthily and slow, as if following in a funeral train, but dancing down the stairs, tripping through the halls, skipping across the floor, and bounding over the grass, they go, never tiring, never ceasing, till the birds and the sun have gone to rest.

And do what she may, the good lady cannot check the gleeful mirth, or hush the clear ringing laughter of one at least of the fair maidens, who, since last we looked upon them, have grown up to womanhood. Wondrously beautiful is Maggie Miller now, with her bright sunny face, her soft, dark eyes and raven hair, so glossy and smooth, that her sister, the pale sad, blue-eyed Theo, likens it to a piece of shining satin. Now, as ever, the pet and darling of the household, she moves among them like a ray of sunshine ; and the servants, when they hear her bird-like voice waking the echoes of the weird old place, pause in their work to listen, blessing Miss Margaret for the joy and gladness her presence has brought to them.

Old Hagar, in her cottage by the mine, has kept her secret well, whispering it only to the rushing wind and the running brook, which have told no tales to the gay, light-hearted girl, save to murmur in her ear that a life, untrammeled by etiquette and form, would be a blissful life indeed. And Maggie, listening to the voices which speak to her so oft in the autumn wind, the running brook, the opening flower and the falling leaf, has learned a lesson different far from those taught her daily by the prim, stiff governess, who, imported from England six years ago, has drilled both Theo and Maggie, in all the prescribed rules of high-life as prac-tised in the old world. She has taught them how to *sit* and how to *stand*, how to *eat* and how to *drink*, as became young ladies of *Conway* blood and birth. And Madam Conway, through her golden spectacles, looks each day to see some good, from all this teaching, come to the bold, dashing, untamable Maggie, who, spurning alike both *birth* and *blood*, laughs at form and etiquette as taught by Mrs. Jeffrey, and winding her arms around her grandmother's neck, crumples her rich lace ruffle with a most *unladylike hug*, and then bounds away to the stables, pretending not to hear the dis-tressed Mrs. Jeffrey calling after her " not to *run*, 'twas so Yankeefied and vulgar ;" or if she did hear, answering back, " I am a *Yankee*, native born, and shall run for all Johnny Bull."

Greatly horrified at this evidence of total depravity, Mrs

Jeffrey brushes down her black silk apron and goes back to Theo, her more tractable pupil ; while Maggie, emerging ere long from the stable, clears the fence with one leap of her high-mettled pony, which John, the coachman, had bought at an enormous price, of a travelling circus, on purpose for his young mistress, who complained that "grandma's horses were all too lazy and aristocratic in their movements for her."

In perfect amazement Madam Conway looked out when first "Gritty," as the pony was called, was led up to the door, prancing, pawing, chafing at the bit and impatient to be off. "Margaret should never mount that animal," she said ; but Margaret had *ruled* for sixteen years, and now, at a sign from John, she sprang gaily upon the back of the fiery steed, who, feeling instinctively that the rider he carried was a stranger to fear, became under her training perfectly gentle, obeying her slightest command, and following her ere long like a sagacious dog. Not thus easily could Madam Conway manage Maggie, and with a groan she saw her each day fly over the garden gate, and out into the woods, which she scoured in all directions.

"She'll break her neck, I know," the disturbed old lady would say, as Maggie's flowing skirt and waving plumes disappeared in the shadow of the trees. "She'll break her neck some day ;" and thinking some one must be in fault, her eyes would turn reprovingly upon Mrs. Jeffrey for having failed in subduing Maggie, whom the old governess pronounced the "veriest mad-cap in the world ; there was nothing like her in all England," she said, "and her low bred ways must be the result of her having been born on American soil."

If Maggie was to be censured, Madam Conway chose to do it herself, and on such occasions she would answer, "*Low-bred*, Mrs. Jeffrey, is not a proper term to apply to

Margaret. She's a little wild, I admit, but no one with *my* blood in their veins can be *low-bred* ;" and in her indignation at the governess, Madam would usually forget to reprove her grand-daughter when she came back from her ride, her cheeks flushed and her eyes shining like stars with the healthful exercise. Throwing herself upon a stool at her grandmother's feet, Maggie would lay her head upon the lap of the proud lady, who, very lovingly would smooth the soft shining hair, " so much like her own," she said.

"Before you had to *color* it, you mean, don't you, grand-ma ?" the mischievous Maggie would rejoin, looking up archly to her grandmother, who would call her a saucy child, and stroke still more fondly the silken locks.

Wholly unlike Maggie was Theo, a pale-faced, fair-haired girl, who was called *pretty*, when not overshadowed by the queenly presence of her more gifted sister. And Theo was very proud of this sister, too ; proud of the beautiful Maggie, to whom, though two years her junior, she looked for counsel, willing always to abide by her judgment ; for what Maggie did must of course be right, and grandma would not scold. So if at any time Theo was led into error, Maggie stood ready to bear the blame, which was never very severe, for Mrs. Jeffrey had learned not to censure her too much, lest by so doing she should incur the displeasure of her employer, who in turn loved Maggie, if it were possible, better than the daughter whose name she bore, and whom Maggie called her mother. Well kept and beautiful was the spot where that mother lay, and the grave was marked by a costly marble, which gleamed clear and white through the surrounding evergreens. This was Maggie's favorite resort, and here she often sat in the moonlight, musing of one who slept there, and who, they said, had held her on her bosom when she died.

At no great distance from this spot, was another grave, where the grass grew tall and green, and where the head-stone, half sunken in the earth, betokened that she who rested there was of humble origin. Here Maggie seldom tarried long. The place had no attraction for her, for rarely now was the name of Hester Hamilton heard at the old stone house, and all, save one, seemed to have forgotten that such as she had ever lived. This was Hagar Warren, who in her cottage by the mine has grown older, and more crazy-like since last we saw her. Her hair, once so much like that which Madame Conway likens to her own, has bleached as white as snow, and her tall form is shrivelled now, and bent. The *secret* is wearing her life away, and yet she does not regret what she has done. She cannot, when she looks upon the beautiful girl, who comes each day to her lonely hut, and whom she worships with a species of wild idolatry. Maggie knows not why it is, and yet to her there is a peculiar fascination about that strange old woman, with her snow-white hair, her wrinkled face, her bony hand, and wild, dark eyes, which, when they rest on her, have in them a look of unutterable tenderness.

Regularly each day when the sun nears the western horizon, Maggie steals away to the cottage, and the lonely woman, waiting for her on the rude bench by the door, can tell her bounding footstep from all others which pass that way. She does not say much now, herself ; but the sound of Maggie's voice, talking to her in the gathering twilight, is the sweetest she has ever heard, and so she sits and listens, while her hands work nervously together, and her whole body trembles with the longing, intense desire she feels, to clasp the young girl to her bosom, and claim her as her own. But this she dare not do, for Madame Conway's training has had its effect, and in Maggie's bearing there is ever a degree of pride which forbids anything like undue familiarity. And it was this very *pride* which Hagar liked to see, whispering often to herself, " Warren *blood* and Conway *airs*—the two go well together."

Sometimes a *word* or a *look*, would make her start, they reminded her so forcibly of the dead ; and once she said involuntarily. " You are like your mother, Maggie. Exactly what she was at your age."

" My mother !" answered Maggie. You never talked to me of her. Tell me of her now, I did not suppose I was like her, in anything."

" Yes, in everything," said old Hagar, " the same dark eyes and hair, the same bright red cheeks, the same—"

" Why Hagar, what *can* you mean ?" interrupted Maggie. " My mother had light blue eyes and fair brown hair, like Theo. Grandma says I am not like her at all, while old Hannah, the cook, when she feels ill-natured, and wishes to tease me, says I am the very image of Hester Hamilton."

" And what if you are ? What if you are ?" eagerly rejoined old Hagar. " Would you feel badly, to know you looked like Hester ?" and the old woman bent anxiously forward, to hear the answer, " Not for myself, perhaps, provided Hester was *handsome*, for I think a good deal of beauty, that's a fact ; but it would annoy grandma terribly to have me look like a servant. She might fancy I was Hester's daughter, for she wonders every day where I get my low-bred ways, as she calls my liking to sing and laugh, and be natural."

" And s'posin' Hester was your mother, would you care ?" persisted Hagar.

" Of course I should," answered Maggie, her large eyes opening wide at the strange question. " I wouldn't for the whole world be anybody but Maggie Miller, just who I am

To be sure I get awfully out of patience with grandma, and Mrs. Jeffrey, for talking so much about *birth* and *blood* and *family*, and all that sort of nonsense, but after all, I wouldn't for anything be poor and work as poor folks do."

"I'll never tell her, never," muttered Hagar; and Maggie continued: "What a queer habit you have of talking to yourself. Did you always do so?"

"Not always. It came upon me with *the secret*," Hagar answered inadvertently; and eagerly catching at the last word, which to her implied a world of romance and mystery, Maggie exclaimed, "The *secret*, Hagar, the *secret !* If there's anything I delight in, it's a *secret !*" and sliding down from the rude bench to the grass plat at Hagar's feet, she continued: Tell it to me, Hagar, that's a dear old woman. I'll never tell anybody as long as I live. I won't upon my word," she continued, as she saw the look of horror resting on Hagar's face; "I'll help you to keep it, and we'll have such grand times talking it over. Did it concern yourself?" and Maggie folded her arms upon the lap of the old woman, who answered in a voice so hoarse and unnatural that Maggie involuntarily shuddered, "Old Hagar would die inch by inch sooner than tell you, Maggie Miller, her secret."

" Was it then so dreadful?" asked, Maggie half fearfully, and casting a stealthy glance at the dim woods, where the night shadows were falling, and whose winding path she must traverse alone, on her homeward route. " Was it then so dreadful?"

"Yes, dreadful, dreadful; and yet, Maggie, I have some times wished you knew it. You would forgive me, perhaps, if you knew how I was tempted," said Hagar, and her voice was full of yearning tenderness, while her bony fingers parted lovingly the shining hair from off the white brow of the young girl, who plead again, "Tell it to me, Hagar."

There was a fierce struggle in Hagar's bosom, but the night wind, moving through the hemlock boughs, seemed to say, "Not yet—not yet," and remembering her vow, she answered. "Leave me, Maggie Miller, I cannot tell *you* the secret. You of all others. You would hate me for it, and that I could not bear. Leave me alone, or the sight of you, so beautiful, pleading for my secret, will kill me dead."

There was command in the tones of her voice, and rising to her feet, Maggie walked away, with a dread feeling at her heart, a feeling which whispered vaguely to her of a *deed of blood ;* for what, save this, could thus affect old Hagar?— Her road home led near the little burying-ground, and impelled by something she could not resist, she paused at her mother's grave. The moonlight was falling softly upon it, and seating herself within the shadow of the monument, she sat a long time, thinking, not of the dead, but of Hagar and the strange words she had uttered. Suddenly, from the opposite side of the graveyard, there came a sound as of some one walking, and looking up, Maggie saw approaching her the bent figure of the old woman, who seemed unusually excited. Her first impulse was to fly, but knowing how improbable it was that Hagar should seek to do her harm, and thinking she might discover some clue to the mystery, if she remained, she sat still, while kneeling on Hester's grave, old Hagar wept bitterly, talking the while, but so incoherently that Maggie could distinguish nothing, save the words, "*You*, Hester, have forgiven me."

"Can it be that she has killed her own child !" thought Mag, and starting to her feet she stood face to face with Hagar, who screamed, "*You* here, Maggie Miller ! Here with the others who know my secret. But you shan't wring

it from me. You shall never know it, unless the dead rise
up to tell you."

"Hagar Warren," said Margaret sternly, "is *murder*
your secret? Did Hester Hamilton die at her mother's
hands?"

With a short gasping moan, Hagar staggered backward
a pace or two, and then standing far more erect than Margaret had ever seen her before, she answered, "No, Maggie
Miller, no; *murder* is *not* my secret. These hands," and she
tossed in the air her shrivelled arms, "these hands are as
free from blood as yours. And now go. Leave me alone
with my dead, and see that you tell no tales. You like
secrets, you say. Let what you have heard to-night, be *your*
secret. Go."

Maggie obeyed, and walked slowly homeward, feeling
greatly relieved that her suspicion was false, and experiencing a degree of satisfaction in thinking that she, too, had
a secret, which she would guard most carefully from her
grandmother and Theo. "She would never tell them what
she had seen and heard—never!"

Seated upon the piazza was Madam Conway and Theo,
the former of whom chided her for staying so late at the
cottage, while Theo asked what queer things the old witch-
woman had said to-night.

With a very expressive look, which seemed to say, "I
know, but I shan't tell," Maggie seated herself at her grandmother's feet, and asked, "how long Hagar had been crazy?
Did it come upon her when her daughter died?" she in
quired; and Madam Conway answered, "yes, about that
time, or more particularly when the baby died. Then she
began to act so strangely that I removed you from her care,
for, from something she said, I fancied she meditated harm
to you."

For a moment Maggie sat wrapt in thought—then clapping her hands together, she exclaimed—"I have it ; I know now what ails her. She felt so badly to see you happy with me, that she tried to *poison me.* She said she was sorely tempted—and that's the secret which is killing her."

"*Secret !* What secret ?" cried Theo ; and womanlike, forgetting her resolution not to *tell,* Mag told what she had seen and heard, adding as her firm belief that Hagar had made an attempt upon her life.

"I would advise you for the future to keep away from her, then," said Madam Conway, to whom the suggestion seemed a very probable one.

But Maggie knew full well that whatever Hagar might once have thought to do, there was no danger to be apprehended from her now, and the next day found her as usual on her way to the cottage. Bounding into the room where the old woman sat at her knitting, she exclaimed, "I know what it is ! I know your secret !"

There was a gathering mist before Hagar's eyes, and her face was deathly white, as she gasped, "*You* know the secret ! How ? where ? Have the dead come back to tell ? Did anybody see me do it ?"

"Why, no," answered Mag, beginning again to grow a little mystified. "The *dead* have nothing to do with it. You tried to poison me when I was a baby, and that's what makes you crazy. *Isn't* it so ? Grandma thought it was, when I told her how you talked last night."

There was a heavy load lifted from Hagar's heart, and she answered calmly, but somewhat indignantly, "So you *told*—I thought I could trust you, Maggie."

Instantly the tears came to Maggie's eyes, and, coloring crimson, she said : "I didn't mean to tell—indeed I didn't, but I forgot all about your charge. Forgive me, Hagar, do," and, sinking on the floor, she looked up in Hagar's face so pleadingly that the old woman was softened, and answered gently, "You are like the rest of your sex, Margaret. No woman but Hagar Warren ever kept a secret; and it's killing her, you see."

"Don't keep it then," said Mag. "Tell it to me. Confess that you tried to poison me because you envied grandma," and the soft eyes looked with an anxious, expectant expression into the dark, wild orbs of Hagar, who replied, "Envy was at the bottom of it all, but I never tried to harm *you*, Margaret, in any way. I only thought to do you good. You have not guessed it. You cannot, and you must not try."

"Tell it to me then. I want to know it *so* badly," persisted Mag, her curiosity each moment increasing.

"*Maggie Miller*," said old Hagar, and the knitting dropped from her fingers, which moved slowly on till they reached and touched the little snow-flake of a hand, resting on her knee; "Maggie Miller, if you knew that the telling of that secret would make you perfectly wretched, would you wish to hear it?"

For a moment Mag was silent, and then, half laughingly, she replied, "I'd risk it, Hagar, for I never wanted to know anything half so bad in all my life. Tell it to me, won't you?"

Very beautiful looked Maggie Miller then. Her straw flat sat jauntily on one side of her head, her glossy hair combed smoothly back, her soft lustrous eyes shining with eager curiosity, and her cheeks flushed with excitement. Very, very beautiful she seemed to the old woman, who, in her intense longing to take the bright creature to her bosom, was, for an instant sorely tempted.

"*Margaret!*" she began, and at the sound of her voice

the young girl shuddered involuntarily. "Margaret!" she said again, but ere another word was uttered, the autumn wind, which for the last half hour had been rising rapidly, came roaring down the wide-mouthed chimney, and the heavy fireboard fell upon the floor with a tremendous crash, nearly crushing old Hagar's foot, and driving for a time all thoughts of the secret from Maggie's mind. "Served me right," muttered Hagar, as Maggie left the room for water with which to bathe the swollen foot. "Served me right, and if *ever* I'm tempted to tell her again may every bone in my body be smashed!"

The foot was carefully cared for. Maggie's own hands tenderly bandaging it up, and then with redoubled zeal she returned to the attack, pressing old Hagar so hard that the large drops of perspiration gathered thickly about her forehead and lips, which were white as ashes. Wearied at last, Mag gave it up for the time being, but her curiosity was thoroughly aroused, and for many days she persisted in her importunity, until at last, in self defence, old Hagar, when she saw her coming, would steal away to the low roofed chamber, and hiding behind a pile of rubbish, would listen breathlessly, while Margaret hunted for her in vain. Then when she was gone, she would crawl out from her hiding-place, covered with cobwebs and dust, and muttering to herself, "I never expected this, and it's more than I can bear. Why will she torment me so, when a knowledge of the secret would drive her mad!"

This, however, Maggie Miller did not know. Blessed with an uncommon degree of curiosity, which increased each time she saw old Hagar, she resolved to solve the mystery, which she felt sure was connected with herself, though in what manner, she could not guess. "But I *will* know," she would say to herself, when returning from a fruitless quizzing of old Hagar, whose hiding-place she had at last discovered ; " I *will* know what 'tis about me. I shall never be *quite* happy till I do."

Ah, Maggie, Maggie, be happy while you can, and leave the secret alone. It will come to you soon enough—aye, soon enough.

CHAPTER V.

TRIFLES.

VERY rapidly the winter passed away, and one morning, early in March, Mag went down to the cottage with the news that Madam Conway was intending to start immediately for England, where she had business which would probably detain her until fall.

" Oh, won't I have fun in her absence !" she cried. " I'll visit every family in the neighborhood. Here she's kept Theo and me, caged up like two wild animals, and now I am going to see a little of the world. I don't mean to study a bit, and instead of visiting you once a day, I shall come at least *three times*."

" The Lord help me !" ejaculated old Hagar, who, much as she loved Maggie, was beginning to dread her daily visits."

" Why, do you want help ?" asked Maggie, laughingly. " Are you tired of me, Hagar ? Don't you like me any more ?"

" *Like you, Maggie Miller ! like you,*" repeated old Hagar, and in the tones of her voice there was a world of tenderness and love. " There is nothing on earth I love as I do you But you worry me to death sometimes."

" Oh, yes, I know," answered Mag ; ' but I'm not going to tease you awhile. I shall have so much else to do when grandma is gone, that I shall forget it. I wish she wasn't

so proud," she continued, after a moment. "I wish she'd
let Theo and me see a little more of the world than she
does. I wonder how she ever expects us to get married, or
be anybody, if she keeps us here in the woods like two
young savages. Why, as true as you live, Hagar, I have
never been anywhere in my life, except to church Sundays,
once to Douglas's store, in Worcester, once to Patty Thomp-
son's funeral, and once to a Methodist camp-meeting ; and
I never spoke to more than a dozen men besides the minister
and the school-boys. It's too bad !" and Maggie pouted
quite becomingly at the injustice done her by her grandmother in keeping her thus secluded. "Theo don't care,"
she said. "She is prouder than I am, and does not wish to
know the *Yankees*, as grandma calls the folks in this country ;
but I'm glad I am a Yankee. I wouldn't live in England
for anything."

"Why don't your gra' mother take you with her ?"
asked Hagar, who in r measure sympathized with Maggie
for being thus isolated.

"She says we are too young to go into society," answered
Mag. "It will be time enough two years hence, when I'm
eighteen and Theo twenty. Then I believe she intends taking us to London, where we can show off our accomplish-
ments, and practise that wonderful courtesy which Mrs.
Jeffrey has taught us. I daresay the queen will be astonished at our qualifications ;" and with a merry laugh, as she
thought of the appearance she should make at the Court of
St. James, Mag leaped on Gritty's back and bounded away,
while Hagar looked wistfully after her, saying as she wiped
the tears from her eyes, "Heaven bless the girl ! She
might sit on the throne of England any day, and Victoria
wouldn't disgrace herself at all by doing her reverence, even
if she be a child of Hagar Warren."

As Maggie had said, Madam Conway was going to England. At first, she thought of taking the young ladies with her, but, thinking they were hardly old enough yet to be emancipated from the school-room, she decided to leave them under the supervision of Mrs. Jeffrey, whose niece she promised to bring with her on her return from America. Upon her departure she bade Theo and Mag a most affectionate adieu, adding :

"Be good girls while I am away," keep in the house, mind Mrs. Jeffrey, and don't fall in love."

This last injunction came involuntarily from the old lady, to whom the idea of their falling in love was quite as preposterous as to themselves.

"Fall in love!" repeated Maggie, when her tears were dried, and she with Theo was driving slowly home. "What could grandma mean! I wonder who there is for us to love, unless it be John the coachman, or Bill the gardener. I 'most wish we could get in love though, just to see how 'twould seem, don't you?" she continued.

"Not with anybody *here*," answered Theo, her nose slightly elevated at the thoughts of people whom she had been educated to despise.

"Why not *here* as well as elsewhere?" asked Maggie. "I don't see any difference. But grandma needn't be troubled, for such things as men's boots never came near our house. I think it's a shame though," she continued, "that we don't know anybody, either male or female. Let's go down to Worcester, some day, and get acquainted. Don't you remember the two handsome young men whom we saw five years ago, in Douglas's store, and how they winked at each other when grandma ran down their goods, and said there were not any darning needles fit to use, this side of the water!"

On most subjects, Theo's memory was treacherous, but
she remembered perfectly well the two young men, particularly the taller one, who had given her a remnant of blue
ribbon, which he said was just the color of her eyes. Still,
the idea of going to Worcester did not strike her favorably.
"She wished Worcester would come to them," she said,
"but she should not dare to go there. They would surely
get lost. Grandma would not like it, and Mrs. Jeffrey
would not let them go, even if they wished."

"A fig for Mrs. Jeffrey," said Maggie. "I shan't mind
her much. I'm going to have a real good time, doing as I
please, and if you are wise, you'll have one too."

"I suppose I shall do what you tell me to—I always do,"
answered Theo, submissively, and there the conversation
ceased.

Arrived at home they found dinner awaiting them, and
Maggie, when seated, suggested to Mrs. Jeffrey that she
should give them a vacation of a few weeks, just long enough
for them to get rested and visit the neighbors. But this
Mrs. Jeffrey refused to do.

"She had her orders to keep them at their books," she
said, and "study was healthful ;" at the same time she bade
them be in the school-room on the morrow. There was a
wicked look in Maggie's eyes, but her tongue told no tales,
and when next morning she went with Theo, demurely to
the school-room, she seemed surprised at hearing from Mrs.
Jeffrey that every book had disappeared from the desk,
where they were usually kept ; and though the greatly disturbed and astonished lady had sought for them nearly an
hour, they were not to be found.

"Maggie has hidden them, I know," said Theo, as she
saw the mischievous look on her sister's face.

"Margaret wouldn't do such a thing, I'm sure," answered

Mrs. Jeffrey, her voice and manner indicating a little doubt, however, as to the truth of her assertion.

But Maggie had hidden them, and no amount of coaxing could persuade her to bring them back. "You refused me a vacation when I asked for it," she said, "so I'm going to have it perforce;" and playfully catching up the little dumpy figure of her governess, she carried her out upon the piazza, and seating her in a large easy-chair, bade her "take *snuff and comfort,* too, as long as she liked."

. Mrs. Jeffrey knew perfectly well that Maggie in reality was mistress of the house, that whatever she did Madam Conway would ultimately sanction ; and as a rest was by no means disagreeable, she yielded with a good grace, dividing her time between sleeping, snuffing and dressing, while Theo lounged upon the sofa and devoured some musty old novels, which Maggie, in her rummaging, had discovered.

Meanwhile Maggie kept her promise of visiting the neighbors, and almost every family had something to say in praise of the merry light-hearted girl, of whom they had heretofore known but little. Her favorite recreation, however, was riding on horseback, and almost every day she galloped through the woods and over the fields, usually terminating her ride with a call upon old Hagar, whom she still continued to tease unmercifully for the secret, and who was glad when at last an incident occurred which for a time drove all thoughts of the secret from Maggie's mind.

CHAPTER VI.

THE JUNIOR PARTNER.

ONE afternoon towards the middle of April, when Maggie as usual was flying through the woods, she paused for a moment beneath the shadow of a sycamore, while Gritty drank from a small running brook. The pony having quenched his thirst, she gathered up her reins for a fresh gallop, when her ear caught the sound of another horse's hoofs; and looking back, she saw approaching her at a rapid rate a gentleman whom she knew to be a stranger. Not caring to be overtaken, she chirruped to the spirited Gritty, who, bounding over the velvety turf, left the unknown rider far in the rear.

"Who can she be?" thought the young man, admiring the utter fearlessness with which she rode; then, feeling a little piqued, as he saw how the distance between them was increasing, he exclaimed, "be she woman, or be she witch, I'll overtake her," and whistling to his own fleet animal, he, too, dashed on at a furious rate.

"Trying to catch me, are you?" thought Maggie. "I'd laugh to see you do it," and entering at once into the spirit of the race, she rode on for a time with headlong speed— then, by way of tantalizing her pursuer, she paused for a moment until he had almost reached her, when at a peculiar whistle Gritty sprang forward, while Maggie's mocking laugh was borne back to the discomfited young man, whose

Interest in the daring girl increased each moment. It was a long, long chase she led him, over hills, across the plains, and through the grassy valley, until she stopped at last within a hundred yards of the deep, narrow gorge, through which the millstream ran.

"I have you now," thought the stranger, who knew by the dull, roaring sound of the water, that a chasm lay between him and the opposite bank.

But Maggie had not yet half displayed her daring feats of horsemanship, and when he came so near that his waving brown locks and handsome dark eyes were plainly discernible, she said to herself, "he rides tolerably well. I'll see how good he is at a leap," and, setting herself more firmly in the saddle, she patted Gritty upon the neck. The well trained animal understood the signal, and rearing high in the air, was fast nearing the bank, when the young man, suspecting her design, shrieked out, "Stop, lady, stop! It's madness to attempt it."

"Follow me if you can," was Maggie's defiant answer, and the next moment she hung in mid air over the dark abyss.

Involuntarily the young man closed his eyes, while his ear listened anxiously for the cry which would come next. But Maggie knew full well what she was doing. She had leaped that narrow gorge often, and now when the stranger's eyes unclosed, she stood upon the opposite bank, caressing the noble animal which had borne her safely there.

"It shall never be said that Henry Warner was beaten by a school-girl," muttered the stranger. "If *she* can clear that, I can, bad rider as I am!" and burying his spurs deep in the sides of his horse, he pressed on while Maggie held her breath in fear, for she knew that without practice no one could do what she had done.

11

There was a partially downward plunge—a fierce struggle on the shelving bank, where the animal had struck a few feet from the top,—then the steed stood panting on terra firma, while a piercing shriek broke the deep silence of the wood, and Maggie's cheeks blanched to a marble hue. The rider, either from dizziness or fear, had fallen at the moment the horse first struck the bank, and from the ravine below there came no sound to tell if yet he lived.

"He's dead ; he's dead !" cried Maggie. "'Twas my own foolishness which killed him," and springing from Gritty's back she gathered up her long riding skirt, and glided swiftly down the bank, until she came to a wide, projecting rock, where the stranger lay, motionless and still, his white face upturned to the sunlight, which came stealing down through the overhanging boughs. In an instant she was at his side, and his head was restng on her lap, while her trembling fingers parted back from his pale brow the damp mass of curling hair.

"The fall alone would not kill him," she said, as her eye measured the distance, and then she looked anxiously round for water, with which to bathe his face.

But water there was none, save in the stream below, whose murmuring flow fell mockingly on her ears, for it seemed to say she could not reach it. But Maggie Miller was equal to any emergency, and venturing out to the very edge of the rock, she poised herself on one foot, and looked down the dizzy height, to see if it were possible to descend.

"I can try at least," she said, and glancing at the pale face of the stranger, unhesitatingly resolved to attempt it

The descent was less difficult than she had anticipated, and in an incredibly short space of time, she was dipping her tasteful velvet cap in the brook, whose sparkling foam had never before been disturbed by the touch of a hand as soft and fair as hers. To ascend was not so easy a matter ; but chamois-like, Maggie's feet trod safely the dangerous path, and she soon knelt by the unconscious man, bathing his forehead in the clear cold water,. until he showed signs of returning life. His lips moved slowly, at last, as if he would speak ; and Maggie, bending low to catch the faint-est sound, heard him utter the name of " Rose." In Mag-gie's bosom, there was no feeling for the stranger, save that of pity, and yet, that one word " Rose," thrilled her with a strange undefinable emotion, awaking at once a yearning desire to know something of her who bore that beautiful name, and who, to the young man, was undoubtedly the one in all the world most dear.

" Rose," he said again, "·is it you ?" and his eyes, which opened slowly, scanned with an eager, questioning look, the face of Maggie, who, open-hearted and impulsive as usual, answered somewhat sadly : " I am nobody but Maggie Miller. I am not Rose, though I wish I was, if you would like to see her.

The tones of her voice recalled the stranger's wandering mind, and he answered : " Your voice is like Rose, but I would rather see *you*, Maggie Miller. I like your fearlessness, so unlike most of your sex. Rose is far, more gentle, more feminine than you, and if her very life depended upon it, she would never dare leap that gorge."

The young man intended no reproof ; but Maggie took his words as such,, and for the first time in her life, began to 'think that possibly her manner was not always as womanly as might be. At all events she was not like the gentle Rose, whom she instantly invested with every possible grace and beauty, wishing that she herself was like her, instead of the wild mad-cap she was. Then thinking her conduct required some apology, she answered, as none save one as fresh and ingemuous as Maggie Miller would have answered, "I don't know any better than to behave as I do. I've always lived in the woods—have never been to school a day in my life—never been anywhere except to camp meeting, and once to Douglas's store in Worcester!"

This was entirely a new phase of character to the man of the world, who laughed aloud, and at the mention of *Douglas's* store, started so quickly, that a spasm of pain distorted his features, causing Maggie to ask if he were badly hurt.

"Nothing but a broken leg," he answered ; and Maggie to whose mind broken bones conveyed a world of pain and suffering, replied. "Oh, *I am so sorry for you*, and it's my fault, too. Will you forgive me ?" and her little chubby hands clasped his so pleadingly, that raising himself upon his elbow, so as to obtain a better view of her bright face, he answered ; "I'd willingly break a hundred bones for the sake of meeting a girl like you, Maggie Miller."

Maggie was unused to flattery, save as it came from her grandmother, Theo, or old Hagar, and now paying no heed to his remark, she said, "Can you stay here alone, while I go for help? our house is not far away."

"I'd rather *you* would remain with me," he replied ; "but as you cannot do both, I suppose you must go."

"I shan't be gone long," said Maggie, "and I'll send old Hagar to keep you company ;" so saying, she climbed the bank, and mounting Gritty, who stood quietly awaiting her, she seized the other horse by the bridle, and rode swiftly away, leaving the young man to meditate upon the novel situation in which he had so suddenly been placed.

"Ain't I in a pretty predicament ?" said he, as he tried in vain to move his swollen limb, which was broken in two places, but which being partially benumbed, did not now pain him much. "But it serves me right for chasing a harum-scarum thing, when I ought to have been minding my own ousiness, and collecting bills for Douglas & Co. And she says she's been there, too. I wonder who she is, the handsome sprite. I believe I made her more than half jealous, talking of my golden-haired Rose ; but she is far more beautiful than Rose, more beautiful than any one I ever saw. I wish she'd come back again," and shutting his eyes, he tried to recall the bright, animated face, which had so lately bent anxiously above him. "She tarries long," he said, at last, beginning to grow uneasy. "I wonder how far it is, and where the deuce can this old Hagar be, of whom she spoke."

"She's here," answered a shrill voice, and looking up, he saw before him the bent form of Hagar Warren, at whose door Maggie had paused for a moment, while she told of the accident, and begged of Hagar to hasten.

Accordingly, equipped with a blanket and pillow, a brandy bottle and the camphor, old Hagar had come, but when she offered the latter for the young man's acceptance, he pushed it from him, saying, "Camphor was his detestation, but he shouldn't object particularly to smelling of the other bottle !"

"No you don't," said Hagar, who thought him in not quite so deplorable a condition as she had expected to find him. "My creed is never to give young folks brandy. except in cases of emergency ; so saying she made him more comfortable by placing a pillow beneath his head, and then thinking possibly, that this, to herself, was "a case of emergency," she withdrew to a little distance, and sitting down upon the gnarled roots of an upturned tree, drank a swallow of the old Cognac, while the young man, maimed and disabled, looked wistfully at her !

Not that he cared for the brandy, of which he seldom

tasted ; but he needed something to relieve the deathlike
faintness which occasionally came over him, and which old
Hagar, looking only at his mischievous eyes, failed to
observe.   Only those who knew Henry Warner intimately
gave him credit for the many admirable qualities he really
possessed ; so full was he of *fun*.   It was in his merry eyes,
and about his quizzically-shaped mouth, that the principal
difficulty lay ; and most persons, seeing him for the first
time, fancied that, in some way, he was making sport of
them.   This was old Hagar's impression, as she sat there in
dignified silence, rather enjoying, than otherwise, the occasional groans which came from his white lips.   There were
intervals, however, when he was comparatively free from
pain, and these he improved by questioning her with regard
to Maggie, asking who she was, and where she lived.

"She is *Maggie Miller*, and she lives in a *house*," answered
the old woman, rather pettishly.

"Ah, indeed—snappish are you?" said the young man,
attempting to turn himself a little, the better to see his companion.   "Confound that leg !" he continued, as a fierce
twinge gave him warning not to try many experiments.   "I
know her name is Maggie Miller, and I supposed she lived
in a house ; but who is she, any way, and what is she?"

"If you mean is she *anybody*, I can answer that question
quick," returned Hagar.   "She calls Madam Conway her
grandmother, and Madam Conway came from one of the
best families in England—that's who she is ; and as to what
she is, she's the finest, handsomest, smartest girl in
America ; and as long as old Hagar Warren lives, no city
chap with strapped down pantaloons and sneering mouth is
going to fool with her either !"

"Confound my mouth !   It's always getting me into
trouble," thought the stranger, trying in vain to smooth

down the corners of the offending organ, which in spite of him would curve with what Hagar called a sneer, and from which there finally broke a merry laugh, sadly at variance with the suffering expression of his face.

"Your leg must hurt you mightily, the way you go on," muttered Hagar, and the young man answered : "It does almost murder me, but when a laugh is in a fellow, he can't help letting it out, can he? But where the plague can that witch of a——I beg your pardon, Mrs. Hagar," he added hastily, as he saw the frown settling on the old woman's face, "I mean to say where can Miss Miller be? I shall faint away unless she comes soon, or you give me a taste of the brandy!"

This time there was something in the tone of his voice which prompted Hagar to draw near, and she was about to offer him the brandy, when Maggie appeared, together with three men, bearing a litter, or small cot-bed. The sight of her produced a much better effect upon him than Hagar's brandy would have done, and motioning the old woman aside, he declared himself ready to be removed.

"Now, John, do pray be careful and not hurt him much," cried Maggie, as she saw how pale and faint he was, while even Hagar forgot the curled lip, which the young man bit until the blood started through, so intense was his agony when they lifted him upon the litter. "The camphor, Hagar, the camphor," said Maggie, and the stranger did not push it aside when her hand poured it on his head ; but the laughing eyes, now dim with pain, smiled gratefully upon her, and the quivering lips once murmured as she walked beside him, "Heaven bless you, Maggie Miller!"

Arrived at Hagar's cottage, the old woman suggested that he be carried in there, saying as she met Maggie's questioning glance, "I can take care of him better than any one else."

The pain by this time was intolerable, and scarcely know-ing what he said, the stranger whispered, "Yes, yes, leave me here."

For a moment the bearers paused, while Maggie, bending over the wounded man, said softly. "Can't you bear it a little longer, until our house is reached? You'll be more comfortable there. Grandma has gone to England, and I'll take care of you myself!"

This last was perfectly in accordance with Maggie's frank, impulsive character, and it had the desired effect. Henry Warner would have borne almost death itself for the sake of being nursed by the young girl beside him, and he signi-fied his willingness to proceed, while at the same time his hand involuntarily grasped that of Maggie, as if in the touch of her snowy fingers there were a mesmeric power to soothe his pain. In the meantime a hurried consultation had been held between Mrs. Jeffrey and Theo, as to the room suitable for the stranger to be placed in.

"It's not likely he is much," said Theo, "and if grandma were here I presume she would assign him the chamber over the kitchen. The wall is low on one side I know, but I dare say he is not accustomed to anything better."

Accordingly several articles of stray lumber were removed from the chamber, which the ladies arranged with care, and which, when completed, presented quite a respectable appear-ance. But Maggie had no idea of putting her guest, as she considered him, in the kitchen chamber; and when, as the party entered the house, Mrs. Jeffrey, from the head of the stairs, called out, "This way, Maggie, tell them to come this way," she waved her aside, and led the way to a large airy room over the parlor, where, in a high, old fashioned bed, surrounded on all sides by heavy damask curtains, they laid the weary stranger. The village surgeon arriving soon after, the fractured bones were set, and then, as perfect quiet seemed necessary, the room was vacated by all save Maggie, who glided noiselessly around the apartment, while the eyes of the sick man followed her with eager, admiring glances, so beautiful she looked to him in her new capacity of nurse.

Henry Warner, as the stranger was called, was the junior partner of the firm of Douglas & Co., Worcester, and his object in visiting the Hillsdale neighborhood was to collect several bills which for a long time had been due. He had left the cars at the depot, and hiring a livery horse was taking the shortest route from the east side of town to the west, when he came accidentally upon Maggie Miller, and as we have seen, brought his ride to a sudden close. All this he told to her on the morning following the accident, retaining until the last the name of the firm of which he was a member.

"And you were once there at our store," he said. "How long ago?"

"Five years" answered Maggie, "when I was eleven, and Theo thirteen;" then, looking earnestly at him she exclaimed, "and you are the very one, the clerk with the *saucy eyes* whom grandma disliked so much, because she thought he made fun of her; but we didn't think so—Theo and I," she added hastily, as she saw the curious expression on Henry's mouth, and fancied he might be displeased. "We liked them both very much, and knew they must of course be annoyed with grandma's English whims."

For a moment the saucy eyes studied intently the fair girlish face of Maggie Miller, then slowly closed, while a train of thought something like the following passed through the young man's mind; "a woman and yet a perfect child, innocent and unsuspecting as little Rose herself It one

11*

respect they are alike, knowing no evil and expecting none ;
and if I, Henry Warner, do aught by thought or deed to
injure this young girl, may I never again look on the light
of day or breathe the air of heaven."

The vow had passed his lips. Henry Warner never broke
his word, and henceforth Maggie Miller was as safe with
him as if she had been an only and well beloved sister.
Thinking him to be asleep, Maggie started to leave the
room, but he called her back, saying. "Don't go ; stay
with me, won't you ?"

"Certainly," she answered, drawing a chair to the bedside.
"I supposed you were sleeping."

"I was not," he replied. "I was thinking of you and of
Rose. Your voices are much alike. I thought of it yesterday when I lay upon the rock."

"Who is *Rose*?" trembled on Maggie's lips, while at the
sound of that name, she was conscious of the same undefinable emotion she had once before experienced. But the question was not asked. "If she were his sister he would tell
me," she thought ; "and if she is not his sister "——

She did not finish the sentence, neither did she understand that if Rose to him was something dearer than a
sister, she, Maggie Miller, did not care to know it.

"Is she beautiful as her name, this Rose?" she asked at
last.

"She is beautiful, but not so beautiful as you. There are
few who are," answered Henry ; and his eyes fixed themselves upon Maggie, to see how she would bear the compliment.

But she scarcely heeded it, so intent was she upon knowing something more of the mysterious Rose. "She is beautiful, you say. Will you tell me how she looks ?" she continued ; and Henry Warner answered, " she is a frail, deli

cate little creature, almost dwarfish in size, but perfect in form and feature."

Involuntarily Maggie shrunk back in her chair, wishing her own queenly form had been a very trifle shorter, while Mr. Warner continued, "She has a sweet, angel face, Maggie, with eyes of lustrous blue, and curls of golden hair."

"You must love her very dearly," said Maggie, the tone of her voice indicating a partial dread of what the answer might be.

"I do indeed love her," was Mr. Warner's reply, " love her better than all the world beside. And she has made me what I am ; but for her, I should have been a worthless dissipated fellow. It's my natural disposition ; but Rose has saved me, and I almost worship her for it. She is my good angel—my darling—my "——

Here he paused abruptly, and leaning back upon his pillows rather enjoyed than otherwise the look of disappointment plainly visible on Maggie's face. She had fully expected to learn who Rose was ; but this knowledge he purposely kept from her. It did not need a very close observer of human nature, to read at a glance the ingenuous Maggie, whose speaking face betrayed all she felt. She was unused to the world. He was the first young gentleman whose acquaint-she had ever made, and he knew that she already felt for him a deeper interest than she supposed. To increase this interest was his object, and this he thought to do by withholding from her, for a time, a knowledge of the relation existing between him and the Rose of whom he had talked so much. The ruse was successful, for during the remainder of the day, thoughts of the golden-haired Rose were running through Maggie's mind, and it was late that night ere she could compose herself to sleep, so absorbed was she in wondering "*what* Rose was to Henry Warner. Not that she cared particularly," she tried to persuade herself; "but she would like to be at ease upon that subject."

To Theo she had communicated the fact, that their guest was a partner of Douglas & Co. and this tended greatly to raise the young man in the estimation of a young lady like Theo Miller. Next to rank and station *money* was with her the one thing necessary to make a person *somebody*. Douglas, she had heard, was an immensely wealthy man; possibly the junior partner was wealthy, too ; and if so, the parlor chamber, to which she had at first objected, was none too good for his aristocratic bones. She would go herself and see him in the morning.

Accordingly, on the morning of the second day she went with Maggie to the sick room, speaking to the stranger for the first time ; but keeping still at a respectful distance, until she should know something definite concerning him.

"We have met before, it seems," he said, after the first interchange of civilities was over ; "but I did not think our acquaintance would be renewed in this manner."

No answer from Theo, who, like many others, had taken a dislike to his *mouth,* and felt puzzled to know whether he intended ridiculing her or not.

"I have a distinct recollection of your grandmother," he continued, "and now I think of it, I believe Douglas has once or twice mentioned the elder of the two girls. That must be you ?" and he looked at Theo, whose face brightened perceptibly

"*Douglas,*" she repeated. "He is the owner of the store, and the one I saw, with black eyes and black hair was only a clerk."

"The veritable man himself," cried Mr. Warner. "George Douglas, the *senior partner* of the firm, said by some to be worth two hundred thousand dollars, and only twenty-eight years old, and the best fellow in the world, except that he pretends to dislike women."

By this time, Theo's proud blue eyes shone with delight, and when, after a little further conversation, Mr. Warner expressed a wish to write to his partner, she brought her own rose-wood writing-desk for him to use, and then seating herself by the window, waited until the letter was written.

"What shall I say for you, Miss Theo?" he asked, near the close ; and coloring slightly, she answered, " Invite him to come out and see you."

"Oh, that will be grand!" cried Maggie, who was far more enthusiastic, though not more anxious than her sister.

Of *her*, Henry Warner did not ask any message. He would not have written it had she sent one ; and folding the letter, after adding Theo's invitation, he laid it aside.

"I must write to Rose next," he said, "'Tis a whole week since I have written, and she has never been so long without hearing from me."

Instantly there came a shadow over Maggie's face, while Theo, less scrupulous, asked, " who Rose was."

"A very dear friend of mine," said Henry, and, as Mrs. Jeffrey just then sent for Theo, Maggie was left with him alone.

"Wait one moment," she said, as she saw him about to commence the letter. "Wait till I bring you a sheet of gilt-edged paper. It is more worthy of Rose, I fancy, than the plainer kind."

"Thank you," he said. "I will tell her of your suggestion."

The paper was brought, and then seating herself by the window, Maggie looked out abstractedly, seeing nothing, and hearing nothing save the sound of the pen, as it wrote down words of love, for the gentle Rose. It was not a long epistle ; and, as at the close of the Douglas letter he had asked a message from Theo, so now at the close of this, he claimed one from Maggie.

"What shall I say for you?" he asked ; and coming toward him, Margaret answered, "Tell her I love her, though I don't know who she is !"

"Why have you never asked me?" queried Henry, and coloring crimson, Maggie answered hesitatingly, "I thought you would tell me if you wished me to know."

"Read this letter and that will explain who she is," the young man continued, offering the letter to Maggie, who, grasping it eagerly, sat down opposite, so that every motion of her face was visible to him.

The letter was as follows :

"MY DARLING LITTLE ROSE :

"Do you fancy some direful calamity has befallen me, because I have not written to you for more than a week? Away with your fears, then, for nothing worse has come upon me than a badly broken limb, which will probably keep me a prisoner here for two months or more. Now don't be frightened, Rosa. I am not crippled for life, and even if I were, I could love you just the same, while you, I'm sure, would love me more.

' As you probably know, I left Worcester on Tuesday morning for the purpose of collecting some bills in this neighborhood. Arrived at Hillsdale I procured a horse, and was sauntering leisurely through the woods, when I came suddenly upon a *flying witch* in the shape of a beautiful young girl. She was the finest rider I ever saw, and such a chase as she led me, until at last, to my dismay, she leaped across a chasm, down which a nervous little creature like you would be afraid to look. Not wishing to be out-done, I followed her, and, as a matter of course, broke my bones.

"Were it not that the accident will somewhat incommode Douglas, and greatly fidget you, I should not much regret it, for to me there is a peculiar charm about this old stone house and its quaint surroundings. But the greatest charm of all, perhaps, lies in my fair nurse, Maggie Miller, for whom I risked my neck. You two would be fast friends in a mo-ment, and yet you are totally dissimilar, save that your voices are much alike.

"Write to me, soon, dear Rose, and believe me ever

"Your affectionate brother,

"HENRY."

"Oh," said Maggie, catching her breath, which for a time had been partially suspended, "Oh ;" and in that sin-gle monosyllable, there was to the young man watching her, a world of meaning. "She's your *sister*, this little Rose ;" and the soft dark eyes, flashed brightly upon him.

"What did you suppose her to be?" he asked, and Mag-gie answered, "I thought she might be your wife, though I should rather have her for a sister, if I were you."

The young man smiled involuntarily, thinking to himself how his fashionable city friends would be shocked at such perfect frankness, which meant no more than their own studied airs.

"You are a good girl, Maggie," he said, at last, "and I would not for the world deceive you ; Rose is my step-sister. We are in no way connected save by a marriage, still I love her all the same. We were brought up together by a lady who is aunt to both, and Rose seems to me like an own dear sister. She has saved me from almost everything. I once loved the wine cup ; but her kindly words and gentle influence won me back, so that now I seldom taste it. And once I thought to run away to sea, but Rose found it out, and meeting me at the gate, persuaded me to return. It is wonderful, the influence she has over me, keeping my wild spirits in check, and if I am ever anything, I shall owe it all to her."

"Does she live in Worcester ?" asked Maggie ; and Henry answered, "No, in Leominster, which is not far distant. I go home once a month, and I fancy I can see Rose now, just as she looks when she comes tripping down the walk to meet me, her blue eyes shining like stars, and her golden curls blowing over her pale forehead. She is very, very frail : and sometimes when I look upon her, the dread fear steals over me, that there will come a time, ere long, when I shall have no sister."

There were tears in Maggie's eyes, tears for the fair young girl whom she had never seen, and she felt a yearning desire to look once on the beautiful face of her whom Henry War-ner called his sister. "I wish she would come here, I want to see her," she said, at last, and Henry replied, "She does not go often from home. But I have her daguerreo-type in Worcester. I'll write to Douglas to bring it," and opening the letter, which was not yet sealed, he added a few lines. "Come, Maggie," he said, when this was finished, "you need exercise. Suppose you ride over to the office with these letters."

Maggie would rather have remained with him : but she expressed her willingness to go, and in a few moments was seated on Gritty's back, with the two letters clasped firmly in her hand. At one of these, the one bearing the name of *Rose Warner*, she looked often and wistfully ; "'twas a most beautiful name," she thought, "and she who bore it was beautiful too." And then there arose within her a wish, shadowy and undefined to herself, it is true—but still a wish that she, Maggie Miller, might one day call that gentle Rose her *sister*. "I shall see her sometimes, any way, she thought, "and this George Douglas, too. I wish they'd visit us together," and having by this time reached the post office, she deposited the letters, and galloped rapidly toward home.

CHAPTER VII.

THE SENIOR PARTNER.

THE large establishment of Douglas & Co. was closed for the night. The clerks had gone each to his own place; old Safford, the poor relation, the man of all work, who attended faithfully to everything, groaning often and praying oftener, over the careless habits of "the boys," as he called the two young men, his employers, had sought his comfortless bachelor attic, where he slept always with one ear open, listening for any burglarious sound which might come from the store below, and which had it come to him listening thus, would have frightened him half to death. George Douglas, too, the senior partner of the firm, had retired to his own room, which was far more elegantly furnished than that of the old man in the attic, and now in a velvet easy chair, he sat reading the letter from Hillsdale, which had arrived that evening, and a portion of which we subjoin for the reader's benefit.

After giving an account of his accident, and the manner in which it occurred, Warner continued:

"They say 'tis a mighty bad wind which blows no one any good, and so, though I verily believe I suffer all a man can suffer with a broken bone, yet, when I look at the fair face of Maggie Miller, I feel that I would not exchange this high old bed, to enter which, needs a short ladder, even for a seat by you on that three-legged stool, behind the old writing-desk. I never saw anything like her in my life. Everything she thinks, she says, and as to flattering her, it can't be done. I've told her a dozen times at least that she was beautiful, and she didn't mind it any more than Rose does, when I flatter her. Still, I fancy if I were to talk to her of love, it might make a difference, and perhaps I shall, ere I leave the place.

"You know, George, I have always insisted there was but one female in the world fit to be a *wife*, and as that one was my sister, I should probably never have the pleasure of paying any bills for *Mrs. Henry Warner ;* but I've half changed my mind, and I'm terribly afraid this Maggie Miller, not content with breaking my bones, has made sad work with another portion of the body, called by physiologists, the heart. I don't know how a man feels when he is in love ; but when this Maggie Miller looks me straight in the face with her sunshiny eyes, while her little soft white hand pushes back my hair (which by the way, I slily disarrange on purpose) I feel the blood tingle to the ends of my toes, and still I dare not hint such a thing to her. 'Twould frighten her off in a moment, and she'll send in her place either an old hag of a woman, called Hagar, or her proud sister Theo, whom I cannot endure.

"By the way, George, this Theo will just suit you, who are fond of aristocracy. She's proud as Lucifer, thinks because she was born in England, and sprung from a high family, that there is no one in America worthy of her ladyship's notice, unless indeed they chance to have money. You ought to have seen how her eyes lighted up when I told her you were said to be worth $200,000. She told me directly to invite you out here, and this, I assure you, was a good deal for her to do. So don your best attire, not forgetting the diamond cross, and come for a day or two. Old Saf

ford will attend to the store.   It's what he was made for,
and he likes it.   But as I am a *Warner*, so shall I do my
duty, and *warn* you not to meddle with *Maggie*.   She is my
own exclusive property, and altogether too good for a
worldly fellow like you.   *Theo* will suit you better.   She's
just aristocratic enough in her nature.   I don't see how the
two girls come to be so wholly unlike as they are.   Why,
I'd sooner take Maggie for Rose's sister, than for Theo's.

" Bless me, I had almost forgotten to ask if you remember that stiff old English woman, with the snuff-colored
satin, who came to our store some five years ago, and found
so much fault with *Yankee goods* as she called them?   If
you have forgotten her, you surely remember the two girls
in flats, one of whom seemed so much distressed at her
grandmother's remarks.   *She*, the distressed one, was
Maggie ; the other was Theo, and the old lady was Madam
Conway, who, luckily for me, chances at this time to be in
England, buying up goods I presume.   Maggie says that
this trip to Worcester, together with a camp-meeting held
in the Hillsdale woods last year, is the extent of her travels,
and one would think so to see her.   A perfect child of
nature, full of fun, beautiful as a Hebe and possessing the
kindest heart in the world.   If you wish to know more of
her, come and see for yourself, but again I warn you, hands
off ; nobody is to flirt with her but myself, and it is very
doubtful whether even I can do it peaceably, for that old
Hagar, who by the way is a curious specimen, gave me to
understand when I lay on the rock, with her sitting by as
a sort of ogress, that so long as she lived no city chap with
strapped pants (do, pray, bring me a pair, George, without
straps !) and sneering mouth was going to fool with Mar
garet Miller.

" So you see my mouth is at fault again.   Hang it all, I

can't imagine what ails it that everybody should think I'm
making fun of them. Even old Safford mutters about my
making mouths at *him* when I haven't thought of him in a
month! Present my compliments to the old gentleman,
and tell him one of 'the boys' thinks seriously of following
his advice, which you know is 'to sow our wild oats and
get a wife.' Do pray come, for I am only half myself
without you.

"Yours in the brotherhood,

"HENRY WARNER."

For a time after reading the above, George Douglas sat
wrapt in thought, then bursting into a laugh as he thought
now much the letter was like the jovial, light-hearted fellow
who wrote it, he put it aside, and leaning back in his chair
mused long and silently, not of *Theo*, but of *Maggie*, half
wishing he were in Warner's place instead of being there in
the dusty city. But as this could not be, he contented himself with thinking that at some time not far distant he would
visit the old stone house—would see for himself this wonderful *Maggie*—and, though he had been warned against it,
would possibly win her from his friend, who, unconsciously
perhaps, had often crossed his path, watching him jealously
lest he should look too often and too long upon the fragile
Rose, blooming so sweetly in her bird's-nest of a home 'mong
the tall old trees of Leominster.

"But he need not fear," he said somewhat bitterly, "he
need not fear for her, for it is over now. She has refused
me, this Rose Warner, and though it touched my pride to
hear her tell me *no*, I cannot hate her for it. 'She had
given her love to another,' she said, and Warner is blind or
crazy that he does not see the truth. But it is not for me
to enlighten him. He may call her sister if he likes, though

there is no tie of blood between them. I'd far rather it
would be thus, than something nearer;" and slowly rising
up, George Douglas retired to dream of a calm, almost heavenly face, which but the day before had been bathed in
tears as he told to Rose Warner the story of his love.
Mingled too with that dream was another face, a laughing,
sparkling, merry face, upon which no man ever yet had
looked and escaped with a whole heart.

The morning light dispelled the dream, and when in the
store old Safford inquired "what news from the boy?" the
senior partner answered gravely that he was lying among
the Hillsdale hills, with a broken leg caused by a fall from
his horse.

"Always was a careless rider," muttered old Safford,
mentally deploring the increased amount of labor which
would necessarily fall upon him, but which he performed
without a word of complaint.

The fair May blossoms were faded, and the last June
roses were blooming ere George Douglas found time or inclination to accept the invitation indirectly extended to him
by Theo Miller. Rose Warner's refusal had affected him
more than he chose to confess, and the wound must be
slightly healed ere he could find pleasure in the sight of
another. Possessed of many excellent qualities, he had unfortunately fallen into the error of thinking that almost
any one whom he should select would take him for his
money. And when Rose Warner, sitting by his side in the
shadowy twilight, had said, "I cannot be your wife," the
shock was sudden and hard to bear. But the first keen bitterness was over now, and remembering "the wild girls of
the woods," as he mentally styled both Theo and Maggie,
he determined at last to see them for himself.

Accordingly, on the last day of June, he started for Hills

dale, where he intended to remain until after the 4th. To find the old house was an easy matter, for almost every one in town was familiar with its locality, and towards the close of the afternoon, he found himself upon its broad steps applying vigorous strokes to the ponderous brass knocker, and half hoping the summons would be answered by Maggie herself. But it was not, and in the bent, white-haired woman who came with measured footsteps we recognize old Hagar, who spent much of her time at the house, and who came to the door in compliance with the request of the young ladies, both of whom, from an upper window, were curiously watching the stranger.

"Just the old witch one would expect to find in this out of the way place," thought Mr. Douglas, while at the same time he asked "if this were Madam Conway's residence, and if a young man by the name of Warner were staying here?"

"Another city beau!" muttered Hagar, as she answered in the affirmative, and ushered him into the parlor. "Another city beau—there'll be high carryings on now, if he's anything like the other one, who's come mighty nigh turning the house upside down."

"What did you say?" asked George Douglas, catching the sound of her muttering, and thinking she was addressing himself.

"I wasn't speaking to you. I was talking to a likelier person," answered old Hagar, in an under tone, as she shuffled away in quest of Henry Warner, who by this time was able to walk with the help of a cane.

The meeting between the young men was a joyful one, for though George Douglas was a little sore on the subject of Rose, he would not suffer a matter like that to come between him and Henry Warner, whom he had known and liked from boyhood. Henry's first inquiries were naturally of a business character, and then George Douglas spoke of the young ladies, saying he was only anxious to see *Mag*, for he knew of course, he should dislike the other.

Such, however, is wayward human nature, that the fair, pale face, and quiet, dignified manner of Theo Miller had greater attractions for a person of George Douglas's peculiar temperament than had the dashing, brilliant Mag. There was a resemblance, he imagined, between Theo and Rose, and this of itself was sufficient to attract him towards her. Theo, too, was equally pleased ; and when, that evening, Madam Jeffrey faintly interposed her fast departing authority, telling her quondam pupils it was time they were asleep, Theo did not, as usual, heed the warning, but sat very still beneath the vine-wreathed portico, listening while George Douglas told her of the world which she had never seen. She was not proud towards him, for he possessed the charm of money, and as he looked down upon her, conversing with him so familiarly, he wondered how Henry could have called *her cold and haughty*—she was merely *dignified, high-bred*, he thought, and George Douglas liked anything which savored of aristocracy.

Meanwhile, Henry and Mag had wandered to a little summer-house, where, with the bright moonlight falling upon them, they sat together, but not exactly as of old, for Maggie did not now look up into his face as she was wont to do, and if she thought his eye was resting upon her, she moved uneasily, while the rich blood deepened on her cheek. A change has come over Maggie Miller ; it is the old story, too—old to hundreds of thousands, but new to her, the blushing maiden. Theo calls her *nervous*—Mrs. Jeffrey calls her *sick*—the servants call her *mighty queer*—while old Hagar, hovering ever near, and watching her with a jealous eye, knows *she is in love*.

Faithfully and well had Hagar studied Henry Warner, to see if there were aught in him of evil; and though he was not what she would have chosen for the queenly Mag, she was satisfied if Margaret loved him and he loved Margaret. "But did he? He had never told her so;" and in Hagar Warren's wild black eyes, there was a savage gleam, as she thought, "he'll rue the day that he dares trifle with Maggie Miller."

But Henry Warner was not trifling with her. He was only waiting a favorable opportunity for telling her the story of his love; and now, as they sit together in the moonlight, with the musical flow of the millstream falling on his ear, he essays to speak—to tell how she has grown into his heart; to ask her to go with him where he goes; to make his home her home, and so be with him always; but ere the first word was uttered, Maggie asked if Mr. Douglas had brought the picture of his sister.

"Why, yes," he answered, "I had forgotten it entirely. Here it is;" and taking it from his pocket, he passed it to her.

It was a face of almost ethereal loveliness, which through the moonlight looked up to Maggie Miller, and again she experienced the same undefinable emotion, a mysterious, invisible something, drawing her towards the original of the beautiful likeness.

"It is strange how thoughts of Rose always affect me," she said, gazing earnestly upon the large eyes of blue, shadowed forth upon the picture. "It seems as though she must be nearer to me than an unknown friend."

"Seems she like a sister?" asked Henry Warner, coming so near that Maggie felt his warm breath upon her cheek.

"Yes, yes, that's it," she answered, with something of her olden frankness. "And had I somewhere in the world an unknown sister, I should say it was Rose Warner!"

12

There were a few low, whispered words, and when the full moon which for a time, had hidden itself behind the clouds, again shone forth in all its glory, Henry had asked Maggie Miller to be the sister of Rose Warner, and Maggie had answered "yes !"

That night, in Maggie's dreams, there was a strange commingling of thought. Thoughts of Henry Warner, as he told her of his love—thoughts of the gentle girl whose eyes of blue had looked so lovingly up to her, as if between them there was indeed a common bond of sympathy—and stranger far than all, thoughts of the little grave beneath the pine, where slept the so-called child of Hester Hamilton —the child defrauded of its birth-right, and who, in the misty vagaries of dreamland, seemed alone to stand between her and the beautiful Rose Warner !

CHAPTER VIII.

STARS AND STRIPES.

On the rude bench by her cabin door, sat Hagar Warren, her black eyes peering out into the woods, and her quick ear turned to catch the first sound of bounding footsteps, which came at last, and Maggie Miller was sitting by her side.

"What is it, darling?" Hagar asked, and her shrivelled hand smoothed, caressingly, the silken hair, as she looked into the glowing face of the young girl and half guessed what was written there.

To Theo, Mag had whispered the words, "I am engaged," and Theo had coldly answered, "Pshaw? Grandma will quickly break that up. Why, Henry Warner is comparatively poor. Mr. Douglas told me so, or rather I quizzed him until I found it out. He says, though, that Henry has rare business talents, and he could not do without him."

To the latter part of Theo's remark, Maggie paid little heed; but the mention of her grandmother troubled her. She would oppose it, Mag was sure of that, and it was to talk on this very subject she had come to Hagar's cottage.

"Just the way I s'posed it would end," said Hagar, when Mag, with blushing, half-averted face, told the story of her engagement; "Just the way I s'posed 'twould end, but I didn't think 'twould be so quick."

"Two months and a half is a great while, and then we have been together so much," replied Maggie, at the same time asking if Hagar did not approve her choice.

"Henry Warner's well enough," answered Hagar. "I've watched him close and see no evil in him; but he isn't the one for you, nor are you the one for him. You are both too wild, too full of fun, and if yoked together will go to destruction, I know. You need somebody to hold you back, and so does he."

Involuntarily, Maggie thought of Rose, mentally resolving to be, if possible, more like her.

"You are not angry with me?" said Hagar, observing Maggie's silence. "You asked my opinion, and I gave it to you. You are too young to know who you like. Henry Warner is the first man you ever knew, and, in two years' time you'll tire of him."

"Tire of him, Hagar? Tire of Henry Warner!" cried Mag, a little indignantly. "You do not know me, if you think I'll ever tire of him; and then, too, did I tell you grandma keeps writing to me about a Mr. Carrollton, who she says is wealthy, fine looking, highly educated, and very aristocratic, and that last makes me hate him! I've heard so much about aristocracy, that I'm sick of it, and just for that reason I would not have this Mr. Carrollton, if I knew he'd make me Queen of England. But grandma's heart is set upon it, I know, and she thinks of course he would marry me—says he is delighted with my daguerreotype—that awful one, too, with the staring eyes. In grandma's last letter, he sent me a note. 'Twas beautifully written, and I dare say he is a fine young man, at least he talks *common sense*, but I shan't answer it; and if you'll believe me, I used part of it in lighting Henry's cigar, and with the rest I shall light *fire-crackers* on the 4th of July; Henry has bought a lot of them, and we're going to have fun. How grandma would scold!—-but I shall marry Henry Warner, any way. Do you think she will oppose me, when she sees how determined I am?"

"Of course she will," answered Hagar, "I know these Carrolltons; they are a haughty race, and if your grandmother has one of them in view she'll turn you from her door sooner than see you married to another, and an American, too."

There was a moment's silence, and then with an unnatural gleam in her eye, old Hagar turned towards Mag, and grasping her shoulder, said, "If she does this thing, Maggie Miller—if she casts you off, will you take *me* for your grandmother? Will you let *me* live with you? I'll be your drudge, your slave; say, Maggie, may I go with you? Will you call *me* grandmother? I'd willingly die if only once I could hear you speak to me 'thus, and know it was in love."

For a moment Mag looked at her in astonishment; then thinking to herself, "She surely is half-crazed," she answered laughingly, "Yes, Hagar, if grandma casts me off, you may go with me. I shall need your care, but I can't promise to call you *grandma*, because you know you are not."

The corners of Hagar's mouth worked nervously, but her teeth shut firmly over the thin, white lip, forcing back the wild words trembling there, and the secret was not told.

"Go home, Maggie Miller," she said, at last, rising slowly to her feet. "Go home now, and leave me alone. I am willing you should marry Henry Warner, nay, I wish you to do it; but you must remember your promise."

Maggie was about to answer, when her thoughts were directed to another channel by the sight of George Douglas and Theo, coming slowly down the shaded pathway, which led past Hagar's door. Old Hagar saw them, too, and, whispering to Maggie, said, " there's another marriage brewing, or the signs do not tell true, and madam will sanction this one, too, for there's money there, and *gold* can purify any blood."

Ere Maggie could reply, Theo called out, "you here, Mag, as usual ?" adding, aside, to her companion, " she has the most unaccountable taste, so different from me, who cannot endure anything low and vulgar. Can you ? But I need not ask," she continued, "for your associations have been of a refined nature."

George Douglas did not answer, for his thoughts were back in the brown farmhouse at the foot of the hill, where his boyhood was passed, and he wondered what the high-bred lady at his side would say if she could see the sun-burnt man and plain, old-fashioned woman, who called him their son, *George Washington !* He would not confess that he was ashamed of his parentage, for he tried to be a kind and dutiful child, but he would a little rather that Theo Miller should not know how democratic had been his early training. So he made no answer, but, addressing himself to Mag, asked " how she could find it in her heart to leave her patient so long ?"

" I'm going back directly," she said, and donning her flat, she started for home, thinking she had gained but little satisfaction from Hagar, who, as Douglas and Theo passed on, resumed her seat by the door, and listening to the sound of Margaret's retreating footsteps, muttered, " the old light-heartedness is gone. There are shadows gathering round her ; for once in love, she'll never be as free and joyous again. But it can't be helped ; it's the destiny of women, and I only hope this Warner is worthy of her, but he ain't

He's too wild—too full of what Hagar Warren calls *bedevilment*. And Mag does everything he tells her to do. Not content with tearing down his bed-curtains, which have hung there full twenty years, she's set things all cornerwise, because the folks do so in Worcester, and has turned the parlor into a smoking room, till all the air of Hillsdale can't take away that tobacco scent. Why, it almost knocks me down !" and the old lady groaned aloud, as she recounted to herself the recent innovations upon the time-honored habits of her mistress's house.

Henry Warner was, indeed, rather a fast young man, but it needed the suggestive presence of George Douglas to bring out his true character ; and for the four days succeeding the arrival of the latter, there were rare doings at the old stone house, where the astonished and rather delighted servants looked on in amazement, while the young men sang their jovial songs and drank of the rare old wine, which Mag, utterly fearless of what her grandmother might say, brought from the cellar below. But when, on the morning of the 4th, Henry Warner suggested that they have a *celebration*, or, at least, hang out the American flag by way of showing their patriotism, there were signs of rebellion in the kitchen, while even Mrs. Jeffrey, who had long since ceased to interfere, felt it her duty to remonstrate. Accordingly, she descended to the parlor, where she found George Douglas and Mag dancing to the tune of Yankee Doodle, which Theo played upon the piano, while Henry Warner whistled a most stirring accompaniment ! To be heard above that din was impossible, and involuntarily patting her own slippered foot to the lively strain, the distressed little lady went back to her room, wondering what Madam Conway would say if she knew how her house was being desecrated.

But Madam Conway did not know. She was three

thousand miles away, and with this distance between them, Maggie dared do anything ; so when the flag was again mentioned, she answered apologetically, as if it were something of which they ought to be ashamed : " We never had any, but we can soon make one, I know. 'Twill be fun to see it float from the house-top !" and, flying up the stairs to the dusty garret, she drew from a huge oaken chest, a scarlet coat, which had belonged to the former owner of the place, who little thought, as he sat in state, that his favorite coat would one day furnish materials for the emblem of American freedom !

No such thought as this, however, obtruded itself upon Mag, as she bent over the chest. "The coat is of no use," she said, and gathering it up, she ran back to the parlor, where, throwing it across Henry's lap, she told how it had belonged to her great-great-grandfather, who, at the time of the Revolution, went home to England. The young men exchanged a meaning look, and then burst into a laugh, but the cause of their merriment they did not explain, lest the prejudices of the girls should be aroused.

"This is just the thing," said Henry, entering heart and soul into the spirit of the fun. " This is grand. Can't you find some blue for the ground-work of the stars ?"

Mag thought a moment, and then exclaimed, " Oh, yes, I have it, grandma has a blue satin bodice, which she wore when she was a young lady. She once gave me a part of the back for my dolly's dress. , She won't care if I cut up the rest for a banner."

" Of course not," answered George Douglas. " She'll be glad to have it used for such a laudable purpose," and walking to the window, he laughed heartily as he saw in fancy the wrath of the proud English woman, when she learned the use to which her satin bodice had been appropriated.

The waist was brought in a twinkling, and then, when Henry asked for some white, Mag cried, "A sheet will be just the thing—one of grandma's small linen ones. It won't hurt it a bit," she added, as she saw a shadow on Theo's brow, and, mounting to the top of the high chest of drawers, she brought out a sheet of finest linen, which, with rose leaves, and fragrant herbs, had been carefully packed away.

It was a long, delightful process, the making of that banner, and Maggie's voice rang out loud and clear, as she saw how cleverly Henry Warner managed the shears, cutting the red coat into stripes. The arrangement of the satin fell to Maggie's lot, and, while George Douglas made the stars, Theo looked on, a little doubtfully, not that her nationality was in any way affected, for what George Douglas sanctioned was by this time right with her; but she felt some misgiving as to what her grandmother might say; and thinking if she did nothing but look on and laugh, the blame would fall on Mag, she stood aloof, making occasionally a suggestion, and seeming as pleased as any one, when, at last, the flag was done. A quilting frame served as a flag-staff, and Mag was chosen to plant it upon the top of the house, where was a cupola, or miniature tower, overlooking the surrounding country. Leading to this tower was a narrow staircase, and up these stairs Mag bore the flag, assisted by one of the servant girls, whose birth-place was green Erin, and whose broad, good-humored face shone with delight, as she fastened the pole securely in its place, and then shook aloft her checked apron, in answer to the cheer which came up from below, when first the American banner waved over the old stone house.

Attracted by the noise, and wondering what fresh mischief they were doing, Mrs. Jeffrey went out into the yard just in time to see the flag of freedom as it shook itself out in the summer breeze.

" Heaven help me !" she ejaculated ; " Stars and Stripes, on Madam Conway's house !" and resolutely shutting her eyes, lest they should look again, on what to her seemed sacrilege, she groped her way back to the house, and retiring to her room, wrote to Madam Conway an exaggerated account of the proceedings, bidding her hasten home, or Mag and Theo would be ruined.

The letter being written, the good lady felt better—so much better, indeed, that after an hour's deliberation she concluded not to send it, inasmuch as it contained many complaints against the young lady Margaret, who she knew was sure in the end to find favor in her grandmother's eyes. This was the first time Mrs. Jeffrey had attempted a letter to her employer, for Maggie had been the chosen correspondent, Theo affecting to dislike anything like letter-writing. On the day previous to Henry Warner's arrival at the stone house, Mag had written to her grandmother, and ere the time came for her to write again, she had concluded to keep his presence there a secret : so Madam Conway was, as yet, ignorant of his existence ; and while in the homes of the English nobility, she bore herself like a royal princess, talking to young Arthur Carrollton of her beautiful granddaughter, she little dreamed of the real state of affairs at home.

But it was not for Mrs. Jeffrey to enlighten her, and tearing her letter in pieces, the governess sat down in her easy-chair by the window, mentally congratulating herself upon the fact that " the two young savages," as she styled Douglas and Warner, were to leave on the morrow. This last act of theirs, the hoisting of the banner, had been the culminating point, and too indignant to sit with them at the

same table, she resolutely kept her room throughout the
entire day, poring intently over "Baxter's Saint's Rest,"
her favorite volume when at all flurried or excited. Occasionally, too, she would stop her ears with jeweller's cotton, te
shut out the sound of *Hail Columbia* as it came up to her
from the parlor below, where the young men were doing
their best to show their patriotism.

Towards evening, alarmed by a whizzing sound, which
seemed to be often repeated, and wishing to know the cause,
she stole half way down the stairs, when the mischievous
Mag greeted her with a *serpent*, which hissing beneath her
feet, sent her quickly back to her room, from which she did
not venture again. Mrs. Jeffrey was very good natured,
and reflecting that " young folks must have fun," she became
at last comparatively calm, and at an early hour sought her
pillow. But thoughts of "*stars and stripes*" waving directly
over her head, as she knew they were, made her nervous,
and the long clock struck the hour of two, while she was
yet restless and wakeful.

" Maybe the *Saint's Rest* will quiet me a trifle," she
thought, and striking a light, she attempted to read ; but in
vain, for every word was a *star*, every line a *stripe*, and
every leaf a *flag*. Shutting the book and hurriedly pacing
the floor, she exclaimed, " It's of no use trying to sleep, or
meditate either. Baxter himself couldn't do it with that
thing over his head, and I mean to take it down. It's a
duty I owe to King George's memory, and to Madam Conway ;" and stealing from her room, she groped her way up
the dark, narrow stairway, until emerging into the bright
moonlight, she stood directly beneath the American banner,
waving so gracefully in the night wind. "It's a clever
enough device," she said, gazing rather admiringly at it.
" And I'd let it be if I s'posed I could sleep a wink ; but *I*

can't. It's worse for my nerves than strong green tea, and
I'll not lie awake for all the Yankee flags in Christendom ;"
so saying, the resolute little woman tugged at the quilt-
frame until she loosened it from its fastenings, and then
started to return.

But, alas ! the way was narrow and dark, the banner was
large and cumbersome, while the lady that bore it was nervous and weak. It is not strange, then, that Maggie, who
slept at no great distance, was awakened by a tremendous
crash, as of some one falling the entire length of the tower
stairs, while a voice, frightened and faint, called out, "Help
me, Margaret, do ! I am dead ! I *know* I am !"

Striking a light, Maggie hurried to the spot, while her
merry laugh aroused the servants, who came together in a
body. Stretched upon the floor, with one foot thrust
entirely through the banner, which was folded about her
so that the quilt-frame lay directly upon her bosom, was
Mrs. Jeffrey, the broad frill of her cap standing up erect,
and herself asserting with every breath that "she was dead
and buried, she knew she was." ·

"Wrapped in a winding sheet, I'll admit," said Maggie,
"but not quite dead, I trust ;" and putting down her light,
she attempted to extricate her governess, who continued to
apologize for what she had done. "Not that I cared so
much about your *celebrating America ;* but I couldn't sleep
with the thing over my head ; I was going to put it back in
the morning before you were up. There ! there ! careful !
It's broken short off !" she screamed, as Maggie tried to release her foot from the rent in the linen sheet, a rent which
the frightened woman persisted in saying, "she could darn
as good as new," while at the same time she implored of
Maggie to handle carefully her ankle, which had been
sprained by the fall.

Maggie's recent experience in broken bones had made her quite an adept, and taking the slight form of Mrs. Jeffrey in her arms, she carried her back to her room, where growing more quiet, the old lady told her how she happened to fall, saying, "she never thought of stumbling, until she fancied that Washington and all his regiment were after her, and when she turned her head to see, she lost her footing, and fell.

Forcing back her merriment, which in spite of herself would occasionally burst forth, Maggie made her teacher as comfortable as possible, and then staid with her until morning, when, leaving her in charge of a servant, she went below to say farewell to her guests. Between George Douglas and Theo, there were a few low spoken words, she granting him permission to write, while he promised to visit her again in the early autumn. He had not yet talked to her of love, for Rose Warner had still a home in his heart, and she must be dislodged ere another could take her place. But his affection for her was growing gradually less. Theo suited him well, her family suited him better, and when at parting he took her hand in his, he resolved to ask her for it, when next he came to Hillsdale.

Meanwhile, between Henry Warner and Maggie there was a far more affectionate farewell, he whispering to her of a time not far distant, when he would claim her as his own, and she should go with him. He would write to her every week, he said, and Rose should write, too. He would see her in a few days, and tell her of his engagement, which he knew would please her.

"Let me send her a line," said Maggie, and on a tiny sheet of paper, she wrote, "*Dear Rose:* Are you willing I should be your sister, Maggie ?"

Half an hour later, and Hagar Warren, coming through

the garden gate, looked after the carriage which bore the gentlemen to the depot, muttering to herself, " I'm glad the high bucks have gone. A good riddance to them both."

In her disorderly chamber, too, Mrs. Jeffrey hobbled on one foot to the window, where, with a deep sigh of relief, she sent after the young men a not very complimentary adieu, which was echoed in part by the servants below, while Theo, on the piazza, exclaimed against "the lonesome old house, which was never so lonesome before," and Maggie seated herself upon the stairs and cried !

CHAPTER IX.

ROSE WARNER.

Nᴇsᴛʟᴇᴅ among the tall old trees which skirt the borders of Leominster village, was the bird's-nest of a cottage, which Rose Warner called her home, and which, with its wealth of roses, its trailing vines and flowering shrubs, seemed fitted for the abode of one like her. Slight as a child twelve summers old, and fair as the white pond lily, when first to the morning sun it unfolds its delicate petals, she seemed too frail for earth, and both her aunt and he whom she called brother, watched carefully lest the cold north wind should blow too rudely on the golden curls, which shaded her childish brow. Very, very beautiful was little Rose, and yet few ever looked upon her without a feeling of sadness ; for in the deep blue of her eyes, there was a mournful, dreamy look, as if the shadow of some great sorrow were resting thus early upon her.

And Rose Warner had a sorrow, too, a grief which none save one had ever suspected. To him it had come with the words, "I cannot be your wife, for I love another ; one who will never know how dear he is to me."

The words were involuntarily spoken, and George Douglas, looking down upon her, guessed rightly that he "who would never know how much he was beloved," was *Henry Warner.* To her the knowledge that Henry was something dearer than a brother had come slowly, filling her heart

with pain, for she well knew that whether he clasped her to
his bosom, as he often did, or pressed his lips upon her brow,
he thought of her only as a brother thinks of a beautiful
and idolized sister.   It had heretofore been some consolation
to know that his affections were untrammelled with thoughts
of another, that she alone was the object of his love, and
hope had sometimes faintly whispered of what perchance
might be ; but from that dream she was waking now, and
her face grew whiter still, as there came to her from time
to time letters fraught with praises of *Margaret Miller ;* and
if in Rose Warner's nature, there had been a particle of bitterness, it would have been called forth toward one who,
she foresaw, would be her rival.   But Rose knew no malice,
and she felt that she would sooner die than do aught to mar
the happiness of Maggie Miller.

For nearly two weeks she had not heard from Henry, and
she was beginning to feel very anxious, when one morning,
two or three days succeeding the memorable Hillsdale celebration, as she sat in a small arbor so thickly overgrown with
the Michigan rose as to render her invisible at a little distance, she was startled by hearing him call her name, as he
came in quest of her down the garden walk.   The next moment he held her in his arms, kissing her forehead, her lips,
her cheek ; then holding her off, he looked to see if there
had been in her aught of change since last they met.

"You are paler than you were, Rose darling," he said,
"and your eyes look as if they had of late been used to tears.
What is it dearest ?   What troubles you ?"

Rose could not answer immediately, for his sudden coming
had taken away her breath, and as he saw a faint blush
stealing over her face, he continued, "Can it be my little
sister has been falling in love during my absence ?"

Never before had he spoken to her thus ; but a change

had come over him, his heart was full of a beautiful image, and fancying Rose might have followed his example, he asked her the question he did, without, however, expecting or receiving a definite answer.

" I am so lonely, Henry, when you are gone and do not write to me!" she said ; and in the tones of her voice, there was a slight reproof which Henry felt keenly.

He had been so engrossed with Maggie Miller, and the free joyous life he led in the Hillsdale woods, that for a time he had neglected Rose, who, in his absence, depended so much on his letters for comfort.

"I have been very selfish, I know," he said ; " but I was so happy, that for a time I forgot everything save Maggie Miller."

An involuntary shudder ran through Rose's slender form ; but conquering her emotion, she answered calmly. " What of this Maggie Miller ? Tell me of her, will you ?"

Winding his arm around her waist, and drawing her closely to his side, Henry Warner rested her head upon his bosom; where it had often lain, and smoothing her golden curls, told her of Maggie Miller, of her queenly beauty, of her dashing, independent spirit ; her frank, ingenuous manner; her kindness of heart, and last of all, bending very low, lest the vine leaves and the fair blossoms of the rose should hear, he told her of his love, and Rose, the fairest flower of all which bloomed around that bower, clasped her hand upon her heart, lest he should see its wild throbbings, and forcing back the tears which moistened her long eyelashes, listened to the knell of all her hopes. Henceforth her love for him must be an idle mockery, and the time would come, when to love him as she loved him then, would be a sin, a wrong to herself, a wrong to him, and a wrong to Maggie Miller.

"You are surely not asleep," he said at last, as she made him no reply, and bending forward, he saw the tear drops resting on her cheek. "Not asleep, but *weeping!*" he exclaimed. "What is it, darling? What troubles you?" And lifting up her head, Rose Warren answered, "I was thinking how this new love of yours would take you from me and I should be alone."

"No, not alone," he said, wiping her tears away. "Maggie and I have arranged that matter. You are to live with us, and instead of losing me, you are to gain another— a sister, Rose. You have often wished you had one, and you could surely find none worthier than Maggie Miller."

"Will she watch over *you*, Henry? Will she be to you what *your* wife should be?" asked Rose; and Henry answered, "She is not at all like you, my little sister. She relies implicitly upon my judgment; so you see I shall need your blessed influence all the same, to make me what your brother and Maggie's husband ought to be."

"Did she send me no message?" asked Rose; and taking out the tiny note, Henry passed it to her, just as his aunt called to him from the house, whither he went, leaving her alone.

There were blinding tears in Rose's eyes as she read the few lines, and involuntarily she pressed her lips to the paper, which she knew had been touched by Maggie Miller's hands.

"*My sister*,—sister Maggie," she repeated, and at the sound of that name her fast-beating heart grew still, for they seemed very sweet to her, those words "my sister," thrilling her with a new and strange emotion, and awakening within her a germ of the deep, undying love, she was yet to feel for her who had traced those words, and asked to be her sister, "I will do right," she thought, "I will

conquer this foolish heart of mine, or break it in the struggle, and Henry Warner shall never know how sorely it was
wrung."

The resolution gave her strength, and rising up, she too
sought the house, where, retiring to her room, she penned a
hasty note to Maggie, growing calmer with each word she
wrote.

"I grant your request," she said, "and take you for a
sister well beloved. I had a half-sister once, they say, but
she died when a little babe. I never looked upon her face,
and connected with her birth there was too much of sorrow
and humiliation for me to think much of her, save as of one
who, under other circumstances, might have been dear to
me. And yet, as I grow older, I often find myself wishing
she had lived, for my father's blood was in her veins. But
I do not even know where her grave was made, for we only
heard one winter morning, years ago, that she was dead,
with the mother who bore her. Forgive me, Maggie dear,
for saying so much about that little child. Thoughts of
you, who are to be my sister, make me think of her, who,
had she lived, would have been a young lady now, nearly
your own age. So in the place of *her*, whom, knowing, I
would have loved, I adopt you, sweet Maggie Miller, my
sister and my friend. May heaven's choicest blessings rest
on you forever, and no shadow come between you and the
one you have chosen for your husband. To my partial eyes
he is worthy of you, Maggie, royal in bearing and queenly
in form though you be, and that you may be happy with
him will be the daily prayer of   'ROSE.'"

The letter was finished, and Rose gave it to her brother,
who, after its perusal, kissed her saying, "It is right, my

darling. I will send it to-morrow with mine ; and now fot
a ride. I will see what a little exercise can do for you. I
do not like the color of your face."

But neither the fragrant summer air, nor yet the presence
of Henry Warner, who tarried several days, could rouse
the drooping Rose ; and when at last she was left alone,
she sought her bed, where for many weeks she hovered between life and death, while her brother and her aunt hung
over her pillow, and Maggie, from her woodland home, sent
many an anxious inquiry and message of love to the sick
girl. In the close atmosphere of his counting-room, George
Douglas, too, again battled manfully with his olden love,
listening each day to hear that she was dead. But not thus
early was Rose to die, and with the waning summer days
she came slowly back to life. More beautiful than ever,
because more ethereal and fair, she walked the earth like
one who, having struggled with a mighty sorrow, had won
the victory at last ; and Henry Warner, when he looked on
her sweet, placid face, and listened to her voice as she made
plans for the future, when " Maggie would be his wife,"
dreamed not of the grave hidden in the deep recesses of
her heart, where grew no flower of hope or semblance of
earthly joy.

Thus little know mankind of each other !

CHAPTER X.

EXPECTED GUESTS.

On the Hillsdale hills the October sun was shining, and the forest trees were donning their robes of scarlet and brown, when again the old stone house presented an air of joyous expectancy. The large, dark parlors were thrown open, the best chambers· were aired, the bright, autumnal flowers were gathered and in tastefully arranged bouquets adorned the mantels, while Theo and Maggie, in their best attire, flitted uneasily from room to room, running sometimes to the gate to look down the grassy road, which led from the highway, and again mounting the tower stairs to obtain a more extended view.

In her pleasant apartment, where last we left her with a sprained ankle, Mrs. Jeffrey, too, fidgeted about, half sympathizing with her pupils in their happiness, and half regretting the cause of that happiness, which was the expected arrival of George Douglas and Henry Warner, who, true to their promise, were coming again "to try for a week the Hillsdale air, and retrieve their character as fast young men." So, at least, they told Mrs. Jeffrey, who, mindful of her exploit with the banner and wishing to make some amends, met them alone on the threshold, Maggie having at the last moment *ran away*, while Theo sat in a state of dignified perturbation upon the sofa.

A few days prior to their arrival, letters had been received from Madam Conway, saying she should probably remain in England two or three weeks longer, and thus the house was again clear to the young men, who, forgetting to retrieve their characters, fairly outdid all they had done before. The weather was remarkably clear and bracing, and the greater part of each day was spent in the open air, either in fishing, riding, or hunting ; Maggie teaching Henry Warner how to ride and leap, while he in turn taught her to shoot a bird upon the wing, until the pupil was equal to her master ! In these out-door excursions George Douglas and Theo did not always join, for he had something to say, which he would rather tell her in the silent parlor, and which, when told, furnished food for many a quiet conversation ; so Henry and Maggie rode oftentimes alone ; and old Hagar, when she saw them dashing past her door, Maggie usually taking the lead, would shake her head and mutter to herself "'Twill never do—that match. He ought to hold her back, instead of leading her on. I wish Madam Conway *would* come home and end it."

Mrs. Jeffrey wished so too, as night after night her slumbers were disturbed by the sounds of merriment which came up to her from the parlor below, where the young people were "enjoying themselves," as Maggie said, when reproved for the noisy revel. The day previous to the one set for their departure chanced to be Henry Warner's twenty-seventh birth-day, and this Maggie resolved to honor with an extra supper, which was served at an unusually late hour in the dining-room, the door of which opened out upon a closely latticed piazza.

"1 wish we could think of something new to do," said Maggie as she presided at the table, "something real funny;" then, as her eyes fell upon the dark piazza, where a single light was burning dimly ; sheexclaimed, "Why can't we get up tableaux ? There are heaps of the queerest clothes in the big oaken chest in the garret. The servants can be audience, and they need some recreation !"

The suggestion was at once approved, and in half an hour's time the floor was strewn with garments of every con-conceivable fashion, from long stockings and small-clothes to scarlet cloaks and gored skirts, the latter of which were immediately donned by Henry Warner, to the infinite delight of the servants, who enjoyed seeing the grotesque costumes, even if they did not exactly understand what the tableaux were intended to represent. The banner, too, was brought out, and after bearing a conspicuous part in the performance, was placed at the end of the dining-room, where it would be the first thing visible to a person opening the door opposite. At a late hour the servants retired, and then George Douglas, who took kindly to the luscious old wine, which Maggie again had brought from her grandmother's choicest store, filled a goblet to the brim, and pledging first the health of the young girls, drank to " the old lady across the water," with whose goods they were thus making free !

Henry Warner rarely tasted wine, for though miles away from Rose, her influence was around him—so, filling his glass with water, he, too, drank to the wish that " the lady across the sea would remain there yet awhile, or at all events not stumble upon us to-night !"

"What if she should !" thought Maggie, glancing around at the different articles scattered all over the floor, and laughing as she saw in fancy her grandmother's look of dismay, should she by any possible chance obtain a view of the room, where perfect order and quiet had been wont to reign. But the good lady was undoubtedly taking her morning

nap on the shores of old England.   There was no danger to
be apprehended from her unexpected arrival, they thought ;
and just as the clock struck one, the young men sought their
rooms, greatly to the relief of Mrs. Jeffrey, who in her long
night robes, with streaming candle in hand, had more than
a dozen times leaned over the banister, wondering "if the
carouse would ever end."

It did end at last, and tired and sleepy, Theo went
directly to her chamber, while Maggie staid below, thinking
to arrange matters a little, for their guests were to leave on
the first train, and she had ordered an early breakfast.
But it was a hopeless task, the putting of that room to
rights ; and trusting much to the good nature of the housekeeper, she finally gave it up and went to bed, forgetting in
her drowsiness to fasten the outer door, or yet to extinguish
the lamp which burned upon the side-board.

CHAPTER XI.

UNEXPECTED GUESTS.

AT the delightful country seat of Arthur Carrollton, Madam Conway had passed many pleasant days, and was fully intending to while away several more, when an unexpected summons from his father made it necessary for the young man to go immediately to London, and as an American steamer was about to leave the port of Liverpool, Madam Conway determined to start for home at once. Accordingly she wrote for Anna Jeffrey, whom she had promised to take, with her, to meet her in Liverpool, and a few days previous to the arrival of George Douglas and Henry Warner at Hillsdale, the two ladies embarked with an endless variety of luggage, to say nothing of Miss Anna's guitar-case, bird-cage and favorite lap-dog "Lottie"

Once fairly on the sea, Madam Conway became exceedingly impatient and disagreeable, complaining both of fare and speed, and at length came on deck one morning with the firm belief that something dreadful had happened to Maggie! She was dangerously sick, she knew, for never but once before had she been visited with a like presentiment, and that was just before her daughter died. Then it came to her just as this had done, in her sleep, and very nervously the lady paced the vessel's deck, counting the days as they passed, and almost weeping for joy when told

13

Boston was in sight. Immediately after landing, she made inquiries as to when the next train passing Hillsdale station would leave the city, and though it was midnight, she resolved at all hazards to go on, for if Maggie were really ill, there was no time to be lost !

Accordingly, when at four o'clock A.M. Maggie, who was partially awake, heard in the distance the shrill scream of the engine, as the night express thundered through the town, she little dreamed of the boxes, bundles, trunks and bags, which lined the platform of Hillsdale station, nor yet of the resolute woman in brown, who persevered until a rude one horse wagon was found in which to transport herself and her baggage to the old stone house. The driver of the vehicle in which, under ordinary circumstances, Madam Conway would have scorned to ride, was a long, lean, half-witted fellow, utterly unfitted for his business. Still, he managed quite well until they turned into the grassy by-road, and Madam Conway saw through the darkness the light which Maggie had inadvertently left within the dining-room !

There was no longer a shadow of uncertainty ; "Margaret was dead," and the lank Tim was ordered to drive faster, or the excited woman, perched on one of her travelling trunks, would be obliged to foot it ! A few vigorous strokes of the whip set the sorrel horse into a canter, and as the night was dark, and the road wound round among the trees, it is not at all surprising that Madam Conway, with her eye still on the beacon light, found herself seated rather unceremoniously in the midst of a *brush heap*, her goods and chattels rolling promiscuously around her, while lying across a log, her right hand clutching at the bird-cage, and her left grasping the shaggy hide of Lottie, who yelled most furiously, was Anna Jeffrey, half blinded with mud, and bitterly denouncing American drivers and Yankee roads ! To gather themselves together was not an easy matter, but the *ten pieces* were at last all told, and then, holding up her skirts, bedraggled with dew, Madam Conway resumed her seat in the wagon, which was this time driven in safety to her door. Giving orders for her numerous boxes to be safely bestowed, she hastened forward and soon stood upon the threshold.

" *Great Heaven!*" she exclaimed, starting backward so suddenly that she trod upon the foot of Lottie, who again sent forth an outcry, which Anna Jeffrey managed to choke down. " Is this bedlam or what ?" and stepping out upon the piazza, she looked to see if the blundering driver had made a mistake. But no, it was the same old grey stone house she had left some months before ; and again pressing boldly forward, she took the lamp from the side-board and commenced to reconnoitre. " My mother's wedding dress, as I live ! and her scarlet broadcloth, too !" she cried, holding to view the garments which Henry Warner had thrown upon the arm of the long settee. A turban or cushion, which she recognized as belonging to her grandmother, next caught her view, together with the small-clothes of her sire.

" *The entire contents of the oaken chest,*" she continued, in a tone far from being calm and cool. " What can have happened ! It's some of that crazy Hagar's work, I know. I'll have her put in the "——but whatever the evil was which threatened Hagar Warren, it was not defined by words, for at that moment the indignant lady caught sight of an empty bottle, which she instantly recognized as having held her very oldest, choicest wine. " The Lord help me !" she cried, " I've been *robbed ;*" and grasping the bottle by the neck, she leaned up against the banner which she had not yet descried.

" In the name of wonder, what's *this* ?" she almost

screamed, as the full blaze of the lamp fell upon the flag, revealing the truth at once, and partially stopping her breath.

Robbery was nothing to insult, and forgetting entirely the wine, she gasped, "*stars and stripes* in this house ! In the house of my grandfather, as loyal a subject as King George ever boasted ! What can Margaret be doing to suffer a thing like this ?"

A few steps further on, and Margaret herself might have been seen peering out into the darkened upper hall, and listening anxiously to her grandmother's voice. The sound of the rattling old wagon had aroused her, and curious to know who was stirring at this early hour, she had cautiously opened her window, which overlooked the piazza, and to her great dismay, had recognized her grandmother as she gave orders concerning her baggage. Flying back to her room, she awoke her sister, who, springing up in bed, whispered faintly, "*Will* she kill us dead, Maggie ? Will she kill us dead ?"

"Pshaw ! no," answered Maggie, her own courage rising with Theo's fears. "She'll have to scold a spell, I suppose, but I can coax her, I know !"

By this time the old lady was ascending the stairs, and closing the door, Maggie applied her eye to the key-hole, listening breathlessly for what might follow. George Douglas and Henry Warner occupied separate rooms, and their boots were now standing outside their doors, ready for the chore boy, Jim, who thus earned a quarter every day. Stumbling first upon the pair belonging to George Douglas, the lady took them up, ejaculating, "*Boots ! boots ! Yes, men's boots*, as I'm a living woman ! The like was never seen by me before in this hall. *Another pair !*" she contin-ued, as her eye fell on those of Henry Warner. "Another

pair, and in the best chamber, too ! What will come next ?"
And setting down her light, she wiped the drops of perspiration from her face, at the same time looking around in
some alarm, lest the owners of said boots should come
forth.

Just at that moment Mrs. Jeffrey appeared. Alarmed by
the unusual noise, and fancying the young gentlemen might
be robbing the house, as a farewell performance, she had
donned a calico wrapper, and tying a black silk handker-
chief over her cap, had taken her scissors, the only weapon
of defence she could find, and thus equipped for battle, she
had sallied forth. She was prepared for burglars—nay, she
would not have been disappointed, had she found the
young men busily engaged in removing the ponderous
furniture from their rooms ; but the sight of Madam Conway, at that unseasonable hour, was wholly unexpected,
and in her fright she dropped the lamp which she had lighted in place of her candle, and which was broken in frag-
ments, deluging the carpet with oil, and eliciting a fresh
groan from Madam Conway.

" *Jeffrey, Jeffrey !*" she gasped, " what *have* you done ?"

" Great goodness !" ejaculated Mrs. Jeffrey, remembering
her adventure when once before she left her room in the night.
" I certainly am the most unfortunate of mortals. Catch me
out of bed again, let what will happen ;" and turning, she
was about to leave the hall, when Madam Conway, anxious
to know what had been done, called her back, saying rather
indignantly, " I'd like to know whose house I am in ?"

" A body would suppose 'twas Miss Margaret's, the way
she's conducted," answered Mrs. Jeffrey ; and Madam Conway continued, pointing to the *boots*, " Who have we here ?
These are not Margaret's, surely ?"

" No, ma'am, they belong to the young men, who have

turned the house topsy-turvey, with their tableaux, their *Revolution* celebration, their banner, and carousing generally," said Mrs. Jeffrey, rather pleased than otherwise at being the first to tell the news.

" *Young men !*" repeated Madam Conway, "what young men ? Where did they come from, and why are they here?"

" They are *Douglas & Warner,*" said Mrs. Jeffrey, " two as big scapegraces as there are this side of Old Bailey— that's *what* they are. They came from Worcester, and if I've any discernment, they are after *your girls*, and your girls are after *them.*"

" *After my girls ! After Maggie !* It can't be possible !" gasped Madam Conway, thinking of Arthur Carrollton.

" It's the very truth, though," returned Mrs. Jeffrey. " Henry Warner, who, in my opinion, is the worst of the two, got to chasing Margaret in the woods, as long ago as last April; she jumped Gritty across the gorge, and he, like a fool, jumped after, breaking his leg "——

" Pity it hadn't been his neck," interrupted Madam Conway, and Mrs. Jeffrey continued, " Of course he was brought here, and Margaret took care of him. After a while, his comrade Douglas came out, and of all the carousals you ever thought of, I reckon they had the worst 'Twas the 4th of July, and if you'll believe it, they made a banner, and Maggie planted it herself on the housetop. They went off next morning ; but now they've come again, and last night the row beat all. I never got a wink of sleep till after two o'clock."

Here, entirely out of breath, the old lady paused, and going to her room, brought out a basin of water and a towel, with which she tried to wipe off the oil. But Madam Conway paid little heed to the spoiled carpet, so engrossed was she with what she had heard.

"I'm astonished at Margaret's want of discretion," said she, "and I depended so much upon her, too."

"I always knew you were deceived by her," said Mrs. Jeffrey, still bending over the oil; "but it wasn't for me to say so, for you are blinded towards that girl. She's got some of the queerest notions, and then she's so high strung. She won't listen to reason. But I did my country good service once. I went up in the dead of night to take down the flag, and I don't regret it either, even if it did pitch me to the bottom of the stairs, and sprained my ankle."

"Served you right," interposed Madam Conway, who, not at all pleased at hearing Margaret thus censured, now turned the full force of her wrath upon the poor little governess, blaming her for having suffered such proceedings. "What did Margaret and Theo know, young things as they were? and what was Mrs. Jeffrey there for if not to keep them circumspect! But instead of doing this, she had undoubtedly encouraged them in their folly, and then charged it upon Margaret."

It was in vain that the greatly distressed and astonished lady protested her innocence, pleading her sleepless nights and lame ankle as proofs of having done her duty; Madam Conway would not listen. "Somebody was of course to blame," and as it is a long established rule, that a part of every teacher's duty is to be responsible for the faults of the pupils, so Madam Conway now continued to chide Mrs. Jeffrey as the prime mover of everything, until that lady, overwhelmed with the sense of injustice done her, left the oil and retired to her room, saying as she closed the door, "I was never so injured in all my life—never, to think that after all my trouble she should charge it to *me!* It will break my heart, I know. Where shall I go for comfort or *rest?*"

This last word was opportune and suggestive. If *rest* could not be found in *Baxter's Saints' Rest,* it was not by her to be found at all ; and sitting down by the window in the grey dawn of the morning, she strove to draw comfort from the words of the good divine, but in vain. It had never failed her before ; but never before had she been so deeply injured, and closing the volume at last, she paced the floor in a very perturbed state of mind.

Meantime, Madam Conway had sought her granddaughter's chamber, where Theo in her fright had taken refuge under the bed, while Maggie feigned a deep, sound sleep. A few vigorous shakes, however, aroused her, when greatly to the amazement of her grandmother, she burst into a merry laugh, and winding her arms around the highly scandalized lady's neck, said, " Forgive me, grandma, I've been awake ever since you came home. I did not mean to leave the dining-room in such disorder, but I was *so* tired, and we had *such* fun— hear me out," she continued, laying her hand over the mouth of her grandmother, who attempted to speak ; " Mrs. Jeffrey told you how Mr. Warner broke his leg, and was brought here. He is a real nice young man, and so is Mr. Douglas, who came out to see him. They are partners in the firm of Douglas & Co. Worcester."

" Henry Warner is nothing but the *Co.* though, Mr. Douglas owns the store, and is worth two hundred thousand dollars !" cried a smothered voice from under the bed ; and Theo emerged into view, with a feather or two ornamenting her hair, and herself looking a little uneasy and frightened.

The 200,000 dollars produced a magical effect upon the old lady, exonerating George Douglas at once from all blame. But towards Henry Warner she was not thus lenient ; for, cowardlike, Theo charged him with having suggested everything, even to the cutting up of the red coat for a banner !

"What !" fairly screamed Madam Conway, who in her hasty glance at the flag, had not observed the material, "not taken my *grandfather's coat* for a banner !"

" Yes, he did," said Theo, " and Maggie cut up your blue satin bodice for *stars*, and took one of your fine linen sheets for the foundation."

"The wretch !" exclaimed Madam Conway, stamping her foot in her wrath, and thinking only of Henry Warner. " I'll turn him from my door instantly. My blue satin bodice, indeed !"

" 'Twas I, grandma—'twas I," interrupted Maggie, looking reproachfully at Theo. " 'Twas I, who cut up the bodice. I, who brought down the scarlet coat."

"And *I* didn't do a thing but look on," said Theo. " I knew you'd be angry, and I tried to make Maggie behave, but she wouldn't."

" I don't know as it is anything to you what *Maggie* does, and I think it would look quite as well in you, to take part of the blame yourself, instead of putting it all upon your sister," was Madam Conway's reply ; and feeling almost as deeply injured as Mrs. Jeffrey herself, Theo began to cry, while, Maggie with a few masterly strokes, succeeded in so far appeasing the anger of her grandmother, that the good lady consented for the young gentlemen to stay to breakfast, saying, though, that "they should decamp immediately after, and never darken her doors again."

" But Mr. Douglas is *rich*," sobbed Theo from behind her pocket handkerchief, " immensely rich and of a very aristocratic family, I'm sure, else where did he get his money ?"

This remark was timely, and when, fifteen minutes later, Madam Conway was presented to the gentlemen in the hall,

Ler manner was far more gracious towards George Douglas than it was towards Henry Warner, to whom she merely nodded, deigning no answer whatever to his polite apology for having made himself so much at home in Ler house. The expression of his mouth was as usual against him, and fancying he intended adding insult to injury by laughing in her face, she coolly turned her back upon him ere he had finished speaking, and walked down stairs, leaving him to wind up his speech with *"an old she dragon!"*

By this time both the sun and the servants had arisen, the former shining into the disorderly dining-room, and disclosing to the latter the weary jaded Anna, who, while Madam Conway was exploring the house, had thrown herself upon the lounge, and had fallen asleep.

"Who is she, and where did she come from?" was anxiously inquired, and they were about going in quest of Margaret, when their mistress appeared suddenly in their midst, and their noisy demonstrations of joyful surprise awoke the sleeping girl, who, rubbing her red eyelids, asked for her aunt, and why she did not come to meet her.

"She has been a little excited, and forgot you, perhaps," answered Madam Conway, at the same time bidding one of the servants to show the young lady to Mrs. Jeffrey's room.

The good lady had recovered her composure somewhat, and was just wondering why her niece did not come with Madam Conway as had been arranged, when Anna appeared, and in her delight at once more beholding a child of her only sister, and her husband's brother, she forgot in a measure how injured she had felt. Ere long the breakfast bell rang; but Anna declared herself too weary to go down, and as Mrs. Jeffrey felt that she could not yet meet Madam Conway face to face, they both remained in their room,

Anna again falling away to sleep, while her aunt grown more calm, sought, and this time found, comfort in her favorite volume. Very cool, indeed, was that breakfast, partaken in almost unbroken silence below. The toast was cold, the steak was cold, the coffee was cold, and frosty as an icicle was the lady who sat where the merry Maggie had heretofore presided. Scarcely a word was spoken by any one; but in the laughing eyes of Maggie there was a world of fun, to which the mischievous mouth of Henry Warner responded, by a curl exceedingly annoying to his stately hostess, who, in passing him his coffee, turned her head in another direction lest she should be *too civil!*

Breakfast being over, George Douglas, who began to understand Madam Conway tolerably well, asked of her a private interview, which was granted, when he conciliated her first by apologizing for anything ungentlemanly he might have done in her house, and startled her next by asking for Theo, as his wife.

"You can," said he, " easily ascertain my character and standing in Worcester, where for the last ten years I have been known first as clerk, then as junior partner, and finally as proprietor of the large establishment which I now conduct."

Madam Conway was at first too much astonished to speak. Had it been *Maggie* for whom he asked, the matter would have been decided at once, for *Maggie* was her *pet, her pride,* the intended bride of Arthur Carrollton; but Theo was a different creature altogether, and though the *Conway blood* flowing in her veins entitled her to much consideration, she was neither showy nor brilliant, and if she could marry 200,000 dollars, even though it were *American coin,* she would perhaps be doing quite as well as could be expected! So Madam Conway replied at last, that " she would con sider the matter, and if she found that Theo's feelings were fully enlisted, she would perhaps return a favorable answer "I know the firm of Douglas & Co. by reputation," said she, "and I know it to be a wealthy firm; but with me, *family* is quite as important as money."

"My family, madam, are certainly respectable," interrupted George Douglas, a deep flush overspreading his face.

He was indignant at her presuming to question his respectability, Madam Conway thought, and so she hastened to appease him, by saying, "Certainly, I have no doubt of it. There *are* marks by which I can *always* tell."

George Douglas bowed low to the far-seeing lady, while a train of thought, not altogether complimentary to her discernment in this case, passed through his mind.

Not thus lenient would Madam Conway have been towards Henry Warner, had he presumed to ask her that morning for Maggie, but he knew better than to broach the subject then. "He would write to her," he said, immediately after his return to Worcester, and in the meantime, Maggie, if she saw proper, was to prepare her grandmother for it by herself announcing the engagement. This, and much more he said to Maggie, as they sat together in the library, so much absorbed in each other as not to observe the approach of Madam Conway, who entered the door just in time to see Henry Warner with his arm around Maggie's waist. She was a woman of bitter prejudices, and had conceived a violent dislike for Henry, not only on account of the stars and stripes, but because she read to a certain extent the true state of affairs. Her suspicions were now confirmed, and rapidly crossing the floor, she confronted him, saying, "let my grand-daughter alone, young man, both now, and forever."

Something of Hagar's fiery spirit flashed from Maggie's

dark eyes, but forcing down her anger, she answered half earnestly, half playfully, " I am nearly old enough, grandma, to decide that matter for myself."

A fierce expression of scorn passed over Madam Conway's face, and harsh words might have ensued had not the carriage at that moment been announced. Wringing Maggie's hand, Henry arose and left the room, followed by the indignant lady, who would willingly have suffered *him* to walk, but thinking 200,000 dollars quite too much money to go on foot, she had ordered her carriage, and both the senior and junior partner of Douglas & Co. were ere long riding a second time away from the old house by the mill.

CHAPTER XII.

THE WATERS ARE TROUBLED.

"GRANDMA wishes to see you, Maggie, in her room," said Theo to her sister one morning, three days after the departure of their guests.

"Wishes to see *me!* For what?" asked Maggie; and Theo answered, "I don't know, unless it is to talk with you about Arthur Carrollton."

"Arthur Carrolton!" repeated Maggie. "Much good it will do her to talk to me of him. I hate the very sound of his name;" and rising, she walked slowly to her grandmother's room, where in her stiff brown satin dress, her golden spectacles planted firmly upon her nose, and the Valenciennes border of her cap shading but not concealing the determined look on her face, Madam Conway sat erect in her high backed chair, with an open letter upon her lap.

It was from *Henry.* Maggie knew his handwriting in a moment, and there was another, too, for her; but she was too proud to ask for it, and seating herself by the window, she waited for her grandmother to break the silence, which she did ere long as follows:

"I have just received a letter from that Warner, asking me to sanction an engagement which he says exists between himself and you. Is it true? Are you engaged to him?"

" *I am,*" answered Maggie, playing nervously with the

tassel of her wrapper, and wondering why Henry had written so soon, before she had prepared the way by a little judicious coaxing.

"Well then," continued Madam Conway, "the sooner it is broken the better. I am astonished that you should stoop to such an act, and I hope you are not in earnest."

"*But I am*," answered Maggie, and in the same cold, decided manner, her grandmother continued: "Then nothing remains for me, but to forbid your having any communication whatever with one whose conduct in my house has been so unpardonably rude and vulgar. You will never marry him, Margaret, never ! Nay, I would sooner see you dead than the wife of that *low, mean, impertinent* fellow."

In the large dark eyes there was a gleam decidedly *Hagarish* as Maggie arose, and standing before her grandmother, made answer: "You must not, in my presence, speak thus of Henry Warner. He is neither low, mean, vulgar, nor impertinent. You are prejudiced against him, because you think him comparatively poor, and because he has dared to look at me, who have yet to understand why the fact of my being a *Conway*, makes me any better. I have promised to be Henry Warner's wife, and Margaret Miller never yet has broken her word."

"But in this instance *you will*," said Madam Conway, now thoroughly aroused. "I will never suffer it; and to prove I am in earnest, I will here, before your face, burn the letter he has presumed to send you ; and this I will do to any others which may come to you from him."

Maggie offered no remonstrance ; but the fire of a volcano burned within, as she watched the letter blackening upon the coals ; and when next her eyes met those of her grandmother, there was in them a fierce, determined look, which prompted that lady at once to change her tactics, and try the power of persuasion, rather than of force. Feigning a smile, she said, " What ails you, child? You look to me like Hagar. It was wrong in me, perhaps, to turn your letter, and had I reflected a moment, I might not have done it ; but I cannot suffer you to receive any more. I have other prospects in view for you, and have only waited a favorable opportunity to tell you what they are. Sit down by me, Margaret, while I talk with you on the subject."

The burning of her letter had affected Margaret strangely, and with a benumbed feeling at her heart, she sat down without a word, and listened patiently to praises long and praises loud of Arthur Carrollton, who was described as being every way desirable, both as a friend and a husband. " His father, the elder Mr. Carrollton, was an intimate friend of my husband," said Madam Conway, " and wishes our families to be more closely united, by a marriage between you and his son Arthur, who is rather fastidious in his taste, and though twenty-eight years old, has never yet seen a face which suited him. But he is pleased with you, Maggie. He liked your picture, imperfect as it is, and he liked the tone of your letters, which I read to him. They were so original, he said, so much like what he fancied you to be. He has a splendid country seat, and more than one nobleman's daughter would gladly share it with him ; but I think he fancies *you*. He has a large estate near Montreal, and some difficulty connected with it will ere long bring him to America. Of course he will visit here, and with a little tact on your part, you can, I'm sure, secure one of the best matches in England. He is fine looking, too. I have his daguerreotype," and opening her work-box, she drew it forth, and held it before Maggie, who resolutely shut her eyes, lest she *should* see the face of one she was so deter mined to dislike

"What do you think of him?" asked Madam Conway, as her arm began to ache, and Maggie had not yet spoken.

"I haven't looked at him," answered Maggie, "I hate him, and if he comes here after me, I'll tell him so, too. I hate him because he is an Englishman. I hate him because he is aristocratic. I hate him for everything, and before I marry him I'll run away!"

Here, wholly overcome, Maggie burst into tears, and precipitately left the room. An hour later, and Hagar, sitting by her fire, which the coolness of the day rendered necessary, was startled by the abrupt entrance of Maggie, who, throwing herself upon the floor, and burying her face in the old woman's lap, sobbed bitterly.

"What is it, child? What is it, darling?" asked Hagar; and in a few words Maggie explained the whole. "She was persecuted, *dreadfully* persecuted. Nobody before ever had so much trouble as she. Grandma had burned a letter from Henry Warner, and would not give it to her. Grandma said, too, she should never marry him, should never write to him, nor see anything he might send to her. Oh, Hagar, Hagar, isn't it cruel?" and the eyes, whose wrathful, defiant expression was now quenched in tears, looked up in Hagar's face for sympathy.

The right chord was touched, and much as Hagar might have disliked Henry Warner, she was his fast friend now. Her mistress's opposition and Maggie's tears had wrought a change, and henceforth all her energies should be given to the advancement of the young couple's cause.

"I can manage it," she said, smoothing the long silken tresses which lay in disorder upon her lap. "Richland post office is only four miles from here; I can walk double that distance easy. Your grandmother never thinks of going there, neither am I known to any one in that neighborhood

Write your letter to Henry Warner, and before the sun goes down, it shall be safe in the letter box. He can write to the same place, but he had better direct to me, as your name might excite suspicion."

This plan seemed perfectly feasible ; but it struck Maggie unpleasantly. She had never attempted to deceive in her life, and she shrunk from the first deception. She would rather, she said, try again to win her grandmother's consent But this she found impossible, Madam Conway was determined, and would not listen.

"It grieved her sorely," she said, "thus to cross her favorite child, whom she loved better than her life ; but 'twas for her good, and must be done."

So she wrote a cold, and rather insulting letter to Henry Warner, bidding him, as she had once done before, "let her grand-daughter alone," and saying "it was useless for him to attempt anything secret, for Maggie would be closely watched, the moment there were indications of a clandestine correspondence."

This letter, which was read to Magaret, destroyed all hope, and still she wavered, uncertain whether it would be right to deceive her grandmother. But while she was yet undecided, Hagar's fingers, of late unused to the pen, traced a few lines to Henry Warner, who acting at once upon her suggestion, wrote to Margaret a letter, which he directed to "Hagar Warren, Richland."

In it he urged so many reasons why Maggie should avail herself of this opportunity for communicating with him, that she yielded at last, and regularly each week, old Hagar toiled through sunshine and through storm to the Richland post office, feeling amply repaid for her trouble, when she saw the bright expectant face which almost always greeted her return. Occasionally, by way of lulling the suspicious of

Madam Conway, Henry would direct a letter to Hillsdale, knowing full well it would never meet the eyes of Margaret, over whom, for the time being, a *spy* had been set, in the person of Anna Jeffrey.

This young lady, though but little connected with our story, may perhaps deserve a brief notice Older than either Theo or Margaret, she was neither remarkable for beauty or talent. Dark haired, dark eyed, dark browed, and as the servants said, "dark in her disposition," she was naturally envious of those whose rank in life entitled them to more attention than she was herself accustomed to receive. For this reason, Maggie Miller had from the first been to her an object of dislike, and she was well pleased when Madam Conway, after enjoining upon her the strictest secrecy, appointed her to watch that young lady, and see that no letter was ever carried by her to the post office which Madam Conway had not first examined. In the snaky eyes there was a look of exultation, as Anna Jeffrey promised to be faithful to her trust, and for a time she became literally Maggie Miller's shadow, following her here, following her there, and following her everywhere, until Maggie complained so bitterly of the annoyance, that Madam Conway at last, feeling tolerably sure that no counterplot was intended, revoked her orders, and bade Anna Jeffrey leave Margaret free to do as she pleased.

Thus relieved from espionage, Maggie became a little more like herself, though a sense of the injustice done her by her grandmother, together with the deception she knew she was practising, wore upon her ; and the servants at their work listened in vain for the merry laugh they had loved so well to hear. In the present state of Margaret's feelings, Madam Conway deemed it prudent to say nothing of Arthur Carrollton, whose name was never mentioned

save by Theo and Anna, the latter of whom had seen him in
England, and was never so well pleased as when talking of
his fine country seat, his splendid park, his handsome horses,
and last, though not least, of himself. "He was," she said,
"without exception, the most elegant and aristocratic young
man she had ever seen ;" and then for more than an hour, she
would entertain Theo with a repetition of the many agreeable things he had said to her during the one day she had
spent at his house, while Madam Conway was visiting
there.

In perfect indifference, Maggie, who was frequently present, would listen to these stories, sometimes listlessly turning the leaves of a book, and again smiling scornfully as she
thought how impossible it was that the fastidious Arthur
Carrollton should have been at all pleased with a girl like
Anna Jeffrey ; and positive as Maggie was that she *hated*
him, she insensibly began to feel a very slight degree of interest in him, "at least, she would like to know how he
looked ;" and one day when her grandmother and Theo
were riding, she stole cautiously to the box where she knew
his picture lay, and taking it out, looked to see, "if he were
so very fine looking."

"*Yes he was*," Maggie acknowledged that ; and sure that
she hated him terribly, she lingered long over that picture,
admiring the classically shaped head, the finely cut mouth,
and more than all the large dark eyes which seemed so full
of goodness and truth. "Pshaw !" she exclaimed, at last,
restoring the picture to its place, "If Henry were only a
little taller, and had as handsome eyes, he'd be a great deal
better looking. Any way, I like him, and I *hate* Arthur
Carrollton, who I know is domineering, and would try to
make me mind. He has asked for my daguerreotype,
grandma says, one which looks as I do now. I'll send it

too," and she burst into a loud laugh at the novel idea which had crossed her mind.

That day when Madam Conway returned from her ride, she was surprised at Maggie's proposing that Theo and herself should have their likenesses taken for Arthur Carrollton.

"If he wants my picture," said she, "I am willing he shall have it. It is all he'll ever get."

Delighted at this unexpected concession, Madam Conway gave her consent, and the next afternoon found Theo and Maggie at the daguerrean gallery in Hillsdale, where the latter astonished both her sister and the artist by declaring her intention of not only sitting with her bonnet and shawl on ; but also of turning her *back* to the instrument ! It was in vain that Theo remonstrated ! "That position or none," she said ; and the picture was accordingly taken, presenting a very correct likeness when finished, of a *bonnet*, a *veil*, and a *shawl*, beneath which Maggie Miller was supposed to be.

Strange as it may seem, this freak struck Madam Conway favorably. Arthur Carrollton knew that Maggie was unlike any other person, and the joke, she thought, would increase rather than diminish the interest he already felt in her. So she made no objection, and in a few days it was on its way to England, together with a lock of Hagar's snow white hair, which Maggie had coaxed from the old lady, and unknown to her grandmother, placed in the casing at the last moment.

Several weeks passed away, and then there came an answer —a letter so full of wit and humor that Maggie confessed to herself that he must be very clever to write so many shrewd things, and be withal so perfectly refined. Accompanying the package, was a small rosewood box, containing a most exquisite little pin made of *Hagar's frosty hair*, and

richly ornamented with gold. Not a word was written con
cerning it, and as Maggie kept her own counsel, both Thea
and her grandmother marvelled greatly, admiring its beauty
and wondering for whom it was intended.

"For me, of course," said Madam Conway. "The hair
is Lady Carrollton's, Arthur's grandmother. I know it by its
soft silky look. She has sent it as a token of respect, for
she was always fond of me;" and going to the glass,
she very complacently ornamented her Honiton collar with
Hagar's hair, while Maggie, bursting with fun, beat a hasty
retreat from the room, lest she should betray herself.

Thus the winter passed away, and early in the spring,
George Douglas, to whom Madam Conway had long ago
sent a favorable answer, came to visit his betrothed, bringing to Maggie a note from Rose, who had once or twice
sent messages in Henry's letters. She was in Worcester
now, and her health was very delicate. "Sometimes," she
wrote, "I fear I shall never see you, Maggie Miller—shall
never look into your beautiful face, or listen to your voice ;
but whether in heaven or on earth I am first to meet with
you, my heart claims you as a *sister*, the one whom of all the
sisters in the world I would rather call my own."

"Darling Rose !" murmured Maggie, pressing the delicately traced lines to her lips, "how near she seems to me !
nearer almost than Theo ;" and then involuntarily her
thoughts went backward to the night when Henry Warner
first told her of his love, and when in her dreams there had
been a strange blending together of herself, of Rose, and
the little grave beneath the pine !

But not yet was that veil of mystery to be lifted. Hagar's
secret must be kept a little longer, and unsuspicious of the
truth, Maggie Miller must dream on of sweet Rose Warner,
whom she hopes one day to call her sister !

There was also a message from Henry, and this George Douglas delivered in secret, for he did not care to displease his grandmother elect, who, viewing him through a golden setting, thought he was not to be equalled by any one in America. "So gentlemanly," she said, "and so modest, too," basing her last conclusion upon his evident unwillingness to say very much of himself or his family. Concerning the latter she had questioned him in vain, eliciting nothing save the fact that they lived in the country several miles from Worcester, that his father always staid at home, and consequently his mother went but little into society.

"Despises the vulgar herd, I dare say," thought Madam Conway, contemplating the pleasure she should undoubtedly derive from an acquaintance with Mrs. Douglas, senior !

"There was a sister, too," he said, and at this announcement Theo opened wide her blue eyes, asking her name, and " why he had never mentioned her before."

"I call her Jenny," said he, coloring slightly, and adding playfully, as he caressed Theo's smooth, round cheek, " wives do not usually like their husband's sisters."

"But I shall like *her*, I know," said Theo. " She has a beautiful name, *Jenny Douglas*—much prettier than *Rose Warner*, about whom Maggie talks to me so much."

A gathering frown on her grandmother's face warned Theo that she had touched upon a forbidden subject, and as Mr. Douglas manifested no desire to continue the conversation, it ceased for a time, Theo wishing "she could see Jenny Douglas," and George wondering what she would say when she did see her !

For a few days longer he lingered, and ere his return, it was arranged that early in July, Theo should be his bride. On the morning of his departure, as he stood upon the steps alone with Madam Conway, she said, " I think I can rely upon you, Mr. Douglas, not to carry either letter, note, or message from Maggie to that young Warner. I've forbidden him my house, and I mean what I say."

"I assure you, madam, she has not asked me to carry either," answered George; who, though he knew perfectly well of the secret correspondence, had kept it to himself. "You mistake Mr. Warner, I think," he continued, after a moment. "I have known him long and esteem him highly."

"Tastes differ," returned Madam Conway, coldly. "No man of good breeding would presume to cut up my grandfather's coat, or drink up my best wine."

"He intended no disrespect, I'm sure," answered George. "He only wanted a little *fun* with the stars and stripes."

"It was fun for which he will pay most dearly though," answered Madam Conway, as she bade Mr. Douglas good bye; then walking back to the parlor, she continued speaking to herself, "*Stars and stripes!*" I'll teach him to cut up my blue bodice for *fun*. I wouldn't give him Margaret if his life depended upon it;" and sitting down she wrote to Arthur Carrollton, asking if he really intended visiting America, and when.

CHAPTER XIII.

SOCIETY.

DURING the remainder of the spring, matters at the old stone house proceeded about as usual, Mag writing regularly to Henry, who as regularly answered, while old Hagar managed so adroitly, that no one suspected the secret correspondence, and Madam Conway began to hope her granddaughter had forgotten the foolish fancy. Arthur Carrollton had replied that his visit to America, though sure to take place, was postponed indefinitely, and so the good lady had nothing, in particular, with which to busy herself, save the preparations for Theo's wedding, which was to take place near the first of July.

Though setting a high value upon money, Madam Conway was not penurious, and the bridal trousseau far exceeded anything which Theo had expected. As the young couple were not to keep house for a time, a most elegant suite of rooms had been selected in a fashionable hotel ; and determining that Theo should not, in point of dress, be rivalled by any of her fellow-boarders, Madam Conway spared neither time nor money in making the outfit perfect. So, for weeks, the old stone house presented a scene of great confusion. Chairs, tables, lounges and piano, were piled with finery, on which Anna Jeffrey worked industriously, assisted sometimes by her aunt, whom Madam Conway pro

14

nounced altogether too superannuated for a governess, and
who, though really an excellent scholar, was herself far better pleased with muslin robes and satin bows, than with
French idioms and Latin verbs.   Perfectly delighted, Mag
joined in the general excitement, wondering occasionally
when, and *where* her own bridal would be.   Once she ventured to ask if Henry Warner and his sister might be
invited to Theo's wedding ; but Madam Conway answered
so decidedly in the negative, that she gave it up, consoling
herself with thinking that she would sometime visit her sister, and see Henry, in spite of her grandmother.

The marriage was very quiet, for Madam Conway had no
acquaintance, and the family alone witnessed the ceremony.
At first Madam Conway had hoped that Mr. and Mrs.
Douglas, senior, together with their daughter Jenny, would
be present, and she had accordingly requested George to
invite them, feeling greatly disappointed when she learned
that they could not come.

"I wanted so much to see them," she said to Mag, "and
know whether they are worthy to be related to the Conways
—but of course they are, as much so as any American
family.   George has every appearance of refinement and
high-breeding."

"But his family, for all that, may be as ignorant as
farmer Canfield's," answered Mag ; to which her grandmother replied, "you needn't tell me that, for *I'm* not to be
deceived in such matters.   I can tell at a glance if a person
is *low-born*, no matter what their education or advantages
may have been.—Who's that ?" she added, quickly and
turning round she saw old Hagar, her eyes lighted up, and
her lips moving with an incoherent sound, not easily understood.

Hagar had come up to the wedding, and had reached the

door of Madam Conway's room just in time to hear the last remark, which roused her at once.

"Why don't she discover *my secret*, then," she muttered, "if she has so much discernment? Why don't she see the *Hagar* blood in her? for it's there, plain as day;" and she glanced proudly at Mag, who, in her simple robe of white was far more beautiful than the bride.

And still Theo, in her handsome travelling dress, was very fair to look upon, and George Douglas felt proud, that she was his, resolving, as he kissed away the tears she shed at parting, that the vow he had just made should never be broken. A few weeks of pleasant travel westward, and then the newly-wedded pair came back to what, for a time, was to be their home.

George Douglas was highly respected in Worcester, both as a man of honor and a man of wealth; consequently, every possible attention was paid to Theo, who was petted and admired, until she began to wonder why neither Mag, nor yet her all-discerning grandmother, had discovered how charming and faultless she was!

Among George's acquaintance, was a Mrs. Morton, a dashing, fashionable woman, who determined to honor the bride with a party, to which all the *élite* of Worcester were invited, together with many of the Bostonians Madam Conway and Mag were of course upon the list, and as timely notice was given them by Theo, Madam Conway went twice to Springfield in quest of a suitable dress for Mag. "She wanted something becoming," she said, and a delicate rose-colored satin, with a handsome overskirt of lace, was, at last, decided upon.

"She must have some pearls for her hair," thought Madam Conway, and when next Maggie, who, girl-like, tried the effect of her first party dress at least a dozen times, stood before the glass to see "if it were exactly the right length," she was presented with the pearls, which Anna Jeffrey, with a feeling of envy at her heart, arranged in the shining braids of her hair.

"Oh, isn't it perfectly splendid!" cried Mag, herself half inclined to compliment the beautiful image reflected in the mirror.

"You ought to see Arthur Carrollton's sister, when she is dressed, if you think you look handsome," answered Anna, adding that "*diamonds* were much more fashionable than *pearls.*"

"You have attended a great many parties and seen a great deal of fashion, so I dare say you are right," Mag answered, ironically; and then, as through the open window she saw Hagar approaching, she ran out upon the piazza to see what the old woman would say.

Hagar had never seen her thus before, and now, throwing up her hands in astonishment, she involuntarily dropped upon her knees, and while the tears rained over her time-worn face, whispered, "Hester's child—*my grand-daughter*—heaven be praised!"

"Do I look pretty?" Margaret asked; and Hagar answered, "More beautiful than any one I ever saw. I wish your mother could see you now."

Involuntarily Maggie glanced at the tall marble gleaming through the distant trees, while Hagar's thoughts were down in that other grave—the grave beneath the pine. The next day was the party, and at an early hour. Madam Conway was ready. Her rich purple satin and Valenciennes laces, with which she hoped to impress Mrs. Douglas senior, were carefully packed up together with Maggie's dress; and then, shawled and bonneted, she waited impatiently for her carriage, which she preferred to the cars. It came at last, but in place of John, the usual coachman, Mike, a rather wild youth of twenty, was mounted upon the box. His father, he said, had been taken suddenly ill, and had deputed him to drive.

For a time Madam Conway hesitated, for she knew Mike's one great failing, and she hardly dared risk herself with him, lest she should find a seat less desirable even than the memorable brush-heap. But Mike protested loudly to having joined the "Sons of Temperance" only the night before, and as in his new suit of blue, with shining brass buttons, he presented a more stylish appearance than his father, his mistress finally decided to try him, threatening all manner of evil if, in any way, he broke his pledge, either to herself or the " Sons," the latter of whom had probably never heard of him. He was perfectly sober now, and drove them safely to Worcester, where they soon found themselves in Theo's handsome rooms. Her wrappings removed and herself snugly ensconced in a velvet-cushioned chair, Madam Conway asked, " How long before Mrs. Douglas, senior, would probably arrive."

A slight shadow, which no one observed, passed over Theo's face as she answered, " George's father seldom goes into society, and consequently, his mother will not come."

" Oh, I am so sorry," replied Madam Conway, thinking of the purple satin, and continuing, " Nor the young lady, either ?"

" None of them," answered Theo, adding hastily, as if to change the conversation, " Isn't my piano perfectly elegant ?' and she ran her fingers over an exquisitely carved instrument, which had inscribed upon it simply "Theo ;" and then, as young brides sometimes will, she expatiated upon the kindness and generosity of George, showing, withal, that her love for her husband was founded upon something far more substantial than family or wealth.

Her own happiness, it would seem, had rendered her less selfish and more thoughtful for others; for once that after-noon, on returning to her room after a brief absence, she whispered to Mag that " *some one* in the parlor below wished to see her."

Then seating herself at her grandmother's feet, she enter-tained her so well with a description of her travels, that the good lady failed to observe the absence of Mag, who, face to face with Henry Warner, was making amends for their long separation. Much they talked of the past, and then Henry spoke of the future; but of this Mag was less hopeful. Her grandmother would never consent to their marriage, she knew—the *stars* and *stripes* had decided that matter, even though there were no Arthur Carrollton across the sea, and Mag sighed despondingly as she thought of the long years of single-blessedness in store for her.

" There is but one alternative left then," said Henry. " If your grandmother refuses her consent altogether, I must take you without her consent."

" I shan't run away," said Mag; " I shall live an old maid, and you must live an old bachelor, until grandma"——

She did not have time to finish the sentence ere Henry commenced unfolding the following plan :—

" It was necessary," he said, " for either him or Mr. Doug-las to go to Cuba; and, as Rose's health made a change of climate advisable for her, George had proposed to him to go, and take his sister there for the winter. And, Maggie," he continued, "will you go, too? We are to sail the middle of October, stopping for a few weeks in Florida, until the unhealthy season in Havana is passed. I will see your grandmother to-morrow morning—will once more honorably ask her for your hand, and if she still refuses, as you think she will, it cannot surely be wrong in you to consult your own happiness instead of her prejudices. I will meet you at old Hagar's cabin at the time appointed. Rose and my aunt, who is to accompany her, will be in New York, whither we will go immediately. A few moments more and you will be my wife, and beyond the control of your grand-mother, Do you approve my plan, Maggie, darling? Will you go."

Maggie could not answer him then, for an elopement was something from which she instinctively shrunk, and with a faint hope that her grandmother might consent, she went back to her sister's room, where she had not yet been missed. Very rapidly the remainder of the afternoon passed away, and at an early hour, wishing to know "exactly how she was going to look," Mag commenced her toilet. Theo, too, desirous of displaying her white satin as long as possible, began to dress; while Madam Conway, in no haste to don her purple satin, which was uncomfortably tight, amused herself by watching the passers by, nodding at intervals, in her chair.

While thus occupied, a perfumed note was brought to her, the contents of which elicited from her an exclamation of surprise.

"*Can it be possible!*" she said; and thrusting the note into her pocket, she hastily left the room.

She was gone a long, long time ; and when at last she re-turned, she was evidently much excited, paying no attention whatever to Theo, who, in her bridal robes, looked charm ingly, but minutely inspecting Mag, to see if in her adorn-ings there was aught out of its place. Her dress was fault less, and she looked so radiantly beautiful, as she stood before her grandmother, that the old lady kissed her foudly.

whispering, as she did so, " You are indeed beautiful." It was a long time ere Madam Conway commenced her own toilet, and then she proceeded so slowly that George Douglas became impatient, and she finally suggested that he and Theo should go without her, sending the carriage back for herself and Mag. To this proposition he at last yielded ; and when they were left alone, Madam Conway greatly accelerated her movements, dressing herself in a few moments, and then, much to Mag's surprise, going below without a word of explanation. A few moments only elapsed ere a servant was sent to Mag saying that her presence was desired at No. 40, a small private parlor, adjoining the public drawing-rooms.

" What can it mean ? Is it possible that *Henry* is there?" Mag, asked herself, as with a beating heart she descended the stairs.

A moment more, and Mag stood on the threshold of No. 40. Seated up on the sofa was Madam Conway, her purple satin seeming to have taken a wide sweep, and her face betokening the immense degree of satisfaction she felt in being there thus with the stylish, elegant looking stranger who stood at her side, with his deep, expressive eyes fixed upon the door expectantly. Maggie knew him in a moment— knew it was *Arthur Carrollton ;* and, turning pale, she started backward, while he advanced forward and offering her his hand, looked down upon her with a winning smile, saying, as he did so, " Excuse my familiarity. You are Maggie Miller, I am sure."

For an instant Mag could not reply, but soon recovering her composure, she received the stranger gracefully, and then taking the chair he politely brought her, she listened while her grandmother told that " he had arrived at Montreal two weeks before ; that he had reached Hillsdale that morning, an hour or two after their departure, and learning their destination, had followed them in the cars; that she had taken the liberty of informing Mrs. Morton of his arrival, and that lady had of course extended to him an invitation to be present at her party."

"Which invitation I accept, provided Miss Maggie allows me to be her escort," said the young man, and again his large, black eyes rested admiringly upon her.

Mag had anticipated a long, quiet talk with Henry Warner, and, wishing the Englishman anywhere but there, she answered coldly, "I cannot well decline your escort, Mr. Carrollton, so of course I accept it."

Madam Conway bit her lip, but Mr. Carrollton, who was prepared for anything from Maggie Miller, was not in the least displeased, and, consulting his diamond-set watch, which pointed to nearly ten, he asked "if it were not time to go."

"Certainly," said Madam Conway. "You remain here, Maggie; I will bring down your shawl," and she glided from the room, leaving them purposely alone.

Mag was a good deal astonished, slightly embarrassed and a little provoked, all of which Arthur Carrollton readily saw; but this did not prevent his talking to her, and during the few minutes of Madam Conway's absence, he decided that neither Margaret's beauty, nor yet her originality, had been overrated by her partial grandmother, while Mag, on her part, mentally pronounced him "the finest looking, the most refined, the most gentlemanly, the proudest, and *the atefullest* man she had ever seen!"

Wholly unconscious of her cogitation, he wrapped her shawl very carefully about her, taking care to cover her white shoulders from the night air; then offering his arm to her grandmother, he led the way to the carriage, whither

14*

she followed him, wondering if Henry would be jealous, and thinking her first act would be to tell him "how she *hated* Arthur Carrollton, and *always should !*"

It was a gay, brilliant scene which Mrs. Morton's drawing-rooms presented, and as yet the centre of attraction, Theo, near the door, was bowing to the many strangers who sought her acquaintance. Greatly she marvelled at the long delay of her grandmother and Maggie, and she had just suggested to Henry that he should go in quest of them, when she saw her sister ascending the stairs.

On a sofa across the room, sat a pale, young girl, arrayed in white, her silken curls falling around her neck like a golden shower, and her mournful eyes of blue, scanning eagerly each new comer, then with a look of disappointment drooping beneath the long lashes which rested wearily upon her colorless cheek. It was Rose Warner, and the face she sought was Maggie Miller's. She had seen no semblance of it yet, for Henry had no daguerreotype. Still, she felt sure she would know it, and when at last, in all her queenly beauty, Maggie came, leaning on Arthur Carrollton's arm, Rose's heart made ready answer to the oft repeated question, " who is she ?"

"Beautiful, gloriously beautiful," she whispered softly, while, from the grave of her buried hopes, there came one wild heart-throb, one sudden burst of pain caused by the first sight of her rival, and then Rose Warner grew calm again, and those who saw the pressure of her hand upon her side, dreamed not of the fierce pang within. She had asked her brother not to tell Maggie she was to be there. She would rather watch her awhile, herself unknown ; and now with eager, curious eyes, she followed Maggie, who was quickly surrounded by a host of admirers.

It was Maggie's first introduction into society, and yet, so perfect was her intuition of what was proper, that neither by word or deed did she do aught to shock the most fastidious. It is true her merry laugh more than once rang out above the din of voices ; but it was so joyous that no one objected, particularly when they looked in her bright and almost childish face. Arthur Carrollton, too, acting as her escort, aided her materially, for it was soon whispered around that he was a wealthy Englishman, and many were the comments made upon the handsome couple, who seemed singularly adapted to each other. A glance had convinced Arthur Carrollton, that Maggie was by far the most beautiful lady present, and feeling that on this, her first introduction into society, she needed some one to shield her, as it were, from the many foolish, flattering speeches which were sure to be made in her hearing, he kept her at his side, where she was nothing loth to stay ; for notwithstanding that she " *hated him so,*" there was about him a fascination she did not try to resist.

" They are a splendid couple," thought Rose, and then she looked to see how Henry was affected by the attentions of the handsome foreigner.

But Henry was not jealous, and standing a little aloof, he felt more pleasure than pain in watching Maggie as she received the homage of the gay throng. Thoughts similar to those of Rose, however, forced themselves upon him as he saw the dignified bearing of Mr. Carrollton, and for the first time in his life he was conscious of an uncomfortable feeling of inferiority to something or somebody, he hardly knew what. This feeling, however, passed away when Maggie came at last to his side, with her winning smile, and playful words

Very closely Madam Conway watched her now; but Maggie did not heed it, and leaning on Henry's arm, she seemed oblivious to all save him. After a time, he led her out upon a side piazza, where they would be comparatively alone. Observing that she seemed a little chilly, he left her for a moment, while he went in quest of her shawl. Scarcely was he gone when a slight, fairy form came flitting through the moonlight to where Maggie sat, and twining its snow white arms around her neck, looked lovingly into her eyes, whispering soft and low, "My sister."

"*My sister!*" How Maggie's blood bounded at the sound of that name, which even the night wind, sighing through the trees, seemed to take up and repeat, "My sister!" What was there in those words thus to affect her? Was that fair young creature, who hung so fondly over her, naught to her save a common stranger? Was there no tie between them, no bond of sympathy and love? We ask this of you, our reader, and not of Maggie Miller, for to her there came no questioning like this. She only knew that every pulsation of her heart responded to the name of *sister*, when breathed by sweet Rose Warner, and folding her arms about her, she pillowed the golden head upon her bosom, and pushing back the clustering curls, gazed long and earnestly into a face which seemed so heavenly and pure.

Few were the words they uttered at first, for the *mysterious, invisible something* which prompted each to look into the other's eyes, to clasp the other's hands, to kiss the other's lips, and whisper the other's name.

"I have wished so much to see you, to know if you are worthy of my noble brother," said Rose at last, thinking she must say something on the subject uppermost in both their minds

"And am I worthy?" asked Maggie, the bright blushes stealing over her cheek. "Will you let me be your sister?"

"My heart would claim you for that, even though I had no brother," answered Rose, and again her lips touched those of Maggie.

Seeing them thus together, Henry tarried purposely a long time, and when at last he rejoined them, he proposed returning to the drawing-room, where many inquiries were making for Maggie.

"I have looked for you a long time, Miss Maggie," said Mr. Carrollton. "I wish to hear you play," and taking her arm in his, he led her to the piano.

From the moment of her first introduction to him, Maggie had felt that there was something commanding in his manner, something she could not disobey ; and now, though she fancied it was impossible to play before that multitude, she seated herself mechanically, and while the keys swam before her eyes, went through with a difficult piece, which she had never but once before executed correctly.

"You have done well, much better than I anticipated," said Mr. Carrollton, again offering her his arm ; and though a little vexed, those few words of commendation were worth more to Maggie than the most flattering speech which Henry Warner had ever made to her.

Soon after leaving the piano, a young man approached, and invited her to waltz. This was something in which Maggie excelled ; for two winters before, Madam Conway had hired a teacher to instruct her grand-daughters in dancing, and she was about to accept the invitation, when, drawing her arm still closer within his own, Mr. Carrollton looked down upon her, saying softly, "I wouldn't."

Maggie had often waltzed with Henry at home. He saw no harm in it, and now when Arthur Carrollton objected, she was provoked, while at the same time she felt constrained to decline.

"Sometime, when I know you better, I will explain to you *why* I do not think it proper for young girls to waltz with every one," said Mr. Carrollton; and leading her from the drawing-room, he devoted himself to her for the remainder of the evening, making himself so perfectly agreeable, that Maggie forgot everything, even Henry Warner, who in the meantime had tried to recognize Madam Conway as an acquaintance.

A cool nod, however, was all the token of recognition she had to give him. This state of feeling augured ill for the success of his suit; but when at a late hour that night, in spite of grandmother or Englishman, he handed Maggie to the carriage, he whispered to her softly, "I will see her to-morrow morning, and know the worst."

The words caught the quick ear of Madame Conway ; but not wishing Mr. Carrollton to know there was anything particular between her grand-daughter and Henry Warner, she said nothing, and when arrived at last at the hotel, she asked an explanation, Maggie, who hurried off to bed, was too sleepy to give her any answer.

"I shall know before long, any way, if he sees me in the morning," she thought, as she heard a distant clock strike two, and settling her face into the withering frown with which she intended to annihilate Henry Warner, the old lady was herself, ere long, much faster asleep than the young girl at her side, who was thinking of Henry Warner, wishing he was three inches taller, or herself three inches shorter, and wondering if his square shoulders would not be somewhat improved by *braces!*

"I never noticed how *short* and *crooked* he was," she thought, "until I saw him standing by the side of Mr

Carrollton, who is such a splendid figure, so tall and straight; but big, overgrown girls like me, always get short husbands, they say," and satisfied with this conclusion, she fell asleep.

CHAPTER XIV.

MADAM CONWAY'S DISASTERS.

AT a comparatively early hour Madam Conway arose, and going to the parlor, found there Arthur Carrollton, who asked if Margaret were not yet up. "Say that I wish her to ride with me on horseback," said he. "The morning air will do her good;" and quite delighted, Madam Conway carried the message to her grand-daughter.

"Tell him I shan't do it," answered the sleepy Maggie, adjusting herself for another nap. Then, as she thought how his eyes probably looked as he said, "I wish her to ride," she felt impelled to obey, and greatly to her grand-mother's surprise, she commenced dressing.

Theo's riding dress was borrowed, and though it did not fit her exactly, she looked unusually well, when she met Mr Carrollton in the lower hall, and once mounted upon the gay steed, and galloping away into the country, she felt more than repaid for the loss of her morning slumber.

"You ride well," said Mr. Carrollton, when at last they paused upon the brow of a hill, overlooking the town, "but you have some faults, which, with your permission I will correct," and in the most polite and gentlemanly manner, he proceeded to speak of a few points wherein her riding might be improved.

Among other things, he said she rode too fast for a lady ;

and biting her lip, Maggie thought, " If I only had Gritty here, I'd lead him such a race as would either break his *bones* or his *neck*, I'm not particular which."

Still, she followed his directions implicitly, and when, ere they reached home, he told her that she excelled many who had been for years to riding schools, she felt repaid for his criticisms, which she knew were just, even if they were not agreeable. Breakfast being over, he announced his inten· tention of going down to Boston, telling Maggie he should probably return that evening and go with her to Hillsdale on the morrow.

Scarcely had he gone when Henry Warner appeared, asking an interview with Madam Conway, who haughtily led the way into a private room. Very candidly and honorably Henry made known to her his wishes, whereupon a most stormy scene ensued, the lady so far forgetting herself as to raise her voice several notes above its usual pitch, while Henry, angered by her insulting words, bade her take the consequences of her refusal, hinting that girls had been known to marry without their guardian's consent.

" An elopement, hey ? He threatens me with an elope-ment, does he ?" said Madam Conway, as the door closed after him. · " I am glad he warned me in time," and then trembling in every limb lest Maggie should be spirited away before her very eyes, she determined upon going home immediately, and leaving Arthur Carrollton to follow in the cars

Accordingly Maggie was bidden to pack her things at once, the excited old lady keeping her eye constantly upon her to see that she did not disappear through the window or some other improbable place. In silence Maggie obeyed, pouting the while a very little, partly because she should not again see Henry, partly because she had confidently ex pected to ride home with Mr. Carrollton ! and partly be cause she wished to stay to the firemen's muster, which had long been talked about, and was to take place on the morrow. They were ready at last, and then in a very perturbed state of feeling, Madam Conway waited for her carriage, which was not forthcoming, and upon inquiry, George Douglas learned that, having counted upon another day in the city, Mike was now going through with a series of *plunge baths*, by way of sobering himself ere appearing before his mistress. This, however George kept from Madam Conway, not wishing to alarm her ; and when, after a time, Mike appeared, sitting bolt upright upon the box, with the lines grasped firmly in his hands, she did not suspect the truth, nor know that he, too, was angry for being thus compelled to go home before he saw the firemen.

Thinking him sober enough to be perfectly safe, George Douglas felt no fear, and bowing to his new relatives, went back to comfort Theo, who, as a matter of course cried a little when the carriage drove away. Worcester was left behind, and they were far out in the country ere a word was exchanged between Madam Conway and Maggie ; for while the latter was pouting behind her veil, the former was wondering what possessed Mike to drive into every rut and over every stone.

"You, Mike," she exclaimed at last leaning from the window. " What ails you ?"

"Nothing, as I'm a living man," answered Mike, halting so suddenly as to jerk the lady backwards and mash the crown of her bonnet.

Straightening herself up, and trying in vain to smooth the *jam*, Madam Conway continued, " In liquor, I know I wish I had staid at home ;" but Mike loudly denied the charge, declaring " he had spent the blessed night at a meeting of the *Sons*, where they passed round nothing stronger than lemons and water, and if the horses chose to run off the track, 'twasn't his fault—he couldn't help it," and with the air of one deeply injured, he again started forward, turning off ere long into a cross road, which, as they advanced, grew more stony and rough, while the farm-houses, as a general thing, presented a far less respectable appearance than those on the Hillsdale route

"Mike, you villain!" ejaculated the lady, as they ran down into a ditch, and she sprang to one side to keep the carriage from going over.

But ere she had time for anything further, one of the axle-trees snapped asunder, and to proceed further in their present condition was impossible. Alighting from the carriage, and setting her little feet upon the ground with a vengeance, Madam Conway first scolded Mike unmercifully for his carelessness, and next chided Maggie for manifesting no more concern.

"You'd as lief go to destruction as not, I do believe!" said she, looking carefully after the bandbox containing her purple satin.

"I'd rather go *there* first," answered Maggie, pointing to a brown, old-fashioned farmhouse, about a quarter of a mile away.

At first, Madam Conway objected, saying she preferred sitting on the bank to intruding herself upon strangers; but as it was now noon-day, and the warm September sun poured fiercely down upon her, she finally concluded to follow Maggie's advice, and gathering up her box and parasol started for the house, which, with its tansy patch on the right, and its single poplar tree in front, presented rather an uninviting appearance.

"Some vulgar creatures live there, I know. Just hear

that old tin horn," she exclaimed, as a blast, loud and shrill
blown by practised lips, told to the men in a distant field
that dinner was ready.

A nearer approach disclosed to view a slanting roofed
farm-house, such as is often found in New England, with
high, narrow windows, small panes of glass, and the most
indispensable paper curtains of blue, closely shading the windows of what was probably "the best room." In the apartment opposite, however, they were rolled up, so as to show
the old-fashioned drapery of dimity, bordered with a netted
fringe. Half a dozen broken pitchers and pots held gerani-
ums, verbenas and other plants, while the well kept beds of
hollyhocks, sunflowers and poppies, indicated a taste for
flowers in some one. Everything about the house was
faultlessly neat. The door-sill was scrubbed to a chalky-
white, while the uncovered floor wore the same polished hue.

All this Madam Conway saw at a glance, but it did not
prevent her from holding high her aristocratic skirts, lest
they should be contaminated, and when, in answer to her
knock, an odd-looking, peculiarly dressed woman appeared,
she uttered an exclamation of disgust, and turning to Maggie, said, " You talk—I can't!"

But the woman did not stand at all upon ceremony.
For the last ten minutes she had been watching the strangers as they toiled over the sandy road, and when sure they
were coming there, had retreated into her bed-room, donning
a flaming red calico, which, guiltless of hoops, clung to her
tenaciously, showing her form to good advantage, and rous-
ing at once the risibles of Maggie. A black lace cap, ornamented with ribbons of the same fanciful color as the dress,
adorned her head ; and with a dozen or more pins in her
mouth, she now appeared, hooking her sleeve and smooth
ing down the black collar upon her neck.

In a few words, Maggie explained to her their misfortune, and asked permission to tarry there until the carriage was repaired.

"Certing, certing," answered the woman, courtesying almost to the floor. "Walk right in, if you can git in. It's my cheese day, or I should have been cleared away sooner. Here Betsey Jane, you have prinked long enough ; come and hist the winders in t'other room, and wing 'em off, so the ladies can set in there out of this dirty place," then turning to Madam Conway, who was industriously freeing her French kids from the sand they had accumulated during her walk, she continued. "Have some of my shoes to rest your feet a spell ;" and diving into a recess or closet she brought forth a pair of slippers large enough to hold both of Madam Conway's feet at once.

With a haughty frown the lady declined the offer, while Maggie looked on in delight, pleased with an adventure which promised so much fun. After a moment, Betsey Jane appeared, attired in a dress similar to that of her mother, for whose lank appearance she made ample amends in the wonderful expansion of her robes, which minus gather or fold at the bottom, set out like a miniature tent, upsetting at once the band-box which Madam Conway had placed upon a chair, and which, with its contents, rolled promiscuously over the floor !

"*Betsey Jane!* How can you wear them abominable things !" exclaimed the distressed woman, stooping to pick up the purple satin which had tumbled out.

A look from the more fashionable daughter, as with a swinging sweep she passed on into the parlor, silenced the mother on the subject of *hoops*, and thinking her guests must necessarily be thirsty after their walk, she brought them a pitcher of water, asking if " they'd chuse it clear, or with a

little ginger and molasses," at the same time calling to Betsey Jane to know if them windows was *wung* off!

The answer was in the affirmative, whereupon the ladies
were invited to enter, which they did the more willingly, as
through the open door they had caught glimpses of what
proved to be a very handsome Brussels carpet, which in
that room seemed a little out of place, as did the sofa, and
handsome hair-cloth rocking chair.   In this last Madam
Conway seated herself, while Maggie reclined upon a lounge,
wondering at the difference in the various articles of furniture, some of which were quite expensive, while others were
of the most common kind.

"Who can they be?   She looks like some one I have
seen," said Maggie as Betsey Jane left the room.   "I mean
to ask their names;" but this her grandmother would not suffer.   "It was too much like familiarity," she said, "and
she did not believe in putting one's self on a level with such
people."

Another loud blast from the horn was blown, for the bustling woman of the house was evidently getting uneasy, and
ere long three or four men appeared, washing themselves
from the spout of the pump, and wiping upon a coarse towel,
which hung upon a roller near the back door.

"I shan't eat at the same table with those creatures,"
said Madam Conway, feeling intuitively that she would be
invited to dinner.

"Why, grandma, yes you will, if she asks you to," answered Maggie.   "Only think how kind they are to us perfect strangers!"

What else she might have said was prevented by the entrance of Betsey Jane, who informed them that "dinner was
ready;" and with a mental groan, as she thought how she
was about to be martyred, Madam Conway followed her to

the dining-room, where a plain substantial farmer's meal was spread. Standing at the head of the table, with her good-humored face all in a glow, was the hostess, who pointing Madam Conway to a chair, said, "Now set right by, and make yourselves to hum. Mebby I orto have set the table over, and I guess I should if I had anything fit to eat. Be you fond of biled victuals?" and taking it for granted they were, she loaded both Madam Conway's and Maggie's plate with every variety of vegetables used in the preparation of the dish known everywhere as "boiled victuals."

By this time the men had ranged themselves in respectful silence upon the opposite side of the table, each stealing an admiring though modest glance at Maggie ; for the masculine heart, whether it beat beneath a homespun frock or coat of finest cloth, is alike susceptible to glowing, youthful beauty like that of Maggie Miller. The head of the house was absent—"had gone to town with a load of wood," so his spouse informed the ladies, at the same time pouring out a cup of tea, which she said she had tried to make strong enough to bear up an egg. "Betsey Jane," she continued, casting a deprecating glance, first at the blue sugar bowl and then at her daughter, "what possessed you to put on this brown sugar, when I told you to get crush?—Have some of the apple sass? it's new—made this morning. Dew have some," she continued as Madam Conway shook her head. "Mebby it's better than it looks. Seem's ef you wasn't goin' to eat nothin'. Betsey Jane, now you're up after the crush, fetch them china sassers for the cowcumbers. Like enough she'll eat some of them."

But affecting a headache, Madam Conway declined everything, save the green tea and a Boston cracker, which, at the first mention of headache, the distressed woman had brought her. Suddenly remembering Mike, who having fixed the carriage, was fast asleep on a wheelbarrow under the wood-shed, she exclaimed, "For the land of massy, if I hain't forgot that young gentleman! Go, William and call him this minute. Are you sick at your stomach?" she asked, turning to Madam Conway, who, at the thoughts of eating with her drunken coachman, had uttered an exclamation of disgust. "Go, Betsey Jane, and fetch the camphire, quick!"

But Madam Conway did not need the camphor, and so she said, adding that Mike was better where he was. Mike thought so too, and refused to come, whereupon the woman insisted that he must. "There was room enough," she said, "and no kind of sense in Betsey Jane's taking up the hull side of the table with them ratans. She could set nearer the young lady."

"Certainly," answered Maggie, anxious to see how the *ratans* would manage to squeeze in between herself and the table-leg, as they would have to do if they came an inch nearer.

This feat could not be done, and in attempting it Betsey Jane upset Maggie's tea upon her handsome travelling dress, eliciting from her mother the exclamation, "*Betsey Jane Douglas*, you allus was the blunderin'est girl!"

This little accident diverted the woman's mind from Mike, while Madam Conway, starting at the name of *Douglas*, thought to herself, "Douglas!—Douglas! I did not suppose 'twas so common a name. But then it don't hurt George any, having these creatures bear his name."

Dinner being over, Madam Conway and Maggie returned to the parlor, where, while the former resumed her chair, the latter amused herself by examining the books and odd-looking daguerreotypes which lay upon the table.

"Oh, *grandmother!*" she almost screamed, bounding to

that lady's side, "as I live, here's a picture of *Theo and George Douglas* taken together," and she held up a handsome casing before the astonished old lady, who donning her golden spectacles in a twinkling saw for herself that what Maggie said was true.

"They *stole* it," she gasped. "We are in a den of thieves! Who knows what they'll take from my bandbox?" and she was about to leave the room, when Maggie, whose quick mind saw farther ahead, bade her stop.

"I may discover something more," said she, and taking a handsomely bound volume of Lamb, she turned to the flyleaf, and read, "*Jenny Douglas*, from her brother George, Worcester, Jan. 8th."

It was plain to her now; but any mortification she might otherwise have experienced was lost in the one absorbing thought, "*What will grandma say?*"

"Grandmother," said she, showing the book, "don't you remember the mother of that girl called her *Betsey Jane Douglas?*"

"Yes, yes," gasped Madam Conway, raising both hands, while an expression of deep, intense anxiety was visible upon her face.

"And don't you know, too," continued Maggie, "that George always seemed inclined to say as little as possible f his parents? Now, in this country, it is not unusual for he sons of just such people as these to be among the most wealthy and respectable citizens."

"Maggie, Maggie," hoarsely whispered Madam Conway, grasping Maggie's arm, "*do* you mean to insinuate—am I to understand that you believe that odious woman and hideous girl to be the mother and sister of George Douglas?"

"I haven't a doubt of it," answered Maggie. "'Twas the
15

resemblance between Betsey Jane and George, which I observed at first."

Out of her chair to the floor tumbled Madam Conway, fainting entirely away, while Maggie, stepping to the door, called for help.

"I mistrusted she was awful sick at dinner," said Mrs. Douglas, taking her hands from the dishwater, and running to the parlor. "I wish she'd smelt of the camphor, as I wanted her to. Does she have such spells often?"

By this time Betsey Jane had brought a basin of water, which she dashed in the face of the unconscious woman, who soon began to revive.

"Pennyryal tea'll settle her stomach quicker'n anything else," said Mrs. Douglas. "I'll clap a little right on the stove;" and helping Madam Conway to the sofa, she left the room.

"There may possibly be a mistake, after all," thought Maggie. "I'll question the girl," and turning to Betsey Jane, she said, taking up the book which had before attracted her attention, "Is this, Jenny Douglas, intended for you?"

"Yes, ma'am," answered the girl, coloring slightly. "Brother George calls me Jenny, because he thinks *Betsey* so old fashioned."

An audible groan from the sofa, and Maggie continued, "Where does your brother live?"

"In Worcester, ma'am. He keeps a store there," answered Betsey, who was going to say more, when her mother reëntering the room, took up the conversation by saying, "Was you tellin' 'em about *George Washington?* Wal, he's a boy no mother need to be ashamed on, though my old man sometimes says he's ashamed of us, we are so different. But then he orto consider the advantages he's had. We only brung him up till he was ten years old, and then an uncle he was named after took him, and gin him a college schoolin', and then put him into his store in Worcester. Your head aches *wus*, don't it? Poor thing! The pennyryal will be steeped directly," she added, in an aside to Mada n Conway, who had groaned aloud as if in pain. Then resuming her story, she continued, "Better'n six year ago, Uncle George, who was a bachelder, died, leaving the heft of his property, seventy-five thousand dollars, or more, to my son, who is now top of the heap in the store, and worth $100,000, I presume; some say, $200,000: but that's the way some folks have of *agitatin'* things."

" Is he married?" asked Maggie, and Mrs. Douglas, mistaking the motive which prompted the question, answered, "Yes, dear, he is. If he wan't, I know of no darter-in-law I'd as soon have as *you*. I don't believe in finding fault with my son's wife; but there's a proud look in her face, I don't like. This is her picter," and she passed to Maggie the daguerreotype of Theo.

" I've looked at it before," said Maggie, and the good woman proceeded. " I hain't seen her yet; but he's goin' to bring her to Charlton bimeby. He's a good boy, George is, free as water;—gave me this carpet, the sofy and chair, and has paid Betsey Jane's schoolin' one winter at Leicester. But Betsey don't take to books much. She's more like me, her father says. They had a big party for George last night, but I wasn't invited. Shouldn't a' gone if I had been; but for all that, a body don't wan't to be slighted, even if hey don't belong to the quality. If I'm good enough to be George's mother I'm good enough to go to a party with his wife. But she wan't to blame, and I shan't lay it up against her. I shall see her to-morrow, pretty likely, for Sam Babbit's wife and I are goin' down to the firemen's muster

You've heard on't, I s'pose. The different engines are goin' to see which will shute water the highest over a 180 foot pole. I wouldn't miss goin' for anything, and of course I shall call on *Theodoshy*. I calkerlate to like her, and when they go to housekeepin', I've got a hull chest full of sheets, and piller-biers, and towels I'm goin' to give her, besides three or four bed quilts I pieced myself, two in herrin'-bone pattern, and one in risin' sun. I'll show 'em to you," and leaving the room, she soon returned with three patch-work quilts, wherein were all possible shades of color, red and yellow predominating, and in one the "rising sun" forming a huge centre piece.

"Heavens!" faintly articulated Madam Conway, pressing her hands upon her head, which was supposed to be aching dreadfully. The thought of *Theo* reposing beneath the "risin' sun," or yet the "herrin'-bone," was intolerable; and looking beseechingly at Maggie, she whispered, "*Do see* if Mike is ready."

"If it's the carriage you mean," chimed in Mrs. Douglas, "it's been waiting quite a spell, but I thought you warn't fit to ride yet, so I didn't tell you."

Starting to her feet, Madam Conway's bonnet went on in a trice, and taking her shawl in her hand, she walked out doors, barely expressing her thanks to Mrs. Douglas, who, greatly distressed at her abrupt departure, ran for the herb tea, and taking the tin cup in her hand, followed her guest to the carriage, urging her to "take a swaller just to keep from vomiting."

"She's better without it," said Maggie. "She seldom takes medicine," and politely expressing her gratitude to Mrs. Douglas for her kindness, she bade Mike drive on.

"Some crazy critter just out of the Asylum, I'll bet," said Mrs Douglas, walking back to the house with her pennyroyal tea. "How queer she acted! but that girl's a lady, every inch of her, and so handsome, too, I wonder who she is?"

"Don't you believe the old woman felt a little above us?" suggested Betsey Jane, who had more discernment than her mother.

"Like enough she did, though I never thought on't. But she needn't. I'm as good as she is, and I'll warrant as much thought on, where I'm known;" and quite satisfied with her own position, Mrs. Douglas went back to her dishwashing, while Betsey Jane stole away up stairs to try the experiment of arranging her hair after the fashion in which Margaret wore hers.

In the meantime, Mike, perfectly sobered, had turned his horses' heads in the direction of Hillsdale, when Madame Conway called out, "To Worcester, Mike—to Worcester, as fast as you can drive."

"*To Worcester!* For what?" asked Maggie, and the excited woman answered. "*To stop it. To forbid the bans.* I should think you'd ask *for what?*"

"To stop it," repeated Maggie. "I'd like to see you stop it, when they've been married two months!"

"So they have, *so they have,*" said Madam Conway, wringing her hands in her despair, and crying out, "that a *Conway* should be so disgraced. What shall I do? What shall I do?"

"Make the best of it, of course," answered Maggie. "I don't see as George is any worse for his parentage. He is evidently greatly respected in Worcester, where his family are undoubtedly known. He is educated and refined, if they are not. Theo loves him, and that is sufficient, unless I add that he has money."

"But not as much as I supposed," moaned Madam Conway. "Theo told me $200,000; but that woman said *one*

Oh what will become of me? Give me the hartshorn, Mag
gie. I feel *so* faint!"

The hartshorn was handed her, but it could not quiet her
distress. Her family pride was sorely wounded, and had
Theo been dead, she would hardly have felt worse than she
did.

"How *will* she bear it when it comes to her knowledge,
as it necessarily must? It will kill her, I know," she exclaimed, after Maggie had exhausted all her powers of reasoning in vain; then, as she remembered the woman's
avowed intention of visiting her daughter-in-law on the morrow, she felt that she *must* turn back; she *must* see Theo
and break it to her gently, or "the first sight of that odious
creature, claiming her for a daughter, might be of incalcula-
ble injury."

"Stop, Mike," she was about to say; but ere the words
passed her lips, she reflected that to take Maggie back to
Worcester, was to throw her again in Henry Warner's way,
and this she could not do. There was then but one alternative. She could stop at the Charlton depot, not far distant,
and wait for the downward train, while Mike drove Maggie
home, and this she resolved to do. Mike was accordingly
bidden to take her at once to the depot, which he did, while
she explained to Maggie, her reason for returning.

"Theo is much better alone, and George will not thank
you for interfering," said Maggie, not at all pleased with
her grandmother's proceedings.

But the old lady was determined. "It was her duty,"
she said, "to stand by Theo in trouble, and if a visit from
that horrid creature wasn't *trouble*, she could not well define
it."

"When will you come home?" asked Maggie.

"Not before to-morrow night. Now I have undertaken

the matter, I intend to see it through," said Madam Conway, referring to the expected visit of " Mrs. Douglas, senior."

But Mike did not thus understand it, and thinking her only object in turning back was, " to see the doin's," as he designated the " Fireman's Muster," he muttered long and loud about " being thus sent home, while his madam went to see the *fun.*"

In the meantime, on a hard settee, at the rather uncomfortable depot, Madam Conway awaited the arrival of the train, which came at last, and in a short time, she found herself again in Worcester   Once in a carriage, and on her way to the " Bay State," she began to feel a little nervous, half-wishing she had followed Maggie's advice, and left Theo alone.   But it could not now be helped, and while trying to think what she should say to her astonished grand-daughter, she was set down at the door of the hotel, slightly bewildered, and a good deal perplexed, a feeling which was by no means diminished when she learned that Mr. and Mrs. Douglas were both out of town.

" Where *have* they gone, and when will they return ?" she gasped, untying her bonnet strings for an easier respiration.

To these queries the clerk replied, that he believed Mr. Douglas had gone to Boston on business, that he might be at home that night ; at all events, he would probably return in the morning ; she could find Mr. Warner, who would tell her all about it.   " Shall I send for him ?" he continued, as he saw the scowl upon her face.

• " Certainly not," she answered, and taking the key, which had been left in his charge, she repaired to Theo's rooms, and sinking into a large easy-chair, fanned herself furiously, wondering if they *would* return that night, and what they would say when they found *her* there.   " *But I don't care,*" she continued, speaking aloud and shaking her head very decidedly at the excited woman whose image was reflected by the mirror opposite, and who shook her head as decidedly in return! "George Douglas has deceived us shamefully, and I'll tell him so, too. I wish he'd come this minute!"

But George Douglas knew well what he was doing. Very gradually was he imparting to Theo a knowledge of his parents, and Theo, who really loved her husband, was learning to prize him for himself and not for his family. Feeling certain that the firemen's muster would bring his mother to town, and knowing that Theo was not yet prepared to see her, he was greatly relieved at Madam Conway's sudden departure, and had himself purposely left home, with the intention of staying away until Friday night. This, however, Madam Conway did not know, and very impatiently she awaited his coming, until the lateness of the hour precluded the possibility of his arrival, and she retired to bed, but not to sleep, for the city was full of firemen, and one company, failing of finding lodgings elsewhere, had taken refuge in an empty carriage shop near by. The hard, bare floor was not the most comfortable bed imaginable, and preferring the bright moonlight and open air, they made the night hideous with their noisy shouts, which the watchmen tried in vain to hush. To sleep in that neighborhood was impossible, and all night long Madam Conway vibrated between her bed and the window, from which latter point she frowned wrathfully down upon the red coats below, who, scoffing alike at law and order as dispensed by the police kept up their noisy revel, shouting lustily for " Chelsea, No. 4," and "Washington, No. 2," until the dawn of day.

"I wish to mercy I'd gone home, !" sighed Madam Conway, as weak and faint she crept down to the breakfast tab.c, doing but little justice to anything, and returning to her room, pale, haggard and weary.

Ere long, however, she became interested in watching the crowds of people, who at an early hour filled the streets; and when at last the different fire companies of the State paraded the town in a seemingly never ending procession, she forgot in a measure her trouble, and drawing her chair to the window, sat down to enjoy the brilliant, scene, involuntarily nodding her head to the stirring music, as troop after troop passed by. Up and down the street, as far as the eye could reach, the sidewalks were crowded with men, women and children, all eager to see the sight. There were people from the city and people from the country, the latter of whom, having anticipated the day for weeks and months, were now unquestionably enjoying it.

Conspucious among these was a middle aged woman, who elicited remarks from all who beheld her, both from the peculiarity of her dress, and the huge, blue cotton umbrella she persisted in hoisting, to the great annoyance of those in whose faces it was thrust, and who forgot in a measure their vexation when they read the novel device it bore. · Like many other people who can sympathize with the good woman, she was always losing her umbrella, and at last, in self-defence, had embroidered upon the blue in letters of white :

"Steal me not, for fear of shame,
For here you see my owner's name.
"CHARITY DOUGLAS."

As the lettering was small and not very distinct, it required a close observation to decipher it ; but the plan was a successful one, nevertheless, and for four long years the blue umbrella had done good service to its mistress, shielding her alike from sunshine and from storm, and now in the

15*

crowded city it performed a double part, preventing its nearest neighbors from seeing, while at the same time it kept the dust from settling on the thick green veil and leghorn bonnet of its owner. At Betsey Jane's suggestion she wore a hoop to-day on Theo's account, and that she was painfully conscious of the fact, was proved by the many anxious glances she cast at her chocolate colored muslin, through the thin folds of which it was plainly visible.

"I wish I had left the pesky thing to hum," she thought, feeling greatly relieved when at last, as the crowd became greater, it was broken in several pieces and ceased to do its duty.

From her seat near the window, Madam Conway caught sight of the umbrella as it swayed up and down amid the multitude, but she had no suspicion that she who bore it thus aloft had even a better right than herself to sit where she was sitting. In her excitement she had forgotten Mrs. Douglas's intended visit, to prepare Theo for which she had returned to Worcester, but it came to her at length, when as the last fire company passed, the blue umbrella was closed, and the leghorn bonnet turned in the direction of the hotel. There was no mistaking the broad good-humored face which looked so eagerly up at "George's window," and involuntarily Madam Conway glanced under the bed with the view of fleeing thither for refuge !

"What shall I do ?" she cried, as she heard the umbrella on the stairs. "I'll lock her out," she continued; and in an instant the key was in her pocket, while, trembling in every limb, she awaited the result.

Nearer and nearer the footsteps came ; there was a knock upon the door, succeeded by a louder one, and then, as both these failed to elicit a response, the handle of the umbrella was rigorously applied. But all in vain, and Madam

Conway heard the discomfited outsider say, "They told me Theodoshy's *grandmarm* was here, but I guess she's in the street. I'll come agin bime-by," and Mrs. Douglas senior walked disconsolately down the stairs, while Madam Conway thought it doubtful whether she gained access to the room *that day*, come as often as she might.

Not long after, the gong sounded for dinner, and unlocking the door, Madam Conway was about descending to the dining-room, when the thought burst upon, "What if she should be at the table? It's just like her."

The very idea was overwhelming, taking from her at once all desire for dinner ; and returning to her room, she tried, by looking over the books, and examining the carpet, to forget how hungry and faint she was. Whether she would have succeeded is doubtful, had not an hour or two later brought another knock from the umbrella, and driven all thoughts of eating from her mind. In grim silence she waited until her tormentor was gone, and then wondering if it was not time for the train, she consulted her watch. But alas ! 'twas only *four ;* the cars did not leave until *six,* and so another weary hour went by. At the end of that time, however, thinking the depot preferable to being a prisoner there, she resolved to go ; and leaving the key with the clerk, she called a carriage and was soon on her way to the cars.

As she approached the depot, she observed an immense crowd of people, gathered together, among which the red coats of the firemen were conspicuous. A fight was evidently in progress, and as the horses began to grow restive, she begged of the driver to let her alight, saying she could easily walk the remainder of the way. Scarcely, however, was she on *terra firma,* when the yelling crowd made a precipitate rush towards her, and in much alarm, she climbed for safety into an empty buggy, whereupon the horse, equally alarmed, began to rear, and without pausing an instant, the terrified lady sprang out on the side opposite to that by which she had entered, catching her dress upon the seat, and tearing half the gathers from the waist.

"Heaven help me!" she cried, picking herself up, and beginning to wish she had never troubled herself with Theo's mother-in-law.

To reach the depot was now her great object, and as the two belligerent parties occupied the front, she thought to effect an entrance at the rear. But the doors were *locked*, and as she turned the corner of the building, she suddenly found herself in the thickest of the fight. To advance was impossible, to turn back equally so, and while meditating some means of escape, she lost her footing and fell across a wheelbarrow, which stood upon the platform, crumpling her bonnet, and scratching her face upon a nail which protruded from the vehicle. Nearer dead than alive, she made her way at last into the depot, and from thence into the cars, where, sinking into a seat, and drawing her shawl closely around her, the better to conceal the sad condition of her dress, she indulged in meditations not wholly complimentary to firemen in general, and her late comrades in particular.

For half an hour she waited impatiently, but though the cars were filling rapidly there were no indications of starting; and it was almost seven, ere the long and heavily loaded train moved slowly from the depot. About fifteen minutes previous to their departure, as Madam Conway was looking ruefully out upon the multitude, she was horrified at seeing directly beneath her window, the veritable woman from whom, through the entire day, she had been hiding. Involuntarily she glanced at the vacant seat in front of her, which, as she feared, was soon occupied by Mrs. Douglas and her companion, who, as Madam Conway divined, was "Sam Babbit's wife."

Trembling nervously lest she should be discovered, she drew her veil closely over her face, keeping very quiet, and looking intently from the window into the gathering darkness without. But her fears were groundless, for Mrs Douglas had no suspicion that the crumpled bonnet and sorry figure, sitting so disconsolately in the corner, was the same which but the day before had honored her with a call. She was in high spirits, having had, as she informed her neighbor, "a tip-top time." On one point, however, she was disappointed. "She meant as much as could be to have seen Theodoshy, but she wan't to hum. Her grandmarm was in town," said she, "but if she was in the room, she must have been asleep, or dreadful deaf, for I pounded with all my might. I'm sorry, for I'd like to scrape acquaintance with her, bein' we're connected."

An audible groan came from beneath the thick brown veil, whereupon both ladies turned their heads. But the indignant woman made no sign, and in a whisper loud enough for Madam Conway to hear, Mrs. Douglas said, "Some Irish critter in liquor, I presume. Look at her jammed bonnet."

This remark drew from Mrs. Babbit a very close inspection of the veiled figure, who, smothering her wrath, felt greatly relieved when the train started, and prevented her from hearing anything more. At the next station, however, Mrs. Douglas showed her companion a crochet collar, which she had purchased for two shillings, and which, she said, "was almost exactly like the one worn by the woman who stopped at her house the day before."

Leaning forward, Madam Conway glanced contemptuously at the coarse knit thing, which bore about the same resemblance to her own handsome collar, as cambric does **to** satin.

"Vulgar, ignorant creatures!" she muttered, while Mrs. Babbit, after duly praising the collar, proceeded to make some inquiries concerning the strange lady who had shared Mrs. Douglas's hospitality.

"I've no idee who she was," said Mrs. Douglas ; "but I think it's purty likely she was some crazy critter they was takin' to the hospital."

Another groan from beneath the brown veil, and turning around, the kind hearted Mrs. Douglas asked if she was sick, adding in an aside, as there came no answer, "been fightin' I'll warrant!"

Fortunately for Madam Conway, the cars moved on, and when they stopped again, to her great relief, the owner of the blue umbrella, together with "Sam Babbit's wife," alighted, and amid the crowd assembled on the platform she recognized Betsey Jane, who had come down to meet her mother. The remainder of the way seemed tedious enough, for the train moved but slowly, and it was near 10 o'clock ere they reached the Hillsdale station, where, to her great delight, Madam Conway found Margaret awaiting her, together with Arthur Carrollton. The moment she saw the former, who came eagerly forward to meet her, the weary, worn-out woman burst into tears; but at the sight of Mr. Carrollton, she forced them back, saying in reply to Maggie's inquiries, that Theo was not at home, that she had spent a dreadful day, and been knocked down in a fight at the depot, in proof of which she pointed to her torn dress, her crumpled bonnet, and scratched face. Maggie laughed aloud in spite of herself, and though Mr. Carrollton's eyes were several times turned reprovingly upon her, she continued to laugh at intervals at the sorry, forlorn appearance presented by her grandmother, who for several days was confined to her bed, from the combined effects of *fasting, fright, firemen's muster*, and her late encounter with Mrs. Douglas, senior !

CHAPTER XV.

ARTHUR CARROLLTON AND MAGGIE.

Mr. CARROLLTON had returned from Boston on Thursday afternoon, and finding them all gone from the hotel, had come on to Hillsdale in the evening train, surprising Maggie as she sat in the parlor alone, wishing herself in Worcester, or in some place where it was not as lonely as there. With his presence the loneliness disappeared, and in making his tea and listening to his agreeable conversation, she forgot everything, until, observing that she looked weary, he said, "Maggie, I would willingly talk to you all night, were it not for the bad effect it would have you on to-morrow. You must go to bed now," and he showed her his watch, which pointed to the hour of midnight.

Exceedingly mortified, Maggie was leaving the room, when noticing her evident chagrin, Mr. Carrollton came to her side and laying his hand very respectfully on hers, said kindly, "It is my fault, Maggie, keeping you up so late, and I only send you away now, because those eyes are growing heavy, and I know that you need rest. Good night to you, and pleasant dreams."

He went with her to the door, watching her until she disappeared up the stairs ; then half wishing he had not sent her from him, he, too, sought his chamber; but not to sleep, for Maggie, though absent, was with him still in fancy. For more than a year he had been haunted with a bright, sunshiny face, whose owner embodied the dashing, independent spirit, and softer qualities which made Maggie Miller so attractive.   Of this face he had often thought, wondering if the real would equal the ideal, and now that he had met with her, had looked into her truthful eyes, had gazed upon her sunny face, which mirrored faithfully her every thought and feeling, he was more than satisfied, and to love that beautiful girl seemed to him an easy matter.   She was so childlike, so artless, so different from any one whom he had ever known, that he was interested in her at once.   But Arthur Carrollton never did a thing precipitately.   She might have many glaring faults, he must see her more, must know her better, ere he lavished upon her the love whose deep fountains had never yet been stirred.

After this manner he reasoned as he walked up and down his chamber, while Maggie, on her sleepless pillow, was thinking, too, of him, wondering if she did hate him as much as she intended, and if Henry would be offended at her sitting up with him until after twelve o'clock.

It was nearly half-past nine when Maggie awoke next morning, and making a hasty toilet, she descended to the dining-room, where she found Mr. Carrollton awaiting her. He had been up a long time; but when Anna Jeffrey, blessed with an uncommon appetite, fretted at the delay of breakfast, and suggested calling Margaret, he objected, saying she needed rest, and must not be disturbed.   So, in something of a pet, the young lady breakfasted alone with her aunt, Mr. Carrollton preferring to wait for Maggie.

"I am sorry I kept you waiting," said Maggie, seating herself at the table, and continuing to apologize for her tardiness.

But Mr. Carrollton felt more than repaid by having her thus alone with him, and many were the admiring glances he cast towards her, as with her shining hair, her happy face, her tasteful morning gown of pink, and her beautiful white hands which handled so gracefully the silver coffee-urn, she made a living, glowing picture, such as any man might delight to look upon. Breakfast being over, Mr. Carroll-ton proposed a ride, and as Anna Jeffrey at that moment entered the parlor, he invited her to accompany them. There was a shadow on Maggie's brow, as she left the room to dress, a shadow which had not wholly disappeared when she returned; and observing this, Mr. Carrollton said, "Were I to consult my own wishes, Maggie, I should leave Miss Jeffrey at home; but she is a poor girl whose enjoy-ments are far less than ours, consequently I invited her for this once, knowing how fond she is of riding."

"How thoughtful you are of other people's happiness!" said Maggie, the shadow leaving her brow at once.

"I am glad that *wrinkle* has gone, at all events," returned Mr. Carrollton, laughingly, and laying his hand upon her forehead, he continued: "Were you my sister Helen, I should probably *kiss* you for having so soon got over your *pet*; but as you are Maggie Miller, I dare not," and he looked earnestly at her, to see if he had spoken the truth.

Coloring crimson as it became the affianced bride of Henry Warner to do, Maggie turned away, thinking Helen must be a happy girl, and half wishing she, too, were Arthur Carrollton's sister. It was a long, delightful excur-sion they took, and Maggie, when she saw how Anna Jeffrey enjoyed it, did not altogether regret her presence. On their way home she proposed calling upon Hagar, "whom she had not seen for three whole days."

"And who, pray, is Hagar?" asked Mr. Carrollton; and Maggie replied, "She is my old nurse,—a strange, crazy creature, whom they say I somewhat resemble."

By this time they were near the cottage, in the door of which old Hagar was standing, with her white hair falling round her face.

"I see by your looks, you don't care to call, but I shall," said Maggie, and bounding from her saddle, she ran up to Hagar, pressing her hand and whispering in her ear, that it would soon be time to hear from Henry.

"Kissed her, I do believe!" said Anna Jeffrey. "She must have admirable taste!"

Mr. Carrollton thought so too, and with a half comical, half displeased expression, he watched the interview between that weird old woman, and fair young girl, little suspecting how nearly they were allied.

"Why didn't you come and speak to her?" said Maggie, as he alighted to assist her in again mounting Gritty. "She used to see you in England, when you were a baby, and if you won't be angry, I'll tell you what she said, it was, that you were the crossest, ugliest young one she ever saw! There, there, don't set me down so hard!" and the saucy eyes looked mischievously at the proud Englishman, who, truth to say, *did* place her in the saddle with a little more force than was at all necessary.

Not that he was angry. He was only annoyed for what he considered Maggie's undue familiarity with a person like Hagar, but he wisely forbore making any comments in Anna Jeffrey's presence, except, indeed, to laugh heartily at Hagar's complimentary description of himself when a baby. Arrived at home, and alone again with Maggie, he found her so very good-natured and agreeable, that he could not chide her for anything, and Hagar was for a time forgotten.

That evening, as the reader knows, they went together to the depot, where they waited four long hours, but not impatiently; for sitting there in the moonlight, with the winding

Chicopee full in view, and Margaret Miller at his side, Arthur Carrollton forgot the lapse of time, especially when
Maggie, thinking no harm, gave a most ludicrous description
of her call upon Mrs. Douglas senior, and of her grandmother's distress at finding herself so nearly connected with
what she termed "a low, vulgar family."

Arthur Carrollton was very proud, and had Theo been *his*
sister, he might, to some extent, have shared in Madam
Conway's chagrin ; and so he said to Maggie, at the same
time fully agreeing with her that George Douglas was a refined, agreeable man, and as such entitled to respect.   Still,
had Theo known of his parentage, he said, it would probably
have made some difference ; but now that it could not be
helped, it was wise to make the best of it.

These words were little heeded then by Maggie, but with
most painful distinctness they recurred to her in the after
time, when, humbled in the very dust, she had no hope that
the highborn, haughty Carrollton would stoop to a child of
Hagar Warren !   But no shadow of the dark future was
over her now, and very eagerly she drank in every word and
look of Arthur Carrollton, who, all unconsciously, was tram-
pling on another's rights, and gradually weakening the fancied love she bore for Henry Warner.

The arrival of the train brought their pleasant conversation to a close, and for a day or two Maggie's time was
wholly occupied with her grandmother, to whom she frankly
acknowledged having told Mr. Carrollton of Mrs. Douglas
and her daughter Betsey Jane.   The fact that *he* knew of
her *disgrace* and did not despise her was of great benefit to
Madam Conway, and after a few days she resumed her usual
spirits, and actually told of the remarks made by Mrs. Douglas concerning herself and the *fight* she had been in !   As
time passed on she became reconciled to the Douglases, hav

ing, as she thought, some well-founded reasons for believing that for Theo's disgrace, Maggie would make amends by marrying Mr. Carrollton, whose attentions each day became more and more marked, and were not apparently altogether disagreeable to Maggie. On the contrary, his presence at Hillsdale was productive of much pleasure to her, as well as of a little annoyance.

From the first he seemed to exercise over her an influence she could not well resist—a power to make her do whatever he willed that she should do ; and though she sometimes rebelled, she was pretty sure in the end to yield the contest, and submit to one who was evidently the ruling spirit. As yet nothing had been said of the hair ornament which, out of compliment to him, her grandmother wore every morning in her collar, but at last, one day Madam Conway spoke of it herself, asking "if it were, as she had supposed, his grandmother's hair ?"

"Why, no," he answered involuntarily ; "it is a lock Maggie sent me in that wonderful daguerreotype !"

"The stupid thing !" thought Maggie, while her eyes fairly danced with merriment, as she anticipated the question she fancied was sure to follow, but did not.

One glance at her tell-tale face was sufficient for Madam Conway. In her whole household there was but one head with locks as white as that, and whatever her thoughts might have been, she said nothing, but from that day forth, *Hagar's hair* was never again seen ornamenting her person ! That afternoon Mr. Carrollton and Maggie went out to ride, and in the course of their conversation he referred to the pin, asking whose hair it was and seeming much amused when told that it was Hagar's.

"But why did you not tell her when it first came," he said ; and Maggie answered, "Oh, it was such fun to see her sporting Hagar's hair, when she is so proud. It didn't hurt her either, for Hagar is as good as anybody. I don't believe in making such a difference because one person chances to be richer than another."

"Neither do I," returned Mr. Carrollton. "I would not esteem a person for wealth alone, but there are points of difference which should receive consideration. For instance, this old Hagar may be well enough in her way, but suppose she were nearly connected to you—your *grandmother* if you like—it would certainly make some difference in your position. You would not be Maggie Miller, and I "——

"Wouldn't ride with me, I dare say," interrupted Maggie; to which he replied, "I presume not," adding as he saw slight indications of pouting, "and therefore I am glad you are Maggie Miller, and not Hagar's grandchild."

Mentally pronouncing him a "proud hateful thing," Maggie rode on a while in silence. But Mr. Carrollton knew well how to manage her, and he, too, was silent until Maggie, who could never refrain from talking any length of time, forgot herself and began chatting away as gaily as before. During their excursion they came near to the gorge of Henry Warner memory, and Maggie, who had never quite forgiven Mr Carrollton for criticising her horsemanship, resolved to show him what she could do. The signal was accordingly given to Gritty, and ere her companion was aware of her intention she was tearing over the ground at a speed he could hardly equal. The ravine was just on the border of the wood, and without pausing an instant, Gritty leaped across it, landing safely on the other side, where he stopped, while half fearfully, half exultingly, Maggie looked back to see what Mr. Carrollton would do. At first he had fancied Gritty beyond her control, and when he saw her directly over the deep chasm he shuddered, involuntarily stretching out his arms to save her ; but the look she gave him as she turned around, convinced him that the risk she had run was done on purpose. Still he had no intention of following her, for he feared his horse's ability as well as his own to clear that pass.

"Why don't you jump ? Are you afraid ?" and Maggie's eyes looked archly out from beneath her tasteful riding cap.

For half a moment he felt tempted to join her, but his better judgment came to his aid, and he answered, "Yes, Maggie, *I am afraid*, having never tried such an experiment. But I wish to be with you in some way, and as I cannot come to you, I ask you to come to me. You seem accustomed to the leap !"

He did not praise her. Nay, she fancied there was more of censure in the tones of his voice ; at all events, he had asked her rather commandingly to return, and "she wouldn't do it." For a moment she made no reply, and he said again, "Maggie, will you come ?" then half playfully, half reproachfully, she made answer, "A gallant Englishman indeed ! willing I should risk my neck where you dare not venture yours. No, I shan't try the leap again to-day, I don't feel like it ; but I'll cross the long bridge half a mile from here—good bye," and fully expecting him to meet her, she galloped off, riding, ere long, quite slowly, "so he'd have a nice long time to wait for her !"

How then was she disappointed, when, on reaching the bridge, there was nowhere a trace of him to be seen, neither could she hear the sound of his horse's footsteps, though she listened long and anxiously.

"He is certainly the most provoking man I ever saw ;" she exclaimed, half crying with vexation. "Henry wouldn't have served me so, and I'm glad I was engaged to him be fore I saw this hateful Carrollton, for grandma might possibly have coaxed me into marrying him, and then wouldn't *Mr. Dog* and *Mrs. Cat* have led a stormy life ! No, we wouldn't," she continued ; " I should in time get accustomed to minding him, and then I think he'd be splendid, though no better than Henry. I wonder if Hagar has a letter for me !" and chirruping to Gritty, she soon stood at the door of the cabin.

"Have you two been qarrelling ?" asked Hagar, noticing Mag's flushed cheeks. "Mr. Carrollton passed here twenty minutes, or more, ago, looking mighty sober, and here you are with your face as red—What has happened ?"

"Nothing," answered Mag, a little testily, " only he's the meanest man !—Wouldn't follow me, when I leaped the gorge, and I know he could, if he had tried."

"Showed his good sense," interrupted Hagar, adding that Maggie mustn't think every man was going to risk his neck for her.

"I don't think so, of course," returned Maggie ; " but he might act better—almost commanded me to come back and join him, as though I was a little child ; but I wouldn't do it. I told him I'd go down to the long bridge and cross, expecting, of course, he'd meet me there ; and instead of that, he has gone off home. How did he know what accident would befall me ?"

"Accident !" repeated Hagar ; "accident befall you, who know every crook and turn of these woods so much better than he does ?"

"Well, any way, he might have waited for me," returned Mag. "I don't believe he'd care if I were to get killed. I mean to scare him and see ;" and springing from Gritty's back, she gave a peculiar whistling sound, at which the pony bounded away towards home while she followed Hagar into the cottage, where a letter from Henry awaited her.

They were to sail for Cuba on the 15th of October, and he now wrote, asking if Maggie would go without her grandmother's consent. But, though irresolute when he before broached the subject, Mag was *decided* now. " She would not run away," and so she said to Hagar, to whom she confided the whole affair.

"I do not think it would be right to elope," she said. " In three years more, I shall be twenty-one, and free to do as I like ; and if grandma will not let me marry Henry, now, he must wait. I can't run away. *Rose* would not approve of it, I'm sure, and I 'most know Mr. Carrollton would not."

" I can't see how his approving, or *not* approving can affect you," said Hagar ; then bending down, so that her wild eyes looked full in Maggie's eyes, she said, " Are you beginning to like this Englishman ?"

" *Why, no, I guess I ain't,*" answered Mag, coloring slightly. " I dislike him dreadfully, he's so proud. Why, he did the same as to say, that if I were your grandchild, he would not ride with me."

" *My grandchild,* Maggie Miller !—*my grandchild!*" shrieked Hagar. " What put that into his head ?"

Thinking her emotion caused by anger at Arthur Carrollton, Mag mentally chided herself for having inadvertently said what she did, while, at the same time, she tried to soothe old Hagar, who rocked to and fro, as was her custom when her " crazy spells" were on. Growing a little more composed, she said, at last, " Marry Henry Warner, by all means, Maggie ; he ain't as proud as Carrollton—he would not care as much if he knew it."

" Know what ?" asked Mag; and, remembering herself in

16

time, Hagar answered, adroitly, "knew of your promise to
let me live with you. You remember it, don't you?" and
she looked wistfully towards Mag, who, far more intent
upon something else, answered, "Yes, I remember. But
hush! don't I hear horses' feet coming rapidly through the
woods?" and running to the window, she saw Mr. Carrollton,
mounted upon Gritty, and riding furiously towards the house.

"You go out, Hagar, and see if he is looking for me,"
whispered Mag, stepping back, so he could not see.

"Henry Warner must snare the bird quick, or he will
lose it," muttered Hagar, as she walked to the door, where,
evidently much excited, Mr. Carrollton asked if "she knew
aught of Miss Miller, and why Gritty had come home alone?
It is such an unusual occurrence," said he, "that we felt
alarmed, and I have come in quest of her."

From her post near the window, Maggie could plainly see
his face, which was very pale, and expressive of much concern, while his voice, she fancied, trembled as he spoke her
name.

"He does care," she thought; woman's pride was satisfied, and ere Hagar could reply, she ran out saying laughingly, "And so you thought maybe I was killed, but I'm
not. I concluded to walk home and let Gritty go on in advance. I did not mean to frighten grandma."

"She was not as much alarmed as myself," said Mr. Carrollton, the troubled expression of his countenance changing
at once. "You do not know how anxious I was, when I
saw Gritty come riderless to the door, nor yet how relieved
I am in finding you thus unharmed."

Maggie knew she did not deserve this, and blushing like a
guilty child, she offered no resistance when he lifted her in
the saddle gently—tenderly, as if she had indeed escaped
from some great danger.

"It is time you were home," said he, and throwing the bridle across his arm, he rested his hand upon the saddle and walked slowly by her side.

All his fancied coldness was forgotten ; neither was the leap nor yet the bridge once mentioned, for he was only too happy in having her back alive, while she was doubting the propriety of an experiment which, in the turn matters had taken, seemed to involve deception. Observing at last that he occasionally pressed his hand upon his side, she asked the cause, and was told that he had formerly been subject to a pain in his side, which excitement or fright greatly augmented. "I hoped I was free from it," he said, "but the sight of Gritty dashing up to the door without you, brought on a slight attack ; for I knew if you were harmed, the fault was mine for having rather unceremoniously deserted you."

This was more than Mag could endure in silence. The frank ingenuousness of her nature prevailed, and turning towards him her dark, beautiful eyes, in which tears were shining, she said : "Forgive me, Mr. Carrollton. I sent Gritty home on purpose to see if you would be annoyed, for I felt vexed because you would not humor my whim and meet me at the bridge. I am sorry I caused you any uneasiness," she continued, as she saw a shadow flit over his face "Will you forgive me ?"

Arthur Carrollton could not resist the pleading of those lustrous eyes, nor yet refuse to take the ungloved hand she offered him ; and if, in token of reconciliation, he did press t a little more fervently than Henry Warner would have thought at all necessary, he only did what, under the circumstances, it was very natural he should do. From the first Maggie Miller had been a puzzle to Arthur Carrollton : but he was fast learning to read her—was beginning to un

derstand how perfectly artless she was—and this little incident increased, rather than diminished, his admiration.

"I will forgive you, Maggie," he said, on one condition
"You must promise never again to experiment with my
feelings, in a similar manner."

The promise was readily given and then they proceeded
on as leisurely as if at home, there was no anxious grandmother vibrating between her high-backed chair and the
piazza, nor yet an Anna Jeffrey, watching them enviously as
they came slowly up the road.

That night there came to Mr. Carrollton a letter from
Montreal, saying his immediate presence was necessary there,
on a business matter of some importance, and he accordingly
decided to go on the morrow.

"When may we expect you back?" asked Madam Conway, as in the morning he was preparing for his journey.

"It will, perhaps, be two months at least, before I
return," said he, adding that there was a possibility of his
being obliged to go immediately to England.

In the recess of the window Mag was standing, thinking
how lonely the house would be without him, and wishing
there was no such thing as parting from those she liked—
even as *little* as she did Arthur Carrollton.

"I won't let him know that I care, though," she thought,
and forcing a smile to her face, she was about turning to
bid him good bye, when she heard him tell her grandmother
of the possibility there was that he would be obliged to go
directly to England from Montreal.

"Then I may never see him again," she thought, and her
tears burst forth involuntarily, at the idea of parting with
him forever.

Faster and faster they came, until at last, fearing lest he
should see them, she ran away up stairs, and mounting to

the roof, sat down behind the chimney, where, herself unob-served, she could watch him far up the road. From the half-closed door of her chamber, Anna Jeffrey had seen Mag stealing up the tower stairs ; had seen, too, that she was weeping, and suspecting the cause, she went quietly down to the parlor to hear what Arthur Carrollton would say. The carriage was waiting, his trunk was in its place, his hat was in his hand ; to Madam Conway he said good bye ; to Anna Jeffrey, too, and still he lingered, looking wistfully round in quest of something, which evidently was not there.

"Where's Margaret ?" he asked at last, and Madam Con-way answered, " surely, where can she be ? Have you seen her, Anna ?"

"I saw her on the stairs some time ago," said Anna, adding that possibly she had gone to see Hagar, as she usually visited her at this hour.

A shade of disappointment passed over Mr. Carrollton's face, as he replied, "tell her I am sorry she thinks more of Hagar than of me."

The next moment he was gone, and leaning against the chimney, Mag watched with tearful eyes the carriage as it wound up the grassy road. On the brow of the hill, just before it would disappear from sight, it suddenly stopped. Something was the matter with the harness, and while John was busy adjusting it, Mr. Carrollton leaned from the win-dow, and looking back, started involuntarily as he caught sight of the figure so clearly defined upon the house-top. A slight suspicion of the truth came upon him, and kissing his hand, he waved it gracefully towards her. Mag's handker-chief was wet with tears, but she shook it out in the morn-ing breeze, and sent to Arthur Carrollton, as she thought, her last good bye.

Fearing lest her grandmother should see her swollen eyes, she stole down the stairs, and taking her shawl and bonnet from the table in the hall, ran off into the woods, going to a pleasant, mossy bank, not far from Hagar's cottage, where she had more than once sat with Arthur Carrollton, and where she fancied she would never sit with him again.

"I don't believe it's for *him*, that I am crying," she thought, as she tried in vain to stay her tears; "I always intended to hate him, and I 'most know I do; I'm only feeling badly, because I *won't* run away, and Henry and Rose will go without me so soon!" And fully satisfied at having discovered the real cause of her grief, she laid her head upon the bright autumnal grass, and wept bitterly, holding her breath, and listening intently as she heard, in the distance, the sound of the engine, which was bearing Mr. Carrollton away.

It did not occur to her that he could not yet have reached the depot, and as she knew nothing of a change in the time of the trains, she was taken wholly by surprise, when, fifteen minutes later, a manly form bent over her, as she lay upon the bank, and a voice, earnest and thrilling in tones, murmured softly, "Maggie, are those tears for me?"

When about halfway to the station, Mr. Carrollton had heard of the change of the time, and knowing he should not be in season, had turned back, with the intention of waiting for the next train, which would pass in a few hours. Learning that Maggie was in the woods, he had started in quest of her, going naturally to the mossy bank, where, as we have seen, he found her weeping on the grass. She was weeping for him—he was sure of that. He was not indifferent to her, as he had sometimes feared, and for an instant he felt tempted to take her in his arms and tell her how dear she was to him.

"I will speak to her first," he thought, and so he asked 'if the tears were for him." ' '

Inexpressibly astonished and mortified at having him see her thus, Maggie started to her feet, while angry words at being thus intruded upon, trembled on her lips. But winding his arm around her, Mr. Carrollton drew her to his side, explaining to her in a few words how he came to be there, and continuing, "I do not regret the delay, if by its means I have discovered what I very much wish to know. Maggie, *do* you care for me? Were you weeping because I had left you?"

He drew her very closely to him—looking anxiously into her face, which she covered with her hands. *She knew he was in earnest*, and the knowledge that he loved her thrilled her for an instant with indescribable happiness. A moment, however, and thoughts of her engagement with another flashed upon her. "She must not sit there thus with Arthur Carrollton—she would be true to Henry," and with mingled feelings of sorrow, regret and anger—though why she should experience either she did not then understand—she drew herself from him, and when he said again, "Will Maggie answer? Are those tears for me?" she replied petulantly, "*No;* can't a body *cry* without being bothered for a reason? I came down here to be alone?"

"I did not mean to intrude, and I beg your pardon for having done so," said Mr. Carrollton, sadly, adding, as Maggie made no reply, "I expected a different answer, Maggie; I almost hoped you liked me, and I believe now that you do."

In Maggie's bosom there was a fierce struggle of feeling She *did* like Arthur Carrollton—and she *thought* she liked Henry Warner—at all events she was engaged to him, and half angry at the former for having disturbed her, and still

more angry at herself for being thus disturbed, she exclaimed
as he again placed his arm around her, "Leave me alone,
Mr. Carrollton. I *don't* like you. I don't like anybody!"
and gathering up her shawl, which lay upon the grass, she
ran away to Hagar's cabin, hoping he would follow her.
But he did not. It was his first attempt at love-making,
and very much disheartened, he walked slowly back to the
house; and while Maggie, from Hagar's door, was looking
to see if he were coming, he, from the parlor window, was
watching, too, for her, with a shadow on his brow and a load
upon his heart. Madam Conway knew that something was
wrong, but it was in vain that she sought an explanation.
Mr. Carrollton kept his own secret, and consoling herself with
his volunteered assurance that in case it became necessary
for him to return to England, he should, before embarking,
visit Hillsdale, she bade him a second adieu.

In the meantime, Maggie, having given up all hopes of
again seeing Mr. Carrollton, was waiting impatiently the
coming of Hagar, who was absent, having, as Maggie
readily conjectured, gone to Richland. It was long past
noon when she returned, and by that time the stains had
disappeared from Maggie's face, which looked nearly as
bright as ever. Still, it was with far less eagerness than
usual that she took from Hagar's hand the expected letter
from Henry. It was a long, affectionate epistle, urging her
once more to accompany him, and saying if she still refused
she must let him know immediately, as they were intending
to start for New York in a few days.

"I can't go," said Maggie; "it would not be right."
And going to the time-worn desk, where, since her secret
correspondence, she had kept materials for writing, she
wrote to Henry a letter, telling him she felt badly to disappoint him, but she deemed it much wiser to defer their mar-

riage until her grandmother felt differently, or at least unti she was at an age to act for herself. This being done, she went slowly back to the house, which to her seemed desolate indeed. Her grandmother saw readily that something was the matter, and rightly guessing the cause, she forebore questioning her, neither did she once that day mention Mr. Carrollton, although Anna Jeffrey did, telling her what he had said about her "thinking more of Hagar than of himself," and giving as her opinion that he was much displeased at her rudeness in running away.

"Nobody cares for his displeasure," answered Maggie, greatly vexed at Anna, who took especial delight in annoying her.

Thus a week went by, when one evening, as Madam Conway and Maggie sat together in the parlor, they were surprised by the sudden appearance of Henry Warner. He had accompanied his aunt and sister to New York, where they were to remain for a few days, and then impelled by a strong desire to see Margaret once more, he had come with the vain hope that at the last hour she would consent to fly with him, or her grandmother consent to give her up. All the afternoon he had been at Hagar's cottage waiting for Maggie, and at length determining to see her, he had ventured to the house. With a scowling frown, Madam Conway looked at him through her glasses, while Maggie, half joyfully, half fearfully, went forward to meet him. In a few words he explained why he was there, and then again asked of Madam Conway if Margaret could go.

"I do not believe she cares to go," thought Madam Conway, as she glanced at Maggie's face ; but she did not say so, lest she should awaken within the young girl a feeling of opposition.

She had watched Maggie closely, and felt sure that her

16*

affection for Henry Warner was neither deep nor lasting Arthur Carrollton's presence had done much towards weak- ening it, and a few months more would suffice to wear it away entirely. Still, from what had passed, she fancied that opposition alone would only make the matter worse by rous- ing Maggie at once. She knew far more of human nature than either of the young people before her ; and after a little reflection, she suggested that Henry should leave Mag- gie with her for a year, during which time no communica- tion whatever should pass between them, while she would promise faithfully not to influence Margaret either way.

"If at the end of the year," said she, " you both retain for each other the feelings you have now, I will no longer object to the marriage, but will make the best of it."

At first, Henry spurned at the proposition, and when he saw that Margaret thought well of it, he reproached her with a want of feeling, saying "she did not love him as she had once done."

" I shall not forget you, Henry," said Maggie, coming to his side and taking his hand in hers, "neither will you for- get me ; and when the year has passed away, only think how much pleasanter it will be for us to be married here at home, with grandma's blessing on our union !"

"If I only knew you would prove true !" said Henry, who missed something in Maggie's manner.

"I *do* mean to prove true," she answered sadly, though at that moment another face, another form, stood between her and Henry Warner, who, knowing that Madam Conway would not suffer her to go with him on any terms, concluded at last to make a virtue of necessity, and accordingly ex- pressed his willingness to wait, provided Margaret were al- lowed to write occasionally either to himself or Rose.

But to this Madam Conway would not consent. "She

wished the test to be perfect," she said, "and unless he accepted her terms, he must give Maggie up, at once and forever."

As there seemed no alternative, Henry rather ungraciously yielded the point, promising to leave Maggie free for a year, while she, too, promised not to write either to him or to Rose, except with her grandmother's consent. Maggie Miller's word once passed, Madam Conway knew it would not be broken, and she unhesitatingly left the young people together while they said their parting words. A message of love from Maggie to Rose—a hundred protestations of eternal fidelity, and then they parted ; Henry, sad and disappointed, slowly wending his way back to the spot where Hagar impatiently awaited his coming, while Maggie, leaning from her chamber window, and listening to the sound of his retreating footsteps, brushed away a tear, wondering the while why it was that *she felt so relieved.*

CHAPTER XVI.

PERPLEXITY.

HALF in sorrow, half in joy, old Hagar listened to the story which Henry told her, standing at her cottage door. In sorrow, because she had learned to like the young man, learned to think of him as Maggie's husband, who would not wholly cast her off, if her secret should chance to be divulged; and in joy, because her idol would be with her yet a little longer.

"Maggie will be faithful quite as long as you," she said, when he expressed his fears of her forgetfulness; and trying to console himself with this asshrance, he sprang into the carriage in which he had come, and was driven rapidly away.

He was too late for the night express, but taking the early morning train, he reached New York just as the sun was setting.

"Alone ! my brother, alone ?" queried Rose, as he entered the private parlor of the hotel where she was staying with her aunt.

"Yes, alone, just as I expected," he answered, somewhat bitterly.

Then very briefly he related to her the particulars of his adventure, to which she listened eagerly, one moment chiding herself for the faint, shadowy hope which whispered that possibly Maggie Miller would never be his wife, and again sympathizing in his disappointment.

"A year would not be very long," she said "and in the new scenes to which he was going," a part of it would pass rapidly away;" and then in her childlike, guileless manner, she drew a glowing picture of the future, when, her own health restored, they would return to their old home in Leominster, where, after a few months more, he would bring 'o them his bride.

"You are my comforting angel, Rose," he said, folding her lovingly in his arms, and kissing her smooth white cheek. "With such a treasure as you for a sister, I ought not to repine, even though Maggie Miller should never be mine."

The words were lightly spoken, and by him soon forgotten, but Rose remembered them long, dwelling upon them in the wearisome nights, when in her narrow berth, she listened to the swelling sea, as it dashed against the vessel's side. Many a fond remembrance, too, she gave to Maggie Miller, who, in her woodland home, thought often of the travellers on the sea, never wishing that she was with them; but experiencing always a feeling of pleasure in knowing that she was Maggie Miller yet, and should be until next year's autumn leaves were falling.

Of Arthur Carrollton she thought frequently, wishing she had not been so rude that morning in the woods, and feeling vexed because in his letters to her grandmother, he merely said, Remember me to Margaret."

"I wish he would write something besides *that*," she thought, "for I remember him now altogether too much for my own good;" and then she wondered "what he *would* have said that morning, if she had not been so cross."

Very little was said to her of him by Madam Conway, who, having learned that he was not going to England, and would ere long return to them, concluded for a time to let the matter rest, particularly as she knew how much Maggie was already interested in one whom she had resolved to hate. Feeling thus confident that all would yet end well, Madam Conway was in unusually good spirits, save when thoughts of Mrs. Douglas senior obtruded themselves upon her. Then, indeed, in a most unenviable state of mind, she repined at the disgrace which Theo had brought upon them, and charged Maggie repeatedly to keep it a secret from Mrs. Jeffrey and Anna, the first of whom made many inquiries concerning the family, which she supposed of course was very aristocratic.

One day towards the last of November, there came to Madam Conway a letter from Mrs. Douglas senior, wonderful alike in composition and appearance. Directed wrong side up, sealed with a wafer, and stamped with a thimble, it bore an unmistakable resemblance to its writer, who expressed many regrets that "she had not known in the time on't, who her illustrious visitors were."

"If I had known," she wrote, "I should have sot the table in the parlor certing, for though I'm plain and home-spun, I know as well as the next one what good manners is, and do my endeavors to practise it. But do tell a body," she continued, "where you was, muster day in Wooster. I knocked and pounded enough to raise the dead, and nobody answered. I never noticed you was deaf when you was here, though Betsey Jane thinks she did. If you be, I'll send you up a receipt for a kind of intment which Miss Sam Babbit invented, and which cures everything.

"Theodoshy has been to see us, and though in my way of thinkir', she ain't as handsome as Margaret, she looks as well as the ginerality of women. I liked her, too, and as

soon as the men's winter clothes is off my hands, I calkerlate to have a quiltin', and finish up another bedquilt to
send her, for manlike, George has furnished up his rooms
with all sorts of nicknacks, and got only two blankets, and
two Marsales spreads for his bed. So I've sent 'em down
the herrin'-bone and risin' sun quilts for every day wear, as
I don't believe in usin' your best things all the time. My
old man says I'd better let 'em alone ; but he's got some
queer ideas, thinks you'll sniff your nose at my letter, and
all that, but I've more *charity* for folks, and well I might
have, bein' that's my name.

" CHARITY DOUGLAS."

To this letter were appended three different postscripts.
In the *first* Madam Conway and Maggie were cordially
invited to visit Charlton again ; in the *second* Betsey June
sent her *regrets ;* while in the *third* Madam Conway was
particularly requested to excuse haste and a bad pen.

"Disgusting creature !" was Madam Conway's exclamation, as she finished reading the letter, then tossing it into
the fire she took up another one, which had come by the
same mail, and was from Theo herself.

After dwelling at length upon the numerous calls she
made, the parties she attended, the compliments she received,
and her curiosity to know why her grandmother came back
that day, she spoke of her recent visit in Charlton.

"You have been there, it seems," she wrote, "so I need
not particularize, though I know how shocked and disappointed you must have been ; and I think it very kind in
you not to have said anything upon the subject, except that
you had called there, for George reads all my letters, and I
would not have his feelings hurt. He had prepared me in
a measure for the visit, but the reality was even worse than

I anticipated. And still they are the kindest hearted people in the world, while Mr. Douglas is a man, they say, of excellent sense. George never lived at home much, and their heathenish ways mortify him I know, though he never says a word, except that they are his parents.

"People here respect George, too, quite as much as if he were a *Conway*, and I sometimes think they like him all the better for being so kind to his old father, who comes frequently to the store. Grandma, I begin to think differently of some things from what I did. Birth and blood do not make much difference in this country, at least ; and still I must acknowledge that I should feel dreadfully if I did not love George and know that he is the kindest husband in the world."

The letter closed with a playful insinuation that as Henry Warner had gone, Maggie might possibly marry Arthur Carrollton, and so make amends for the disgrace which Theo had unwittingly brought upon the Conway line.

For a long time after finishing the above, Madam Conway sat rapt in thought. Could it be possible that during all her life, she had labored under a mistake? Were birth and family rank really of no consequence? Was George just as worthy of respect as if he had descended directly from the Scottish race of Douglas, instead of belonging to that vulgar woman? "It may be so in America," she sighed ; "but it is not true of England," and sincerely hoping that Theo's remark concerning Mr. Carrollton might prove true, she laid aside the letter, and for the remainder of the day, busied herself with preparations for the return of Arthur Carrollton, who had written that he should be with them on the first of December.

The day came, and, unusually excited, Maggie flitted from

room to room, seeing that everything was in order, wonder
ing how he would meet her and if he had forgiven her
for having been so cross at their last interview in the woods
The effect of every suitable dress in her wardrobe was tried,
and she decided at last upon a crimson and black merino,
which harmonized well with her dark eyes and hair.   The
dress was singularly becoming, and feeling quite well satisfied with the face and form reflected by her mirror, she
descended to the parlor, where any doubts she might have
had concerning her personal appearance were put to flight
by Anna Jeffrey, who, with a feeling of envy, asked " if she
had the scarlet fever !" referring to her bright color, and
saying, she "did not think too red a face becoming to any
one, particularly to Margaret, to whom it gave a *blowsy*
look, such as she had more than once heard Mr. Carrollton
say he did not like to see !"

Margaret knew well that the dark-browed girl would give
almost anything for the roses blooming on her cheeks ; so
she made no reply, but simply wished Anna would return to
England, as for the last two months she had talked of doing
It was not quite dark, and Mr. Carrollton, if he came that
night, would be with them soon.   The car whistle had
sounded some time before, and Maggie's quick ear caught at
last the noise of the bells in the distance.   Nearer and
nearer they came ; the sleigh was at the door, and forgetting everything but her own happiness, Maggie ran out to
meet their guest, nor turned her glowing face away when he
stooped down to kiss her.   He had forgiven her ill-nature,
she was certain of that, and very joyfully she led the way
to the parlor, where as the full light of the lamp fell upon
him she started involuntarily, he seemed so changed.

" Are you sick ?" she asked, and her voice expressed the
deep anxiety she felt.

Forcing back a slight cough and smiling down upon her he answered cheerfully, "Oh no, not sick. Canada air does not agree with me; that's all. I took a severe cold, soon after my arrival in Montreal," and the cough he had attempted to stifle, now burst forth, sounding to Maggie, who thought only of consumption, like an echo from the grave.

"Oh, I am so sorry," she answered sadly, and her eyes filled with tears, which she did not try to conceal, for looking through the window across the snow-clad field on which the winter moon was shining, she saw instinctively another grave beside that of her mother.

Madam Conway had not yet appeared, and as Anna Jeffrey just then left the room, Mr. Carrollton was for some moments alone with Maggie. Winding his arm around her waist, and giving her a most expressive look, he said, "Maggie, are those tears for me?"

Instantly the bright blushes stole over Maggie's face and neck, for she remembered the time when once before he had asked her a similar question. Not now, as then, did she turn from him away, but she answered frankly, "Yes, they are. You look so pale and thin, I'm sure you must be very ill."

Whether Mr. Carrollton liked *blowsy* complexions or not, he certainly admired Maggie's at that moment, and drawing her closer to his side, he said, half playfully, half earnestly, "To see you thus anxious for me, Maggie, more than atones for your waywardness when last we parted. You are forgiven, but you are unnecessarily alarmed. I shall be better soon. Hillsdale air will do me good, and I intend remaining here until I am well again. Will you nurse me, Maggie, just as my sister Helen would do, were she here?"

The right chord was touched, and all the soft, womanly

qualities of Maggie Miller's nature were called forth by Arthur Carrollton's failing health. For several weeks after his arrival at Hillsdale he was a confirmed invalid, lying all-day upon the sofa in the parlor, while Maggie read to him from books which he selected, partly for the purpose of amusing himself, and more for the sake of benefiting her and improving her taste for literature. At other times, he would tell her of his home beyond the sea, and Maggie, listening to him while he described its airy halls, its noble parks, its shaded walks and musical fountains, would sometimes wish aloud that she might one day see that spot which seemed to her so much like paradise. He wished so, too, and often-times when, with half-closed eyes, his mind was wandering amid the scenes of his youth, he saw at his side a queenly figure with features like those of Maggie Miller, who each day was stealing more and more into his heart, where love for other than his nearest friends had never before found entrance. She had many faults, he knew, but these he possessed both the will and the power to correct, and as day after day she sat reading at his side, he watched her bright, animated face, thinking what a splendid woman she would make, and wondering if an American rose like her would bear transplanting to English soil.

Very complacently Madam Conway looked on, reading aright the admiration which Arthur Carrollton evinced for Margaret, who in turn was far from being uninterested in him. Anna Jeffrey, too, watched them jealously, ponder-ing in her own mind some means by which she could, if possible, annoy Margaret. Had she known how far matters had gone with Henry Warner, she would unhesitatingly have told it to Arthur Carrollton; but so quietly had the affair been managed that she knew comparatively but little. This little, however, she determined to tell him, together with any embellishments she might see fit to use. Accordingly one afternoon, when he had been there two months or more, and Maggie had gone with her grandmother to- ride, she went down to the parlor under pretence of getting a book to read. He was much better now, but feeling somewhat fatigued from a walk he had taken in the yard, he was re- clining upon the sofa. Leaning over the rocking-chair which stood near by, Anna inquired for his health, and then asked how long since he had heard from home.

He liked to talk of England, and as there was nothing to him particularly disagreeable in Anna Jeffrey, he bade her be seated. Very willingly she complied with his request, and after talking awhile of England, announced her inten- tion of returning home the last of March. " My aunt prefers remaining with Madam Conway, but I don't like America," said she, " and I often wonder why I am here."

" I supposed you came to be with your aunt, who, I am told, has been to you a second mother," answered Mr. Car- •
rollton ; and Anna replied, " You are right. She could not be easy until she got me here, where I know I am not wanted ; at least *one* would be glad to have me leave."

Mr. Carrollton looked inquiringly at her, and Anna con- tinued : " I fully supposed I was to be a companion for Mar- garet ; but instead of that she treats me with the utmost coolness, making me feel keenly my position as a dependent."

" That does not seem at all like Maggie," said Mr. Car- rollton, and with a meaning smile far more expressive than words, Anna answered, " She may not always be alike, but hush ! don't I hear bells ?" and she ran to the window, say- ing as she resumed her seat, " I thought they had come, but I was mistaken. I dare say Maggie has coaxed her grandmother to drive by the post office, thinking there might be a letter from Henry Warner.

Her manner affected Mr. Carrollton perceptibly, but he made no reply; and Anna asked "if he knew Mr. Warner?"

"I saw him in Worcester, I believe," he said, and Anna continued, "Do you think him a suitable husband for a gir like Maggie?"

There was a deep flush on Arthur Carrollton's cheek, and his lips were whiter than their wont as he answered, "I know nothing of him, neither did I suppose Miss Miller ever thought of him for a husband."

"I know she did at one time," said his tormentor, turning the leaves of her book, with well feigned indifference. "It was not any secret, or I should not speak of it; of course Madam Conway was greatly opposed to it, too, and forbade her writing to him; but how the matter is now, I do not positively know, though I am quite sure they are engaged."

"Isn't it very close here? Will you please to open the hall door?" said Mr. Carrollton, suddenly panting for breath; and satisfied with her work, Anna did as desired and then left him alone.

"Maggie engaged!" he exclaimed, "engaged, when I was hoping to win her for myself!" and a sharp pang shot through his heart as he thought of giving to another the beautiful girl who had grown so into his love. "But I am glad I learned it in time," he continued, hurriedly walking the floor, "knew it ere I had done Henry Warner a wrong, by telling her of my love, and asking her to go with me to my English home, which will be desolate without her. This is why she repulsed me in the woods. She knew I ought not to speak of *love* to *her*. Why didn't I see it before, or why has not Madam Conway told me the truth! *She* at least has deceived me," and with a feeling of keer disappointment, he continued to pace the floor, one moment resolving to leave Hillsdale at once, and again thinking how impossible it was to tear himself away.

Arthur Carrollton was a perfectly honorable man, and once assured of Maggie's engagement, he would neither by word or deed do aught to which the most fastidious lover could object, and Henry Warner's rights were as safe with him as with the truest of friends. But was Maggie really engaged? Might there not be some mistake? He hoped so at least, and alternating between hope and fear, he waited impatiently the return of Maggie, who, with each thought of losing her, seemed tenfold dearer to him than she had ever been before; and when at last she came bounding in, he could scarcely refrain from folding her in his arms, and asking of her to think again ere she gave another than himself the right of calling her his bride. But she is not mine, he thought, and so he merely took her cold hands within his own, rubbing them until they were warm. Then seating himself by her side upon the sofa, he spoke of her ride, asking casually if she called at the post office.

"No, we did not drive that way," she answered readily, adding that the post office had few attractions for her now, as no one wrote to her save Theo.

She evidently spoke the truth, and with a feeling of relief Mr. Carrollton thought that possibly Miss Jeffrey might have been mistaken; but he would know at all hazards, even though he ran the risk of being thought extremely rude. Accordingly that evening, after Mrs. Jeffrey and Anna had retired to their room, and while Madam Conway was giving some household directions in the kitchen, he asked her to come and sit by him as he lay upon the sofa, himself placing her chair where the lamp light would fall fully upon her face and reveal its every expression. Closing the piano, she complied with his request, and then awaited in silence for what he was to say.

"Maggie," he began, "you may think me bold, but there is something I very much wish to know, and which you, if you choose, can tell me. From what I have heard, I am led to think you are engaged. Will you tell me if this is true ?"

The bright color faded out from Maggie's cheek, while her eyes grew darker than before, and still she did not speak. Not that she was angry with him for asking her that question ; but because the answer, which, if made at all, must be yes, was hard to utter. And yet why should she hesitate to tell him the truth at once ?

Alas, for thee, Maggie Miller ! The fancied love you feel for Henry Warner is fading fast away. Arthur Carrollton is a dangerous rival, and even now, you cannot meet the glance of his expressive eyes without a blush ! Your better judgment acknowledged his superiority to Henry long ago, and now in your heart there is room for none save him.

"Maggie," he said, again stretching out his hand to take the unresisting one which lay upon her lap, "you need not make me other answer save that so plainly written on your face. You are engaged, and may heaven's blessing attend both you and yours."

At this moment Madam Conway appeared, and fearing her inability to control her feelings longer, Maggie precipitately left the room. Going to her chamber, she burst into a passionate fit of weeping, one moment blaming Mr. Carrollton for having learned her secret, and the next chiding herself for wishing to withhold from him a knowledge of her engagement.

"It is not that I love Henry less, I am sure," she thought,

and laying her head upon her pillow, she recalled everything which had passed between herself and her affianced husband, trying to bring back the olden happiness with which she had listened to his words of love. But it would not come ; there was a barrier in the way, Arthur Carrollton as he looked when he said so sadly, "You need not tell me, Maggie."

"Oh, I wish he had not asked me that question," she sighed. "It has put such dreadful thoughts into my head. And yet I love Henry as well as ever ; I know I do, I am sure of it, or if I do not, *I will*," and repeating to herself again and again the words, "I will, I will," she fell asleep

Will, however, is not always subservient to one's wishes, and during the first few days succeeding the incident of that night, Maggie often found herself wishing Arthur Carrollton had never come to Hillsdale, he made her so wretched, so unhappy. Insensibly, too, she became a very little unamiable, speaking pettishly to her grandmother, disrespectfully to Mrs Jeffrey, haughtily to Anna, and rarely to Mr. Carrollton, who, after the lapse of two or three weeks, began to talk of returning home in the same vessel with Anna Jeffrey, at which time his health would be fully restored. Then, indeed, did Maggie awake to the reality that while her hand was plighted to one, she loved another—not as in days gone by she had loved Henry Warner, but with a deeper, more absorbing love. With this knowledge, too, there came the thought that Arthur Carrollton had once loved her, and but for the engagement now so much regretted, he would ere this have told her so. But it was *too late, too late*. He would never feel toward her again as he once had felt, and bitter tears she shed as she contemplated the fast coming future, when Arthur Carrollton would be gone, or shudderingly thought of the time when Henry Warner would return to claim her promise.

"I cannot, cannot marry him," she cried, "until I've torn that other image from my heart," and then for many days she strove to recall the olden love in vain ; for, planted on the sandy soil of childhood, as it were, it had been outgrown, and would never again spring into life. "I will write to him exactly how it is," she said at last; "will tell him that the affection I felt for him, could not have been what a wife should feel for her husband. I was young, had seen nothing of the world, knew nothing of gentlemen's society, and when he came with his handsome face, and winning ways, my interest was awakened. Sympathy, too, for his misfortune, increased that interest, which grandma's opposition tended in no wise to diminish. But it has died out, that fancied love, and I cannot bring it back. Still, if he insists, I will keep my word, and when he comes next autumn, I will not tell him, No."

Maggie was very calm when this decision was reached, and opening her writing desk she wrote just as she said she would, begging of him to forgive her if she had done him wrong, and beseeching Rose to comfort him as only a sister like her could do. "And remember," she wrote at the close, "remember that sooner than see you *very* unhappy, I will marry you, will try to be a faithful wife ; though, Henry, I would rather not—oh, so much rather not."

The letter was finished, and then Maggie took it to her grandmother, who read it eagerly, for in it she saw a fulfillment of her wishes. Very closely had she watched both Mr. Carrollton and Maggie, readily divining the truth, that something was wrong between them. But from past experience, she deemed it wiser not to interfere directly. Mr. Carrollton's avowed intention of returning to England, how ever, startled her, and she was revolving some method of procedure when Margaret brought to her the letter.

"I am happier than I can well express," she said, when she had finished reading it. "Oh course you have my permission to send it. But what has changed you, Maggie? Has another taken the place of Henry Warner?"

"Don't ask me, grandma," cried Mag, covering her face with her hands, "don't ask me, for indeed I can only tell you that I am very unhappy."

A little skillful questioning on Madam Conway's part, sufficed to explain the whole—how constant association with Arthur Carrollton had won for him a place in Maggie's heart, which Henry Warner had never filled ; how the knowledge that she loved him as she could love no other one had faintly revealed itself to her, on the night when he asked if she were engaged, and had burst upon her with overwhelming power, when she heard that he was going home.

"He will never think of me again, I know," she said ; "but, with my present feelings, I cannot marry Henry, unless he insists upon it."

"Men seldom wish to marry a woman who says she does not love them, and Henry Warner will not prove an exception," answered Madam Conway ; and, comforted with this assurance, Mag folded up her letter, which was soon on its way to Cuba.

The next evening, as Madam Conway sat alone with Mr. Carrollton, she spoke of his return to England, expressing her sorrow, and asking why he did not remain with them longer.

"I will deal frankly with you, Madam," said he, " and say that if I followed my own inclination I should stay, for Hillsdale holds for me an attraction which no other spot possesses. I refer to your grand-daughter, who, in the little time I have known her, has grown very dear to me; so dear, that I dare not stay longer where she is, lest I should love her too well, and rebel against yielding her to another."

For a moment, Madam Conway hesitated; but thinking the case demanded her speaking, she said, "Possibly, Mr. Carrollton, I can make an explanation which will show some points in a different light from that in which you now see them. Margaret is engaged to Henry Warner, I will admit; but the engagement has become irksome, and yesterday she wrote, asking a release, which he will grant, of course."

Instantly, the expression of Mr. Carrollton's face was changed, and very intently he listened, while Madam Conway frankly told him the story of Margaret's engagement up to the present time, withholding from him nothing, not even Mag's confession of the interest she felt in him, an interest which had weakened her girlish attachment for Henry Warner.

"You have made me very happy," Mr. Carrollton said to Madam Conway, as, at a late hour, he bade her good night, "happier than I can well express; for, without Margaret, life to me would be dreary, indeed."

The next morning, at the breakfast table, Anna Jeffrey, who was in high spirits with the prospect of having Mr. Carrollton for a fellow-traveller, spoke of their intended voyage, saying she could hardly wait for the time to come, and asking if he were not equally impatient to leave so *horrid* a country as America.

"On the contrary," he replied, "I should be sorry to leave America just yet. I have, therefore, decided to remain a little longer," and his eyes sought the face of Mag

who, in her joyful surprise, dropped the knife with which
she was helping herself to butter ; while Anna Jeffrey, quite
as much astonished, upset her coffee, exclaiming, " *No*
going home ! What has changed your mind ?"

Mr. Carrollton made her no direct reply, and she continued her breakfast in no very amiable mood ; while Maggie, too much overjoyed to eat, managed, ere long, to find
an excuse for leaving the table. Mr. Carrollton wished to
do everything honorably, and so he decided to say nothing
to Mag of the cause of this sudden change in his plan, until
Henry Warner's answer was received, as she would then
feel freer to act as she felt. His resolution, however, was
more easily made than kept, and during the succeeding
weeks, by actions, if not by words, he more than once told
Maggie Miller how much she was beloved ; and Maggie,
trembling with fear lest the cup of happiness just within her
grasp should be rudely dashed aside, waited impatiently for
the letter which was to set her free. But weeks went by,
and Maggie's heart grew sick with hope deferred, for there
came to her no message from the distant Cuban shore
where, in another chapter, we will for a moment go.

CHAPTER XVII.

BROTHER AND SISTER.

Brightly shone the moonlight on the sunny isle of Cuba, dancing lightly on the wave, resting softly on the orange groves, and stealing gently through the casement, into the room where a young girl lay, whiter far than the flowers strewn upon her pillow. From the commencement of the voyage, Rose had drooped, growing weaker every day, until at last all who looked upon her, felt that the home, of which she talked so much, would never again be gladdened by her presence. Very tenderly, Henry Warner nursed her, bearing her often in his arms upon the vessel's deck, where she could breathe the fresh morning air as it came rippling o'er the sea. But neither ocean breeze, nor yet the fragrant breath of Florida's aromatic bowers, where for a time they stopped, had power to rouse her ; and when at last Havana was reached, she laid her weary head upon her pillow, whispering to no one of the love which was wearing her life away. With untold anguish at their hearts, both her aunt and Henry watched her, the latter shrinking ever from the thoughts of losing one who seemed a part of his very life.

"I cannot give you up, my Rose. I cannot live without you," he said, when once she talked to him of death. "You are all the world to me," and laying his head upon her pillow, he wept as men will sometimes weep over their first great sorrow.

"Don't, Henry," she said, laying her tiny hand upon his hair "Maggie will comfort you when I am gone She will talk to you of me, standing at my grave, for, Henry, you must not leave me here alone. You must carry me home and bury me in dear old Leominster, where my child-hood was passed, and where I learned to love you so much; oh, so much!"

There was a mournful pathos in the tone with which the last words were uttered, but Henry Warner did not under stand it, and covering the little blue veined hand with kisses, he promised that her grave should be made at the foot of the garden in their far off home, where the sunset-light fell softly, and the moonbeams gently shone. That evening, Henry sat alone by Rose, who had fallen into a disturbed slumber. For a time he took no notice of the dis-connected words she uttered in her dreams, but when, at last, he heard the sound of his own name, he drew near, and bending low, listened with mingled emotions of joy, sorrow and surprise to a secret which, waking, she would never have told to *him*, above all others. She loved him—the fair girl he called his sister—but not as a sister loves, and now, as he stood by her, with the knowledge thrilling every nerve, he remembered many by-gone scenes, where, but for his blindness, he would have seen how every pulsa-tion of her heart throbbed alone for him, whose hand was plighted to another, and that other no unworthy rival. Beautiful, very beautiful, was the shadowy form which, at that moment, seemed standing at his side, and his heart went out towards her as the one above all others to be his bride.

"Had I known it sooner," he thought, "known it before I met the peerless Mag, I might have taken Rose to my bosom and loved her, it may be, with a deeper love than that I feel for Maggie Miller, for Rose is everything to me She has made and keeps me what I am, and how can I let her die, when I have the power to save her ?"

There was a movement upon the pillow. Rose was waking, and as her soft blue eyes unclosed and looked up in his face, he wound his arms around her, kissing her lips, as never before he had kissed her. She was not his *sister* now—the veil was torn away—a new feeling had been awakened, and as days and weeks went by there gradually crept in between him and Maggie Miller a new love—even a love for the fair-haired Rose, to whom he was kinder, if possible, than he had been before, though he seldom kissed her lips, or caressed her in any way.

"It would be wrong," he said, "a wrong to himself—a wrong to her—and a wrong to Maggie Miller, to whom his troth was plighted," and he did not wish it otherwise, he thought ; though insensibly there came over him a wish that Maggie herself might weary of the engagement, and seek to break it. "Not that he loved *her* the less," he reasoned, "but that he *pitied* Rose the more."

In this manner time passed on, until at last there came to him Maggie's letter which had been a long time on the sea.

"I expected it," he thought, as he finished reading it, and though conscious for a moment of a feeling of disappointment, the letter brought him far more pleasure than pain.

Of Arthur Carrollton no mention had been made, but he readily guessed the truth; and thinking "it is well," he laid the letter aside and went back to Rose, deciding to say nothing to her then. He would wait until his own feelings were more perfectly defined. So a week went by, and again, as he had often done before, he sat with her alone in the stilly night, watched her as she slept, and thinking how beautiful she was, with her golden hair shading her childish face, her long eyelashes resting on her cheek, and her little hands folded meekly upon her bosom.

"She is too beautiful to die," he murmured, pressing a kiss upon her lips.

This act awoke her, and turning towards him she said, "Was I dreaming, Henry, or did you kiss me as you used to do?"

"Not dreaming, Rose," he answered—then rather hurriedly he added, "I have a letter from Maggie Miller, and ere I answer it, I would read it to you. Can you hear it now?"

"Yes, yes," she whispered faintly, "read it to me, Henry;" and turning her face away, she listened, while he read that Maggie Miller, grown weary of her troth, asked a release from her engagement.

He finished reading, and then waited in silence to hear what Rose would say. But for a time she did not speak. All hope for herself had long since died away, and now she experienced only sorrow for Henry's disappointment.

"My poor brother," she said at last, turning her face towards him and taking his hand in hers; "I am sorry for you—to lose us both, Maggie and me. What will you do?"

"Rose," he said, bending so low that his brown locks mingled with the yellow tresses of her hair, "Rose, I do not regret Maggie Miller's decision, neither do I blame her for it. She is a noble, true-hearted girl, and so long as I live I shall esteem her highly; but I, too, have changed—have learned to love another. Will you sanction this new love, dear Rose? Will you say that it is right?"

The white lids closed wearily over the eyes of blue, but they could not keep back the tears which rolled down her face, as she answered somewhat sadly, "Who is it, Henry?"

There was another moment of silence, and then he whispered in her ear, "People call her Rose; *I* once called her *sister*; but my heart now claims her for something nearer. My Rose," he continued, "shall it be? Will you live for my sake? Will you be my wife?"

The shock was too sudden—too great, and neither on that night, nor yet the succeeding day, had Rose the power to answer. But as the dew of heaven is to the parched and dying flower, so were these words of love to her, imparting at once new life and strength, making her as it were another creature. The question asked that night so unexpectedly, was answered at last; and then with almost perfect happiness at her heart, she, too, added a few lines to the letter which Henry sent to Maggie Miller, over whose pathway, hitherto so bright, a fearful shadow was falling.

CHAPTER XVIII.

THE PEDDLER.

It was a rainy April day—a day which precluded all out door exercise, and Hagar Warren, from the window of her lonely cabin, watched in vain for the coming of Maggie Miller. It was now more than a week since she had been there, for both Arthur Carrollton and herself had accompanied the disappointed Anna Jeffrey to New York, going with her on board the vessel which was to take her from a country she so affected to dislike.

"I dare say you'll be Maggie *somebody else* ere I meet you again," she said to Maggie, at parting, and Mr. Carrollton, on her journey home, found it hard to keep from asking her if for the "somebody else," she would substitute his name and so be "Maggie Carrollton."

This, however, he did not do ; but his attentions were so marked, and his manner toward her so affectionate, that ere Hillsdale was reached, there was in Maggie's mind no longer a doubt as to the nature of his feelings toward her. Arrived at home, he kept her constantly at his side, while Hagar, who was suffering from a slight attack of rheumatism, and could not go up to the stone house, waited and watched, thinking herself almost willing to be teased for the *secret*, if she could once more hear the sound of Maggie's voice. The secret, however, had been forgotten in the exciting scenes, through which Maggie had passed since first she learned of its existence ; and it was now a long, long time since she had mentioned it to Hagar, who each day grew more and more determined never to reveal it.

"My life is almost ended," she thought, "and the secret shall go with me to my grave. Margaret will be happier without it, and it shall not be revealed."

Thus she reasoned on that rainy afternoon, when she sat waiting for Maggie, who, she heard, had returned the day before. Slowly the hours dragged on, and the night shadows fell at last upon the forest trees, creeping into the corners of Hagar's room, resting upon the hearth-stone falling upon the window pane, creeping up the wall, and affecting Hagar with a nameless fear of some impending evil. This fear not even the flickering flame of the lamp, which she lighted at last, and placed upon the mantel, was able to dispel, for the shadows grew darker, folding themselves around her heart, until she covered her eyes with her hands, lest some goblin shape should spring into life before her.

The sound of the gate latch was heard, and footsteps were approaching the door ; not the bounding step of Maggie, but a tramping tread, followed by a heavy knock, and the next moment a tall, large man appeared before her, asking shelter for the night. The pack he carried showed him at once to be a peddler, and upon a nearer view, Hagar recognized in him a stranger who, years before, had craved her hospitality. He had been civil to her then ; she did not fear him now, and she consented to his remaining, thinking his presence there might dispel the mysterious terror hanging around her. But few words passed between them that night, for Martin, as he called himself, was tired, and after partaking of the supper she prepared, he retired to rest The

next morning, however, he was more talkative, kindly en
lightening her with regard to his business, his family and
his place of residence, which last he said was in Meriden,
Connecticut.

It was a long time since Hagar had heard that name, and
now, turning quickly towards him, she said, "*Meriden*?
That is where my Hester lived, and where her husband died."

"I want to know," returned the Yankee peddler. "What
might have been his name?"

"Hamilton, Nathan Hamilton. Did you know him?
He died nineteen years ago, this coming summer."

"*Egzactly!*" ejaculated the peddler, setting down his pack,
and himself taking a chair, preparatory to a long talk
"Egzactly; I knowed him like a book. *Old Squire* Hampleton, the biggest man in Meriden, and you don't say his
last wife, that tall, handsome gal, was your darter?"

"Yes, she was my daughter," answered Hagar, her whole
face glowing with the interest she felt, in talking for the
first time in her life with one who had known her daughter's
husband, Maggie's father. "You knew her. You have
seen her?" she continued; and Martin answered, "Seen her
a hundred times, I'll bet. Any how, I sold her the weddin'
gown, and now I think on't, she favored you. She was a
likely person, and I allus thought that proud sister of his'n,
the widder Warner, might have been in better business than
takin' them children away as she did, because he married
his hired gal. But it's as well for them, I s'pose, particularly for the boy, who is one of the fust young men in
Wooster, now. Keeps a big store!"

"*Warner, Warner!*" interrupted old Hagar, the nameless
terror of the night before creeping again into her heart.
"Whose name did you say was Warner?"

"The hull on 'em, boy, girl and all, is called Warner

now—one Rose, and t'other Henry," answered the peddler, perfectly delighted with the interest manifested by his auditor, who, grasping at the bedpost and moving her hand rapidly before her eyes, as if to clear away a mist which had settled there, continued, " I remember now Hester told me of the children ; but one, she said, was a step-child, that was the boy, wasn't it ?" and her wild, black eyes had in them a look of unutterable anxiety, wholly incomprehensible to the peddler, who, instead of answering her question said, " What ails you woman ?   Your face is as white as a piece of paper ?"

" Thinking of Hester always affects me so," she answered; and stretching her hands beseechingly towards him, she entreated him to say if Henry were not the step-child.

" *No marm, he warn't,*" answered the peddler, who, like a great many talkative people, pretended to know more than he really did, and who in this particular instance, was certainly mistaken.   " I can tell you egzactly how that is ; Henry was the son of Mr. Hampleton's first marriage, *Henry Hampleton.*   The second wife, the one your darter lived with, was the *widder Warner,* and had a little gal, *Rose,* when she married Mr. Hampleton.   This widder Warner's husband's brother married Mr. Hampleton's *sister,* the woman who took the children, and had Henry change his name to Warner.   The Hampletons and Warners were mighty big feelin' folks, and the old Squire's match mortified 'em dreadfully."

" Where are they now ?" gasped Hagar, hoping there might be some mistake.

" There you've got me !" answered Martin.   " I haven't seen 'em this dozen year ; but the last I heard, Miss Warner and Rose was livin' in Leominster, and Henry was in a big store in Wooster   But what the plague is the matter ?" he continued, alarmed at the expression of Hagar's face, as well as at the strangeness of her manner.

Wringing her hands as if she would wrench her fingers from their sockets, she clutched at her long white hair, and rocking to and fro, moaned " woe is me, and woe the day when I was born."

From every one save her grandmother, Margaret had kept the knowledge of her changed feelings towards Henry Warner ; and looking upon a marriage between the two as an event surely expected, old Hagar was overwhelmed with grief and fear.   Falling at last upon her knees, she cried, " Had you cut my throat from ear to ear, old man, you could not have hurt me more.   Oh, that I had died years and years ago ! but I must *live* now, *live !*" she screamed, springing to her feet—" live to prevent the wrong my own wickedness has caused."

Perfectly astonished at what he saw and heard, the peddler attempted to question her, but failing to obtain any satisfactory answers, he finally left, mentally pronouncing her, " as crazy as a loon."   This opinion was confirmed by the people on whom he next called, for, chancing to speak of Hagar, he was told that nothing which she did or said was considered strange, as she had been called insane for years. This satisfied Martin, who made no further mention of her, and thus the scandal, which his story might otherwise have produced, was prevented.   .

In the meantime, on her face old Hagar lay, moaning bitterly.   " My sin has found me out, found me out ; and just when I thought it never need be known.   For myself, I do not care ; but *Maggie, Maggie,* how can I tell her that she is bone of *my* bone, blood of *my* blood, flesh of *my* flesh — and me, old Hagar Warren !"

It would be impossible to describe the scorn and intense

loathing concentrated in the tones of Hagar's voice as she uttered these last words, "*and me, old Hagar Warren!*" Had she indeed been the veriest wretch on earth, she could not have hated herself more than she did in that hour of her humiliation, when, with a loud voice, she cried, "let me die, oh, let me die, and it will never be known!" Then, as she reflected upon the terrible consequence which would ensue were she to die and make no sign, she wrung her hands despairingly, crying, "Life, life, yes, give me life to tell her of my guilt; and then it will be a blessed rest to die. Oh, Margaret, my precious child, I'd give my heart's blood, drop by drop, to save you; but it can't be; you must not wed your father's son; oh, *Maggie, Maggie, Maggie!*"

Fainter and fainter grew each succeeding word, and when the last was spoken, she fell again upon her face, unconscious and forgetful of her woe. Higher and higher in the heavens rose the morning sun, stealing across the window-sill, and shining aslant the floor, where Hagar still lay in a deep, deathlike swoon. An hour passed on, and then the wretched woman came slowly back to life, her eyes lighting up with joy, as she whispered, "it *was* a dream, thank heaven, 'twas a dream;" and then growing dim with tears, as the dread reality came over her. The first fearful burst of grief was passed, for Hagar now could weep, and tears did her good, quelling the feverish agony at her heart. Not for herself did she suffer so much as for Mag, trembling for the effect the telling of the secret would have on her. For it *must* be told. She knew that full well, and as the sun fast neared the western horizon, she murmured, "Oh, *will* she come to-night, will she come to-night?"

Yes, Hagar, she will. Even now her feet, which, when they backward turn, will tread less joyously, are threading

the woodland path. The half-way rock is reached—neaɪcɪ
and nearer she comes—her shadow falls across the floor—
her hand is on your arm—her voice is in your ear—·Maggie
Miller is at your side—Heaven help you both !

CHAPTER XIX.

THE TELLING OF THE SECRET.

"Hagar! Hagar!" exclaimed Mag, playfully bounding
.o her side, and laying her hand upon her arm; "What ail-
eth thee, Hagar?"

The words were mete, for never Hagar in the desert,
thirsting for the gushing fountain, suffered more than did
she who sat with covered face and made no word of answer.
Maggie was unusually happy that day, for but a few hours
before she had received Henry's letter, making her free—
free to love Arthur Carrollton, who she well knew only
waited a favorable opportunity to tell her his love; so
with a heart full of happiness she had stolen away to visit
Hagar, reproaching herself as she came for having neglected
her so long. "But I'll make amends, by telling her what
I'm sure she must have guessed," she thought, as she entered the cottage, where, to her surprise, she found her
weeping. Thinking the old woman's distress might possibly
be occasioned by her neglect, she spoke again—"Are you
crying for me, Hagar?"

"Yes, Maggie Miller, for *you*—for *you!*" answered Hagar,
lifting up a face so ghastly white, that Maggie started back
in some alarm.

"Poor Hagar, you are ill," she said, and advancing nearer
she wound her arms around the trembling form, and pillow

ing the snowy head upon her bosom, continued soothingly, "I did not mean to stay away so long. I will not do it again, but I am so happy, Hagar, *so* happy that I half forgot myself."

For a moment Hagar let her head repose upon the bosom of her child, then murmuring softly, "it will never lie there again," she arose, and, confronting Maggie, said, "Is it love which makes you so happy?"

"Yes, *Hagar, love*," answered Margaret, the deep blushes stealing over her glowing face.

"And is it your intention to marry the man you love?" continued Hagar, thinking only of Henry Warner, while Margaret, thinking only of Arthur Carrollton, replied, "If he will marry me, I shall most surely marry him."

"It is enough. I must tell her," whispered Hagar; while Maggie asked, "Tell me what?"

For a moment the wild eyes fastened themselves upon her with a look of yearning anguish, and then Hagar answered slowly, "Tell you what you've often wished to know—*my secret!*" the last word dropping from her lips more like a warning hiss than like a human sound. It was long since Mag had teased for the secret, so absorbed had she been in other matters, but now that there was a prospect of knowing it, her curiosity was reawakened, and while her eyes glistened with expectation, she said, "Yes, tell it to me, Hagar, and then I'll tell you mine;" and all over her beautiful face there shone a joyous light as she thought how Hagar, who had once pronounced Henry Warner unworthy, would rejoice in her new love.

"Not here, Maggie—not here in this room can I tell you," said old Hagar; "but out in the open air, where my breath will come more freely;" and leading the way, she hobbled to the mossy bank, where Mag had sat with Ar thur Carrollton on the morning of his departure for Montreal.

Here she sat down, while Maggie threw herself upon the damp ground at her feet, her face lighted with eager curiosity and her lustrous eyes bright as stars with the excitement. For a moment Hagar bent forward, and folding her hands one above the other, laid them upon the head of the young girl as if to gather strength for what she was to say. But all in vain ; for when she essayed to speak, her tongue clave to the roof of her mouth, and her lips gave forth unmeaning sounds.

" It must be something terrible to affect her so," thought Mag, and taking the bony hands between her own, she said, " I would not tell it, Hagar ; I do not wish to hear."

The voice aroused the half-fainting woman, and withdrawing her hand from Maggie's grasp, she replied, " Turn away your face, Margaret Miller, so I cannot. see the hatred settling over it, when I tell you what I must."

"Certainly ; my back if you prefer it," answered Mag, half playfully ; and turning around, she leaned her head against the feeble knees of Hagar.

" *Maggie, Maggie*," began the poor old woman, lingering long and lovingly over that dear name, " nineteen years ago, next December, I took upon my soul the secret sin which has worn my life away, but I did it for the love I had for you. Oh, Margaret, believe it, for the love I had for *you*, more than for my own ambition ;" and the long fingers slid nervously over the bands of shining hair just within her reach.

At the touch of those fingers, Mag shuddered involuntarily. There was a vague, undefined terror stealing over her, and impatient to know the worst, she said, " Go on, tell me what you did."

"*I can't—I can't*—and yet I *must*," cried Hagar. "You were a beautiful baby, Mag, and the other one was sickly, pinched and blue. I had you both in my room the night after Hester died ; and the *devil*—Maggie, do you know how the devil *will* creep into the heart, and whisper, *whisper* till the brain is all on fire ? This thing he did to me, Maggie, nineteen years ago, he whispered—whispered dreadful things, and his whisperings were of *you*."

"Horrible ! Hagar," exclaimed Maggie. . "Leave the devil, and tell me. of yourself."

"That's it," answered Hagar. "If I had but left him then, this hour would never have come to me; but I listened, and when he told me that a handsome, healthy child, would be more acceptable to the Conways than a weakly, fretful one—when he said that Hagar Warren's grandchild had far better be a lady than a drudge—that no one would ever know it, for none had noticed either—*I did it, Maggie Miller ; I took you from the pine board cradle, where you lay—I dressed you in the other baby's clothes—I laid you on her pillow—I wrapped her in your coarse white frock—I said that she was mine, and Margaret—oh Heaven ! can't you see it ? Don't you know that I, the shrivelled, skinny hag, who tells you this,* AM YOUR OWN GRANDMOTHER ! !"

There was no need for Maggie Miller to answer that appeal. The words had burned into her soul—scorching her very life-blood, and maddening her brain. It was a fearful blow—crushing her at once. She saw it all, under-stood it all, and knew there was no hope. The family pride, at which she had often laughed, was strong within her and could not at once be rooted out. All the fond household memories, though desecrated and trampled down, were not so soon to be forgotten. She could not own that half-crazed woman for her grandmother ! As Hagar talked, she had risen to her feet, and now, tall and erect as the mountain ash which grew on her native hills, she stood before her, every vestige of color faded from her face, her eyes dark as midnight and glowing like coals of living fire, while her hands, locked despairingly together, moved slowly towards Hagar, as if to thrust her aside.

"Oh, speak again," she said, "but not the dreadful words you said to me just now. Tell me they are false—say that my father perished in the storm, that my mother was she who held me on her bosom when she died—that I—oh, Hagar, *I am not—I will not be the creature you say I am.* Speak to me," she continued, "*tell me, is it true?*" and in her voice there was not the olden sound.

Hoarse—hollow—full of reproachful anguish it seemed, and bowing her head in very shame, old Hagar made her answer : "Would to heaven 'twere not true—but 'tis—it is ! Kill me, Maggie," she continued, "strike me dead, if you will, but take your eyes away. You must not look thus at *me,* a heart-broken wretch."

But not of Hagar Warren was Maggie thinking then. The past, the present, and the future were all embodied in her thoughts. She had been an intruder all her life ; had ruled with a high hand people on whom she had no claim, and who, had they known her parentage, would have spurned her from them. Theo, whom she had held in her arms so oft, calling her sister and loving her as such, was hers no longer ; nor yet the fond woman who had cherished her so tenderly—neither were hers ; and in fancy she saw the look of scorn upon that woman's face, when she should hear the tale, for it *must* be told, and *she* must tell it too. She would not be an impostor ; and then there flashed upon her the agonizing thought, before which all else seemed as naught—in the proud heart of Arthur Carrollton was there a place for Hagar Warren's grandchild? *"No no! no!"* she moaned; and the next moment she lay at Hagar's feet, white, rigid and insensible.

"She's dead!" cried Hagar; and for one brief instant she hoped that it was so.

But not then and there was Margaret to die; and slowly she came back to life, shrinking from the touch of Hagar's hand, when she felt it on her brow.

"There may be some mistake," she whispered; but Hagar answered, "there is none;" at the same time relating so minutely the particulars of the deception, that Maggie was convinced, and covering her face with her hands, sobbed aloud, while Hagar, sitting by in silence, was nerving her-self to tell the rest.

The sun had set, and the twilight shadows were stealing down upon them, when creeping abjectly upon her knees towards the wretched girl, she said, "There is *more*, Maggie, *more*—I have not told you all."

But Maggie had heard enough, and exerting all her strength, she sprang to her feet, while Hagar clutched eagerly at her dress, which was wrested from her grasp, as Maggie fled away—away—she knew not, cared not whither, so that she were beyond the reach of the trembling voice, which called after her to return. Alone in the deep woods, with the darkness falling around her, she gave way to the mighty sorrow which had come so suddenly upon her. She could not doubt what she had heard. She knew that it was true, and as proof after proof crowded upon her, until the chain of evidence was complete, she laid her head upon the rain-wet grass, and shudderingly stopped her ears, to shut out, if possible, the memory of the dreadful words, "I, the shrivelled, skinny hag, who tells you this, am your own grand-mother." For a long time she lay there thus, weeping till the fountain of her tears seemed dry ; then weary, faint, and sick, she started for her home. Opening cautiously the outer door, she was gliding up the stairs, when Madam Conway, entering the hall with a lamp, discovered her, and uttered an exclamation of surprise at the strangeness of her appearance. Her dress, be-draggled and wet, was torn in several places by the briery bushes she had passed ; her hair, loosened from its confinement, hung down her back, while her face was so white and ghastly, that Madam Conway in much alarm followed her up the stairs, asking what had happened.

"Something dreadful came to me in the woods," said Maggie, " but I can't tell you to-night. To-morrow I shall be better—or dead—oh, *I wish I could be dead*—before you hate me so; *dear grand*——No I didn't mean that—you *ain't*; forgive me, do," and sinking to the floor, she kissed the very hem of Madam Conway's dress.

Unable to understand what she meant, Madam Conway divested her of her damp clothing, and placing her in bed, sat down beside her, saying gently, " Can you tell me now what frightened you ?"

A faint cry was Maggie's only answer, and taking the lady's hand, she laid it upon her forehead, where the drops of perspiration were standing thickly. All night long Madam Conway sat by her, going once to communicate with Arthur Carrollton, who, anxious and alarmed, came often to the door, asking if she slept. She did sleep at last—a fitful fever-ish sleep ; but ever at the sound of Mr. Carrollton's voice a spasm of pain distorted her features, and a low moan came from her lips. Maggie had been terribly excited, and when next morning she awoke, she was parched with burning fever, while her mind at intervals seemed wandering ; and ere two days were passed, she was raving with delirium, brought on, the physician said, by some sudden shock, the nature of which no one could even guess.

For three weeks she hovered between life and death, whispering oft of the "horrid shape which had met her in the woods, robbing her of happiness and life." Winding her feeble arms around Madam Conway's neck, she would beg of her most piteously "not to cast her off—not to send her away from the only home she had ever known—for I couldn't help it," she would say. "I didn't know it, and I've loved you all so much—so much! Say, grandma, may I call you *grandma* all the same? *Will* you love *poor Maggie* a little?" and Madam Conway, listening to words whose meaning she could not fathom, would answer by laying the aching head upon her bosom, and trying to soothe the excited girl. Theo, too, was summoned home, but at her Maggie at first refused to look, and covering her eyes with her hand she whispered scornfully, "*pinched* and *blue*, and *pale;* that's the very look. I couldn't see it when I called you sister."

Then her mood would change, and motioning Theo to her side, she would say to her, "Kiss me once, Theo, just as you used to do when I was Maggie Miller."

Towards Arthur Carrollton she from the first manifested fear, shuddering whenever he approached her, and still exhibiting signs of uneasiness if he left her sight. "He hated her," she said, "hated her for what she could not help;" and when, as he often did, he came to her bedside, speaking to her words of love, she would answer mournfully, "Don't, Mr. Carrollton; your pride is stronger than your love. You will hate me when you know it all."

Thus two weeks went by, and then with the first May day, reason returned again, bringing life and strength to the invalid, and joy to those who had so anxiously watched over her. Almost her first rational question was for *Hagar*, and if she had been there.

"She is confined to her bed with inflammatory rheumatism," answered Madam Conway, "but she inquires for you every day, they say; and once when told you could not live, she started to crawl on her hands and knees to see you, but fainted near the gate and was carried back."

"Poor old woman!" murmured Maggie, the tears rolling down her cheeks, as she thought how strong must be the love that half crazed creature bore her, and how little it was returned, for every feeling of her nature revolted from claiming a near relationship with one whom she had hitherto regarded as a servant. The secret, too, seemed harder to divulge, and day by day she put it off, saying to them when they asked what had so much affected her, that "she could not tell them yet—she must wait till she was stronger."

So Theo went back to Worcester as mystified as ever, and Maggie was left much alone with Arthur Carrollton, who strove in various ways to win her from the melancholy into which she had fallen. All day long she would sit by the open window, seemingly immovable, her large eyes, now intensely black, fixed upon vacancy, and her white face giving no sign of the fierce struggle within, save when Madam Conway, coming to her side, would lay her hand caressingly on her in token of sympathy. Then, indeed, her lips would quiver, and turning her head away, she would say, "Don't touch me—don't."

To Arthur Carrollton she would listen with apparent composure, though often as he talked, her long, tapering nails left their impress in her flesh, so hard she strove to seem indifferent. Once when they were left together alone he drew her to his side, and bending very low, so that his lips almost touched her marble cheek, he told her of his

love, and how full of anguish was his heart when he thought
that she would die.

"But God kindly gave you back to me," he said ; " and
now, my precious Margaret, will you be my wife ? Will you
go with me to my English home, from which I've tarried
now too long, because I would not leave you ? Will Maggie
answer me ?" and he folded her lovingly in his arms.

Oh, how could she tell him " *No*," when every fibre of
her heart thrilled with the answer " *Yes !*" She mistook
him—mistook the character of Arthur Carrollton, for though
pride was strong within him, he loved the beautiful girl who
lay trembling in his arms, better than he loved his pride ;
and had she told him then, who and what she was, he would
not have deemed it a disgrace to love a child of Hagar
Warren. But Margaret did not know him, and when he
said again, " will Maggie answer me ?" there came from her
lips a piteous, wailing cry, and turning her face away, she
answered mournfully, " No, Mr. Carrollton, no, I cannot be
your wife. It breaks my heart to tell you so ; but if you
knew what I know, you would never have spoken to me
words of love. You would have rather thrust me from you,
for indeed I am unworthy."

"Don't you love me, Maggie ?" Mr. Carrollton said, and
in the tones of his voice there was so much of tenderness
that Maggie burst into tears, and involuntarily resting her
head upon his bosom, answered sadly, " I love you so much,
Arthur Carrollton, that I would die a hundred deaths could
that make me worthy of you, as not long ago I thought I was
But it cannot be. Something terrible has come between us.'

"Tell me what it is. Let me share your sorrow." he
said ; but Maggie only answered, " Not yet, not yet. Let
me live where you are a little longer. Then I will tell you
all, and go away forever."

This was all. the satisfaction he could obtain ; but after a time she promised that if he would not mention the subject to her until the first of June, she would then tell him every-thing ; and satisfied with a promise which he knew would be kept, Mr. Carrollton waited impatiently for the appointed time, while Maggie, too, counted each sun as it rose and set, bringing nearer and nearer a trial she so much dreaded.

CHAPTER XX.

THE RESULT.

Two days only remained ere the first of June, and in the solitude of her chamber, Maggie was weeping bitterly. " How can I tell them who I am ?" she thought. " How bear their pitying scorn, when they learn that she whom they call Maggie Miller has no right to that name ?—that Hagar Warren's blood is flowing in her veins—and Madam Conway thinks so much of that ! Oh, why was Hagar left to do me this great wrong ? why did she take me from the pine-board cradle, where she says I lay, and make me what I was not born to be ?" and falling on her knees the wretch-ed girl prayed that it might prove a dream, from which she would ere long awake.

Alas for thee, poor Maggie Miller ! It is not a dream, but a stern reality, and you who oft have spurned at *birth* and *family*, why should you murmur now when both are taken from you ? Are you not still the same, beautiful, accomplished and refined, and can you ask for more ? Strange that theory and practice so seldom should accord. And yet it was not the degradation which Maggie felt so keenly, it was rather the loss of love she feared ; and with-out that, the blood of royalty could not avail to make her happy.

Maggie was a warm-hearted girl, and she loved the stately lady she had been wont to call her grandmother with a filial, clinging love, which could not be severed, and still this love was naught compared to what she felt for Arthur Carrollton, and the giving up of him was the hardest part of all. But it must be done, she thought ; he had told her once that were she Hagar Warren's grandchild, he should not be riding with her—how much less then would he make that child *his wife !* and rather than meet the look of proud disdain his face would wear, when first she stood confessed before him, she resolved to go away where no one had ever heard of her or Hagar Warren. She would leave behind a letter telling why she went, and commending to Madam Conway's care poor Hagar, who had been sorely punished for her sin. "But whither shall I go, and what shall I do, when I get there ?" she cried, trembling at the thoughts of a world of which she knew so little. Then, as she remembered how many young girls of her age went out as teachers, she determined to go at all events. "It will be better than staying here where I have no claim," she thought, and nerving herself for the task, she sat down to write the letter, which, on the first of June, should tell to Madam Conway and Arthur Carrollton the story of her birth.

It was a harder task than she supposed, the writing that farewell, for it seemed like severing every hallowed tie. Three times she wrote, "My dear grandma," then with a throb of anguish, she dashed her pen across the revered name, and wrote simply, "Madam Conway." It was a rambling, impassioned letter, full of tender love—of hope destroyed—of deep despair—and though it shadowed forth no expectation that Madam Conway or Mr. Carrollton would ever take her to their hearts again, it begged of them most touchingly to think sometimes of *"Maggie,"* when she was gone forever. Hagar was then commended to Madam Con way's forgiveness and care. "She is old," wrote Maggie, "her life is nearly ended, and if you have in your heart one feeling of pity for her, who used to call you grandma. bestow it, I pray you, on poor old Hagar Warren."

The letter was finished, and then suddenly remember ing Hagar's words, that "all had not been told," and feeling it her duty to see once more the woman who had brought her so much sorrow, Maggie stole cautiously from the house, and was soon walking down the woodland road, slowly, sadly, for the world had changed to her since last she trod that path. Maggie, too, was changed, and when at last she stood before Hagar, who was now able to sit up, the latter could scarcely recognize in the pale, haggard woman, the blooming, merry-hearted girl, once known as Maggie Miller.

"Margaret," she cried, "you have come again—come to forgive your poor old grand——No, no," she added, as she saw the look of pain flash over Maggie's face, "I'll never insult you with *that name*. Only say that you forgive, me, will you, Miss Margaret?" and the trembling voice was choked with sobs, while the aged form shook as with a palsied stroke.

Hagar had been ill. Exposure to the damp air on that memorable night had brought on a second severe attack of rheumatism, which had bent her nearly double. Anxiety for Margaret, too, had wasted her to a skeleton, and her thin, sharp face, now of a corpse-like pallor, contrasted strangely with her eyes, from which the wildness all was gone Touched with pity, Maggie drew a chair to her side, and thus replied, "I do forgive you, Hagar, for I know that what you did was done in love; but by telling me what you have, you've ruined all my hopes of happiness. In the new scenes to which I go, and the new associations I shall form, I may become contented with my lot, but never can I forget that I once was Maggie Miller."

"Margaret," gasped Hagar, and in her dim eye there was something of its olden fire, "if by new associations you mean *Henry Warner*, it must not be. Alas, that I should tell this! but Henry is your *brother*—your father's only son. Oh, horror, horror!" and dreading what Margaret would say, she covered her face with her cramped, distorted hands.

But Margaret was not so much affected as Hagar had anticipated. She had suffered severely, and could not now be greatly moved. There was an involuntary shudder as she thought of her escape, and then her next feeling was one of satisfaction in knowing that she was not quite friendless and alone, for Henry would protect her, and Rose, indeed, would be to her a sister.

"Henry Warner my brother!" she exclaimed, "how came you by this knowledge?" And very briefly Hagar explained to her what she knew, saying that Hester had told her of two young children, but she had forgotten entirely their existence, and now that she was reminded of it, she could not help fancying that Hester said the step-child was a boy. But the peddler knew, of course, and she must have forgotten.

"When the baby they thought was you, died," said Hagar, "I wrote to the minister in Meriden, telling him of it, but I did not sign my name, and I thought that was the last I should ever hear of it. Why don't you curse me?" she continued. "Haven't I taken from you your intended husband, as well as your name?"

Maggie understood perfectly now why the secret had been revealed, and involuntarily she exclaimed, "Oh, had I told you first, this never need have been;" and then hurriedly she explained to the repentant Hagar how at the very moment when the dread confession was made, she, Maggie Miller, was free from Henry Warner.

From the window Maggie saw in the distance the servant who had charge of Hagar, and dreading the presence of a third person, she arose to go. Offering her hand to Hagar she said, " Good bye. I may never see you again, but if I do not, remember that I forgive you freely."

" You are not going away, Maggie. Oh, *are* you going away !" and the crippled arms were stretched imploringly towards Maggie, who answered, "Yes, Hagar, I must go. Honor requires me to tell Madam Conway who I am, and after that, you know that I cannot stay. I shall go to my brother."

Three times old Hagar essayed to speak, and at last, between a whisper and a moan, she found strength to say, " Will you kiss me once, Maggie darling ? 'Twill be something to remember, in the lonesome nights when I am all alone. *Just once*, Maggie. *Will you ?*"

Maggie could not refuse, and gliding to the bowed woman's side, she put back the soft hair from off the wrinkled brow, and left there token of her forgiveness.

———

The last May sun had set, and ere the first June morning rose Maggie Miller would be nowhere found in the home her presence had made so bright. Alone, with no eye upon her save that of the Most High, she had visited the two graves, and while her heart was bleeding at every pore, had wept her last adieu over the sleeping dust so long held sacred as her mother's. Then kneeling at the other grave, she murmured, " Forgive me, Hester Hamilton, if in this parting hour my heart clings most to her whose memory I was first taught to revere ; and if in the better world you know and love each other, oh, will both bless and pity me, poor, wretched Maggie Miller !"

Softly the night air moved through the musical pine over shadowing the humble grave, while the moonlight, flashing from the tall marble, which stood a sentinel over the other mound, bathed Maggie's upturned face as with a flood of glory, and her throbbing heart grew still as if indeed at that hushed moment the two mothers had come to bless their child. The parting with the dead was over, and Margaret sat again in her room, waiting until all was still about the old stone house. She did not add to her letter another line telling of her discovery, for she did not think of it ; her mind was too intent upon escaping unobserved ; and when sure the family had retired, she moved cautiously down the stairs, noiselessly unlocked the door, and without once daring to look back, lest she should waver in her purpose, she went forth, heart-broken and alone, from what for eighteen happy years had been her home. Very rapidly she proceeded, coming at last to an open field through which the railroad ran, the depot being nearly a quarter of a mile away. Not until then had she reflected that her appearance at the station at that hour of the night would excite suspicion, and she was beginning to feel uneasy, when suddenly around a curve the cars appeared in view. Fearing lest she should be too late, she quickened her footsteps, when to her great surprise, she saw that the train was stopping ! But not for her they waited, in the bright moonlight the engineer had discovered a body lying across the track and had stopped the train in time to save the life of the man, who, stupefied with drunkenness, had fallen asleep. The movement startled the passengers, many of whom alighted and gathered around the inebriate.

In the meantime, Margaret had come near, and knowing she could not now reach the depot in time, she mingled unobserved in the crowd, and entering the rear car, took her seat near the door. The train at last moved on, and as at the station no one save the agent was in waiting, it is not strange that the conductor passed unheeded the veiled figure which in the dark corner sat ready to pay her fare.

"He will come to me by and by," thought Maggie, but he did not, and when Worcester was reached, she was still debtor to the Boston & Albany Railroad for the sum of seventy cents. Bewildered and uncertain what to do next, she stepped upon the platform, deciding finally to remain at the depot until morning, when a train would leave for Leominster, where she confidently expected to find her brother. Taking a seat in the ladies' room, she abandoned herself to her sorrow, wondering what Theo would say could she see her then. But Theo, though dreaming it may be of Maggie, dreamed not that she was near, and so the night wore on, Margaret sleeping towards daylight, and dreaming, too, of Arthur Carrollton, who she thought had followed her—nay, was bending over her now and whispering in her ear, "Wake, Maggie, wake."

Starting up, she glanced anxiously around, uttering a faint cry when she saw that it was not Arthur Carrollton, but a dark, rough-looking stranger, who rather rudely asked "where she wished to go?"

"To Leominster," she answered, turning her face fully towards the man, who became instantly respectful, telling her when the train would leave, and saying that she must go to another depot, at the same time asking if she had not better wait at some hotel.

But Maggie preferred going at once to the Fitchburg depot, which she accordingly did, and drawing her veil over her face, lest some one of her few acquaintances in the city should recognize her, she sat there until the time appointed for the cars to leave. Then, weary and faint, she entered the train, her spirits in a measure rising as she felt that she was, drawing near to those who would love her for what she was and not for what she had been. *Rose* would comfort her, and already her heart bounded with the thought of seeing one whom she believed to be *her brother's wife*, for Henry had written that ere this his homeward voyage was made, Rose would be his bride.

Ah, Maggie ! there is for you a greater happiness in store —not a *brother*, but a *sister*—your father's child is there to greet your coming. And even at this early hour, her snow white fingers are arranging the fair June blossoms into bouquets, with which she adorns her house, saying to him who hovers at her side, " that somebody, she knows not whom, is surely coming there to-day;" and then, with a blush stealing over her cheek, she adds : " I wish it might be Margaret;" while Henry, with a peculiar twist of his comical mouth, winds his arm around her waist, and playfully responds, " Any one save her."

CHAPTER XXI.

THE SISTERS.

On a cool piazza overlooking a handsome flower garden, the breakfast table was tastefully arranged. It was Rose's idea to have it there, and in her cambric wrapper, her golden curls combed smoothly back, and her blue eyes shining with the light of a new joy, she occupies her accustomed seat beside one who for several happy weeks has called her his, loving her more and more each day, and wondering how thoughts of any other could ever have filled his heart. There was much to be done about his home, so long deserted, and as Rose was determined upon a trip to the sea side, he had made arrangements to be absent from his business for two months or more, and was now enjoying all the happiness of a quiet, domestic life, free from care of any kind. He had heard of Maggie's illness, but she was better now, he supposed, and when Theo hinted vaguely that a marriage between her and Arthur Carrollton was not at all improbable, he hoped it would be so, for the Englishman, he knew, was far better adapted to Margaret than he had ever been. Of Theo's hints he was speaking to Rose, as they sat together at breakfast, and she had answered, "It will be a splendid match," when the door-bell rang, and the servant announced, "a lady in the parlor, who asked for Mr. Warner."

"I told you some one would come," said Rose; "do pray see who it is. How does she look, Janet?"

"Tall, white as a ghost, with big, black eyes," wa-

Janet's answer; and with his curiosity awakened, Henry Warner started for the parlor, Rose following on tiptoe, and listening through the half closed door to what their visitor might say.

Margaret had experienced no difficulty in finding the house of Mrs. Warner, which seemed to her a second Paradise, so beautiful and cool it looked, nestled amid the tall, green forest trees. Everything around it betokened the fine taste of its occupants, and Maggie, as she reflected that she, too, was nearly connected with this family, felt her wounded pride in a measure soothed, for it was surely no disgrace to claim such people as her friends. With a beating heart, she rang the bell, asking for Mr. Warner, and now, trembling in every limb, she awaited his coming. He was not prepared to meet her, and at first he did not know her, she was so changed ; but when, throwing aside her bonnet, she turned her face so the light from the window opposite shone fully upon her, he recognized her in a moment, and exclaimed, " Margaret, Margaret Miller ! why are you here ?"

The words reached Rose's ear, and darting forward, she stood within the door, just as Margaret, staggering a step or two towards Henry, answered passionately, " I have come to tell you what I myself but recently have learned ;" and wringing her hands despairingly, she continued, " I am not Maggie Miller, I am not anybody, I am Hagar Warren's grandchild, the offspring of her daughter and your own father! Oh, Henry, don't you see it ? I am your sister. Take me as such, will you ? Love me as such, or I shall surely die. I have nobody now in the wide world but you. They are all gone, all—Madam Conway, Theo too, and—and "——She could not speak that name. It died upon her lips, and tottering to a chair she would have fallen had not Henry caught her in his arms.

Leading her to the sofa, while Rose, perfectly confounded still stood within the door, he said to the half crazed girl, "Margaret, I do not understand you. I never had a sister, and my father died when I was six months old. There must be some mistake. Will you tell me what you mean ?"

Bewildered and perplexed, Margaret began a hasty repetition of Hagar's story, but ere it was three-fourths told, there came from the open door a wild cry of delight, and quick as lightning, a fairy form flew across the floor, white arms were twined round Maggie's neck, kiss after kiss was pressed upon her lips, and Rose's voice was in her ear, never before half so sweet as now, when it murmured soft and low to the weary girl, *My sister Maggie*—mine you are—the child of my own father, for I was *Rose Hamilton*, called Warner, first to please my aunt, and next to please my Henry. Oh, Maggie darling, I am so happy now ;" and the little snowy hands smoothed caressingly the bands of hair, so unlike her own fair waving tresses.

It was, indeed, a time of almost perfect bliss to them all, and for a moment Margaret forgot her pain, which, had Hagar known the truth, need not have come to her. But she scarcely regretted it now, when she felt Rose Warner's heart throbbing against her own, and knew their father was the same.

"You are tired," Rose said, at length, when much had been said by both. "You must have rest, and then I will bring to you my aunt, our aunt, Maggie—our father's sister. She has been a mother to me. She will be one to you. But stay," she continued, "you have had no breakfast. I will bring you some," and she tripped lightly from the room.

Maggie followed her with swimming eyes, then turning to Henry, she said. "You are very happy, I am sure."

"Yes, very," he answered, coming to her side. "Happy in my wife, happy in my newly found sister," and he laid his hand on hers, with something of his former familiarity.

But the olden feeling was gone, and Maggie could now meet his glance without a blush, while he could talk with her as calmly as if she had never been aught to him save the sister of his wife. Thus often changeth the human heart's first love.

After a time, Rose returned, bearing a silver tray heaped with the most tempting viands ; but Maggie's heart was too full to eat, and after drinking a cup of the fragrant black tea, which Rose herself had made, she laid her head upon the pillow, which Henry brought, and with Rose sitting by, holding lovingly her hand, she fell into a quiet slumber. For several hours she slept, and when she awoke at last, the sun was shining in at the western window, casting over the floor a glimmering light, and reminding her so forcibly of the dancing shadows on the grass which grew around the old stone house, that her eyes filled with tears, and thinking herself alone, she murmured, "Will it never be my home again ?"

A sudden movement, the rustling of a dress startled her, and lifting up her head, she saw standing near, a pleasant-looking, middle aged woman, who, she rightly guessed, was Mrs Warner, her own aunt.

"Maggie," the lady said, laying her hand on the fevered brow, "I have heard a strange tale to-day. Heretofore I had supposed Rose to be my only child, but though you take me by surprise, you are not the less welcome. There is room in my heart for you, Maggie Miller, room for the youngest born of my only brother. You are somewhat like him, too," she continued, "though more like your mother;"

and with the mention of that name, a flush stole over the lady's face, for she, too, was very proud, and her brother's marriage with a servant girl had never been quite forgiven.

Mrs. Warner had seen much of the world, and Maggie knew her to be a woman of refinement, a woman of whom even Madam Conway would not be ashamed ; and winding her arms around her neck, she said impulsively, " I am glad *you* are my aunt, and you will love me, I am sure, even if I am poor Hagar's grandchild."

Mrs. Warner knew nothing of Hagar, save from Henry's amusing description, the entire truth of which she somewhat doubted ; but she knew that whatever Hagar Warren might be, the beautiful girl before her was not answerable for it, and very kindly she tried to soothe her, telling her how happy they would be together.   " Rose will leave me in the autumn," she said, " and without you I should be all alone."   Of Hagar, too, she spoke kindly, considerately, and Maggie, listening to her, felt somewhat reconciled to the fate which had made her what she was.   Still, there was much of pride to overcome ere she could calmly think of herself as other than Madam Conway's grandchild ; and when that afternoon, as Henry and Rose were sitting with her, the latter spoke of her mother, saying she had a faint remembrance of a tall, handsome girl, who sang her to sleep on the night when her own mother died, there came a visible shadow over Maggie's face, and instantly changing the conversation, she asked why Henry had never told her anything definite concerning himself and family.

For a moment Henry seemed embarrassed.   Both the Hamiltons and the Warners were very aristocratic in their feelings, and by mutual consent, the name of Hester Warren was by them seldom spoken.   Consequently, if there existed a reason for Henry's silence with regard to his own and Rose's history, it was that he disliked bringing up a subject he had been taught to avoid, both by his aunt and the mother of Mr. Hamilton, who for several years after her son's death, had lived with her daughter in Leominster, where she finally died. This, however, he could not say to Margaret, and after a little hesitancy, he answered laughingly, "You never asked me for any particulars ; and then, you know, I was more agreeably occupied than I should have been had I spent my time in enlightening you with regard to our genealogy ;" and the saucy mouth smiled archly first on Rose, and then on Margaret, both of whom blushed slightly, the one suspecting he had not told her the whole truth, and the other knowing he had not.

Very considerate was Rose of Maggie's feelings, and not again that afternoon did she speak of Hester, though she talked much of their father ; and Margaret, listening to his praises, felt herself insensibly drawn towards this new claimant for her filial love. "I wish I could have seen him," she said, and starting to her feet Rose answered, "Strange I did not think of it before. We have his portrait. Come this way," and she led the half unwilling Mag into an adjoining room, where from the wall, a portly, good-humored looking man, gazed down upon the sisters, his eyes seeming to rest with mournful tenderness on the face of her whom in life they had not looked upon. He seemed older than Mag had supposed, and the hair upon his head was white, reminding her of Hagar. But she did not, for this, turn from him away. There was something pleasing in the mild expression of his face, and she whispered faintly, " 'Tis my father."

On the right of this portrait was another, the picture of a woman, in whose curling lip and soft brown eyes, Mag recognized the mother of Henry. To the left was another still, and she gazed upon the angel face, with eyes of violet blue, and hair of golden brown, on which the fading sun light now was falling, encircling it as it were with a halo of glory.

"You are much like her," she said to Rose, who made no answer, for she was thinking of another picture, which years before had been banished to the garret, by her haughty grandmother, as unworthy a place beside him who had petted and caressed the young girl of plebeian birth and kindred.

"I can make amends for it, though," thought Rose, returning with Mag to the parlor : then, seeking out her husband, she held with him a whispered consultation, the result of which was that on the morrow, there was a rummaging in the garret, an absence from home for an hour or two, and when about noon she returned, there was a pleased expression on her face, as if she had accomplished her purpose, whatever it might have been.

All the morning Mag had been restless and uneasy, wandering listlessly from room to room, looking anxiously down the street, starting nervously at the sound of every footstep, while her cheeks alternately flushed and then grew pale as the day passed on. Dinner being over, she sat alone in the parlor, her eyes fixed upon the carpet, and her thoughts away with one who she vaguely hoped would have followed her ere this. True, she had added no postscript to tell him of her new discovery ; but Hagar knew, and he would go to her for a confirmation of the letter. She would tell him where Mag was gone, and he, if his love could survive that shock, would follow her thither ; nay, would be there that very day, and Maggie's heart grew wearier, fainter, as time wore on and he did not come. "I might have known it."

she whispered sadly. "I did know that he would never more think of me," and she wept silently over her ruined love.

"Maggie, sister," came to her ear, and Rose was at her side. "I have a surprise for you, darling. Can you bear it now?"

Oh, how eagerly poor Maggie Miller looked up in Rose's face. The car whistle had sounded half an hour before. Could it be that he had come? *Was he there? Did he love her still?* No, Maggie, no, the surprise awaiting you is of a far different nature, and the tears flow afresh when Rose, in reply to the question, "what is it, darling?" answers "it is this," at the same time placing in Maggie's hand an ambrotype which she bade her examine. With a feeling of keen disappointment, Maggie opened the casing, involuntarily shutting her eyes as if to gather strength for what she was to see.

It was a young face—a handsome face—a face much like her own, while in the curve of the upper lip, and the expression of the large black eyes, there was a look like Hagar Warren. They had met together thus, the one a living reality, the other a semblance of the dead, and she who held that picture trembled violently. There was a fierce struggle within, the wildly beating heart throbbing for one moment with a new-born love, and then rebelling against taking that shadow, beautiful though it was, in place of her whose memory she had so long revered.

"Who is it, Maggie?" Rose asked, leaning over her shoulder.

Maggie knew full well whose face it was she looked upon, but not yet could she speak that name so interwoven with memories of another, and she answered mournfully, "it is Hester Hamilton."

"Yes, Margaret, *your* mother," said Rose. ' I never called her by that name, but I respect her for your sake. She was my father's pet, they say, for he was comparatively old and she his young girl-wife."

"Where did you get this?" Maggie asked; and, coloring crimson, Rose replied, "We have always had her portrait, but grandmother, who was very old and foolishly proud about some things, was offended at our father's last marriage, and when after his death the portraits were brought here, she—forgive her, Maggie—she did not know *you*, or she would not have done it"——

"I know," interrupted Maggie. "She *despised* this Hester Warren; and consigned her portrait to some spot from which you have brought it and had this taken from it."

"Not despised her," cried Rose, in great distress, as she saw a dark expression stealing over the face of Maggie, in whose heart a chord of sympathy had been struck, when she thought of her *mother* banished from her father's side. "Grandma could not despise her," continued Rose, "she was so good, so beautiful."

"Yes, she was beautiful," murmured Maggie, gazing earnestly upon the fair, round face, the soft, black eyes and raven hair of her who for years had slept beneath the shadow of the Hillsdale woods. "Oh, I wish I was dead like her," she exclaimed at last, closing the ambrotype, and laying it upon the table. "I wish I was lying in that little grave in the place of her who should have borne my name, and been what I once was ;" and bowing her face upon her hands she wept bitterly, while Rose tried in vain to comfort her. "I am not sorry *you* are my sister," sobbed Margaret through her tears. "That's the only comfort I have left me now ; but Rose, I love Arthur Carrollton so much---oh so much and how can I give him up ?"

"If he is the noble, true-hearted man he looks to be, he will not give *you* up," answered Rose, and then for the first time since this meeting she questioned Margaret concerning Mr. Carrollton, and the relations existing between them "He will not cast you off," she said, when Margaret had told her all she had to tell, "He may be proud, but he will cling to you still. He will follow you, too—not to-day, perhaps, nor to-morrow, but ere long he will surely come;" and listening to her sister's cheering words, Maggie herself grew hopeful, and that evening talked animatedly with Henry and Rose of a trip to the sea-side they were intending to make.. "You will go, too, Maggie," said Rose, caress ing her sister's pale cheek, and whispering in her ear, "Aunt Susan will be here to tell Mr. Carrollton where you are, if he does not come before wè go, which I am sure he will."

Maggie tried to think so, too, and her sleep that night was sweeter than it had been before for many weeks—but the next day came, and the next, and Maggie's eyes grew dim with watching and with tears, for up and down the road, as far as she could see, there came no trace of him for whom she waited."

"I might have known it ; it was foolish for me to think otherwise," she sighed, and turning sadly from the window where all the afternoon she had been sitting, she laid her head wearily upon the lap of Rose.

"Maggie," said Henry, "I am going to Worcester to-morrow, and perhaps George can tell me something cf Mr Carrollton."

For a moment Maggie's heart throbbed with delight at the thought of hearing from him, even though she heard that he would leave her. But anon her pride rose strong within her. She had told Hagar twice of her destination, Hagar had told him, and if he chose he would have followed her ere this ; so

somewhat bitterly she said, "Don't speak to George of me
Don't tell him I am here. Promise me, will you?"

The promise was given, and the next morning, which was
Saturday, Henry started for Worcester on the early train.
The day seemed long to Maggie, and when at nightfall he
came to them again, it was difficult to tell which was the
more pleased at his return, Margaret or Rose.

"Did you see Theo?" asked the former; and Henry replied, "George told me she had gone to Hillsdale. Madam
Conway is very sick."

"For me! for me! She's sick with mourning for me,"
cried Maggie. "Darling grandma! she does love me still,
and I will go home to her at once."

Then the painful thought rushed over her, "If she wished
for me, she would send. It's the *humiliation*, not the *love*,
that makes her sick. They have cast me off—grandma,
Theo, all, all," and sinking upon the lounge, she wept aloud.

"Margaret," said Henry, coming to her side, "but for
my promise I should have talked to George of you, for
there was a troubled expression on his face when he asked
me if I had heard from Hillsdale."

"What did you say?" asked Maggie, holding her breath
to catch the answer, which was, "I told him you had not
written to me since my return from Cuba, and then he
looked as if he would say more, but a customer called him
away, and our conversation was not resumed."

For a moment Maggie was silent. Then she said, "I am
glad you did not intrude me upon him. If Theo has gone
to Hillsdale, she knows that I am here, and does not care to
follow me. It is the disgrace which troubles them, not the
losing me!" and again burying her head in the cushions of
the lounge, she wept bitterly. It was useless for Henry and
Rose to try to comfort her, telling her it was possible that

Hagar had told nothing; "And if so," said Henry, "you will know that I am the last one to whom you would be expected to flee for protection." Margaret would not listen. She was resolved upon being unhappy, and during the long hours of that night she tossed wakefully upon her pillow, and when the morning came she was too weak to rise ; so she kept her room, listening to the music of the Sabbath bells, which to her seemed sadly saying, " Home, home." " Alas, I have no home," she said, turning away to weep, for in the tolling of those bells there came to her no voice, whispering of the darkness, the desolation, and the sorrow there was in the home for which she so much mourned.

Thus the day wore on, and ere another week was gone, Rose insisted upon a speedy removal to the sea-shore, notwithstanding it was so early in the season, for by this means she hoped that Maggie's health would be improved. Accordingly, Henry went once more to Worcester, ostensibly for money, but really to see if George Douglas now would speak to him of Margaret. But George was in New York, they said ; and somewhat disappointed, Henry went back to Leominster, where everything was in readiness for their journey. Monday was fixed upon for their departure, and at an early hour, Margaret looked back on what had been to her a second home, smiling faintly as Rose whispered to her cheerily, " I have a strong presentiment that somewhere in our travels we shall meet with Arthur Carrollton "

CHAPTER XXII.

THE HOUSE OF MOURNING.

COME now over the hills to the westward. Come to the Hillsdale woods, to the stone house by the mill, where all the day long there is heard but one name, the servants breathing it softly and low, as if she who had borne it were dead, the sister, dim-eyed now, and paler faced, whispering it oft to herself, while the lady, so haughty and proud, repeats it again and again, shuddering as naught but the echoing walls reply to the heart-broken cry of "Margaret, Margaret, where are you now?"

Yes, there was mourning in that household—mourning for the lost one, the darling, the pet of them all.

Brightly had the sun arisen on that June morning which brought to them their sorrow, while the birds in the tall forest tress carolled as gaily as if no storm clond were hovering near. At an early hour Mr. Carrollton had arisen, thinking, as he looked forth from his window, "She will tell me all to-day," and smiling as he thought how easy and pleasant would be the task of winning her back to her olden gaiety. Madam Conway, too, was unusually excited and very anxiously she listened for the first sound of Maggie's footsteps on the stairs.

"She sleeps late," she thought, when breakfast was announced, and taking her accustomed seat, she bade a servant "see if Margaret were ill."

"She is not there," was the report the girl brought back
"Not there !" cried Mr. Carrollton.

"Not there !" repeated Madam Conway, a shadowy foreboding of evil stealing over her. "She seldom walks at
this early hour," she continued, and rising she went herself
to Margaret's room.

Everything was in perfect order, the bed was undisturbed,
the chamber empty, Margaret was gone, and on the dress-
ing-table lay the fatal letter, telling why she went. At
first Madam Conway did not see it ; but it soon caught her
eye, and tremblingly she opened it, reading but the first line:
"I am going away forever."

Then a loud shriek rang through the silent room, pene-
trating to Arthur Carrollton's listening ear, and bringing
him at once to her side. With the letter still in her hand,
and her face of a deathly hue, and her eyes flashing with fear,
Madam Conway turned to him as he entered, saying, "Margaret has gone, left us forever, killed herself it may be—
read ;" and she handed him the letter, herself bending
eagerly forward, to hear what he might say.

But she listened in vain. With lightning rapidity,
Arthur Carrollton read what Mag had written—read that
she, his idol, the chosen bride of his bosom, was the daughter of a *servant*, the grandchild of old *Hagar !* And for
this she had fled from his presence, fled because she knew of
the *mighty pride* which now, in the first bitter moment of his
agony, did indeed rise up a barrier between himself and the
beautiful girl he loved so well. Had she lain dead before
him, dead in all her youthful beauty, he could have folded her
in his arms, and then buried her from his sight, with a feeling of perfect happiness, compared to that which he now felt

"Oh, Maggie, my lost one, can it be ?" he whispered to
himself, and pressing his hand upon his chest, which heaved

19

with strong emotion, he staggered to a seat, while the perspiration stood in beaded drops upon his forehead, and around his lips.

"What is it, Mr. Carrollton? 'Tis something dreadful, sure," said Mrs. Jeffrey, appearing in the door, but Madam Conway motioned her away, and tottering to his side, said, "Read it to me—read."

The sound of her voice recalled his wandering mind, and covering his face with his hands, he moaned in anguish; then, growing suddenly calm, he snatched up the letter, which had fallen to the floor, and read it aloud; while Madam Conway, stupefied with horror, sank at his feet, and clasping her hands above her head, rocked to and fro, but made no word of comment. Far down the long ago her thoughts were straying, and gathering up many by-gone scenes, which told her that what she heard was true.

"Yes, 'tis true," she groaned; and then, powerless to speak another word, she laid her head upon a chair, while Mr. Carrollton, preferring to be alone, sought the solitude of his own room, where unobserved he could wrestle with his sorrow, and conquer his inborn pride, which whispered to him that a Carrollton must not wed a bride so far beneath him.

Only a moment, though, and then the love he bore for Maggie Miller rolled back upon him with an overwhelming power, while his better judgment, with that love, came hand in hand, pleading for the fair young girl, who, now that he had lost her, seemed a thousand fold dearer than before. But he had *not* lost her; he *would* find her. She was Maggie Miller still to him, and though old Hagar's blood were in her veins, he would not give her up. This resolution once made, it could not be shaken, and when half an hour or more was passed, he walked with firm, unfaltering footsteps, back to the apartment where Madam Conway still sat upon the floor, her head resting upon the chair, and her frame convulsed with grief.

Her struggle had been a terrible one, and it was not over yet, for with her it was more than a matter of pride and love. Her daughter's rights had been set at naught; a wrong had been done to the dead; the child who slept beneath the pine had been neglected; nay, in life, had been, perhaps, despised for an intruder, for one who had no right to call *her* grandmother; and shudderingly she cried, "Why was it suffered thus to be?" Then as she thought of white-haired Hagar Warren, she raised her hand to curse her, but the words died on her lips, for Hagar's deed had brought to her much joy; and now, as she remembered the bounding step, the merry laugh, the sunny face, and loving words, which had made her later years so happy, she involuntarily stretched out her arms in empty air, moaning sadly, "I want her here. I want her now, just as she used to be." Then, over the grave of her buried daughter, over the grave of the sickly child, whose thin, blue face came up before her, just as it lay in its humble coffin, over the deception of eighteen years, her heart bounded with one wild, yearning throb, for every bleeding fibre clung with a death-like grasp to her, who had been so suddenly taken from her.

"I love her still," she cried, "but can I take her back?" And then commenced the fiercest struggle of all, the battling of love and pride, the one rebelling against a child of Hagar Warren, and the other clamoring loudly, that without that child the world to her was nothing. It was the hour of Madam Conway's humiliation, and in bitterness of spirit, she groaned, "That I should come to this! Thee first, and Margaret, my bright, my beautiful Margaret next Oh, how can I give her up, when I loved her, best of all— best of all?"

This was true, for all the deeper, stronger love of Madam Conway's nature had gone forth to the merry, gleeful girl, whose graceful, independent bearing she had so often likened to herself, and the haughty race with which she claimed rela tionship. How was this illusion dispelled! Margaret was *not* a Conway, nor yet a Davenport. A servant girl had been her mother, and of her father there was nothing known Madam Conway was one who seldom wept for grief. She had stood calmly at the bedside of her dying husband, had bu- ried her only daughter from her sight, had met with many reverses, and shed for all no tears, but now they fell like rain upon her face, burning, blistering as they fell, but bringing no relief.

"I shall miss her in the morning," she cried, "miss her at noon, miss her in the lonesome nights, miss her every- where—oh, Margaret, Margaret, 'tis more than I can bear! Come back to me now, just as you are. I want you here— here where the pain is hardest," and she clasped her arms tightly over her heaving bosom. Then her pride returned again, and with it came thoughts of Arthur Carrollton. He would scoff at her as weak and sentimental; *he* would never take beyond the sea a bride of *Hagarish* birth; and duty demanded that she, too, should be firm, and sanction his decision. "But when he's gone," she whispered, "when he has left America behind, I'll find her, if my life is spared. I'll find poor Margaret, and see that she does not want, though I must not take her back."

This resolution, however, did not bring her comfort, and the hands pressed so convulsively upon her side could not ease her pain. Sure, never before had so dark an hour enfolded that haughty woman, and a prayer that she might die was trembling on her lips, when a footfall echoed along the hall, and Arthur Carrollton stood before her. His face was very pale, bearing marks of the storm he had passed through ; but he was calm, and his voice was natural as he said, " Possibly what we have heard is false. It may be a vagary of Hagar's half crazed brain."

For an instant Madam Conway had hoped so, too ; but when she reflected, she knew that it was true. Old Hagar had been very minute in her explanations to Margaret, who in turn had written exactly what she had heard, and Madam Conway, when she recalled the past, could have no doubt that it was true. She remembered everything, but more distinctly the change of dress, at the time of the baptism There could be no mistake. *Margaret was not hers*, and so she said to Arthur Carrollton, turning her head away as if she, too, were in some way answerable for the disgrace.

" It matters not," he replied, " *whose* she *has been*. She is *mine*, now, and if you feel able, we will consult together as to the surest method of finding her."

A sudden faintness came over Madam Conway, and while the expression of her face changed to one of joyful surprise, she stammered out, " Can it be I hear aright ? Do I understand you ? Are you willing to take poor Maggie back ?"

" I certainly have no other intention," he answered. " There was a moment the memory of which makes me ashamed, when my pride rebelled ; but it is over now, and though Maggie cannot in reality be again your child, she can be my wife, and I must find her."

" You make me so happy, oh, so happy !" said Madam Conway. " I feared you would cast her off, and in that case it would have been my duty to do so too, though I never loved a human being. as at this moment I love her."

Mr. Carrollton looked as if he did not fully comprehend

the woman, who loving Margaret as she said she did, could yet be so dependent upon his dicision ; but he made no comment, and when next he spoke he announced his intention of calling upon Hagar, who possibly could tell him where Margaret had gone. "At all events," said he, "I may ascertain why the secret, so long kept, was at this late day divulged. It may be well," he continued, "to say nothing to the servants as yet, save that Maggie has gone. Mrs. Jeffrey, however, had better be let into the secret at once. We can trust her, I think."

Madam Conway bowed, and Mr. Carrollton left the room, starting immediately for the cottage by the mine. As he approached the house, he saw the servant who for several weeks had been staying there, and who now came out to meet him, telling him that since the night before, Hagar had been raving crazy, talking continually of Maggie, who, she said, "had gone where none would ever find her."

In some anxiety, Mr. Carrollton pressed on, until the cottage door was reached, where for a moment he stood gazing silently upon the poor woman before him. Upon the bed, her white hair falling over her round, bent shoulders, and her large eyes shining with delirious light, old Hagar sat, weaving back and forth, and talking of Margaret, of Hester, and "the little foolish child," who, with a sneer upon her lip, she said, "was a fair specimen of the Conway race."

"Hagar," said Mr. Carrollton, and at the sound of that voice Hagar turned toward him her flashing eyes, then with a scream, buried her head in the bed-clothes, saying, "Go away, Arthur Carrollton ! Why are you here ? Don't you know *who* I am ? Don't you know *what* Margaret is, and don't you know how *proud* you are ?"

"Hagar," he said again, subduing, by a strong effort, the repugnance he felt at questioning her, "I know all, except where Margaret has gone, and if on this point you can give me any information, I shall receive it most thankfully."

" Gone !" shrieked Hagar, starting up in bed ; " then she *his* gone. The play is played out, the performance is ended, and I sinned for nothing !"

" Hagar, will you tell me where Maggie is ? I wish to follow her," said Mr. Carrollton ; and Hagar answered, " Maggie, Maggie—he said that lovingly enough, but there's a catch somewhere. He does not wish to follow her for any good—and though I know where she has gone, I'll surely never tell. I kept one secret nineteen years. I can keep another as long ;" and folding her arms upon her chest, she commenced singing, " I know full well, but I'll never tell."

Biting his lips with vexation, Mr. Carrollton tried first by persuasion, then by flattery, and lastly by threats, to obtain from her the desired information, but in vain. Her only answer was, " I know full well, but I'll never tell," save once, when tossing towards him her long white hair, she shrieked, " Don't you see a resemblance—only hers is black —and so was mine nineteen years ago,—and so was Hester's too—glossy and black as the raven's wing. The child is like the mother—the mother was like the grandmother, and the grandmother is like—*me*, *Hagar Warren*. Do you understand ?"

Mr. Carrollton made no answer, and with a feeling of disappointment walked away, shuddering as he thought, " and she is Margaret's grandmother."

He found Madam Conway in strong hysterics on Margaret's bed, for she had refused to leave the room, saying, " she would die there or nowhere." Gradually the reality of her loss had burst upon her, and now gasping, choking, and wringing her hands, she lay upon the pillows, while Mrs

Jeffrey, worked up to a pitch of great nervous excitement, fidgeted hither and thither, doing always the wrong thing, fanning the lady when she did not wish to be fanned, and ceasing to fan her just when she was "dying for want of air."

As yet, Mrs. Jeffrey knew nothing definite, except that something dreadful had happened to Margaret ; but very candidly Mr. Carrollton told her all, bidding her keep silent on the subject ; then, turning to Madam Conway, he re· peated to her the result of his call on old Hagar.

"The wretch !" gasped Madam Conway, while Mrs. Jef- frey, running in her fright from the window to the door, and from the door back to the window again, exclaimed, "Mar- garet not a Conway, nor yet a Davenport, after all ! It is just what I expected. I always knew she came honestly by those low-bred ways !"

"Jeffrey," and the voice of the hysterical woman on the bed was loud and distinct, as she grasped the arm of the terrified little governess, who chanced to be within her reach. "Jeffrey," either leave my house at once, or speak more deferentially of *Miss Miller.* You will call her by *that name, too.* It matters not to Mr. Carrollton and myself whose child she has been. She is *ours* now, and must be treated with respect. Do you understand me ?"

"Yes, ma'am," meekly answered Jeffrey, rubbing her dumpy arm which bore the mark of a thumb and finger, and· as her services were not just then required she glided from the room to drown, if possible, her grievance in the leather bound London edition of Baxter !

Meanwhile, Madam Conway was consulting with Mr. Car rollton as to their best mode of finding Margaret. "She took the cars, of course," said Mr. Carrollton, adding that "he should go at once to the depot, and ascertain which way she went. If I do not return to-night you need not be alarmed," he said, as he was leaving the room, whereupon Madam Conway called him back, bidding him "telegraph for Theo at once, as she must have some one with her· besides that vexatious Jeffrey."

Mr. Carrollton promised compliance with her request, and then went immediately to the depot, where he learned that no one had entered the cars from that place on the previous night, and that Maggie, if she took the train at all, must have done so at some other station. This was not unlikely, and before the day was passed, Mr. Carrollton had visited several different stations, and had talked with the conductors of the several trains, but all to no purpose ; and very much disheartened, he returned at nightfall to the old stone house, where to his great surprise, he found both Theo and her husband. The telegram had done its mission, and feeling anxious to know the worst, George had come up with Theo to spend the night. It was the first time Madam Conway had seen him since her memorable encounter with his· mother, for though Theo had more than once been home, he had never before accompanied her, and now when Madam Conway heard his voice in the hall below, she groaned afresh. The sight of his good-humored face, however, and his kind offer to do whatever he could to find the fugitive, restored her composure in a measure, and she partially forgot that he was in any way connected with the *blue umbrella*, or the blue umbrella connected with him ! Never in her life had Theo felt very deeply upon any subject, and now, though she seemed bewildered at what she heard, she manifested no particular emotion, until her grandmother, wringing her hands, exclaimed, "You have *no sister* now, my child, and I no Margaret." Then, indeed, her tears flowed; and when her husband whispered to her, "We will love poor Maggie all the same," she cried aloul, but not quite .

as demonstratively as Madam Conway wished, and in a very unamiable frame of mind, the old lady accused her of being selfish and hard-hearted.

In this stage of proceedings Mr. Carrollton returned, bringing no tidings of Maggie, whereupon another fit of hysterics ensued, and as Theo behaved much worse than Mrs. Jeffrey had done, the latter was finally summoned again to the sick room, where she had last succeeded in quieting the excited woman. The next morning George Douglas visited old Hagar, but he too was unsuccessful, and that afternoon he returned to Worcester, leaving Theo with her grandmother, who, though finding fault with whatever she did, refused to let her go until Margaret was found.

During the remainder of the week, Mr. Carrollton rode through the country, making the most minute inquiries, and receiving always the same discouraging answer. Once he thought to advertise, but from making the affair thus public he instinctively shrank, and resolving to spare neither his time, his money, nor his health, he pursued his weary way alone. Once, too, Madam Conway spoke of Henry Warner, saying it was possible Maggie might have gone to him, as she had thought so much of Rose; but Mr. Carrollton *"knew better."* "A discarded lover," he said, "was the last person in the world to whom a young girl like Margaret would go, particularly as Theo had said that Henry was now the husband of another."

Still the suggestion haunted him, and on the Monday following Henry Warner's first visit to Worcester, he, too, went down to talk with Mr. Douglas, asking him, "if it were possible that Maggie was in Leominster."

"I know she is not," said George, repeating the particulars of his interview with Henry, who, he said, was at the store on Saturday. "Once I thought of telling him all,'

· said he, " and then considering the relations which formerly existed between them, I concluded to keep silent, especially as he manifested no desire to speak of her, but appeared, I fancied, quite uneasy when I casually mentioned Hillsdale."

Thus was that matter decided, and while not many miles away, Maggie was watching hopelessly for the coming of Arthur Carrollton, he, with George Douglas, was devising the best means for finding her, George generously offering to assist in the search, and suggesting finally that he should himself go to New York city, while Mr. Carrollton explored Boston and its vicinity. It seemed quite probable that Margaret would seek some of the large cities, as in her letter she had said she could earn her livelihood by teaching music; and quite hopeful of success, the young men parted, Mr. Carrollton going immediately to Boston, while Mr. Douglas, after a day or two, started for New York, whither, as the reader will remember, he had gone at the time of Henry's last visit to Worcester.

Here, for a time we leave them, Hagar raving mad, Madam Conway in strong hysterics, Theo wishing herself anywhere but at Hillsdale, Mrs. Jeffrey ditto, George Douglas threading the crowded streets of the noisy city, and Mr. Carrollton in Boston, growing paler and sadder as day after day passed by, bringing him no trace of the lost one. Here, I say, we leave them, while in another chapter we follow the footsteps of her for whom this search was made.

CHAPTER XXIII.

NIAGARA.

From the seaside to the mountains, from the mountains to Saratoga, from Saratoga to Montreal, from Montreal to the Thousand Isles, and thence they scarce knew where, the travellers wended their way, stopping not long at any place, for Margaret was ever seeking change. Greatly had she been admired, her pale, beautiful face attracting attention at once; but from all flattery she turned away, saying to Henry and Rose, "Let us go on."

So, onward still onward they went, pausing longest at Montreal, for it was there Arthur Carrollton had been, there a part of his possessions lay, and there Margaret willingly lingered, even after her companions wished to be gone.

"He may be here again," she said; and so she waited and watched, scanning eagerly the passers by, and noticing each new face as it appeared at the table of the hotel, where they were staying. But the one she waited for never came, "and even if he does," she thought, "he will not come for me."

So she signified her willingness to depart, and early one bright July morning, she left, while the singing birds from the tree tops, the summer air from the Canada hills, and, more than all, a warning voice within her, bade her, "Tarry yet a little, stay till the sun was set," for far out in the country and many miles away a train was thundering on

It would reach the city at nightfall, and among its jaded passengers, was a worn and weary man. Hopeless, almost aimless now, he would come, and why he came he scarcely knew. "She would not be there so far from home," he was sure of that, but he was coming for the sake of what he hoped and feared, when last he trod those streets Listlessly he entered the same hotel, from whose windows, for five long days, a fair young face had looked-for him. Listlessly he registered his name, then carelessly turned the leaves backward—backward—backward still, till only one remained between his hand and the page bearing date five days before. He paused and was about to move away, when a sudden breeze from the open window turned the remaining leaf, and his eye caught the name, not of *Maggie Miller*, but of "Henry Warner, lady, and *sister.*"

"Thus it stood, and thus he repeated it to himself, dwelling upon the last words *sister*, as if to him it had another meaning. He had heard from Madam Conway, that neither Henry Warner nor Rose had a sister, but she might be mistaken; probably she was, and dismissing the subject from his mind, he walked away. Still the names haunted him, and thinking at last, that if Mr. Warner were now in Montreal, he would like to see him, he returned to the office, asking the clerk if the occupants of Nos. — were there still.

"Left this morning for the Falls," was the laconic answer, and without knowing why he should particularly wish to do so, Mr. Carrollton resolved to follow them.

He would as soon be at the Falls as at Montreal, he thought. Accordingly he left the next morning for Niagara, taking the shortest route by river and lake, and arriving there on the evening of the second day after his departure from the city. But nowhere could a trace be found of Hen ry Warner, and determining now to wait until he came, Mr. Carrollton took rooms at the International, where after a day or two, worn out with travel, excitement and hope deferred, he became severely indisposed, and took his bed, forgetting entirely both Henry Warner and the sister, whose name he had seen upon the hotel register. Thoughts of Maggie Miller, however, were constantly in his mind, and whether waking or asleep, he saw always *her* face, sometimes radiant with healthful beauty, as when he first beheld her, and again, pale, troubled, and sad, as when he saw her last.

"Oh, shall I ever find her?" he would sometimes say, as in the dim twilight he lay listening to the noisy hum which came up from the public room below.

And once, as he lay there thus, he dreamed, and in his dreams there came through the open window a clear, silvery voice, breathing the loved name of *Maggie.* Again he heard it on the stairs, then little tripping feet went past his door, followed by a slow, languid tread, and with a nervous start, the sick man awoke. The day had been cloudy and dark, but the rain was over now, and the room was full of sunshine—sunshine dancing on the walls, sunshine glimmering on the floor, sunshine everywhere. Insensibly, too, there stole over Mr. Carrollton's senses a feeling of quiet, of rest, and he slept ere long again, dreaming this time that Margaret was there.

Yes, Margaret was there—there, beneath the same roof which sheltered him, and the same sunshine which filled his room with light had bathed her white brow, as leaning from her window, she listened for the roar of the falling water. They had lingered on their way, stopping at the Thousand Isles, for Margaret would have it so; but they had come at last, and the tripping footsteps in the hall, the silvery voice upon the stairs, was that of the golden haired Rose, who watched over Margaret with all a sister's love and a mother's care. The frequent jokes of the fun-loving Henry, too, were not without their good effects, and Margaret was better now than she had been for many weeks.

"I can rest here," she said, and a faint color came to her cheeks, making her look more like herself than she had done before since that night of sorrow in the woods.

And so three days went by, and Mr. Carrollton, on his weary bed, dreamed not that the slender form, which some times through his half closed door, cast a shadow in his room, was that of her for whom he sought. The tripping footsteps, too, went often by, and a merry, childish voice, which reminded him of Maggie, rang through the spacious halls, until at last the sick man came to listen for that party as they passed. They were a merry party, he thought, a very merry party, and he pictured to himself her of the ringing voice ; she was dark eyed, he said, with braids of shining hair, and when, as they were passing once, he asked of his attendant if it were not as he had fancied, he felt a pang of disappointment at the answer which was, "The girl the young gentleman hears so much, has yellow curls and dark blue eyes."

"She is not like Maggie, then," he sighed, and when again he heard that voice, a part of its music was gone. Still it cheered his solitude, and he listened for it again, just as he had done before.

Once, when he knew they were going out, he went to the window to see them, but the large straw flats and close carriage revealed no secret, and disappointed he turned away.

"It is useless to stay here longer," he said ; "I must be about my work. I am able to leave, and I will go to-mor-

row. But first I will visit the Falls once more. I may
never see them again."

Accordingly, next morning, after Margaret and Rose had
left the house, he came down the stairs, sprang into an open
carriage, and was driven to Goat Island, which, until his
illness, had been his favorite resort.

*   *   *   *   *   *

Beneath the tall forest trees which grow upon the island
there is a rustic seat. Just on the brink of the river it
stands, and the carriage road winds by. It is a comparatively retired spot, looking out upon the foaming water rushing so madly on. Here the weary often rest ; here lovers
sometimes come to be alone ; and here Maggie Miller sat
on that summer morning, living over again the past, which
to her had been so bright, and musing sadly of the future,
which would bring her she knew not what.

She had struggled to overcome her pride, nor deemed it
longer a disgrace that she was not a Conway. Of Hagar,
too, she often thought, pitying the poor old half-crazed
woman who for her sake had borne so much. But not of her
was she thinking now. Hagar was shrivelled and bent,
and old, while the image present in Margaret's mind was
handsome, erect and young, *like the gentleman riding by—*
the man whose carriage wheels, grinding into the gravelly
road, attracted no attention. Too intent was she upon a
shadow to heed aught else around, and she leaned against a
tree, nor turned her head aside, as Arthur Carrollton went
by !

A little further on, and out of Maggie's sight, a fairy figure was seated upon the grass ; the flat was thrown aside,
and her curls fell back from her upturned face, as she spoke
to Henry Warner. But the sentence was unfinished, for
the carriage appeared in view, and with woman's quick

perception, Rose exclaims, "'Tis surely Arthur Carroll-ton !"

Starting to her feet, she sprang involuntarily forward to meet him, casting a rapid glance around for Margaret. He observed the movement, and knew that somewhere in the world he had seen that face before—those golden curls- - those deep blue eyes—that childish form—they were not wholly unfamiliar. Who was she, and why did she advance towards him ?

"Rose," said Henry, who would call her back, "Rose !" and looking towards the speaker, Mr. Carrollton knew at once that Henry Warner and his bride were standing there before him.

In a moment he had joined them, and though he knew that Henry Warner had once loved Maggie Miller, he spoke of her without reserve, saying to Rose, when she asked if he were there for pleasure, " I am looking for Maggie Miller. A strange discovery has been made of late, and Margaret has left us."

"She is *here*—here with *us*," cried Rose ; and in tne exuberance of her joy, she was darting away, when Henry held her back until further explanations were made.

This did not occupy them long, for sitting down again upon the bank, Rose briefly told him all she knew ; and when with eager joy he asked " where is she now ?" she pointed towards the spot, and then with Henry walked away, for she knew that it was not for her to witness that glad meeting.

The river rolls on with its heaving swell, and the white foam is tossed towards the shore, while the soft summer air still bears on its wing the sound of the cataract's roar. But Margaret sees it not, hears it not. There is a spell upon her now—a halo of joy, and she only knows that a strong arm is around her, and a voice is in her ear, whispering that the bosom on which her weary head is pillowed shall be her resting-place forever.

It had come to her suddenly, sitting there thus- -the foot-fall upon the sand had not been heard—the shadow upon the grass had not been seen, and his presence had not been felt, till bending low, Mr. Carrollton said aloud, " My Mag-gie !"

Then indeed she started up, and turned to see who it was that thus so much like him had called her name. She saw who it was, and looking in his face, she *knew* she was not hated, and with a moaning cry went forward to the arms extended to receive her.

––––––

Four guests, instead of one, went forth that afternoon from the International—four guests homeward bound, and eager to be there. No more journeying now for happiness ; no more searching for the lost ; for both are found ; both are there—happiness and Maggie Miller.

CHAPTER XXIV

HOME.

IMPATIENT, restless and cross, Madam Conway lay in Margaret's room, scolding Theo, and chiding Mrs. Jeffrey; both of whom, though trying their utmost to suit her, managed unfortunately to do always just what she wished them not to do. Mrs. Jeffrey's hands were usually too cold, while Theo's were too hot. Mrs. Jeffrey made the head of the bed too high. Theo altogether too low. In short, neither of them ever did what Margaret would have done had she been there, and so day after day the lady complained, growing more and more unamiable, until at last Theo began to talk seriously of following Margaret's example, and running away herself, at least as far as Worcester; but the distressed Mrs. Jeffrey, terrified at the thoughts of being left there alone, begged of her to stay a little longer, offering the comforting assurance that "it could not be so bad always, for Madam Conway would either get better—or something."

So Theo staid, enduring with a martyr's patience the caprices of her grandmother, who kept the whole household in a constant state of excitement, and who at last began to blame George Douglas entirely as being the only one in fault. "He didn't half look," she said, "and she doubted whether he knew enough to keep from losing himself in New

York. It was the most foolish thing Arthur Carrollton had ever done, *hiring* George Douglas to search !"

"Hiring him, grandma !" cried Theo, " George offered his services for nothing," and the tears came to her eyes at this injustice done to her husband.

But Madam Conway persisted in being unreasonable, and matters grew gradually worse until the day when Margaret was found at the Falls On that morning Madam Conway determined upon riding—"fresh air would do her good," she said, "and they had kept her in a hot chamber long enough."

Accordingly, the carriage was brought out, and Madam Conway carefully lifted in ; but ere fifty rods were passed, the coachman was ordered to drive back, as " she could not endure the jolt—she told them she couldn't all the time," and her eyes turned reprovingly upon poor Theo, sitting silently in the opposite corner.

" The Lord help me, if she isn't coming back, so soon," sighed Mrs. Jeffrey, as she saw the carriage returning, and went to meet the invalid who had " taken her death cold," just as she knew she should, when they insisted upon her going out.

That day was far worse than any which had preceded it. It was probably her last, Madam Conway said, and numerous were the charges she gave to Theo concerning Margaret, should she ever be found. The house, the farm, the furniture and plate, were all to be hers, while to Theo was given the lady's wardrobe, saving such articles as Margaret might choose for herself, and if she never were found, the house and farm were to be Mr. Carrollton's. This was too much for Theo, who resolved to go home on the morrow at all hazards, and she had commenced making preparations for leaving, when to her great joy her husband came, and in recounting to him her trials, she forgot in a measure how unhappy she had been. George Douglas was vastly amused at what he heard and resolved to experiment a little with the lady, who was so weak as to notice him only with a slight nod when he first entered the room. He saw at a glance that nothing in particular was the matter, and when towards night she lay panting for breath, with her eyes half closed, he approached her and said : "Madam, in case you die "——

"*In case I die,*" she whispered indignantly. "It doesn't admit of a doubt. My feet are as cold as icicles now."

"Certainly," said he. "I beg your pardon ; of course you'll die."

The lady turned away rather defiantly for a dying woman, and George continued : "What I mean to say is this—if Margaret is never found, you wish the house to be Mr. Carrollton's ?"

"Yes, everything, my wardrobe and all," came from beneath the bedclothes, and George proceeded : "Mr. Carrollton cannot of course take the house to England, and as he will need a trusty tenant, would you object greatly, if *my father* and *mother* should come here to live ? They'd like it, I "——

The sentence was unfinished—the bunches in the throat, which for hours had prevented the sick woman from speaking aloud, and were eventually to choke her to death, disappeared ; Madam Conway found her voice, and starting up, screamed out, "That abominable woman and heathenish girl in *this* house, in *my* house ; I'll live forever, first !" and her round bright eyes flashed forth their indignation.

"I thought the mention of *mother* would revive her," said George, aside to Theo, who, convulsed with laughter, had hidden herself behind the window curtain.

Mr. Douglas was right, for not again that afternoon did Madam Conway speak of dying, though she kept her bed until night-fall, when an incident occurred which brought her at once to her feet, making her forget that she had ever been otherwise than well.

In her cottage by the mine, old Hagar had raved, and sung, and wept, talking much of Margaret, but never telling whither she had gone. Latterly, however, she had grown more calm, talking far less than heretofore, and sleeping a great portion of the day, so that the servant who attended her became neglectful, leaving her many hours alone, while she, at the stone house, passed her time more agreeably than at the lonesome hut. On the afternoon of which we write, she was as usual at the house, and though the sun went down, she did not hasten back, for her patient, she said, was sure to sleep, and even if she woke she did not need much care.

Meantime old Hagar slumbered on. It was a deep, refreshing sleep, and when at last she did awake, her reason was in a measure restored, and she remembered everything distinctly, up to the time of Margaret's last visit, when she said she was going away. And Margaret had gone away, she was sure of that, for she remembered Arthur Carrollton stood once within that room, and besought of her to tell if she knew aught of Maggie's destination. She did know, but she had not told, and perhaps they had not found her yet. Raising herself in bed, she called aloud to the servant, but there came no answer; and for an hour or more, she waited impatiently, growing each moment more and more excited. If Margaret were found she wished to know it, and if she were not found, it was surely her duty to go at once, and tell them where she was. But could she walk? She stepped upon the floor and tried. Her limbs trembled beneath her weight, and sinking into a chair, sne cried, "I can't, I can't."

Half an hour later, she heard the sound of wheels. A neighboring farmer was returning home from Richland, and had taken the cross road as his shortest route. "Perhaps he will let me ride," she thought, and hobbling to the door, she called after him, making known her request. Wondering what "new freak" had entered her mind, the man consented, and just as it was growing dark, he set her down at Madam Conway's gate, where, half fearfully, the bewildered woman gazed around. The windows of Margaret's room were open, a figure moved before them, Margaret might be there, and entering the hall door unobserved, she began to ascend the stairs, crawling upon her hands and knees, and pausing several times to rest.

It was nearly dark in the sick-room, and as Mrs. Jeffrey had just gone out, and Theo, in the parlor below, was enjoying a quiet talk with her husband, Madam Conway was quite alone. For a time she lay thinking of Margaret, then her thoughts turned upon George and his "amazing proposition." "Such unheard of insolence!" she exclaimed, and she was proceeding farther with her soliloquy, when a peculiar noise upon the stairs without caught her ear, and raising herself upon her elbow, she listened intently to the sound which came nearer and nearer, and seemed like some one creeping slowly, painfully, for she could hear at intervals a long drawn breath, or groan, and with a vague feeling of uneasiness, she awaited anxiously the appearance of her visitor; nor waited long, for the half closed door swung slowly back, and through the gathering darkness the shape came crawling on, over the threshold, into the room, towards the corner, its limbs distorted and bent, its white hair sweeping the floor. With a smothered cry, Madam Conway hid beneath the bedclothes, looking cautiously out at the singular object which came creeping on until the bed was reached. It touched the counterpane, it was struggling to regain its feet, and with a scream of horror the terrified woman cried out, " Fiend, why are you here ?" while a faint voice replied, " I am looking for Margaret. I thought she was in bed ;" and rising up from her crouching posture, Hagar Warren stood face to face with the woman she had so long deceived.

" Wretch !" exclaimed the latter, her pride returning as she recognized old Hagar, and thought, " She is Maggie's grandmother. Wretch, how dare you come into my pres- ence ? Leave this room at once," and a shrill cry of " Theo, Theo," rang through the house, bringing Theo at once to the chamber, where she started involuntarily at the sight which met her view.

" Who is it ? Who is it ?" she exclaimed.

" It's Hagar Warren. Take her away!" screamed Madam Conway ; while Hagar, raising her withered hand deprecat- ingly, said : " Hear me first. Do you know where Marga- ret is ? Has she been found ?"

" No, no," answered Theo, bounding to her side, while Madam Conway forgot to scream, and bent eagerly forward to listen, her symptoms of dissolution disappearing one by one, as the strange narrative proceeded, and ere its close, she was nearly dressed, standing erect as ever, her face glow- ing, and her eyes lighted up with joy.

" Gone to Leominster ! Henry Warner's half-sister !" she exclaimed. " Why didn't she add a postscript to that let- ter, and tell us so ? though the poor child couldn't think of everything ;" and then, unmindful of George Douglas, who at that moment entered the room, she continued : " I should suppose Douglas might have found it out ere this. But the moment I put my eyes *on that woman,* I knew no child of hers would ever know enough to find Margaret. The *War-ners* are a tolerably good family, I presume. I'll go after her at once. Theo, bring my broché shawl, and wouldn't you wear my satin hood? 'Twill be warmer than my leghorn"

"*Grandma*," said Theo, in utter astonishment, "what d) you mean? You surely are not going to Leominster tonight, as sick as you are?"

"Yes, I am going to Leominster to-night," answered the decided woman, "and this gentleman," waving her hand majestically towards George, "will oblige me much by seeing that the carriage is brought out."

Theo was about to remonstrate, when George whispered "Let her go; Henry and Rose are probably not at home, but Margaret may be there. At all events a little airing will do the old lady good;" and rather pleased than otherwise with the expedition, he went after John, who pronounced his mistress "crazier than Hagar."

But it wasn't for him to dictate, and grumbling at the prospect before him, he harnessed his horses and drove them to the door, where Madam Conway was already in waiting.

"See that everything is in order for our return," she said to Theo, who promised compliance, and then, herself bewildered, listened to the carriage as it rolled away; it seemed so like a dream that the woman, who three hours before could scarcely speak aloud, had now started for a ride of many miles in the damp night-air! But love can accomplish miracles, and it made the eccentric lady strong, buoying up her spirits, and prompting her to cheer on the coachman, until just as the dawn grew rosy in the east, Leominster appeared in view. The house was found, the carriage steps let down, and then with a slight trembling in her limbs, Madam Conway alighted and walked up the gravelled path, casting eager, searching glances around and commenting as follows :

"Everything is in good taste ; they must be *somebody*, these Warners. I'm glad it is no worse." And with each new indication of refinement in Margaret's relatives, the disgrace seemed less and less in the mind of the proud Englishwoman.

The ringing of the bell brought down Janet, who with an inquisitive look at the satin hood and bundle of shawls, ushered the stranger into the parlor, and then went for her mistress. Taking the card her servant brought, Mrs. Warner read with some little trepidation, the name, " MADAM CONWAY, HILLSDALE." From what she had heard, she was not prepossessed in the lady's favor ; but, curious to know why she was there at this early hour, she hastened the making of her toilet, and went down to the parlor, where Madam Conway sat, coiled in one corner of the sofa, which she had satisfied herself was covered with real brocatelle, as were also the chairs within the room. The tables of rosewood and marble, and the expensive curtains had none of them escaped her notice, and in a mood which more common furniture would never have produced, Madam Conway arose to meet Mrs. Warner, who received her politely, and then waited to hear her errand.

It was told in a few words. She had come for *Margaret* —Margaret, whom she had loved for eighteen years, and could not now cast off, even though she were not of the Conway and Davenport extraction.

"I can easily understand how painful must have been the knowledge that Maggie was not your own," returned Mrs. Warner, for she is a girl of whom any one might be proud; but you are laboring under a mistake—Henry is not her brother."

and then, very briefly she explained the matter to Madam
Conway, who having heard so much, was now surprised at
nothing, and who felt, it may be, a little gratified in knowing that Henry was, after all, nothing to Margaret, save the
husband of her sister. But a terrible disappointment awaited her. "Margaret was not there," and so loud were her
lamentations, that some time elapsed ere Mrs. Warner could
make her listen, while she explained, that "Mr. Carrollton
had found Maggie the day previous, at the Falls, that they
were probably in Albany now, and would reach Hillsdale
that very day;" such at least was the import of the telegram
which Mrs. Warner had received the evening before. "They
wish to surprise you undoubtedly," she said, "and consequently have not telegraphed to you."

This seemed probable, and forgetting her weariness, Madam
Conway resolved upon leaving John to drive home at his
leisure, while she took the Leominster cars, which reached
Worcester in time for the upward train. This matter ad-
justed, she tried to be quiet; but her excitement increased
each moment, and when at last breakfast was served, she
did but little justice to the tempting viands which her
hostess set before her. Margaret's chamber was visited
next, and very lovingly she patted and smoothed the downy
pillows, for the sake of the bright head which had rested
there, while to herself she whispered abstractedly, "Yes,
yes," though to what she was giving her assent, she could
not tell. She only knew that she was very happy, and very
impatient to be gone, and when at last she did go, it seemed
to her an age ere Worcester was reached.

Resolutely turning her head away, lest she should see the
scene of her disaster, when last she was in that city, she
walked up and down the ladies' room, her satin hood and
heavy broché shawl, on that warm July morning, attracting

much attention. But little did she care. "Margaret" was the burden of her thoughts, and the appearance of Mrs. Douglas herself, would scarcely have disturbed her. Much less, then, did the presence of a queerly dressed young girl, who, entering the car with her, occupied from necessity the same seat, feeling herself a little annoyed at being thus obliged to sit so near one whom she mentally pronounced "mighty unsociable," for not once did Madam Conway turn her face that way, so intent was she upon watching their apparent speed, and counting the number of miles they had come.

When Charlton was reached, however, she did observe the woman in a shaker, who, with a pail of *huckleberries* on her arm, was evidently waiting for some one.

An audible groan from the depths of the satin hood, as *Betsey Jane* passed out and the cars passed on, showed plainly that the *mother* and *sister* of George Douglas were recognized, particularly as the former wore the red and yellow calico, which, having been used as a "dress up" the summer before, now did its owner service as a garment of every-day wear. But not long did Madam Conway suffer her mind to dwell upon matter so trivial. Hillsdale was not far away, and she came each moment nearer. Two more stations were reached—the haunted swamp was passed—Chicopee River was in sight—the bridge appeared in view—the whistle sounded, and she was there.

Half an hour later, and Theo, looking from her window, started in surprise as she saw the village omnibus drive up to their door.

"'Tis grandmother!" she cried, and running to meet her she asked why she had returned so soon.

"They are coming at noon," answered the excited woman —then, hurrying into the house, and throwing off her hood she continued, " He's found her at the Falls ; they arc between here and Albany now ; tell everybody to hurry as fast as they can ; tell Hannah to make a chicken pie—Maggie was fond of that ; and turkey—tell her to kill a turkey—it's Maggie's favorite dish—and ice cream, too ! I wish I had some this minute," and she wiped the perspiration from her burning face.

No more hysterics now ; no more lonesome nights ; no more thoughts of death—for Margaret was coming home— the best-loved of them all. Joyfully the servants told to each other the glad news, disbelieving entirely the report fast gaining circulation, that the queenly Maggie was lowly born —a grandchild of old Hagar. Up and down the stairs Madam Conway ran, flitting from room to room and tarrying longest in that of Margaret, where the sunlight came in softly through the half closed blinds and the fair summer blossoms smiled a welcome for the expected one.

Suddenly the noontide stillness was broken by a sound, deafening and shrill on ordinary occasions, but falling now like music on Madam Conway's ear, for by that sound she knew that Margaret was near. Wearily went the half hour by, and then, from the head of the tower stairs, Theo cried out, " She is coming !" while the grandmother buried her face in the pillows of the lounge, and asked to be alone when she took back to her bosom the child which was not hers.

Earnestly, as if to read the inmost soul, each looked into the other's eyes—Margaret and Theo—and while the voice of the latter was choked with tears, she wound her arms around the graceful neck, which bent to the caress, and whispered low, " You are my sister still."

Against the vine-wreathed balustrade a fairy form was leaning, holding back her breath lest she should break the

deep silence of that meeting.   In her bosom there was no
pang of fear lest Theo should be loved the best ; and even
had there been, it could not surely have remained, for
stretching out her arm, Margaret drew her to her side, and
placing her hand in that of Theo said, " You are both my
sisters now," while Arthur Carrollton, bending down, kissed
the lips of the three, saying as he did so, " Thus do I
acknowledge your relationship to me."

" Why don't she come ?" the waiting Madam Conway
sighed, just as Theo pointing to the open door, bade Margaret " go in."

There was a blur before the lady's eyes—a buzzing in her
ears—and the footfall she had listened for so long, was now
unheard as it came slowly to her side.   But the light touch
upon her arm—the well remembered voice within her ear,
calling her " Madam Conway," sent through her an electric
thrill, and starting up she caught the wanderer in her arms,
crying imploringly, " Not that name, Maggie darling ; call
me grandma, as you used to do—call me grandma still,"
and smoothing back the long black tresses, she looked to
see if grief had left its impress upon her fair young face.   It
was paler now, and thinner, too, than it was wont to be,
and while her tears fell fast upon it, Madam Conway whispered, " You have suffered much, my child, and so have I.
Why did you go away ?   Say, Margaret, why did you leave
me all alone ?"

" To learn how much you loved me," answered Margaret,
to whom this moment brought happiness second only to that
which she had felt when on the river bank she sat with Arthur Carrollton, and heard him tell how much she had been
mourned—how lonesome was the house without her—and
how sad where all their hearts.

But that was over now ; no more sadness—no more

tears ; the lost one had returned ; Margaret was home again—home in the hearts of all, and nothing could dislodge her—not even the story of her birth, which Arthur Carroll-ton, spurning at further deception, told to the listening servants, who, having always respected old Hagar for her position in the household as well as for her education, so superior to their own, sent up a deafening shout, first for " Hagar's grandchild," and next for " Miss Margaret forever."

CHAPTER XXV.

HAGAR.

By Theo's request, old Hagar had been taken home **the** day before, yielding submissively, for her frenzied mood was over—her strength was gone—her life was nearly spent—and Hagar did not wish to live. That for which she had sinned had been accomplished, and though it had cost her days and nights of anguish, she was satisfied at last. Margaret was coming home again—would be a lady still—the bride of Arthur Carrollton, for George Douglas had told her so, and she was willing now to die, but not until she had seen her once again—had looked into the beautiful face of which she had been so proud.

Not to-day, however, does she expect her; and just as the sun was setting, the sun which shines on Margaret at home, she falls away to sleep. It was at this hour, that Margaret was wont to visit her, and now, as the tree-tops grew red in the day's departing glory, a graceful form came down the woodland path, where for many weeks the grass has not been crushed beneath her feet. They saw her as she left the house, Madam Conway, Theo, all, but none asked whither she was going. They knew, and *one*, who loved her best of all, followed slowly after, waiting in the woods until that interview should end.

Hagar lay calmly sleeping. The servant was as usual

away, and there was no eye watching Margaret as with burning cheeks, and beating heart, she crossed the threshold of the door, pausing not, faltering not, until the bed was reached—the bed where Hagar lay, her crippled hands folded meekly upon her breast, her white hair shading a whiter face, and a look about her half shut mouth, as if the thin pale lips had been much used of late to breathe the word *"forgive."* Maggie had never seen her thus before, and the worn-out, aged face, had something touching in its sad expression, and something startling, too, bidding her hasten, if to that woman she would speak.

"Hagar," she essayed to say, but the word died on her lips, for standing there alone, with the daylight fading from the earth, and the lifelight fading from the form before her, it seemed not meet that she should thus address the sleeper. There was a name however by which she called another—a name of love, and it would make the withered heart of Hagar Warren bound, and beat, and throb with untold joy. And Margaret said that name at last, whispering it first softly to herself; then bending down so that her breath stirred the snow-white hair, she repeated it aloud, starting involuntarily as the rude walls echoed back the name " Grandmother !"

" Grandmother !" Through the senses locked in sleep it penetrated, and the dim eyes, once so fiery and black ; grew large and bright again, as Hagar Warren woke.

Was it a delusion, that beauteous form which met her view, that soft hand on her brow, or was it Maggie Miller ?

" Grandmother," the low voice said again, " I am Maggie, Hester's child. Can you see me ? Do you know that I am here ?"

Yes, through the films of age, through the films of coming death, and through the gathering darkness, old Hagar saw and knew, and with a scream of joy, her shrunken arms wound themselves convulsively around the maiden's neck, drawing her near, and nearer still, until the shrivelled lips touched the cheek of her who did not turn away, but returned that kiss of love.

"Say it again, say that word once more," and the arms closed tighter round the form of Margaret, who breathed it yet again, while the childish woman sobbed aloud : "It is sweeter than the angels' song, to hear you call me so."

She did not ask her when she came—she did not ask her where she had been ; but Maggie told her all, sitting by her side with the poor hands clasped in her own ; then, as the twilight shadows deepened in the room, she struck a light, and coming near to Hagar, said, "Am I much like my mother ?"

"Yes, yes, only more winsome," was the answer, and the half blind eyes looked proudly at the beautiful girl bending over the humble pillow.

"Do you know that ?" Maggie asked, holding to view the ambrotype of Hester Hamilton.

For an instant Hagar wavered, then hugging the picture to her bosom, she laughed and cried together, whispering as she did so, "My little girl, my Hester, my baby that I used to sing to sleep, in our home away over the sea."

Hagar's mind was wandering amid the scenes of bygone years, but it soon came back again to the present time, and she asked of Margaret whence that picture came. In a few words, Maggie told her, and then for a time there was silence, which was broken at last by Hagar's voice, weaker now than when she spoke before.

"Maggie," she said, "what of this Arthur Carrollton ? Will he make you his bride ?"

"He has so promised " answered Mag ; and Hagar con

tinued : "He will take you to England, and you will be a
lady, sure. Margaret, listen to me. 'Tis the last time we
shall ever talk together, you and I, and I am glad that it is
so. I have greatly sinned, but I have been forgiven, and I
am willing now to die. Everything I wished for has come
to pass, even the hearing *you* call me by that blessed name ;
but Maggie, when to-morrow they say that I am dead—
when you come down to look upon me lying here asleep, you
needn't call me 'Grandmother,' you may say 'poor Hagar'
with the rest—and Maggie, is it too much to ask that your
own hands will arrange my hair, fix my cap, and straighten
my poor old crooked limbs for the coffin ? And if I should
look decent, will you, when nobody sees you do it—Madam
Conway, Arthur Carrollton, nobody who is proud—will you,
Maggie, kiss me once for the sake of what I've suffered that
you might be what you are ?"

"Yes, yes, I will," was Maggie's answer, her tears falling
fast, and a fear creeping into her heart, as by the dim candle light, she saw a nameless shadow settling down on
Hagar's face.

The servant entered at this moment, and glancing at old
Hagar, sunk into a chair, for she knew that shadow was
death.

"Maggie," and the voice was now a whisper, "I wish I
could once more see this Mr. Carrollton. 'Tis the nature
of his kin to be sometimes overbearing, and though I am
only old Hagar Warren, he might heed my dying words,
and be more thoughtful of your happiness. Do you think
that he would come ?"

Ere Maggie had time to answer, there was a step upon
the floor, and Arthur Carrollton stood at her side. He had
waited for her long, and growing at last impatient, had
stolen to the open door, and when the dying woman asked

for him, he had trampled down his pride, and entered the humble room. Winding his arm round Margaret, who trembled violently, he said, "Hagar, I am here. Have you aught to say to me?"

· Quickly the glazed eyes turned towards him, and the clammy hand was timidly extended. He took it unhesitatingly, while the pale lips murmured faintly : "Maggie's too." Then holding both between her own, old Hagar said solemnly : "Young man, as you hope for heaven, deal kindly with my child," and Arthur Carrollton answered her aloud : "As I hope for heaven, I will," while Margaret fell upon her knees and wept. Raising herself in bed, Hagar laid her hands upon the head of the kneeling girl, breathing over her a whispered blessing ; then the hands pressed heavily, the fingers clung with a loving grasp, as it were, to the bands of shining hair—the thin lips ceased to move—the head fell back upon the pillow, motionless and still, and Arthur Carrollton, leading Margaret away, told to her gently, that Hagar was dead.

*   *   *   *   *   *

Carefully, tenderly, as if she had been a wounded dove, did the whole household demean themselves towards Margaret, seeing that everything needful was done, but mentioning never in her presence the name of the dead. And Margaret's position was a trying one, for though Hagar had been her grandmother, she had never regarded her as such, and she could not now affect a grief she did not feel. Still, from her earliest childhood she had loved the strange old woman, and she mourned for her now, as friend mourneth for friend, when there is no tie of blood between them.

Her promise, too, was kept, and with her own hands she smoothed the snow-white hair, tied on the muslin cap, folded the stiffened arms, and then, unmindful who was looking on,

kissed twice the placid face, which seemed to smile on her in
death.

———

By the side of Hester Hamilton they made another grave,
and with Arthur Carrollton and Rose standing at either
side, Margaret looked on while the weary and worn was laid
to rest ; then slowly she retraced her steps, walking now
with Madam Conway, for Arthur Carrollton and Rose had
lingered at the grave, talking together of a plan, which had
presented itself to the minds of both as they stood by the
humble stone, which told where Margaret's mother slept.
To Margaret, however, they said not a word, nor yet to
Madam Conway, though they both united in urging the two
ladies to accompany Theo to Worcester for a few days.

"Mrs. Warner will help me keep house," Mr. Carrollton
said, advancing the while so many good reasons why Margaret at least should go, that she finally consented, and
went down to Worcester, together with Madam Conway, George Douglas, Theo and Henry, the latter of whom
seemed quite as forlorn as did she herself, for Rose was left
behind, and without her he was nothing.

Madam Conway had been very gracious to him ; *his family were good*, and when, as they passed the Charlton depot,
thoughts of the leghorn bonnet and blue umbrella intruded
themselves upon her, she half wished that Henry had broken
his leg in Theo's behalf, and so saved her from bearing the
name of Douglas.

The week went by, passing rapidly as all weeks will, and
Margaret was again at home. Rose was there still, and
just as the sun was setting, she took her sister's hand, and
ed her out into the open air, toward the resting-place of
the dead, where a change had been wrought, and Margaret,

leaning over the iron gate, comprehended at once the feeling which had prompted Mr. Carrollton and Rose to desire her absence for a time. The humble stone was gone, and in its place there stood a handsome monument, less imposing, and less expensive than that of Mrs. Miller, it is true ; but still chaste and elegant, bearing upon it simply the names of "Hester Hamilton," and her mother "Hagar Warren," with the years of their death. The little grave, too, where for many years Maggie herself had been supposed to sleep, was not beneath the pine tree now ; that mound was levelled down, and another had been made, just where the grass was growing rank and green beneath the shadow of the taller stone, and there side by side they lay at last together, the mother and her infant child.

"It was kind in you to do this," Margaret said, and then, with her arm round Rose's waist, she spoke of the coming time when the sun of another hemisphere would be shining down upon her, saying she should think often of that hour, that spot, and that sister, who answered : "Every year when the spring rains fall, I shall come to see that the grave has been well kept, for you know that she was *my* mother, too," and she pointed to the name of "Hester," deep cut in the polished marble.

"Not yours Rose, but *mine*," said Maggie. "*My mother*, she was, and as such, I will cherish her memory;" then, with her arm still around her sister's waist, she walked slowly back to the house.

A little later, and while Arthur Carrollton, with Maggie at his side, was talking to her of something which made the blushes burn on her still pale cheeks, Madam Conway herself walked out to witness the improvements, lingering longest at the little grave, and saying to herself, " it was very thoughtful in Arthur, very, to do what I should have done myself ere this, had I not· been afraid of Margaret's feelings."

Then turning to the new monument, she admired its cha: te beauty, but hardly knew whether she was pleased to have it there or not.

"It's very handsome," she said, leaving the yard ; and walking backward to observe the effect. "And it adds much to the looks of the place. There is no question about that. It is perfectly proper, too, or Mr. Carrollton would never have put it here, for he knows what is right, of course," and the still doubtful lady turned away, saying as she did so, "on the whole I think I am glad that Hester has a handsome monument, and I know I am glad that Mrs. Miller's is a little the taller of the two !"

CHAPTER XXVI.

AUGUST EIGHTEENTH, 1858.

YEARS hence, if the cable coil, resting far down in the mermaids' home, shall prove a bond of perfect peace between the mother and her child, thousands will recall the bright summer morning, when through the caverns of the mighty deep, the first electric message came, thrilling the nation's heart, quickening the nation's pulse, and with the music of the deep toned bell, and noise of the cannon's roar, proclaiming to the listening multitude, that the isle beyond the sea, and the lands which to the westward lie, were bound together, shore to shore, by a strange, mysterious tie. And two there are who, in their happy home, will oft look back upon that day, that 18th day of August, which gave to one of Britain's sons as fair and beautiful a bride as e'er went forth from the New England hills to dwell beneath a foreign sky.

They had not intended to be married so soon, for Margaret would wait a little longer; but an unexpected and urgent summons home made it necessary for Mr. Carrollton to go, and so by chance, the bridal day was fixed for the 18th. None save the family were present, and Madam Conway's tears fell fast, as the words were spoken which made them one, for by those words she knew that she and Margaret must part. But not forever; for when the next year's autumn leaves shall fall, the old house by the mill will again be without a mistress, while in a handsome country seat beyond the sea, Madam Conway will demean herself right proudly as becometh the grandmother of Mrs. Arthur Carrollton. Theo, too, and Rose will both be there, for their husbands have so promised, and when the Christmas fires are kindled on the hearth, and the ancient pictures on the wall take a richer tinge from the ruddy light, there will be a happy group. assembled within the Carrollton halls ; and Margaret, the happiest of them all, will then almost forget that ever in the Hillsdale woods, sitting at Hagar's feet, she listened with a breaking heart to the story of her birth.

But not the thoughts of a joyous future could dissipate entirely the sadness of that bridal, for Margaret was well beloved, and the billow which would roll ere long between her and her childhood's home, stretched many, many miles away. Still they tried to be cheerful, and Henry Warner's merry jokes had called forth more than one gay laugh, when the peal of bells and the roll of drums arrested their attention ; while the servants, who had learned the cause of the rejoicing, struck up " God save the Queen," and from an adjoining field a rival choir sent back the stirring note of ' Hail Columbia Happy Land." Mrs. Jeffrey, too, was busy In secret she had labored at the rent made by her foot in the flag of bygone days, and now, perspiring at every pore, she dragged it up the tower stairs, planting it herself upon the house-top, where side by side with the royal banner, it waved in the summer breeze. And this she did, not because she cared aught for the cable, in which she " didn't believe" and declared " would never work," but because she would celebrate Margaret's wedding day, and so made some amends for her interference when once before the stars and stripes had floated above the old stone house.

And thus it was, amid smiles and tears, amid bells and drums, and waving flags and merry song, amid noisy shout and booming guns, that double bridal day was kept; and when the sun went down, it left a glory on the western clouds as if they, too, had donned their best attire in honor of the union.

*   *   *   *   *   *

It is moonlight on the land, glorious, beautiful moonlight. On Hagar's peaceful grave it falls, and glancing off from the polished stone, shines across the fields upon the old stone house, where all is cheerless now and still.   No life— no sound—no bounding step—no gleeful song.   All is silent, all is sad.   The light of the household has departed ; it went with the ·hour when first to each other the lonesome servants said, " Margaret is gone."

Yes, she is gone, and all through the darkened rooms there is found no trace of her, but away to the eastward the moonlight falls upon the sea, where a noble vessel rides. With sails unfurled to the evening breeze, it speeds away— away from the loved hearts on the shore which after that bark, and its precious freight, have sent many a throb of love.   Upon the deck of that gallant ship there stands a beautiful bride, looking across the water with straining eye, and smiling through her tears on him who wipes those tears away, and whispers in her ear, "I will be more to you, *my wife*, than they have ever been."

So, with the love-light shining on her heart, and the moon· light shining on the wave, we bid adieu to one who bears no more the name of " MAGGIE MILLER."

Mary J. Holmes.

LENA RIVERS.—	. . .	A novel.	12mo. cloth,	$1 50
DARKNESS AND DAYLIGHT.—	.	do. .	do. . .	$1.50
TEMPEST AND SUNSHINE.—	.	do. .	do. . .	$1 50
MARIAN GREY.—	. . .	do. .	do. .	$1 50
MEADOW BROOK.—	. . .	do. .	do. .	$1 50
ENGLISH ORPHANS.—	. . .	do. .	do. .	$1 50
DORA DEANE.—	. .	do. .	do. .	$1 50
COUSIN MAUDE.—	. . .	do. .	do . .	$1 50
HOMESTEAD ON THE HILLSIDE.—		do. .	do. .	$1 50
HUGH WORTHINGTON.—	.	do. .	do. .	$1.50
THE CAMERON PRIDE.—	. .	do. .	do. .	$1.50
ROSE MATHER.—	. . .	do. .	do. .	$1 50
ETHELYN'S MISTAKE.—	.	do. .	do. . .	$1.50
MILLBANK.—	. . .	do. .	do. . .	$1.50
EDNA BROWNING.—	.	*Just Published.*	do. . .	$1.50

Augusta J. Evans.

BEULAH.—	. . .	A novel.	12mo. cloth,	$1.75
MACARIA.—	. . .	do. .	do. . .	$1.75
ST. ELMO.—	. . .	do. .	do. . .	$2.00
VASHTI.—	*Just Published.*	do. .	do. . .	$2.00
INEZ.—	. . .	do. .	do. . .	$1.75

Louisa M. Alcott.

MORNING GLORIES.—By the Author of "Little Women," etc. $1.5

The Crusoe Library.

ROBINSON CRUSOE.—A handsome illus. edition.			12mo.	$1.50
SWISS FAMILY ROBINSON.—	do.	. . .	do.	$1.50
THE ARABIAN NIGHTS.—	do.	. . .	do.	$1.50

Captain Mayne Reid.—Illustrated.

THE SCALP HUNTERS.—		12mo. clo.,	$1.50
THE WAR TRAIL.— .	Far West Series	do.	$1.50
THE HUNTER'S FEAST.— .		do.	$1.50
THE TIGER HUNTER.— .		do.	$1.50
OSCEOLA, THE SEMINOLE.—		do.	$1.50
THE QUADROON. .	Prairie Series	do.	$1.50
RANGERS AND REGULATORS.—		do.	$1.50
THE WHITE GAUNTLET.—		do.	$1.50
WILD LIFE.— . .		do.	$1.50
THE HEADLESS HORSEMAN.—	Pioneer Series	do.	$1.50
LOST LENORE.— . .		do.	$1.50
THE WOOD RANGERS.— .		do.	$1.50
THE WHITE CHIEF.— .		do.	$1.50
THE WILD HUNTRESS.— .	Wild Forest Series	do.	$1.50
THE MAROON.— . .		do.	$1.50
THE RIFLE RANGERS— .		do.	$1.50

Comic Books—Illustrated.

ARTEMUS WARD, His Book.—Letters, etc.   12mo. cl., $1.50
DO.   His Travels—Mormons, etc.   do. $1.50
DO.   In London.—Punch Letters.   do. $1.50
DO.   His Panorama and Lecture.   do. $1.50
DO.   Sandwiches for Railroad. . .   .25
JOSH BILLINGS ON ICE, and other things.—   do. $1.50
DO.   His Book of Proverbs, etc.   do. $1.50
DO.   Farmer's Allmanax. . .   .25
FANNY FERN.—Folly as it Flies. . .   do. $1.50
DO.   Gingersnaps . . . .   do. $1.50
VERDANT GREEN.—A racy English college story.   do. $1.50
MILES O'REILLY.—His Book of Adventures.   do. $1.50
ORPHEUS C. KERR.—Kerr Papers, 4 vols. in one.   do. $2.00
DO.   Avery Glibun. A novel. . . $2.00
DO.   The Cloven Foot. do.   do. $1.50
BALLAD OF LORD BATEMAN.—Illustrated by Cruikshank.   .25

A. S. Roe's Works.

A LONG LOOK AHEAD.—   A novel. .   12mo. cloth, $1.50
TO LOVE AND TO BE LOVED.— do. . .   do. $1.50
TIME AND TIDE.—   do. . .   do. $1.50
I'VE BEEN THINKING.—   do. . .   do. $1.50
THE STAR AND THE CLOUD.— do. . .   do. $1.50
TRUE TO THE LAST.—   do. . .   do. $1.50
HOW COULD HE HELP IT ?—   do. . .   do. $1.50
LIKE AND UNLIKE.—   do. . .   do. $1.50
LOOKING AROUND.—   do. . .   do. $1.50
WOMAN OUR ANGEL.—   do. . .   do. $1.50
THE CLOUD ON THE HEART.— do. . .   do. $1.50
RESOLUTION.—   *Just Published.*   do. $1.50

Joseph Rodman Drake.

THE CULPRIT FAY.—A faery poem, with 100 illustrations. $2.00
DO.   Superbly bound in turkey morocco $5.00

"Brick" Pomeroy.

SENSE.—An illustrated vol. of fireside musings. 12mo. cl. $1.50
NONSENSE.—   do.   do.   comic sketches.   do. $1.50
OUR SATURDAY NIGHTS. do.   pathos and sentiment. $1.50
BRICK DUST.—Comic sketches $1.50
GOLD DUST.—Fireside musings. $1.50

John Esten Cooke.

FAIRFAX.—   A brilliant new novel. .   12mo. cloth. $1.50
HILT TO HILT.—   do. . . .   do. $1.50
HAMMER AND RAPIER.— do. . . .   do. $1.50
OUT OF THE FOAM.—   do.   *Just published.* do. $1.50

Victor Hugo.

LES MISERABLES.—The celebrated novel, 　8vo. cloth. $2.50
　　　　　"　　　　Two vol. edition, fine paper, do. - 5.00
　　　　　"　　　　In the Spanish language, 　do. - 5.00

Algernon Charles Swinburne.

LAUS VENERIS, AND OTHER POEMS.—Elegant new ed. - $1.50
FRENCH LOVE-SONGS.—By the best French Authors. - 1.50

Author "New Gospel of Peace."

THE CHRONICLES OF GOTHAM.—A rich modern satire. - $ .25
THE FALL OF MAN.—A satire on the Darwin Theory. - .50

Julie P. Smith.

WIDOW GOLDSMITH'S DAUGHTER.—A novel. 12mo. cloth. $1.75
CHRIS AND OTHO.—　　　　　　do.　　　do. - 1.75
THE WIDOWER.—　　　　　　　do.　　　do. - 1.75
THE MARRIED BELLE.—　　　　do.　　(in press). - 1.75

Mansfield T. Walworth.

WARWICK.—A new novel. -　　-　　- 12mo. cloth. $1.75
LULU.—　　do.　-　　-　　-　　do. - 1.75
HOTSPUR.—　do.　-　　-　　-　　do. - 1.75
STORMCLIFF.—　do.　-　　-　　-　　do. - 1.75
DELAPLAINE.— do.　　-　　-　　-　　do. - 1.75
BEVERLY.—　do.　*Just Published.*　do. - 1.75

Richard B. Kimball.

WAS HE SUCCESSFUL?— A novel. 　- 12mo. cloth. $1.75
UNDERCURRENTS.—　　　　do.　　　do. - 1.75
SAINT LEGER.—　　　　　do.　　　do. - 1.75
ROMANCE OF STUDENT LIFE. do.　　　do. - 1.75
IN THE TROPICS.—　　　　do.　　　do. - 1.75
HENRY POWERS, Banker.—　do.　　　do. - 1.75
TO-DAY.—　　　　　　　do.　　　do. - 1.75

M. Michelet's Remarkable Works.

LOVE (L'AMOUR).—Translated from the French. 12mo. cl. $1.50
WOMAN (LA FEMME).—　　　do.　-　　do. - 1.50

Ernest Renan.

THE LIFE OF JESUS.—Trans'ted from the French. 12mo. cl. $1.75
LIVES OF THE APOSTLES.—　　　do.　　　do. - 1.75
THE LIFE OF SAINT PAUL—　　　do.　　　do. - 1.75
THE BIBLE IN INDIA—　　　　do.　　of Joccoliot. 2.00

Popular Italian Novels.

DOCTOR ANTONIO.—A love story. By Ruffini. 12mo. cl $1.75
BEATRICE CENCI.—By Guerrazzi, with Portrait. do. - 1.75

Geo. W. Carleton.

OUR ARTIST IN CUBA.—With 50 comic illustrations. - $1.50
OUR ARTIST IN PERU.—　　do.　　　do. - 1.50
OUR ARTIST IN AFRICA.—(In press).　　do. - 1.50

Miscellaneous Works.

THE DEBATABLE LAND.—By Robert Dale Owen. 12mo.	$2.00
RUTLEDGE.—A novel of remarkable interest and power.	1.50
THE SUTHERLANDS.— do. Author of Rutledge.	1.50
FRANK WARRINGTON.— do. do.	1.50
SAINT PHILIP'S.- do do.	1.50
LOUIE.— do. do.	1.50
FERNANDO DE LEMOS.—A novel By Charles Gayaree.	2.00
MAURICE.—A novel from the French of F. Bechard.	1.50
MOTHER GOOSE.—Set to music, and with illustrations.	2.00
BRAZEN GATES.—A new child's book, illustrated.	1.50
THE ART OF AMUSING.—Book of home amusements.	1.50
STOLEN WATERS.—A fascinating novel. Celia Gardner.	1.50
HEART HUNGRY.—A novel. By Maria J. Westmoreland.	1.75
THE SEVENTH VIAL.—A new work. Dr. John Cumming.	2.00
THE GREAT TRIBULATION.—new ed. do.	2.00
THE GREAT PREPARATION.— do. do.	2.00
THE GREAT CONSUMMATION.—do. do.	2.00
THE LAST WARNING CRY.— do. do.	1.50
ANTIDOTE TO "THE GATES AJAR."	25
HOUSES NOT MADE WITH HANDS.—Hoppin's Illus.	1.00
BEAUTY IS POWER.—An admirable book for ladies.	1.50
ITALIAN LIFE AND LEGENDS.—By Anna Cora Ritchie.	1.50
LIFE AND DEATH.—A new American novel.	1.50
HOW TO MAKE MONEY; AND HOW TO KEEP IT.—Davies.	1.50
THE CLOISTER AND THE HEARTH.—By Charles Reade.	1.50
TALES FROM THE OPERAS.—The Plots of all the Operas.	1.50
ADVENTURES OF A HONEYMOON.—A love-story.	1.50
AMONG THE PINES.—Down South. By Edmund Kirke.	1.50
MY SOUTHERN FRIENDS.— do. do.	1.50
DOWN IN TENNESSEE.— do. do.	1.50
ADRIFT IN DIXIE.— do. do.	1.50
AMONG THE GUERILLAS.— do. do.	1.50
A BOOK ABOUT LAWYERS.—Bright and interesting.	2.00
A BOOK ABOUT DOCTORS.— do. do.	2.00
WOMAN, LOVE, AND MARRIAGE.—By Fred. Saunders.	1.50
PRISON LIFE OF JEFFERSON DAVIS.—By J. J. Craven.	1.50
POEMS, BY L. G. THOMAS.—	1.50
PASTIMES WITH MY LITTLE FRIENDS.—Mrs. Bennett.	1.50
THE SQUIBOB PAPERS.—A comic book. John Phœnix.	1.50
COUSIN PAUL.—A new American novel.	1.75
JARGAL.—A novel from the French of Victor Hugo.	1.75
CLAUDE GUEUX.— do. do. do.	1.50
LIFE OF VICTOR HUGO.— do do.	2.00
CHRISTMAS HOLLY.—By Marion Harland, Illustrated.	1.50
THE RUSSIAN BALL.—An illustrated satirical Poem.	.25
THE SNOBLACE BALL.— do. do.	.25
THE PRINCE OF KASHNA.—Edited by R. B. Kimball.	1.75

Miscellaneous Works.

A LOST LIFE.—A novel by Emily H. Moore	$1.50
CROWN JEWELS.— do. Mrs. Emma L. Moffett.	$1 75
ADRIFT WITH A VENGEANCE.— Kinahan Cornwallis. .	$1.50
THE FRANCO-PRUSSIAN WAR IN 1870.—By M. D. Landon.	$2.00
DREAM MUSIC.—Poems by Frederic Rowland Marvin. .	$1.50
RAMBLES IN CUBA.—By an American Lady. . .	$1.50
BEHIND THE SCENES, in the White House.—Keckley. .	$2.00
YACHTMAN'S PRIMER.—For Amateur Sailors.—Warren.	50
RURAL ARCHITECTURE.—By M. Field. With illustrations.	$2.00
TREATISE ON DEAFNESS.—By Dr. E. B. Lighthill. . .	$1.50
WOMEN AND THEATRES.—A new book, by Olive Logan.	$1.50
WARWICK.—A new novel by Mansfield Tracy Walworth.	$1.75
SIBYL HUNTINGTON.—A novel by Mrs. J. C. R. Dorr. .	$1.75
LIVING WRITERS OF THE SOUTH.—By Prof. Davidson. .	$2.00
STRANGE VISITORS.—A book from the Spirit World. .	$1.50
UP BROADWAY, and its Sequel.—A story by Eleanor Kirk.	$1.50
MILITARY RECORD, of Appointments in the U.S. Army.	$5.00
HONOR BRIGHT.—A new American novel. . . .	$1.50
MALBROOK.— do. do. do. . . .	$1.50
GUILTY OR NOT GUILTY.— do. do. . . .	$1.75
ROBERT GREATHOUSE.—A new novel by John F. Swift .	$2.00
THE GOLDEN CROSS, and poems by Irving Van Wart, jr.	$1.50
ATHALIAH.—A new novel by Joseph H. Greene, jr. .	$1.75
REGINA, and other poems.—By Eliza Cruger. . .	$1.50
THE WICKEDEST WOMAN IN NEW YORK.—By C. H. Webb.	50
MONTALBAN.—A new American novel. . . .	$1.75
MADEMOISELLE MERQUEM.—A novel by George Sand. .	$1.75
THE IMPENDING CRISIS OF THE SOUTH.—By H. R. Helper.	$2.00
NOJOQUE—A Question for a Continent.— do. .	$2.00
PARIS IN 1867.—By Henry Morford. . . .	$1.75
THE BISHOP'S SON.—A novel by Alice Cary. . .	$1.75
CRUISE OF THE ALABAMA AND SUMTER.—By Capt. Semmes.	$1.50
HELEN COURTENAY.—A novel, author "Vernon Grove."	$1.75
SOUVENIRS OF TRAVEL.—By Madame Octavia W. LeVert.	$2.00
VANQUISHED.—A novel by Agnes Leonard. . .	$1.75
WILL-O'-THE-WISP.—A child's book, from the German .	$1.50
FOUR OAKS.—A novel by Kamba Thorpe. . .	$1.75
THE CHRISTMAS FONT.—A child's book, by M. J. Holmes.	$1 00
POEMS, BY SARAH T. BOLTON.	$1.50
MARY BRANDEGEE—A novel by Cuyler Pine. . .	$1.75
RENSHAWE.— do. do. . .	$1.75
MOUNT CALVARY.—By Matthew Hale Smith. . .	$2.00
PROMETHEUS IN ATLANTIS.—A prophecy. . .	$2 00
TITAN AGONISTES.—An American novel. . .	$2 00